With his hand, he cupped her nape. Just a light brush before he leaned close and whispered in her ear, "Showtime."

A shiver raced down her spine at the feel of his warm breath against her skin.

"First kiss. Don't screw it up." He pressed his lips to her jaw and for a scant moment she forgot about the reporter snapping away down there. She was too overtaken by the rough scrape of his facial hair on her softer skin, the smell of him enveloping her.

She shut her eyes. This time the flashes of light came from behind her eyelids when his mouth closed over hers. It wasn't hard to lean into him. Her hand grabbed hold of his suit jacket before she realized. And when he slanted his mouth and just the tip of his tongue touched to her bottom lip, she whimpered.

He pulled back too soon. His eyes were heated, his hand moving from her neck and brushing her bared shoulder.

Okay. Kissing Reese Crane was *not* going to be a hardship.

ACCLAIM FOR
JESSICA LEMMON'S NOVELS

A BAD BOY FOR CHRISTMAS

"Shopping for a hot holiday read? Look no further than *A Bad Boy for Christmas*. Actually, it's a terrific read for any time of the year. With charismatic characters, stirring situations, and enough sexy to fill an entire town's worth of stockings, this latest in Lemmon's Second Chance series is 400-plus pages of Christmas magic."

—*USA Today*

"4 stars! Lemmon's contemporary style of storytelling and down-to-earth characters shine through. Lemmon will draw readers into this story because she writes characters whom readers can connect with. Connor and Faith are strong and complement each other, and their chemistry is explosive. Lemmon is an expert at the modern-day romance."

—*RT Book Reviews*

"Lemmon's sexy and well-constructed third Second Chance romance uses a nice reversal: the man wants marriage and the woman is commitment-shy...Likable and realistic characters with believable emotions, and the right balance of fantasy fulfillment, make for some good holiday heat."

—*Publishers Weekly* **(starred review)**

RESCUING THE BAD BOY

"An amazing read and I can't wait for the next installment."
—**TheBookNympho.com**

"Nobody does a bad boy like Jessica Lemmon."
— **HarlequinJunkie.com**

"Lemmon's style of storytelling, coupled with a strong plot, makes this story an amazing read."
— *RT Book Reviews*

BRINGING HOME THE BAD BOY

"Clever, romantic, and utterly unforgettable."
— **Lauren Layne, *USA Today* bestselling author**

"4 ½ stars! A sexy gem of a read that will tug at the heartstrings... A heartfelt plot infused with both emotionally tender and raw moments makes this a story that readers will savor."
— *RT Book Reviews*

THE MILLIONAIRE AFFAIR

"Fast-paced, well-written, and impossible to put down... Jessica writes with humor infused generously throughout in a realistic, entertaining way that really helps to make her characters realistic people you'll want to know... You won't be disappointed!"
— **HarlequinJunkie.com**

"Landon and Kimber's banter is infectious as their chemistry sizzles. Smartly written with a narrative infused with humor and snark, this modern-day romance is a keeper."
— *RT Book Reviews*

"I have always loved Jessica Lemmon's books and have enjoyed reading this series. She has again captured me with her magnificent writing and characters."

—NightOwlReviews.com

HARD TO HANDLE

"[Aiden is] a perfect balance of sensitive, heart-on-his-sleeve guy who is as sexy and 'alpha' as they come...A rare treat."

—PolishedBookworm.com

"[Aiden is] a fantastic character. He is a motorcycle-riding, tattooed, rebel kind of guy with a huge heart. What's not to love?...I really enjoyed this book and I think readers will find it entertaining and heartfelt."

—RomanceRewind.blogspot.com

"I smiled through a lot of it, but seeing Aiden and Sadie deal with all of their hurdles was also incredibly moving and had me tearing up more than once as well...I can't wait to see what Lemmon will bring to the table next."

—HerdingCats-BurningSoup.com

"Aiden has all the characteristics of a bad boy but with the heart of that perfect hero...Their gradual spark leads to some well-written steamier scenes."

—RosieReadsRomance.blogspot.com

CAN'T LET GO

"This novella was long enough to get me hooked on Aiden and Sadie and short enough to leave me wanting more... The chemistry between the characters is fan worthy and the banter is a great addition. The writing style draws readers in."

—BSReviewers.blogspot.com

TEMPTING THE BILLIONAIRE

"A smashing debut! Charming, sexy, and brimming with wit—you'll be adding Jessica Lemmon to your bookshelves for years to come!"

—Heidi Betts, *USA Today* bestselling author

"Lemmon's characters are believable and flawed. Her writing is engaging and witty. If I had been reading this book out in public, everyone would have seen the *huge* grin on my face. I had so much fun reading this and adore it immensely."

—LiteraryEtc.wordpress.com

"The awesome cover opened to even more awesome things inside. It was realistic! Funny! Charming! Sweet!"

—AbigailMumford.com

The
BILLIONAIRE BACHELOR

JESSICA LEMMON

FOREVER

NEW YORK   BOSTON

Copyright © 2016 by Jessica Lemmon
Excerpt from *The Billionaire Next Door* Copyright © 2016 by Jessica Lemmon

Cover illustration by Tony Mauro
Cover design by Elizabeth Turner
Cover copyright © 2016 by Hachette Book Group, Inc.

Forever
Hachette Book Group
1290 Avenue of the Americas
New York, NY 10104
forever-romance.com
twitter.com/foreverromance

First Edition: June 2016

Forever is an imprint of Grand Central Publishing.
The Forever name and logo are trademarks of Hachette Book Group, Inc.

The publisher is not responsible for websites (or their content) that are not owned by the publisher.

The Hachette Speakers Bureau provides a wide range of authors for speaking events. To find out more, go to www.hachettespeakersbureau.com or call (866) 376-6591.

ISBNs: 978-1-4555-6654-9 (mass market), 978-1-4555-6655-6 (ebook)

Printed in the United States of America

OPM

10 9 8 7 6 5 4 3 2 1

ATTENTION CORPORATIONS AND ORGANIZATIONS:

Most Hachette Book Group books are available at quantity discounts with bulk purchase for educational, business, or sales promotional use. For information, please call or write:

Special Markets Department, Hachette Book Group
1290 Avenue of the Americas, New York, NY 10104
Telephone: 1-800-222-6747 Fax: 1-800-477-5925

John Lemmon, thank you for driving me to State Street a few days before Christmas, dropping to one knee, and asking me to be your bride. I've never once regretted saying yes.

ACKNOWLEDGMENTS

Ah, the billionaire! It's like returning to my roots. Whether you've been with me since the beginning or are just now discovering me: thanks a *billion*.

Thank you to Michele Bidelspach for your editorial prowess, Nicole Resciniti for your agent superpowers, and to everyone at Forever Romance who had a part in editing, designing, and producing this book.

As always, thank you to my friends and family and my dear husband, who have to deal with me during deadline time. I'm so lucky you all love me enough to put up with me!

The
BILLIONAIRE
BACHELOR

CHAPTER 1

The Van Heusen Hotel was the love of Merina Van Heusen's life. The historical building dominated the corner of Rush and East Chicago Avenue, regal and beautiful, a living work of art.

Her parents' hotel had once been the Bell Terrace, home away from home to celebrities such as Audrey Hepburn, Sammy Davis Jr., and more recently, Lady Gaga and the late Robin Williams. The original structure perished in the Great Chicago Fire of 1871, only to be resurrected bigger, better, and more beautiful.

There was a life lesson in there.

Latte in hand, Merina breathed in the air in the lobby, a mix of vanilla and cinnamon. Faint but reminiscent of the famed dessert invented in the hotel's kitchen: the snicker-doodle. On her way past Arnold, who stood checking a guest into the hotel, she snagged one of the fresh-baked cookies off a plate and winked at him.

The dark-skinned older man slid her a smile and winked back. Having practically grown up here, the VH was a second home to her. Arnold had started out as a bellman and had worked here for as long she could remember. He was as good as family.

She dumped her purse in her office and finished her cookie, holding on to the latte while she meandered down the hallways, checking to make sure there were no trays outside the doors that needed collecting. At the end of the corridor on the first floor, she saw a man outside one of the rooms, drill whirring away.

"Excuse me," she called. Then had to call again to be heard over the sound. When she came into view, he paused the drilling and looked up at her.

He wore a tool belt and navy uniform, and the antique doorknob was sitting on the floor at his feet along with a small pile of sawdust.

"What are you doing?" she asked, bending to pick up the heavy brass. Her parents had done away with "real keys" the moment they took over, installing the popular keycard entry hotels now used, but the antique doorknobs remained.

"Installing the fingerprint entry." From his pocket, the uniformed man pulled out a small silver pad with a black opening, then went back to drilling.

"No, no, no." She placed the doorknob back on the ground and dusted her hand on her skirt. "We're not doing any fingerprint entry." She offered a patient smile. "You need to double-check your work order."

He gave her a confused look. "Ma'am?" He was looking at Merina, but his voice was raised.

Merina's mother, Jolie, appeared from behind the hotel

room door, her eyebrows raising into hair that used to be the same honeyed shade of blond as Merina's but now was more blond to hide the gray.

"Oh, Merina!" Her mother smiled, but her expression looked a little pained.

"Can you give me a minute with my daughter, Gary?" Like she was Gary's mother, Jolie fished a five-dollar bill from her pocket and pressed it into his palm. "Go to the restaurant and have Sharon make you a caramel macchiato. You won't be sorry."

Gary frowned but took the cash. Merina shook her head as he walked away.

"Sweetheart." Jolie offered another smile. A tight-lipped one meaning there was bad news. Like when Merina's cat, Sherwood, had been hit by a car and Jolie had to break it to her. "Come in. Sit." She popped open the door and Merina entered the guest room.

White duvets and molded woodwork, modern flat-screen televisions and artwork. Red, gold, and deep orange accents added to the richness of the palette and were meant to show that a fire may have taken down the original building but couldn't keep it down.

Jolie gestured to the chair by the desk. Merina refused to sit.

"Mom. What's going on?"

On the end of a sigh that didn't make Merina feel any better, her mother spoke.

"Several changes have been ordered for the Van Heusen in order to modernize it. Fingerprint entry is just one of them. Also, the elevators will be replaced."

"Why?" Merina pictured the gold decorative doors with a Phoenix, the mythical bird that arose from the ashes of its predecessor, emblazoned on them. If there was a beating heart in the Van Heusen, it was that symbol. Her stomach turned.

Instead of answering, Jolie continued. "Then there's the carpeting. The tapestry design won't fit in with the new scheme. And probably the molding and ceiling medallions will all be replaced." She sighed again. "It's a new era."

"When did you take to day-drinking?" Merina asked, only half kidding.

Her mother laughed, but it was brief and faded almost instantly. She touched Merina's arm gently. "Sweetheart. We were going to tell you, but we wanted to make sure there really was no going back. I didn't expect the lock-smith to arrive today." Her eyes strayed to the door.

Merina's patience fizzled. "Tell me what?"

"Your father and I sold the Van Heusen to Alexander Crane six months ago. At the time, he had no plans on making any changes at all, but now that he's retiring, the hotel has fallen to his oldest son. Evidently, Reese had different ideas."

At that pronouncement, Jolie's normally sunny attitude clouded over. Merina knew the Cranes. The Crane Hotel was the biggest corporate hotel outfit in the city, the second biggest in the nation. Alexander (better known as "Big Crane") and his sons ran it, local celebrities of sorts. She'd also read about Big Crane's retirement and Reese's likely ascension to CEO.

But none of that mattered. There was only one newly learned fact bouncing around in her brain. "You sold the Van Heusen?"

She needed that chair after all. She sank into it, mind blanking of everything except for one name: Reese Crane.

"Why didn't you tell me?" Merina stood up again. She couldn't sit. She could not remain still while this was happening. Correction: This *had* happened. "Why didn't you talk to me first?"

"You know we'd never include you in our financial difficulties, Merina." Jolie clucked her tongue.

Financial difficulties?

"Bankruptcy was not an option," her mom said. "Plus, selling gave us the best of both worlds. No financial responsibility and we keep our jobs."

"With Reese Crane as your boss!" Her mind spun after she said it aloud. My God. They would be answering to that arrogant, idiotic . . . "No." Merina shook her head as she strode past her mother. "This is a mistake."

And there had to be a way to undo it.

"Merina!" her mother called after her as Merina bent and collected the discarded doorknob off the ground. She strode through the lobby, dumping the remainder of her latte in the wastebasket by the front desk, and then stomped outside.

As luck would have it, the light drizzle turned into steady rain the second she marched through the crosswalk. Angry as she was, she'd bet that steam rose off her body where the raindrops pelted her.

"That stupid, smarmy jackass!" she said as she pushed through a small crowd of people hustling through the crosswalk. Because seriously, who in their right mind would reconstruct the Van Heusen? Fingerprint entry? This wasn't a James Bond movie! She caught a few sideways glances, but it was hard to tell if they were because she was muttering to herself like a loopy homeless person or because she was carrying a disembodied doorknob around with her.

Could be both.

Her parents had sold the Van Heusen to the biggest, most ostentatious hotel chain in the world. And without telling their own daughter, who also happened to be the hotel's manager! How close to bankruptcy had they been? Couldn't Merina have helped? She'd never know now that they'd sneaked behind her back.

How could they do this to me?

Merina was as much a part of that hotel as they were. Her mother acted as if selling it was nothing more than an inconvenience.

Focus. You're pissed at Crane.

Right. Big Crane may have done her parents a favor buying it, but now that he was about to "peace out," it sounded like Reese had decided to flex his corporate muscle.

"Shit!" She didn't just do that. She did *not* just drown her Louboutin pumps in a deep puddle by the curb. She didn't splurge on much, but her shoes were an indulgence. She shook the rainwater from one pump as best she could and sloshed up Rush Street to Superior, her sights set squarely on the Crane Hotel.

Seventy floors of mirrored glass and as invasive as a visit to the ob-gyn. Given the choice between this monstrosity and the Van Heusen, with its warm cookies and cozy design, she couldn't believe anyone would set foot in the clinical, whitewashed Crane Hotels let alone sleep there.

At the top of that ivory tower, Reese Crane perched like an evil overlord. The oldest Crane son wasn't royalty, but according to the social media and newspaper attention he sure as hell thought he was.

Halfway down Superior, she folded her arms over her shirt, shuddering against the intensifying wind. She really should have grabbed her coat on her way out, but there hadn't been a lot of decision-making going into her process. She'd made it this far, fists balled and steam billowing out of her ears, her ire having kept her warm for the relatively short walk. She should have known better. In Chicago, spring didn't show up until summer.

Finally, she stood face-to-face with the gargantuan, seventy-floor home base. The Crane was not only the premier hotel for the visiting wealthy (and possibly uncultured, given that they stayed *here*), but it was also where Reese slept, in his very own suite on the top floor, instead of his sprawling Lake Shore Drive mansion. She wouldn't be surprised if he slept right at his desk, snuggling his cell phone in one hand and a wad of money in the other.

Stupid billionaires.

Inside, she sucked in a generous breath and shook off her chill. At least there was no wind, and despite the chilling whitewash of furniture, rugs, and modern lighting, it was warm. But only in temperature. The Crane represented everything she hated about modern hotels. And she should know, because she'd worked diligently alongside her parents to keep the integrity of their boutique hotel since she started running it. Her hotel was a place of rich history, beauty, and passion. This place was a tower of glass, made so that the lower echelon of the city could see in but never touch.

Perfect for the likes of Reese Crane.

She walked through the lobby, filled to overflowing with businesspeople of every color, shape, and size. Flashes of suits—black, gray, white—passed in a monochrome blur, as if the Crane Hotel had a dress code and each and every guest here had received the memo. Merina, in her plum silk shirt and dark gray pencil skirt and nude heels, didn't stand out...except for the fact that she resembled a drowned rat.

A few surly glances and cocked brows were her reward for rushing out into the storm. Well. Whatever.

She spotted the elevator leading to Crane's office, catching the door as an older woman was reaching for the button. The woman with coiffed gray hair widened her eyes in alarm, a tiny dog held snuggly in her arms. Merina skated a hand down her skirt and over her hair, wiping the hollows below her eyes to ensure she didn't go to Reese's office with panda eyes.

"Good morning," she greeted.

The older woman frowned. Here was the other problem with the Crane. Its guests were as snooty as the building.

Attitude reflects leadership.

The doors opened only once, to deliver the woman and her dog to the forty-second floor, and then Merina rode the car to the top floor without interruption. She used the time to straighten herself in the blurry, reflective gold doors. No keys or security codes were needed to reach the top of the building. Reese Crane was probably far too smug to believe anyone would dare come up here without an appointment. She'd heard his secretary was more like a bulldog that guarded his office.

The elevator doors slid aside to reveal a woman wearing all black, her grim expression better suited for a funeral home than a hotel.

"May I help you?" the woman asked, her words measured, curt, and not the least bit friendly.

"You can't," Merina said, pleased the rain hadn't completely drowned out her rage. "I need to speak with Mr. Crane."

"Do you have an appoin—"

"No." She supposed she could have made an appointment, could have called ahead, but no sense in robbing Reese Crane of the full effect of her face-to-face fury.

The phone rang and the woman slid her acerbic glare away from Merina. She waited as the other woman answered a call, spoke as slowly as humanly possible, and then returned the receiver to the cradle. The woman folded her hands, waiting.

Even with her nostrils flared, Merina forced a smile. There was only one way past this gatekeeper. She called up an ounce of poise—an ounce being the most she could access at the moment. "Merina Van Heusen to see Reese Crane."

"Ms. Van Heusen," the woman said, her tone flat, her eyes going to the doorknob in Merina's hand. "You're here regarding the changes to the hotel, I presume."

"You got it," Merina said, barely harnessing her anger. How come everyone was so damn calm about dismantling a town landmark?

"Have a seat." Crane's bulldog gestured one manicured hand at a group of cushy white chairs, her mouth frowning in disgust as she took in Merina's dishevelment. "Perhaps I could fetch you a towel first."

"I won't be sitting." She wasn't about to be put in her place by Reese's underling. Then her prayers were answered as the set of gleaming wooden doors behind the secretary's desk parted like the Red Sea.

Jackpot.

Merina barreled forward as the woman at the desk barked, "Excuse me!"

Merina ignored her. She wouldn't be delayed another second...or so she thought. She stopped short when a woman in a very tight red dress, the neckline plunging into plentiful cleavage, her heels even higher and potentially more expensive than Merina's Louboutins, swept out of the office and gave her a slow, mascaraed blink back. Then she sashayed around Merina, past the bulldog, and left behind a plume of perfume.

Interesting.

Reese's latest date? An escort? If Merina believed the local tabloids, one and the same. Paying for dates certainly wasn't above his pay grade.

Before the doors closed, she slipped into Reese's office.

"Ms. Van Heusen!" came a bark behind her, but Reese, who stood facing the windows and looking out upon downtown, said three words that instantly silenced his secretary.

"She's fine, Bobbie."

Merina smirked back at the sour-faced, coal-eyed woman as Reese's office doors whooshed shut.

"Merina, I presume." Reese still hadn't turned. His posture was straight, jacket and slacks impeccably tailored to his muscular, perfectly proportioned body. Shark or not, the man could wear a suit. She'd seen the photos of him in the *Trib* as well as *Luxury Stays*, the hotel industry's leading trade magazine, and like every other woman in Chicago, she hadn't missed the gossip about him online. Like his more professional photos, his hands were sunk into his pant pockets, and his wavy, dark hair was styled and perfect.

Clearly the woman who had just left was here on other

business . . . or past business. If something more clandestine was going on, Reese would appear more mussed. Then again, he probably didn't muss his hair during sex. From what she gleaned about him via the media, Reese probably didn't *allow* his hair to muss.

The snarky thought paired with a vision of him out of that suit, stalking naked and primed, golden muscles shifting with each long-legged step. Sharp, navy eyes focused only on her . . .

He turned to face her and she snapped out of her imaginings and blinked at the stubble covering a perfectly angled jaw. What was it about that hint of dishevelment on his otherwise perfect visage that made her breath catch?

Thick dark brows jumped slightly as his eyes zoomed in on her chest.

She sneered before venturing a glance down at her sodden silk shirt. Where she saw the perfect outline of both nipples. A tinge of heat lit her cheeks, and she crossed her arms haughtily, glaring at him as best she could while battling embarrassment.

"Seems this April morning is colder than you anticipated," he drawled.

And that was when any wayward attraction she might have felt toward him died a quick death. The moment he opened his mouth, her hormones pulled the emergency brake.

"Cut the horseshit, Crane," she snapped.

The edge of Reese's mouth moved sideways, sliding the stubble into an even more appealing pattern. But she wasn't here to be insulted or patronized.

"I heard some news," she said.

He didn't bite.

"Your father purchased the Van Heusen," she continued.

"He added it to the family portfolio, yes," he responded coolly.

Portfolio. She felt her lip curl. To him, the VH was a number on a spreadsheet. Nothing more. Which could also mean he didn't care enough about it to continue with these ridiculous changes.

"There's been an error. My mother is under the impression that many of the nostalgic and antique fixtures in the building will be replaced." She plunked down the heavy doorknob on his desk. A pool of rainwater gathered on his leather blotter.

Reese sucked in a breath through his nose and moved to his desk—a block of black wood the color of his heart—and rested one hand on the back of a shiny leather chair.

"Have a seat." He had manly hands for a guy who spent his days in an office and spare time eating souls, and they were about as disturbingly masculine as the scruff lining his jaw.

She didn't want to sit. She wanted to march over there and slap the pompous smirk off his face. Then she remembered her compromised top, refolded her arms over her breasts, and sat as requested.

You win this round, Crane.

Reese lowered himself into his chair and pressed a button on his phone. "Bobbie, Ms. Van Heusen will need a car in fifteen minutes."

"Yes, sir."

So he'd deigned to carve out fifteen minutes for Merina. Lucky her.

"I don't want a car."

"No? You're planning on walking back?" Even sitting,

he exuded power. Broad, strong shoulders filled out his dark jacket, and a gray tie with a silver sheen arrowed down a crisp white shirt.

"Yes." She wondered what time of day he finally gave up and yanked the perfect knot out of that tie. When he surrendered the top button. Another flare of heat shot through her. She hated the way he affected her. She was just so damn aware of him.

It was unfair. She frowned.

"You were saying something about horseshit," he said smoothly, and she realized she had been sitting there glaring at him in silence for a long while.

She cleared her throat and plowed through what she needed to tell him.

"You can't redesign the Van Heusen Hotel. It's a landmark. Did you know the hotel was the first to install elevators? The hotel's chef created the snickerdoodle. That building is an integral thread woven into the fabric of this city."

She pressed her lips together. Perhaps she was being a tad theatrical, but the Van Heusen did have historical importance to the city, and beyond that, a personal history to her. She'd gone to college straight from high school and graduated with her business degree, her dream to run the Van Heusen. A dream she'd realized and was currently living until this little snafu.

"Born and raised in Chicago, Ms. Van Heusen. You're not telling me anything I don't know," he said, sounding bored.

"Then you know remodeling the Van Heusen makes no sense," she continued, using her best ally: reason. "Our hotel is known for its style. Guests come there to experience a living, breathing piece of Chicago." She stopped short of going into a monologue about how even the fires couldn't destroy the dream but opted against it.

"My hotel, Ms. Van Heusen," he corrected.

His. A fact she'd gleaned only a few minutes ago. A dart of pain shot through the center of her chest. She should have demanded to see the contract her parents signed before sloshing over here in a downpour and parading her nipples for Mr. Suit & Beard. She was almost as pissed at them for keeping this from her as she was for Crane thinking he could strut in and take over.

"No matter who owns the building, you have to know that robbing the Van Heusen of its style will make it just another whitewashed, dull hotel," she said.

Her stomach churned. If she had to bear witness to them ripping up the carpeting and replacing it with white shining tile or see a Dumpster filled with antique doorknobs, she might just lose her mind. The hand-carved molding, the ceiling medallions...each piece of the VH had been preserved to keep the integrity of the past. And now Reese wanted to erase it.

She heard the sadness creep into her voice when she ventured, "Surely there's another way."

He didn't respond to this. Instead he pointed out, "Your parents have been in the red for nearly two years."

She felt her eyes go wide. Two *years*?

"I gather this is news to you," he added, then continued. "Your father's hospital bills put them further in debt."

He was referring to her dad's heart attack last year. Merina had no idea the bills had buried them. She lived in the same house. How had they hidden this from her?

"They came to us to buy the building and we did," Reese

said. "I could have fired them, but I didn't. I offered a generous pension plan if they stayed on through the remodel."

A shake worked up her arms and branched over her shoulders. Pension?

"I take it you didn't know that either."

"They didn't want to worry me," she said flatly, but it didn't take the sting from the truth. They'd kept everything from her.

Her pie-in-the-sky parents who loved that building arguably as much as they loved each other had to have gone to Big Crane as a last resort. They'd overlooked he had Satan for a son.

"They trusted your father to take care of them," she said, her anger blooming anew. "Then you waltz in and wipe them out."

"My father likes your parents, but this isn't about what nice people they are," Satan continued. "He mentioned how well they'd maintained the local landmark with what funds they had available."

Merina's nostrils flared as she inhaled some much-needed oxygen. Her parents had cared for and upgraded the Van Heusen as best they could, but face it, her family didn't have the billion-dollar bankroll the Cranes had.

"Your father is a wise man," she said, pitting the two men against each other. Sure enough, a flicker of challenge shone in Reese's navy eyes. "I doubt his intention when he purchased the Van Heusen was to turn it into a mini-me of the Crane."

"My father is retiring in a few months. He's made it clear the future of the Van Heusen is in my hands." Reese shrugged, which made him look relaxed and made her pulse skyrocket. "I fail to see the charm in the funky, run-down boutique hotel, and I assume most visitors do as well."

Funky? Just who did this jerk-off think he was?

"Do you know how many Hollywood actors have dined in our restaurant?" she blurted. "Hemingway wrote part of his memoir sitting on the velvet chair in the lobby!"

"I thought he mostly wrote in Key West."

"Rumors," she hissed.

A smirk slid over his lips in a look that likely melted his fan club's collective underpants, but it had no effect on her. Not now that she knew how far he was taking this.

"You have outdated heating and air," he said, "elevators that are so close to violating safety codes, you may as well install ladders for the guests on the upper floors, and the wood putty isn't fooling anyone, Merina."

At the cool pronouncement of her name, she sat straighter. She'd been told last month that the building inspector had come by for a reassessment for property value, not that he'd be feeding information to the vulture sitting across from her now.

She'd clearly been left out of a lot of discussions.

"The elevators are original to the building."

"It shows." He offered a slow blink. "The Van Heusen is stodgy and outdated, and revenue is falling more each quarter. I'm doing your parents a favor by offering them a way out of what will be nothing but a future of headaches." Reese folded his hands on the desk blotter, expertly avoiding the water gathered there. A large-faced watch peeked out from the edge of his shirt, the sleeves adorned with a pair of onyx and platinum cuff links. "The Crane branding is strong, our business plan seamless. If you love the building as much as you claim to, you'd support the efforts to increase the traffic. We'll see profits double with an upgrade." He shook his head. "But not with your parents there. And not with you there."

A shiver climbed her spine, the rain and Reese's words having sunk right into her bone marrow. Wait. Was he suggesting...

"You're... firing... me?"

He remained stoically silent.

"My family's goddamn name is on the marquee, Crane!" She shot out of her seat and pressed her fingertips onto his desk. Shining, perfect, unscarred. No character. No soul. No history.

Like Reese Crane himself.

"Your family's name will remain on the building," he stated calmly. And while those words tumbled around her brain and set fire to the fury that he'd put on to sear, he added, "Your parents are getting close to retirement age. Are you sure you swam over here on their behalf? Or is this about you?"

"Of course I'm sure," she said too quickly. She wasn't sure at all. Her world had been upended. Like when she'd learned there was no Santa Claus and that her dad had been sneaking downstairs to eat the Oreos all those years. She thought back to her mom telling her about the sale of the Van Heusen and recalled the dash of hope in Jolie's expression.

Did they want out?

"Think about it, Merina. What I'm offering is more than retirement, and at their age I'm sure they don't want to find work," Reese stated. "Running the Van Heusen is all they've known."

If she had said that, the sentence would have been infused with passion hinting at the fairy tale by which they came to own the Van Heusen. When Reese said it, he made the hotel sound like it was a lame, deaf, blind dog needing to be put down.

No. She would not accept this. Not from Reese. Not from her parents. It was possible they'd forgotten how much the hotel meant to them. Not having money created desperate feelings. Her father wasn't as spry as he once was given his heart condition. Maybe they needed her intrusion.

Reese's phone buzzed and Bobbie stated, "Ms. Van Heusen's town car is here, sir."

"I don't want it," Merina bit out, still leaning over his desk.

He angled his eyes up to her and they stayed locked in a heated staring contest until "Very well" came from the phone's speaker, then clicked off again.

Merina straightened. Outside, the rain started coming down in sheets. Didn't it figure? An involuntary shiver racked her spine, and possibly her lips were turning blue from her wet hair, but she kept her knees locked and her arms folded securely over her peek-a-boo breasts.

"I have an appointment I can't miss, but I won't leave you in suspense." Reese stood, deftly unbuttoned his jacket, and shrugged out of it. Those shoulders. My God. He was a mountain of a man. Tall and broad and the absolute opposite of what anyone might expect a hotel owner-slash-billionaire to look like.

"Suspense?" she repeated, her voice dipping low when he came out from behind the desk. Her eyes screwed up to meet his as he draped his suit jacket over her shoulders.

"I'm not going to put you out on your fantastic ass,

Merina." His lips tipped—lush lips. His was a mouth made for sin. But then, Satan. So it made sense.

She gripped the jacket when he let go. She should be throwing it at him, but it was warm and she was freezing. And it smelled of leather and money and power. Three things she wished didn't make her feel safe. What was it about this man? She'd seen pictures of him before, and yes, noticed he was attractive, but in the flesh there was something about him that made her feel utterly feminine. Even at the worst possible times. Like when he was dangling her job over a lava-filled pit and daring her to grab for it.

"I appreciate your reconsidering. I belong at the Van Heusen." Until she figured out a way to get the hotel back, at least she could be there. She would come up with a way to delay the remodel.

"No, you misunderstand me. I can't keep you there," he said, a frown marring his otherwise perfect brow. "But I can offer you almost any position you'd like at Crane Hotels. We have openings in Wisconsin, Virginia, and Ohio. I know it's not Chicago, but chances are you can stay in the Midwest."

He slid past her while she stared at the sheeting rain, her fingers going numb around the lapels of his jacket. Not only was he firing her, but he expected her to work for him? Expected her to leave Chicago? This was her city, dammit! He didn't reserve the right to boot her out.

When she turned, Reese was pressing a button on the wall. His office doors whispered open.

A balding, smiling man appeared in the doorway and gave Reese a wave of greeting. He noticed her next and offered a nod.

Well. Merina didn't care who he was; he was about to

get an earful. She wouldn't allow Reese Crane to dismiss her after dropping that bomb on her feet.

She stomped over to the doorway between him and his guest.

"You listen to me, you suited sewer rat." Disregarding their current third party, she seethed up at Reese. "I'm going to find a way around your machinations and when I do, I'm going to march back in here with the contract my parents signed and shove it straight up your ass."

Reese's eyebrows rose, his lips with them. Instead of apologizing to his guest, he grinned over at the balding man, who to his testament was appropriately shocked, and said, "You'll have to forgive Ms. Van Heusen. She doesn't like when she doesn't get her way."

The balding man laughed, though it sounded a tad uneasy.

Reese tilted his head at Merina. "Will there be anything else?"

"Your head on a pike." With that parting blow, she left, holding fast to the suit jacket. She wore it on the ride down the elevator, through the bland lobby, and out onto Superior Street, where she wadded it up and threw it into a mud puddle gathering near the curb.

She walked back to the Van Heusen in the rain, telling herself she'd won this round. But Merina didn't feel victorious.

She felt lost.

CHAPTER 2

Reese Crane had nine problems—the other members of the board of directors, now disassembling, murmuring to each other about dinner and drinks downtown. Left in the conference room were his youngest brother, Tag, and their father, Alex.

"That meeting went as well as expected," Reese growled. "Bunch of stodgy old placeholders."

"At least you held it in that long," his father said.

Reese had nearly bitten his tongue to remain silent during the meeting. Now he felt his lip curl as he watched the horde of suits waddle away. He had one seat on the board. His father another. But they were in the minority. Thanks to his great-grandfather, who started Crane Hotels and lost the controlling percentage to the public.

The board had made it clear last month they would not appoint Reese in the position of CEO of Crane Hotels when Alex retired. Apparently, no one had changed their collective minds. They'd always liked Alex but had never warmed to his sons.

"Disloyal pack of jackals," Reese said. They saw him as a spoon-fed brat who'd inherited his way to the top floor of Crane Hotels, which was an oversimplified truth. Yes, he was sitting at the position of chief operations officer because his father had founded Crane Hotels, but it wasn't as if he didn't work. As COO, Reese was in charge of the daily operations of the company, which was no small task.

"You have a flippant, playboy reputation," Alex stated, not for the first time. "They're being careful."

"I work damn near eighty hours a week," Reese all but bellowed. "I bleed over fiscal reports."

"You have to play nice, bro," Tag advised, wearing an easy smile. His facial hair was so heavy, he may as well have been sporting a beard. Reese's youngest brother ran Guest and Restaurant Services for Crane Hotels. He did a lot of travel for hotel openings and bar and restaurant events. Typically, you couldn't get him into a suit. Today, he'd eschewed his usual corporate Indiana Jones look for gray slacks and a white button-down.

All hail the board.

"They don't like you much either," Alex said, tipping his head at his other son.

At that, Tag sat straight in his chair and plucked the pencil out of his low-hanging ponytail-bun hybrid. Tag bucked the system every chance he had, so it wasn't any wonder the board hadn't appreciated his bravado. He worked hard, but his style was more beach bum than corporate and every one of those old crones knew it.

The mess over who would hold the position of CEO was only between Reese and the board. Tag didn't want it. Alex was retiring. Their other brother, Eli, was still stationed in the desert and wasn't interested.

"I have an idea," Reese announced. Something that had been knocking around in his head since a soaking wet Merina Van Heusen had marched into his office and plunked a doorknob onto his desk.

At the mention of an idea, Alex waited. Tag's brow creased.

Tag should know better. Of course Reese would come up with a plan before he gave up on being named CEO. It may be an impromptu, mostly old-fashioned plan, but it was a plan.

"Merina Van Heusen came by my office this morning to speak with me about my plans to remodel the Van Heusen."

Alex's brow went up.

"She left incensed," Reese continued. "Stormed out of my office fifteen minutes later but not before insulting me in front of Phil Lightman."

"You're remodeling the Van Heusen? That place is a landmark," Tag said.

"All aboard the ball-busting train." Reese gave Tag a dry look.

His brother grinned in response. "Well, it is."

"Shit," Alex said with a raspy chuckle. His father was in a sleek gray suit and whimsical checkered tie and wore a full white mustache/goatee combo that complemented his thick white hair. He was former military, brawny, had brains and power, and enough balls to say what he meant.

"Shit is right." Tag winced. "I've met Merina Van Heusen. She loves that hotel. I bet she freaked."

Reese frowned. He'd never met her before this morning. "Where did you meet Merina Van Heusen?"

"Hotel supply conference." Tag shrugged.

Reese shook his head. If there was a party, Tag was there. It's one reason he was damn good at what he did for Crane. No one schmoozed like Tag.

"I spoke to her and her parents about the VH. It was obvious she loved that building for more than its bottom-line potential," Tag said.

"Bad business," Alex put in.

"Merina is more than just a numbers girl," Reese stated, agreeing with both his brother and his father. Her passion for her hotel was a tick in the plus column for Reese, because he had something she wanted. That he'd bet she'd do anything to get back.

"I have a perception problem," Reese said.

Alex grunted his agreement.

"The board sees me as a rich, spoiled prince about to inherit the kingdom. They don't trust me. I'm unsettled. A loner." *A playboy*, the tabloids said. He didn't care for the insulting title, but it wasn't untrue. He enjoyed the company of a number of women, consensually, of course, and he wasn't about to apologize for it.

"A man-whore?" Tag offered.

Reese glared.

"Last one." Tag held up a hand of surrender and smiled around his beard, a flash of straight, white teeth thanks to braces he'd bitched about for two years.

"Bed-hopping" as Frank, the douche bag, had called it during the meeting. Whether Reese agreed or not, the perception was there and wasn't going anywhere. As long as the shareholders remained puritanically dated and the board handed them their balls—female board member Lilith's included, because Reese would bet aces to assholes she had them—Reese was going to have a problem. Which meant he had to change his nefarious ways.

On the outside.

"I have to alter that perception," Reese said. "Go from a man who enjoys the company of many women to a man who enjoys the company of one woman."

"Can you even do that?" Tag smirked.

Smart-ass. Reese ignored him and continued. "Once they see me settled, snuggled into a routine, they'll pay more attention to my achievements. The press will have to report on the woman who tamed me rather than the women I discard." That wasn't how he operated, but there was no convincing the outside world. The women he dated knew the score, enjoyed their time spent, and moved on. But reporters were vampires. They wanted blood and amicability didn't make for interesting headlines.

It was the run-in with Merina that started Reese's gears turning. She was fiery and passionate but also elegant and intelligent. If he were involved with someone like her, the local rags would have no choice but to take notice. One relationship for show could fix all of his problems. It was almost too simple.

He told his brother and father as much, finishing with, "Merina is the whole package."

She'd fit into Reese's world—into his plan—seamlessly. At the mention of package, he pictured her again. She'd been a study in opposites: stylish in understated matching jewelry, high-end name-brand shoes and clothing, yet she'd been borderline unhinged. Soaked to the bone and in complete disarray.

Her honeyed blond hair had begun to dry—the ends

curling against her shoulders, while her silk shirt was plastered to her body, her breasts in particular, nipples erect and staring him in the face. But her fantastic tits didn't have his undivided attention. Through her shirt, he'd been able to see the outline and a dab of color on what appeared to be a tattoo.

A tattoo.

It'd taken Herculean willpower to return his gaze to her strongly arched brows and frowning full lips. And even more willpower to keep his mind from wondering what bit of ink she'd permanently etched onto her skin. A butterfly? A teddy bear? A pair of hearts? Merina was a beautiful woman. Seeing her disheveled and learning that under her prim-and-proper exterior there lived a wild woman was... fascinating.

It'd been a long time since anyone had fascinated him.

"You. Settled?" One of Tag's eyebrows climbed his forehead. "With Merina Van Heusen?"

"That's the gist." Reese nodded.

"How? She has to hate you for trying to disassemble the VH."

"A minor setback."

Tag laughed so hard, he nearly toppled off his chair. By the time he righted himself, he was swiping moisture from his eyes and shaking his head. "Good luck with that, brother."

Reese felt his mouth tug at the corners. He saw no other way. This would have to work.

"Merina sounds like the perfect option," Alex interjected, and Reese breathed a sigh of relief. His father, his hero. If Alex saw this working, it would. They shared a brain for business, for negotiating. "She'll do anything to keep her family's legacy intact. And she's tough enough to handle the press."

"No kidding." Reese grunted. In the short time he'd seen her, she'd barreled into his office unannounced, given his dinner date from last week an icy glare, and called him a suited sewer rat. Plus—

"She used the term *horseshit*," Reese said, drawing the attention of the other men. "Who says that?" As he asked that question, he felt the corner of his mouth lift in amusement. When she said the word *shit*, her upper lip canted to one side, just a tad. Thanks to the rain that had washed away some of her makeup he'd noticed there was a tiny pale freckle at the corner of her mouth.

Sexy.

"Merina is tough, but also soft," he said, dragging his thoughts back on course. "She dresses like a lady, handles herself like a woman, and doesn't allow anyone to boss her around."

"Including you," Alex added. "But if you have her cooperation, sounds like she could smooth out your rough edges in the public eye."

"Agree to what? What are we talking about here?" Tag, who was grinning in confusion, shook his head. "You going to demand she date you?"

"I'm going to ask her to marry me," Reese stated, and his brother's smile erased.

Alex smiled proudly. "Brilliant."

"For six months," Reese said. "An agreement that will end as soon as I've established my CEO status. Then we can quietly divorce, and I'll sign over the Van Heusen."

Jaw ajar, Tag looked from his father to his brother. "You're both insane."

"I'm desperate," Reese said. It was the truth. "If I don't convince the board to give me Dad's position, they will appoint a CEO outside of this family."

"That can't happen." Tag looked appropriately upset. None of them wanted anyone other than a family member running Crane Hotels.

"No," Reese agreed. "It can't."

Alex was retiring in six months. He wouldn't put off his retirement, a move that Reese supported a million percent. His father wouldn't let the board bully him. "Start showing weakness, Reese," he'd said, "and they'll pick at your carcass the rest of your reign. We need them. But they need us more. We just have to make them see it."

It was an irritating corporate chess game, but Reese was learning to toe the line when necessary. He planned on growing Crane Hotels to twice the size his father had, and to do that, he couldn't be a lone wolf. He needed the support of the people who made decisions: the board.

Since his work ethic preceded him and they still didn't trust him, the wolf would have to put on sheep's clothing to make them believe he was one of the herd. A family man. A husband intent on keeping up squeaky-clean public appearances.

Win the press, win the board.

Win the board, win CEO.

But Reese also knew his weaknesses. He needed someone who was his opposite yet equal. He needed someone who could handle pressure elegantly, even while using the word *horseshit.*

He needed Merina Van Heusen.

"I have a dinner date," Alex announced, standing from his chair.

"Who is she?" Tag teased.

Big Crane's sons had all taken after him, none of them planning on settling down—well, until just now. But Reese's would be a marriage on paper—totally different. His father had loved their mother, and after she died, he never found another to fill her shoes. Alex was in his sixties and neither the board nor the media cared if he dated. No, that magnifying glass focus fell on Reese, who was the next in line as heir to the Crane throne. Tag's dating was overlooked because he was the party guy and it was expected. Eli was a nonissue since he was overseas. Maybe when he came home, the press would care who he was fucking.

Reese doubted it. The media had their hooks into him. He was the easy target—the man who'd made tawdry headlines because of the number of women he spent time with—and never spent time with more than once.

"She is a *he*, and he is the linen supplier for the greater Chicago area," Alex answered.

"You're supposed to be retired," Reese said.

"Six months." His father pointed at him. Reese smiled. His old man. Retired but not dead, he often said of his future plans. Alex turned and left the conference room and Reese stood to do the same. It had been a hell of a long day already and was less than half over. He didn't stop at five, unless it was five a.m.

"Explain to me why you have to *marry* Merina Van Heusen?" Tag asked, still lounging in the chair. Even dressed nicely, he resembled a lazy cat. He was damn good, though. Guest and Restaurant Services was not an easy part of the hotel business to keep running, but Tag did it flawlessly. And dressed like a bum half the time. Go figure.

"Because Kate Hudson is taken?"

Tag rolled his eyes. "Why not just date her?"

"The board needs to see I'm serious. Nothing is more serious than marriage. Once I've settled down, they'll see I'm a changed man. Responsible."

"No longer the consummate billionaire bachelor," Tag drawled, quoting one of the gossip rags.

"Right," Reese agreed. "It's a business deal like any other deal." He lifted his iPhone and tucked it into his jacket pocket, then straightened his shirtsleeves. "It has perimeters, an end date, and a goal. I'm going to give her a few days—maybe wait until next week to ask her. After she cools down, Merina will see. She's a smart businesswoman, despite the fact that she's in love with that relic of a hotel."

"Sentimentality isn't a crime."

"It isn't, but it's a tool I can use to my advantage. *Our* advantage," he amended. "This will be advantageous for both of us."

"I'm all for you being in position of CEO, Reese; you know I am. This is your destiny. Your legacy. The board is making a mistake if they look elsewhere," Tag said.

"I appreciate that," Reese said, meaning it. The Crane men had always stuck together. His youngest brother may ride his ass on occasion, but in the clutch, Tag had his back.

"But," Tag continued, his tone cautious, "blackmail is low, bro." He finally stood, slowly, then crossed his arms over his chest. Tag was taller than Reese or Eli, standing close to six-five. Massive shoulders, huge arms, and tree-trunk legs came from their father's side, the towering height from their mother's father. Granddad Weller was huge. Eli and Reese liked to give Tag a hard time about his hair, but Tag refused to cut it. Either he had a Samson complex or he liked looking like a beached merman, it was hard to say.

"It's not blackmail. It's proper motivation."

Tag swept the legal pad off the desk, not a word written on it. Reese had no idea why he brought a pad to meetings except that maybe he thought it made him look like he fit here and not on a biplane in a jungle. Tag scrubbed a hand over his heavy facial hair. "I'm going to grab a burger. You?"

Reese shook his head. He'd eat at his desk like he did every day. Didn't keep Tag from asking. Which he appreciated. As brothers who were musketeers at heart, none of them would ever let the other one remain in solitude.

"I need to make a few phone calls," Reese said as he opened the door.

"Guess so," Tag said, walking out ahead of him; then he threw over his shoulder, "You have a wedding to plan and a bride to propose to. In that order."

CHAPTER 3

Thanks, Heather," Merina said to the Van Heusen's new bartender-slash-waitress as she headed out the door. Flame, the restaurant in the Van Heusen, hadn't been terribly busy tonight, but Heather had handled the bar by herself, and given that she'd only been working for the VH for two weeks, Merina was suitably impressed.

Nearly a week had passed since she'd barged into Reese Crane's office, and neither she nor her parents, as far as she knew, had heard from him again.

After she'd left the hotel's doorknob on Reese's desk, Merina had stomped back into the VH, snatched a few towels off a passing cart, and gone into her office. After snagging a sweater off a hook on the wall and putting it on, she went to her mother's office, only to find her father in there, too, leaning over the computer.

Merina hadn't given them a chance to acknowledge her before she started in on them.

"How could you keep something like this from me?" she'd asked while wringing her hair in the towel.

Her father had straightened and held up a hand. "Honey, take a breath."

"I can't take a breath. I can't even think! You sold the hotel without telling me? How much financial strain were you under? Did you consider asking me for help? How could you go outside the family with this?"

When her emotions got the best of her and tears welled in her eyes, her father eased her down on the sofa in her mother's office and they flanked her on either side.

Then they told her how things had snowballed into an avalanche.

Her father, Mark, had insisted on doing the financials himself and had overlooked many opportunities for write-offs over the years. The new accounting firm discovered back taxes they owed. Then there were the repairs needed. An inspection that didn't go well. A recent turnover in employees because a guy had stolen money from the restaurant cash register. Add in her father's recent hospital expenses and it was a recipe for desperation.

"Big Crane was willing to buy it," Mark had told her, one arm solidly around her back. "As it stood, we would have had to put thousands into it just to sell. And your mother and I would likely be out of jobs."

"But you'll be out of jobs soon!" Merina huffed her frustration. "And so will I."

Her parents hadn't known that part, which made her feel moderately better—at least they hadn't kept that from her too.

"I spoke with him," Merina had confessed. "He won't fire me immediately." She didn't know if that was true, but she intended to speak with him further about it. Next time with a dry shirt.

That day she'd wanted so badly for her parents to share in her outrage. Instead her mother had encouraged her in her typical glass-half-full way by saying, "You're young, you're brilliant, and we have faith that you'll find where you belong, even if it isn't here."

Which made her suspect they were resigned to their plight.

Merina paced through the barren restaurant now, her mind latched onto the past. Reese had made it clear to her he wasn't keeping any of them. Not her parents, not Merina, and she guessed the rest of the building's loyal staff would be in danger of losing their jobs too.

She wasn't foolish enough to believe he'd forgotten about their discussion, but there were no further e-mails or appointments, and the locksmith had replaced the card reader on the hotel room door, only now there was a mismatched doorknob instead of the one she'd gifted to Crane.

No construction workers in hard hats had shown up to destroy the building during that week, so for that, she was grateful. The more Reese Crane dragged his heels, the more time she had to come up with a solution to save her job and the hotel from being turned into a glass shrine.

She flipped the sign around at the threshold of Flame so that it read CLOSED as her cell phone chimed. A text at one a.m.? Had to be Lorelei. Maybe back from a horrific date and ready to share all the gory details. Lore knew Merina didn't go to sleep until three, sometimes four. But a glance at the screen showed that it wasn't her best friend, but an unknown number.

Call me if you're awake.

"Sorry, creeper," she said as she pocketed her phone. "I'm not playing this game." Before she stepped into the lobby, though, her phone chimed again. She dug it out of her pocket.

Reese Crane.

Her heart lifted to her throat. Reese Crane was texting her? He'd ignored her for the last week while she tried not to fret over whether he'd roll a wrecking ball down Rush Street for a surprise hotel smashing, and now he was *texting her*? She stared at the seven words on her screen as if she might consider responding.

Which of course she wouldn't.

What if he'd changed his mind about the Van Heusen? About keeping Merina on as manager?

Don't be ridiculous.

That's not what he wanted. The man was an arrogant, pompous jerk who didn't have any reason to contact her unless he wanted to twist the knife. He could call her during normal business hours.

But even as the thought occurred, she didn't put her phone away. Only bit her lip and continued staring. If something was about to go down with the hotel, or with her job, or if there was a way to prevent things from going south, then she needed to know as soon as possible.

"Everything all right, Ms. Van Heusen?" Arnold asked from the front desk. He'd worked here since she was a little girl. And because she loved the nighttime, and so did he, she had often sneaked down to sit with him while her parents worked instead of stay in bed.

In the end, that memory was what changed her mind. If there was a chance to save their jobs, she owed Arnold and her parents the discomfort of returning Satan Crane's call.

"Everything's fine, Arnold. Thanks for asking. I'm making some tea. Can I get you something?"

"I'm good, but thank you." He grinned, and the wide smile comforted her right to her soul.

"You're welcome." Her returning smile faded as she turned back into the bar area and tapped her phone screen.

"Just as I suspected," Reese answered, his voice a smooth, low timbre.

"Hello to you too," she grumbled. *Arrogant prick.* "What is just as you suspected?"

"That you don't sleep."

"I sleep, but it's early."

"It is."

There was a gap of silence that stretched, and she let it. He was the one who wanted to talk to her. Let him talk.

"I have a proposal for you, but I'd like to deliver it in person."

Behind the bar, she rested a clean mug on the surface. "Okay. Well, I'm free Thursday, or—"

"Now."

"Now?"

"You're at the hotel, I presume."

"Yes, but—"

"See you in ten minutes."

Silence.

She looked at the screen of her phone. *Call ended.* She frowned, not liking that he didn't explain. Not liking how she felt as if she didn't have a choice in the matter. Not liking any of it. Not liking *him.*

She was a big girl. She could take her medicine. Even if her medicine was a prescription written on a pink slip that she'd be out on her "fantastic ass" by the end of this week.

But she really hoped not.

She pulled the lever on a vat of hot water on the industrial coffeemaker, then dunked a tea bag into her mug and decided to run to the bathroom while it steeped.

A quick check confirmed she was as put together as one could expect at this time of night. Sure her hair had gone a little limp and her skirt and shirt were wrinkled from wear, but her makeup was reasonably intact and she'd brushed her teeth after a late dinner.

Not that she was trying to impress Reese Crane.

By the time five minutes was up, she was tossing the tea bag in the trash, and the revolving hotel door was spinning. Reese stepped in, wearing a dark suit and pale butter-yellow tie. In his pocket was a matching kerchief, and shiny black shoes poked out of sharp pants accentuating thick thighs and, yeah, she'd admit it, a nice ass. He'd made good time.

"Welcome to a real hotel, Crane," Merina called from the doorway of the bar. "We can talk about your proposal in here."

He turned to face her, his expression registering surprise that faded quickly into his usual take-charge façade. "Very well."

His steps were sure and strong, his body moving like it'd been crafted to walk toward a woman. Merina expected Reese to look at home only in his whitewashed hotel with no personality. But he also looked like he belonged in the warmth of the Van Heusen, with its deep, rich woods and tapestry-style chairs. The soft lighting warmed his skin and made the flecks of gold stand out in his facial hair.

He was alarmingly attractive tonight, and she decided to

blame that observation on her always-present sleep deprivation.

"How does it feel stepping into a place with soul?" she asked as he followed her in.

"You mean where I'm served milk and cookies rather than aged scotch?"

"We have both."

"I'll have a scotch." With a nod, he moved to the bar.

"Sorry. Bar's closed." She wouldn't allow him to come in here and boss her around. He was on her turf.

For now, anyway.

Glancing at her mug, he looked as if he was weighing his options of whether to argue about the bar being closed or not. He must have decided against it. He said nothing more.

Nothing. Even though he'd called this after-hours meeting.

"Would you like to sit?" May as well start the ball rolling.

His expression turned slightly amused before he nodded. "Sure."

She led him away from the bar—no way was she propping up on one of those hard wooden seats after the day she'd had—and slid into a booth. He sat across from her, and with half the lights off in the lounge, the seating arrangement felt intimate.

He regarded the bar, his mouth twisting in indecision. Like he was debating on what part of it to tear out first.

"Okay," Merina interrupted to take his mind off destroying her second favorite room in the hotel. She wrapped her hands around her mug of steaming tea. "What did you need to see me about?"

"A proposal." His eyes snapped to hers. "I'm willing to

let you and your parents keep your jobs and leave the Van Heusen as bohemian as you like."

It was everything she wanted to hear. Like a miracle had occurred. Had he grown a conscience? Her eyes narrowed in suspicion. "What's the catch?"

He smiled, then said two words that made her go temporarily blind in one eye. "Marry me."

In all the imaginings she'd ever had about a marriage proposal, absolutely zero of them included billionaires she barely knew. A small, slightly hysterical laugh left her lips.

Reese didn't flinch.

"Did you just say..." She closed her eyes and pushed the rest from her constricted chest. "*Marry you*?" Surely not. Surely she'd hallucinated that.

"Yes."

She clutched her mug. Voice tight, she asked, "What in the hell are you talking about?"

"My father is retiring soon. The Crane Holdings board of directors isn't convinced I'll make a good replacement due to my dating habits." He stated it clearly and unapologetically, though really, what did he have to apologize for? He was a grown man who could see whomever he wanted. In her opinion, he saw way too many *whomevers*. A string of silly women who were likely chasing after his wallet. "The shareholders are displeased with the fact that I have a reputation for being..."

"A playboy?" she finished for him.

He curled his lip and corrected with, "Not monogamous."

"Are you capable of being monogamous?" It was easier to needle him than address the gauntlet resting between them like a huge pink elephant.

"I don't prefer it."

Which was no answer at all.

"So this is a bribe."

"It's a proposal." One eyebrow lifted slightly. "In this case, literally."

"You think the first time I walk down an aisle it's going to be an arrangement with a coldhearted snake whose only goal in life is to deepen his pockets?" There was no way. No way she'd agree to this. Even if it meant she was fired, she wouldn't sell her soul. "I'm not going to let you bribe me into marrying you. I don't even like you."

"You don't have to like me. You have to pretend to like me."

My God, he's serious.

"No, I don't." Her neck prickled. Maybe this was an elaborate scheme. "I don't have to do anything."

"You do if you want your job. If you want to keep the Van Heusen intact." He grimaced as he studied the bar. "If you turn me down, I might raze it just for fun."

Her blood moved from chilled to boiling. There were not enough swear words—in every language in the universe—to sum up her feelings. She had to say something, however, so she went with, "You asshole."

"Six months." He dipped his chin and trained those heady navy eyes on her. "We get engaged, then married, make a few public appearances for show. The media starts writing favorable things about me instead of lies, and the board will see I've changed." He shrugged one big shoulder. "Once I land CEO, we quietly divorce."

Six months. For a split second she entertained the idea. Keeping her job and the Van Heusen intact would only cost her half a year of her life.

Wait.

No.

"This isn't the sixteenth century, Crane," she snapped. "Can't you find a woman to date monogamously from the collection of dolls you're always parading around the city? The senator's daughter. That underwear model. Oh, what about that really short, cute niece of the famous designer?"

"No," he answered, his lips cradling the familiar word. "I need someone who will keep up the ruse. Someone who is smart and savvy, who the media will believe I've settled down with long-term."

She was pretty sure there were a few compliments in there, but damned if she knew what to do about them.

"Forget it." She put her hands on the table and moved to stand.

"I'll sign the Van Heusen over to you free and clear," he said, holding her eyes with his.

Her currency. He'd found it.

She lowered to her seat again, palms sweating on the wood where they rested.

"It'll be in your name as a settlement of the divorce. What you do with it—keep it or return it to your parents— is up to you." His gaze stuck to her like superglue. "Every- one wins."

She was completely speechless. Not only would she sal- vage everyone's jobs and retain the integrity of the VH, but she'd also get to own it? It was…well, it was insane is what it was.

Wasn't it?

"Are you seeing anyone?" His voice dipped, slicing her hectic thoughts into more pieces. The energy between them intensified.

There was a charge there. A spark in the air when he

was this close to her. She thought it'd been a by-product of her rage when she'd huffed into his office last week. But no. It was real. Which made his proposition a million times more volatile. Because she did *not* like him—not even a little—yet that hadn't quelled the physical attraction, which was problematic.

"I didn't say yes," she reminded both of them.

"If you are," he continued, ignoring her, "you'll have to break it off. Tomorrow at the latest. Tonight, if possible."

Her jaw softened, her mouth falling open. She wasn't seeing anyone, but what if she was? He expected her to make a phone call in the wee hours to announce they were through? She would have been offended for her boyfriend if there were one.

She thought of the man who delivered fresh, organic produce to the hotel. Miles. He'd asked her out for coffee a few days ago. He was cute in a pair of black-framed glasses and his hipster-wear. She guessed him to be a few years younger than her twenty-nine and probably the only thing they had in common was that they both drank coffee, but he had a nice smile and she'd been flattered. So she'd said yes. If she agreed to do what Crane was asking...well, there was no way she could explore anything with Miles.

With anyone.

"Merina."

"What?" Her eyebrows crashed together.

"Are you dating anyone right now?" he asked. Slowly.

She was having a problem processing his offer. His *proposal*. So she deflected.

"Are *you*?"

He gave her a "you've got to be kidding me" frown.

"Oh, right. Like a million somebodies. Tell me why

you're allergic to seeing a woman more than once. Is it because they find out how lousy you are in bed and then run for the hills?"

At her blatant insult, he didn't balk. "It's because I never call them again and instruct my secretary to send flowers stating as much."

Her head jerked on her neck. Was he serious? With him sitting there in his suit and tie, hands folded in front of him, she shouldn't find it surprising he handled his dates much like a corporate takeover. There was absolutely no way she could marry a man—even for show—with that much ice in his veins.

"What about the woman I saw leaving your office?" she asked before she'd meant to. "She didn't look like a typical businesswoman." Unless her business was escorting the rich and famous for a hefty fee.

"She left her necklace on the hotel nightstand and came to pick it up."

"Surely the Crane has a lost-and-found box," she said with a snort.

"My nightstand," he clarified.

Oh.

She felt her face go red. Of course he'd slept with that woman.

"Everything will be handled by my team. The wedding will be two weeks from now," he said, moving them forward yet again.

"I didn't say yes yet," she murmured. She had to murmur, because her lips were numb. And her fingers. All of her. "Two weeks?"

"The sooner the better." Reese kept plowing through. "It will be a simple affair at my house. My brother and father will be there, a justice of the peace, and a few members of the Crane Holdings board. Keep your invitations essential. Your parents, a best friend, a few close family members. We need to keep this small. You can't tell your family you're marrying for show. There is too big of a chance the truth will come out. I'll have a photographer there who will feed a few pictures to the media for publicity purposes."

Publicity. He really had all of this worked out. And her parents. God. What would her parents say when she announced she was engaged to Satan Crane? Especially since she couldn't tell them the truth. Her hands were again wrapped around her mug, but despite the warmth from the cup, a chill swept through her. Was she actually considering this?

She thought of her parents and how much they loved the Van Heusen. She thought of herself and how she'd grown up in this cherished building. She thought of Arnold out front, who loved coming to work each day.

She didn't want to work anywhere else, let alone for one of Crane's übermodern hotels. And after they parted ways, she'd own the Van Heusen. As offers went, they didn't come packaged prettier.

Still, what Crane was proposing—as he'd put it, a literal proposal—was preposterous.

"It has to appear real, so I've handed the details over to my PR specialist," he said. "I've spoken with her about it already. A few public appearances and you'll move into my Lake Shore Drive mansion. She assures me she can easily spin this as a whirlwind romance to the press."

Her mouth fell open.

He met her expression with a dubious one of his own. "I know. Whirlwind romance. Ridiculous." He pulled in a deep breath, one that expanded his chest, and checked the face of his watch. Why, she didn't know. It was two in the morning. Where else could he possibly have to be? Unless she was one in a line of many women to whom he was making this offer. It alarmed her how not surprising that idea was.

"Call whomever you're dating and let him down easy. We don't need him using your breakup as media fodder. Since the timeline is tight, I'll need to know your answer by the end of the week. Six months, Merina, and you'll get everything you want."

He said her name with warmth, his tone rough and soft at the same time. She met his eyes. Navy. The inside of her sank even as her heart kicked against her rib cage. It was everything she wanted. Her future and her past in her control.

"If you and whoever you're seeing are meant to be," he said, the warmth vanishing from his voice, "I'm sure he'll take you back when you and I don't work out."

"I'm not seeing anyone." Unable to sit any longer, she rose from the table, her hands flattening on the surface. His eyes went to her shirt like they did the day she stomped into his hotel. He really had a boob fetish, didn't he?

Slowly, he raised his eyes to her face. "That makes this easier, then."

Easier. Sure. Just allow herself to be bought off by the misogynistic billionaire who was trying to control every particle of her life for six months. Just marry him. Easy-peasy.

"I...I can't do this right now." That was the most honest thing she'd said since he arrived. She couldn't categorize what he was asking. She couldn't fathom it. She couldn't picture it. Her dating Reese was outrageous. Her living with him? Insane. But marriage . . . God. He was crazy.

"I understand." Unaffected by her reaction, Reese stood with her. "You have my private cell now. Call that number and let me know your decision by Friday." With a curt nod, he turned and started out of the dining room.

"I have until Friday?" she couldn't help asking.

"Yes." He plunged his hands into his pockets and waited for her to say more. So she did.

"You booked everything already?"

"Yes." He canted his head to one side and regarded her. He looked handsome and she tried to see him differently than she had when he'd walked in. As a husband. A man she would live with. The man she would hold hands with and kiss in public for the world to see. It was like she'd fallen down the rabbit hole and was having tea with the Mad Hatter.

Reese started for the exit.

"And if I say no," she called after him, her voice hollow, "do you have a plan B?"

This earned her a slight smile over his shoulder, the edges of his lips tipping. "Believe it or not, my list of potential brides with real estate I can hold over their heads is relatively short. I've thought this through. It's the best course of action for both of us."

He turned on the heel of his expensive leather shoes and exited the Van Heusen, leaving Merina with a million thoughts—one of which she really shouldn't entertain.

She looked into her tepid tea, decided it wasn't strong enough, and went behind the bar for a shot of the scotch she'd refused to serve him.

CHAPTER 4

"You threw Reese Crane's thousand-dollar suit jacket into a mud puddle? That's brilliant." Lorelei's deep brown eyes crinkled around the edges and she threw her head back and laughed.

"I don't know how brilliant it was since I walked back freezing and soaked to the bone." Merina yawned, then drank the coffee she needed more than her next breath. It'd been a sleepless, stressful couple of nights. On a good night, she slept a few hours. This week she was lucky if she'd accumulated a few hours' sleep since Monday.

Lorelei swiped moisture from her inky lashes—and not inky because they were coated in mascara. Inky because they were naturally coal black, like her smoothed-to-perfection shoulder-length hair.

"You look amazing," Merina blurted. Because her best friend did, in fact, look amazing. Her cocoa skin was glowing, her cheeks highlighted with a dab of bronzer, her eyes bright and sparkling. Merina, on the other hand, looked like a hobo brought in to be given a hot meal. "Oh my God," she said, her lazy synapses finally firing. "Did you get laid last night? Are you and Malcolm back togeth—"

"What? No! Neither of those things." Lorelei turned her chin down to examine the printed papers in front of her. "And we're not talking about me. We're talking about you, future *Mrs. Crane*."

Since Merina's parents were at the hotel, she'd taken advantage of the rare bit of privacy at home to have Lorelei over. They sat at the breakfast nook, baked-from-a-box blueberry muffins on a plate between them. Merina had filled Lorelei in on the phone at six this morning, which was about two minutes after Reese e-mailed her a prenuptial agreement, from his personal e-mail no less, that stated, *Need your answer by tomorrow. This is a draft and not finalized.*

"Romantic, right?" Merina grumbled into her coffee.

The night he'd stopped by the VH, she'd slept fitfully, grabbing twenty minutes here, five minutes there. She'd stumbled through the next few days on autopilot trying to figure out a way around what Reese was asking. He'd told her she couldn't tell anyone, but the prenup's arrival in her inbox required a lawyer's expertise. Her lawyer also happened to be her very best friend. She'd debated for about thirty seconds before giving in and calling her lawyer bestie.

Lorelei had promised to read over the document and arrive at Merina's house within the hour. Now she flipped through the pages casually while Merina waited and watched her facial expressions for any clue as to what she might say.

"So?" Merina prompted. "How badly am I getting screwed here?" Obviously, Reese Crane had more to gain or he never would have come up with the plan. There was something she wasn't seeing; she was sure of it.

"Honestly?" Lorelei straightened the papers, then folded her hands neatly on top of the stack. "I think you're sitting pretty if you take the deal."

Knife hovering over the butter dish, Merina blinked at her friend. She abandoned the utensil, muffin forgotten. "I'm sorry, I swore I thought I heard you imply this is a good idea?"

Lorelei picked a hunk off the edge of her muffin and popped it into her mouth, then gestured around Merina's living quarters. "Beautiful as your parents' house is, I know you're ready to leave."

Merina sighed. She was past ready. Whenever she and Lorelei had lunch or drinks—sadly, it wasn't that often since Lorelei had made partner at her firm—Merina moaned and complained about living with her parents. At age twenty-nine, it wasn't exactly charming to be shacked up with Mom and Dad. She'd made due because the three-story house had a completely private upstairs, and save for the kitchen, she was able to feel as if she were in her own apartment. She now knew (after her mother's reluctant revelation about their finances) that the rent Merina insisted on paying and grocery trips she made every other week had been helping.

Over the last few years, she'd spent so much time at work, she couldn't see the point in moving out until she had a reason. And then she found one. A beautiful apartment close to the Van Heusen in an artsy building near the museum. She'd put down a deposit, intending to move after the holidays, but by last Thanksgiving her father's heart attack had happened and her parents needed her more than ever. Also, the three of them were home together *more than ever*.

"I can move out without Reese Crane," Merina grunted, buttering the muffin after all.

"This is true." Lorelei nodded as she polished off the end of her muffin. "But if you *with this ring, I thee wed*, you can move out sooner, keep the Van Heusen, and you'll be in charge of everyone's jobs, including your own. This arrangement takes care of all your problems. Plus"—she dusted her hands, sending crumbs onto the napkin in front of her—"this would be a great test run for getting back on the horse."

Merina's entire face screwed to the side. "I think I'm about to be offended."

"I'm your best friend," Lore stated, resting a comforting palm over Merina's hand. "I know you've been avoiding getting serious since Corbin. Reese Crane isn't Corbin."

Corbin. At the mention of her ex-boyfriend, Merina closed her eyes. Lorelei's reassuring touch wasn't reassuring at all. Corbin marked the one time in Merina's life she wished she could rewind, erase, then fast-forward back to today.

She'd met him at a mixer at the Van Heusen's former assistant manager's house. She went to Liza's because she was invited and she wanted to be friendly. She had no idea it was a setup until Liza shoved her brother, Corbin, in Merina's face and left them suspiciously alone on the back porch. To her surprise, she liked him. A lot. He was fun and carefree...seemed less high-strung than the business sorts she'd dated in the past. Not that the list was long. It was mainly comprised of a few longish-term boyfriends during her college years, and then Corbin. Six years of semi-serious dating that had not resulted in marriage or even living together and had tied up what she now recalled fondly as her best dating years.

The evening at Liza's led to exchanged phone numbers and from there turned into a few fun dates at Liza's apartment where Corbin lived as her couch-crashing roommate. The third date ended in Merina's bedroom, and she was grateful she had parents who were modern enough not to pry when she had a man over.

The beginning of the end came when Liza announced she was moving to Colorado to care for hers and Corbin's aging mother. Corbin asked to stay with Merina for the short-term and she hesitantly said yes. When a few weeks turned into a few months, Merina started paying extra on her rent and saying it was from Corbin. It wasn't. He was unemployed, and she quickly learned that his lifestyle was so "carefree" because he essentially mooched off whomever was handy.

Six months later, she came home from work one night to find her parents on the sofa and a note on her bed from Corbin that read, "Sorry, babe." She learned the next morning her bank accounts had been drained.

In the quiet of the wee hours, sometimes she regretted not pressing charges, but she'd been too embarrassed to tell anyone else the truth: that Liza had effectively unloaded her loser brother onto Merina and bolted.

Merina opened her eyes and met Lorelei's sweet, concerned gaze. "I don't know if that's a good argument, Lore. Maybe the lesson I'm to learn is don't trust a man who needs something from me."

Lorelei patted Merina's arm, then pulled her hand away.

"Not like Reese is going to clean out your bank account, babe."

"Good point." She'd put that in Crane's plus column.

"I mean, come on. The last date you went on was with who?"

Her lips flattened. She wasn't answering that question. But Lore knew the answer.

"Big teeth martini guy."

Merina laughed, glad for the reprieve. "He didn't have big teeth!"

"They were really, really white, though. Which against his complexion made them look big."

"Yech." Merina couldn't help that reaction. In the blue lights of the bar, Daniel had been attractive and confident. Once back in his apartment, he was a little slimy. She'd had second thoughts, but then she'd been trying to get past Corbin, so she went through with it. "Well, getting on *that* horse wasn't beneficial."

"Should have been perfect," Lorelei said thoughtfully. "With his horse teeth and all."

Merina laughed so hard she had to hold her stomach. Lorelei joined her. Once they sobered, Merina sniffed and sighed and admitted the part about Crane's offer that was eating at her.

"It's not the way I saw myself getting married for the first time."

Not that she'd always dreamed of a poufy gown with bridesmaids and groomsmen flanking her on either side. She had been fairly certain marriage would come as a natural part of a long-lasting relationship. The *right* long-lasting relationship. Certainly not part of a business agreement. She wrinkled her nose.

"That's fair," Lorelei admitted.

"Marriage is supposed to be forever. Engagements are supposed to be overly romantic. Like State Street in the snow around Christmastime," she said of her parents' engagement.

"I hear you. My dad took my mom up in a hot air balloon."

Merina smiled. "And your mom is terrified of heights." She'd heard the story from Lore's parents before. It was always a boisterous story filled with laughter. "But shouldn't it be like that? Uniquely us?"

"Honey, getting married to a billionaire to win your family's hotel back is as unique as it gets. Not everyone has drop-dead romantic weddings. Look at me." Lorelei, ever the pragmatist, shrugged. "Vegas and Malcolm McDowell," she said of her ex-husband. "Life is a series of events. We're never sure which opportunities are going to come our way."

"I've told myself the same thing. It's only six months, right?"

"Six short months. Malcolm and I lasted six *years*. Try explaining that breakup to everyone." She shouldered her purse, a sign she didn't have the time or the desire to talk about her own closet-dwelling skeletons. "I have to meet a client at Starbucks. Another coffee for me. Hopefully I can maintain rather than behave like a hyperactive squirrel."

"Your blood type is caffeine. I'm not concerned." Merina's smile faded. "Thank you for coming by. You can bill me."

"Fine." Lorelei pulled open the front door. "You owe me a dirty martini with extra blue-cheese-stuffed olives." She winked and stepped out into the crisp morning air, then added, "Take the deal, Mer. He's being fair and there is nothing in there about consummation." She shrugged a petite shoulder. "Unless you want there to be."

At her best friend's sly smirk, Merina shook her head adamantly. "I wouldn't sleep with that jerk."

"Well, if I were you, I'd negotiate some jewelry and nice outfits out of it. You will probably have to succumb to a few public kisses, but then you're off the hook and the Van Heusen is yours in the divorce."

"Jewelry," Merina said drily as she leaned on the doorjamb. Because she was not going to admit she'd just pictured Reese Crane's firm mouth surrounded by stubble and wondered how good his lips would feel on hers.

It'd been a while since she'd dated anyone. A longer while since she'd had a good kiss. What was that guy's name who met her for drinks a few months back? Darryl? Dylan? Well, whoever he was, he hadn't been a good kisser.

"Oh, and get some shoes out of it too." Lorelei kissed her hand and waved good-bye. As her Mercedes pulled away from the curb, Merina considered the very real opportunity she'd been handed. Maybe this was her chance to do like her best friend said. Win back the VH, keep their staff intact, and move out of her parents' house with a clean break.

By fall, she could be sitting pretty, the entire debacle a part of her past.

At the kitchen table, she shoved half the muffin into her mouth and swept the prenup into a stack while she chewed. She cradled it to her chest and finished off her coffee.

"Okay, Mer," she said as she watched the wind blow the budding trees outside, "you can do this." But as she looked down at her cell phone, she imagined it'd grown teeth. What was she supposed to do? Call?

Text him?

She didn't owe him an answer until tomorrow, but she wasn't putting off this decision another minute. She'd already spent more time fretting and less time sleeping than she could afford.

If the options were lose the VH—watching her parents be forced into retirement and their staff file for unemployment—or marry Reese Crane, Merina would marry the man.

So. Maybe the best way to handle this was the most succinct way.

She opened the old text message from Reese and punched in one word. Then she stared at it for the count of three, took a deep breath, and hit SEND.

* * *

Fine.

Reese narrowed his eyes at the one word sitting on his phone's screen.

Fine? He assumed that was Merina's way of saying yes. Not the most heartfelt acceptance of his offer, but then he hadn't presented the proposal in a heartfelt way.

Reese was still pursing his lips in thought when Bobbie cut in. "Mr. Crane?"

"Yes," he said, dropping the phone on his desk and meeting her eyes. She'd come in here to review his schedule for next week and probably thought he was ignoring her. But he'd heard every word. And now Merina's message had changed a few things. "Next week's meeting times work, but I need you to reschedule my lunch appointment tomorrow and arrange a meeting with Merina Van Heusen and Penelope Brand instead."

Bobbie's eyebrows shot up, but she didn't argue. "Very well. Here in your office?"

"Yes. No," he amended quickly. "We'll use the conference room. And have my lawyer swing by later this afternoon. I have a contract that needs his immediate attention." He wanted that prenup finalized. The fewer delays the better.

"Yes, sir." Bobbie left his office and Reese leaned back in his leather high-back and propped his elbow on the arm of the chair.

Merina was going to marry him. Looked like she was on board, and that gave him a sense of satisfaction. He knew she'd see things his way.

"Reese's Rocket," Tag announced, barging through Reese's office door. His grin was shit-eating, his beard neatly trimmed for a change, and his clothes just what Reese had come to expect.

"Henley and cargo pants. Are you working on the water heater?"

Tag waggled his phone. "That's one helluva hashtag."

"What are you talking about?" Reese turned his attention to the stack of phone calls he had to return. Bobbie still insisted on jotting down phone numbers of callers on those WHILE YOU WERE OUT papers he hated so much. He had a trashcan filled with wadded up pink notes. "I need to buy Bobbie an iPad."

"She'd use it as a coaster. She wouldn't know what to do with it," Tag said.

"Fact," Reese agreed.

Tag plopped into the guest chair and leaned back, legs spread, mouth still grinning. Giving up the ghost, Reese dropped his stack of missed phone calls and said, "Out with it."

"There are photos of your junk."

"Pardon?"

"Well, not your *junk*," Tag said, shaking his head at his phone's screen. "But the outline of your junk. You either need a better tailor or you need to start wearing briefs." He tossed his phone onto the desk. Reese lifted the device and found a photo of him, cropped to showcase one particular part of him. His...pants. The poster had drawn a giant red circle around Reese's *junk* and added an arrow and three exclamation marks. The hashtag next to it read *#ReesesRocket*.

Reese's...Rocket? Seriously?

"Fantastic." Reese handed back the phone. "On the list of things I do not need, at the top is press focused on my reputation for—"

"Man-whoring?"

"Dating."

"It is fantastic, actually. You can't buy this kind of press. Who's with you?" Tag held the phone up again.

"I went out with Elaine Parker's daughter, Primrose." Reese recognized his suit and the swish of blue dress cut out of the edge of the photo from a charity event last year. He knew exactly who was responsible for this.

"Ah. Primrose. She's young, dumb, and full of—"

"Money," Reese finished for him. Primrose was the "cute niece of that famous designer" Merina had mentioned the other night. She had asked him to attend the event with her, which he would have turned down if it wasn't a charity with Crane Hotels front and center. Turned out she was clingier than he would have expected. Primrose hadn't stopped calling him for four months. And now this.

"Well, she ain't mad at you," his brother said with another grin.

No, she was apparently trying to draw his attention because he was paying her none. "It's not exactly a compliment."

Tag's smile disappeared and he held up a hand. "Excuse me. If she called your dick 'Reese's Rodent,' *that* wouldn't be a compliment. 'Reese's Rocket' insists you know how to use it. That it's a thing of power." He made a fist.

"For the love of— I didn't even sleep with her." He wasn't that lonely. She was too young. Too wide-eyed and too hopeful for his taste. She wasn't the kind of girl who could handle a one-night stand. Hell, they had ended the evening with a chaste kiss and she still tried for a second date. At least this confirmed his instincts were spot-on.

"It doesn't seem to matter," Tag commented, shaking his head at his phone's screen.

"Is this the only reason you came in here?" Reese asked.

"Yeah." Tag offered a shrug as if it was obvious.

Reese's phone lit and he glanced from his brother to a reminder for the lunch tomorrow he'd asked Bobbie to reschedule. She'd probably come in here with a pink slip giving him the details of the new meeting date in a few minutes; then he could tap it into his iPhone and add to the pink trash pile. Glancing back at his brother, Reese thought of the last text message that was on his phone.

"When a woman says 'fine' . . . ," he started.

"Run." Tag's smug expression fell as he sat ramrod

straight. "Like you have zombies on your tail. 'Fine' is not a term of endearment from a woman."

"Yeah, that's what I thought."

Tag's eyes went to Reese's phone. "Who gave you the F-word?"

"Merina. In answer to my marriage proposal." He leaned on his desk, hands folded. "I'm assuming that's a yes."

"You should assume the position, man. That does not sound like a good sign."

Reese let loose a smile. "We're both business professionals. I'm sure she meant what it says. That she looked over the contract and it was...fine."

"Contract." Tag sucked air through his teeth. "You are not a romantic, are you?"

"And you are?"

"Don Juan over here." Tag gestured to the off-white Henley hugging his biceps. If he had a hashtag, it'd be *Tag's Tanks*. That was a good one, actually. Maybe if that went viral, everyone could talk about him instead. "You two get married, Merina will be the one answering for your 'rocket' to the press, not you."

"Seems unfair." He hadn't thought about that. Then again, he'd never imagined someone coining a term for his...his...

The mind boggled.

"The world is unfair, bro."

He supposed that was true.

"I'm going to have her come in tomorrow to sign the prenup," Reese said. "Then we'll have the hard part of this deal over with." And he could take a breath. The rest would be scheduled and orchestrated, and he could go along with the motions. Few things in life were so easy.

"Take her out for dinner before you meet to sign this *contract*. She's probably nervous as hell. Help ease her worries."

Reese's face pinched. He hadn't thought about Merina being nervous. He hadn't really considered her feelings, assuming this would be a deal like any other.

"She's a businesswoman with something to gain," he told his brother. "I think it's best if we sign first and then meet with my PR person."

"PR person?"

"We need guidance to ensure we convince the press."

Tag made a face. "Wow. Are you this clueless about women?"

"In case you haven't noticed, I have a reputation for doing quite well with women." He pointed at Tag's phone. "Someone is posting odes to my rocket."

"Oh, you're a pro at hookups," Tag agreed. "But Merina Van Heusen isn't going to be a one-nighter you can palm cab money in the morning. She's going to be your wife."

At the word *wife*, Reese's breathing went shallow. Of course, marriage and wife went together, but phrased that way, he was reminded of another long-term relationship that hadn't panned out.

"It's a business arrangement," he reminded them both before he puked. He had this. He didn't have to fall in love with Merina; he just had to show up at a few public appearances with her.

"Armande." Tag stood and snapped his fingers.

"What about it?" Reese's neck prickled. Armande was an upscale fusion French/Italian restaurant known for its romantic mood and special menu made up entirely of aphrodisiacs.

"That's where your first big date should be."

"Armande isn't exactly subtle," Reese grumbled. He needed media attention, not overkill.

"Neither is Reese's Rocket," Tag answered.

"It can't look like a stunt."

"Then I suggest you be convincing. I'll tell Bobbie to book you for dinner. Tonight good?"

"Tag—"

"Tonight it is." His brother opened one of the office doors. "Trust me, man," he said, "Armande is the perfect place to introduce the city to your future bride."

Even if he didn't want to do it, maybe a dinner with Merina before they inked the deal wasn't the worst idea in the world.

"Bobbie, gorgeous," Reese heard Tag say as the doors swished shut.

With a sigh, Reese pressed a button on his cell phone, and regarded Merina's message again.

FINE.

Maybe dinner at Armande would be the best way to ease her concerns. Or maybe, he'd have another publicity nightmare to contend with.

As long as it wasn't *#ReesesRocket*, he was good with that.

* * *

Angling around a housekeeper who smiled as she passed with her cart of fluffy white towels, Merina tapped the screen of her ringing phone. THE CRANE HOTEL, the display read.

Oh, fantastic.

"Merina Van Heusen."

"Ms. Van Heusen, this is Bobbie from Mr. Crane's office," came the curt voice. She didn't wait for Merina to respond before she plowed forward. "Mr. Crane has requested you arrive at his private boardroom for a noon appointment tomorrow."

To sign the prenuptial contract, no doubt.

"Of course," Merina answered with fake bravado. She heard the sound of a pen scratching on a notepad. The sooner she signed those papers, the sooner she could move on to Phase 2 of "Operation Arranged Marriage."

"Also, he has scheduled a dinner with you at nine p.m. this evening at Armande. He'll send a car to your residence at eight."

Merina stopped in the middle of the lobby, realized she was in a guest's path to his room, and smiled politely before moving to a section of uninhabited chairs off to the side. She noticed Bobbie didn't ask if she was available for dinner. And Merina didn't like that at all.

Partially because she didn't like conceding control and partially because Reese Crane—her future husband—should be the one doing the asking.

"Tonight's no good for me," Merina clipped. Total lie. She had no plans tonight other than her usual poring over reports and e-mails. Catching up on work over a glass of merlot. "Perhaps if Mr. Crane could call himself, we could find a time that worked for both of us."

You know, like normal human beings.

"Ms. Van Heusen, Armande is the most sought-after restaurant in the city. Securing a reservation is not easy. Many exceptions were made."

"I'm sorry to hear that, but—"

"The car will be at your house by eight p.m. Do you require a stylist?"

"No, I do not 'require a stylist,'" Merina huffed, insulted on too many levels to count. Bobbie was her least favorite person on the planet, second only to her future husband. "I can dress myself."

"The restaurant is formal and known for its—"

"I know what Armande is, Bobbie." Not because she'd been there, but because it was lauded in the *Trib* as the premiere place to see and be seen. Especially for couples. Especially for *celebrity* couples.

Not that Reese Crane was a celebrity, but he was as close as it came to a local one. And now they'd be seen together in Armande. She could only guess this was part of the "whirlwind romance" ruse. If that was the case, and this was a suggestion by his public relations person, maybe Merina shouldn't be difficult after all. Evidently six months of biting her tongue started now.

"Eight o'clock is fine," she clipped.

"Nice to hear," Bobbie said. "I'll e-mail you a packet of information. Please review it carefully and let me know if you have any questions. Good day, Ms. Van Heusen."

And she was gone.

Merina lowered the phone from her ear in time to see a small envelope icon appear on the screen. An e-mail. That woman was fast. What was she supposed to tell her parents about tonight when a car arrived? *I have a date with billionaire Reese Crane. Yes, turns out he loved when I went over there to challenge him. He finds my trucker mouth irresistible.*

Sigh.

This would be so much easier if she could tell them the

truth: that she was marrying to get the Van Heusen Hotel back. That a six-month trade-off would secure her future, and theirs. Granted, the moment her father learned Reese was blackmailing her, he'd take a ball bat to Reese's gonads. So maybe it was better that she had to lie.

As much as she hated lying. Deception in general. She thought of Corbin and her lip curled.

How'd the saying go? You can't make an omelet without breaking a few eggs. A few white lies told over the next half year, and then she could go back to being herself. It was an act. That's all.

She'd have to convince her parents, as well as the press, that she and Reese fell in love. Opposites attract? That was one way to go. Enemies to lovers? That was another.

Still, a ripple of resentment came at how perfect this solution worked out for everyone.

Suddenly, she sympathized with her parents' hiding their financial worries from her. They loved her and likely did it to protect her, much in the way Merina was doing this because she loved and wanted to protect them.

But even with that justification, she was having a hard time forgiving them for hiding this from her for so long. She was an adult; she could handle bad news. Hell, she had handled financial challenges both on a business and a personal scale. Didn't they trust her?

Well.

They would.

After the divorce, they could relax knowing the Van Heusen Hotel was back in the family's "portfolio" rather than a square on Crane's giant Monopoly board.

At her desk, she wiggled her mouse to wake her sleeping computer and dug into her inbox. At the top was the e-mail from Bobbie: a bullet list of items, including the location of the restaurant, make and model of the car coming to pick her up, and a list of places where Merina might procure a manicure, a dress and shoes, and have her hair styled. The personal care items were marked with an asterisk and at the bottom of the list she saw its meaning.

Each of these services will be billed to Crane Hotels at no cost to you.

Be still her heart.

"I'm not having my nails and hair done," she said to the screen. "And I have great shoes." Decisively, she closed the e-mail and, for good measure, deleted it. She would agree to the dinner and to the car picking her up, but she knew damn well how to get ready for a date at a nice restaurant. Could Reese Crane be more insulting? More controlling?

"Goodness. What's happened to you?"

Merina looked up to see her mother leaning into the office, her hand resting on the knob of Merina's open door.

"You look positively ferocious."

"Uh...small overcharge on new linens," Merina lied, transforming her snarl into a smile. "Nothing a quick phone call won't fix."

"All right, then." Her mother returned her smile but Merina saw suspicion resting behind it. Lying wasn't something Merina did on a daily basis, so it was understandable she was bad at it.

"You're sure you're okay?" Jolie pushed.

"Absolutely. Oh, and I'm going to meet Lorelei for dinner, so I may be home later than usual."

Chicken.

"Later than three a.m.?" her mother asked flatly.

Jolie knew her well. Whenever she and Lore went out, they often stayed out until the last possible minute.

"No." Merina closed the window on her computer. "Not later than three a.m."

"I have to run an errand. Can I pick you up a latte on my way back?"

"Sure, Mom. Thanks."

"Welcome, sweetheart." Jolie winked and wiggled her fingers in good-bye and Merina's heart crushed a little more. Reese was making her run a complete scam on her family and for that, she'd never forgive him. She bit her lip. What had she gotten herself into?

Look at it like a six-month sentence, but with lots and lots of amenities.

In the grand scheme of life, six months wasn't a big deal, but right now, she worried she would feel every agonizing minute.

CHAPTER 5

Armande, located on Ontario Street off the Magnificent Mile, was high profile, difficult to get into, and known for its wealthy clientele. Reese had been here once, a long time ago, on non-romantic business. Tag was more of a regular, making it a point to be seen with his date du jour on occasion.

Reese didn't do romance. Dates, yes. Dinners, yes. Charity events, fund-raisers, dinners for work, no problem. He'd attended all of those and more over the years.

He hadn't always been jaded. When he was younger, there'd been a girlfriend who he thought might become more. Gwyneth had moved into his mansion, settled in for what he thought was the long haul, and after four years together, left him for someone else. Someone Reese had trusted, his best friend at the time, Hayes Lerner.

When Reese found out she was cheating, he told her to leave and she tearfully promised to be out in a week.

He didn't spend another second in that house, packing a bag and securing a penthouse suite in his hotel. Thing was, after she did finally move out, he didn't go back to the mansion.

The hotel was more convenient, or so he'd told himself. And it wasn't haunted by ghosts of his past relationships—two of them if you count Hayes.

Gwyneth had cured him of the need to have a permanent partner. Zero interest, never again. In the quiet, ugly hours when he couldn't sleep, sometimes he thought her distance had been partially his fault. That he could have been different, better.

But those thoughts left with the rising of the sun, and by the time he pressed his morning coffee, he reminded himself what he was good at with women: beginnings. The first meeting, the casual dinner, the sex that followed and brought both parties a reprieve from busy lives and busy days.

A way to have it all. As many new starts as possible without investing years before learning his partner's interest had deferred to someone else.

It seemed even that coping mechanism had its flaws. The board didn't approve of his after-hours activities, and that part of his life could cost him his very legacy.

Unacceptable.

Merina was the key to saving that legacy. No chance of her absconding with someone he knew unless she wanted to be sued or lose her hotel. But he couldn't see her straying. First off, she was nothing like Gwyneth. Merina Van Heusen cared about her family and preserving history. His ex made it clear history meant nothing to her the day she ended what she and Reese had for a guy she'd slept with on a whim.

Only that whim had turned into marriage. She and Hayes had the audacity to send him an invitation, and Gwyneth had expressed she'd like to "remain friends," which would have been laughable if he'd been able to feel anything other than deep, dark acrimony.

Hayes, who had worked for Crane Hotels at the time, was offered a hefty severance package and encouraged to leave. Reese supposed he owed Gwyneth a thank-you for that life lesson. If she'd have stayed with him, he might have settled down with a couple of kids and been happy as a clam in the same management position at Crane he'd held nine years ago.

He might have ignored his drive and aspirations to become CEO. Being in charge of one of the most recognized brands in the country didn't allow a lot of time for relationships. If the board could wrangle two or three brain cells together to see things his way, they'd also see that not having relationship entanglements afforded him to work all the hours he wanted. He could stay up as late as he needed and never receive a text asking him to leave early and pick up eggs and milk on his way home.

Like Mom and Dad.

At that thought, his stomach clenched. He had nothing but good memories of his mother and father, of their relationship. They were the ideal. But after trying his hand at attaining ideal, Reese saw that ideal wasn't for everyone. Success didn't come equally in all factions of life. For him, his success was in business, which, face it, wasn't a bad area to excel.

This was better and exactly why their father had never remarried. Alex knew the secret to thriving in business was to stay flexibly single. Reese knew it. Tag knew it. And when Eli returned from overseas and resumed a regular schedule back at Crane, he'd likely follow the same path. It was the family way.

"Scotch, neat," came a warm female voice to his left.

Reese was seated at the bar at Armande awaiting Merina with a full view of the door, so he knew the woman speaking over his shoulder wasn't her. The voice was a purposeful seductive purr when she addressed him properly.

"Reese Crane. You never called."

No, he wouldn't have called. He turned his head, meeting eyes with a tall brunette in a simple black dress. Long chestnut hair grazed her shoulders.

"But I did appreciate the flowers." Her lips curved to the side in a lazy smile and that's when her name came to him. Rebecca. They'd met at a fund-raiser for the art museum over the holidays. She worked there. What a perfect example of why he didn't do more than one date. She was trouble with a capital T if he'd ever seen it.

"Flowers cover a multitude of sins." He accepted the scotch from the bartender with a nod. Rebecca raised her glass of wine in cheers and they drank.

"I have to say," she said, glancing around the bar, "when we met, I was hoping what the media says about you wasn't true."

God help him if she mentioned his hashtag.

"I was sure you'd find the time we spent together good enough to warrant a second date." She swept her hair over her shoulder. With that body and her piercing almond-shaped eyes, Reese hazarded the safe guess that Rebecca hadn't gone home and cried in her Häagen-Dazs. "But I guess not."

"You seem to have landed on your feet," he said casually, checking the door again. "Who are you here with?"

He looked back at her in time to see her wide mouth part into a smile. "Busted. I'm here with Arnie Palatino."

"Mayor's son." He shrugged his mouth. "Not bad."

"Yeah, but"—she looked around conspiratorially before leaning in and murmuring in his ear—"he doesn't have a rocket in his pocket."

That explained the renewed interest. Before he could respond, he caught a flash of honeyed hair and red that drew his eyes to the door. Rebecca had started talking again but her voice faded into the din of diners and waitstaff. Everything in the room fell away as his eyes zoomed in on the woman who'd come here to meet him.

Merina Van Heusen's dark blond hair was down, one side pushed behind her ear. She wore a classy, simple red dress. It wasn't skintight but floated seductively over delicate shoulders, flaring at her hips. A subtle *V* exposed a hint of cleavage, just enough to make his mouth water but not enough to reveal the trace of ink he'd spotted the day she'd come in wearing a see-through wet silk shirt. A long gold necklace with a circle pendant hung between her breasts.

His mind echoed the reminder *business agreement*, but his instincts, the ones he trotted out for his dates, recognized her as one hundred percent woman.

Beside him, he was aware Rebecca had stopped talking. Just as well—they had nothing to say to each other.

"Excuse me," he said, standing from the bar. The moment he was on his feet, Merina spotted him. Her eyes cut to the brunette, then back to him.

He tried to communicate with a subtle headshake. *Relax, she's old business.*

"I guess you're here with someone too," Rebecca murmured.

"I am," he said. "Thanks for the drink."

She lifted her wine in a noncelebratory *cheers*, a tight, bitter smile on her face. By contrast, Merina Van Heusen was polished. Confident. Decked out in simplicity.

She straightened her shoulders as he approached, both hands wrapped around a gold clutch. She wore heels—five inches if he had to guess. The added height put her damn near eye to eye with him. Her amber eyes flashed with a mix of animosity and bravery. Just like the first time he met her.

"Merina." He offered an elbow.

"Reese." She glided her hand over his forearm. He held back a smile at hearing her say his name. At least she hadn't called him "Crane."

"I see you charged a dress to my tab as I recommended," he murmured as they followed the hostess through the restaurant. A few heads turned, and he wasn't surprised. Merina's red dress and elegance were enough to draw many a wandering eye.

"This old thing?" She slanted him a gaze.

This time the smile didn't stay away. He moved his hand to her lower back, a move that shouldn't have set off his pulse like a missile, but with Merina, he was learning nothing about her was expected.

"Your table, Mr. Crane." Tucked into the corner, a cozy table for two stood, a bottle of champagne chilling in a bucket.

"Thank you." He pulled out a chair for Merina before unbuttoning his suit jacket and sitting down across from her.

"Champagne," she said, her eyes going to the bottle. Her

skin was as smooth as porcelain but golden in color in the candlelight.

"Tag's idea, I'm sure," Reese said.

"Your brother?"

"He arranged this evening."

"I thought Bobbie arranged this evening."

"At Tag's request." He didn't want her to have the wrong idea. He didn't come here to seduce her. He flicked his gaze from the necklace that drew his eyes to her breasts. Probably best he remembered that.

An orderly waiter swept in, poured the champagne, and asked if they'd like the chef's selection for the evening. "An array of plates designed to unleash passion and bloom romance."

Jesus.

"Yes, thank you," Reese told him, keeping his internal reaction hidden. The waiter vanished in a puff of efficiency.

"They don't linger here, do they?" Merina cleared her throat, showing the first sign of discomfort when she lifted the champagne flute to her lips. If they were going to make people believe they were in love, they'd have to be together without a buffer.

"One of the draws of Armande. The staff understands diners come here to be left alone." He unfolded his napkin and put it on his lap. "Or rather, left to each other."

Her eyes moved around the room and Reese found he was unwilling to take his eyes off her face. Her makeup was understated, unlike Rebecca's dark eyes and bright lipstick, yet Merina was simply stunning.

"I hear this restaurant is known for its aphrodisiacs," she said. He liked the way her lips pursed when she said *aphrodisiacs*.

"Chocolate. Watermelon. Oysters. Avocado," he answered.

"Watermelon is an aphrodisiac?" Her expression was bemused.

"If you believe in that sort of thing."

"You don't?" She reached for her champagne again. He thought of her as a force to be reckoned with, yet she had the most delicate hands. Long fingers, blunt nails suggesting she did her own hard work, but feminine as proved by the sheen of pale polish. He found the dichotomy tantalizing. And it hadn't required a single oyster to feel that attraction right down to his bones.

"No," he answered. "I don't."

"Well, that's no fun," she said, sipping from her glass. Then her cheeks colored. "I mean, not that I expect... never mind."

What did she think? That he'd brought her here to seduce her and take her back to his room and...best not to chase that thought to its inevitable ending. This romance was for show, not indulgence.

The first course came via one of the waitstaff, who set Merina's plate in front of her, then Reese's in front of him. "Pan-seared mochi with avocado and a yuzu sesame dressing," the waiter announced.

"Wow. This is adorable," Merina said, staring down at the single block of mochi and small square of avocado sitting on the center of a gold-edged white plate.

"Good too." He lifted a pair of chopsticks from the table and ate it in one bite. After watching him, she did the same. He sipped his champagne and enjoyed the show. He liked her mouth. Liked her appetite. For business and for food.

After she swallowed and dabbed her mouth, he filled her champagne glass, figuring the more of it they drink, the better. This was beyond awkward for two people who didn't know each other.

"Did you know you have a hashtag?" she asked, licking her lips after another sip.

"Not you too," he said, his tone dry.

She gave him a flirty smile.

"I know I have a hashtag," he muttered, refilling his own glass and placing the bottle in the ice bucket.

"Do you know who started it?" she asked.

"I have a good idea."

"Well, at least it's flattering."

"If you find objectification flattering," he challenged. "Would you like it if someone gave a hashtag to your..." He gestured to her chest.

She tilted her head in thought rather than offense. "Hmm. Fair point. I thought men liked to be told how large their penises are."

A smile tickled the side of his mouth. Leave it to Merina to use the word *penises* as casually as she'd used the word *horseshit*.

"See? You do like it."

"I'm attached to it."

Her eyes brightened, and he felt a charge of pride in drawing forth the reaction. Then she laughed, just a small one, and that was even better. The women he normally dated were with him because of who he was, so getting them to laugh—charming them—wasn't a challenge. But Merina was with him in spite of who he was, so getting that reaction from her was genuinely rewarding.

"You have a lighter side," she said. "Who knew?"

"Don't tell anyone. You'll ruin my reputation." The air between them was warm and alive. He could continue this for a while longer.

But then her eyes went to Rebecca and her date being seated at a small table in the middle of the restaurant and her smile faded. A disapproving grunt sounded from her throat.

"That woman," she said, turning back to him. "Friend of yours?"

"No." His friends were business colleagues, and even then "friends" wasn't the right term for who they were. The women he dated, well, the only friendly thing between them was the way they parted after both parties received what they needed.

"But you did sleep with her," Merina blurted.

"I don't sleep with my friends."

"Only strangers?" She rested her glass on the white tablecloth.

That warm attraction between them didn't fizzle out, but burned hot. She wanted to play hardball? He could do that.

"Who do you sleep with, Merina?"

"Excuse me?" Dark rose colored her cheekbones.

"You brought it up." He leaned forward. "Just making conversation."

She shook her head as her eyes darted to the side. "I shouldn't have, I suppose. I find your love life fascinating."

"You, the media, and Crane Holdings board of directors." He sat back, feeling the weight of that admission. How had everything he'd achieved, everything he'd strived for, been watered down to who he had sex with? It was insulting. "I don't understand. What's the draw?"

"Are you kidding? A wealthy man who dates a parade of

beautiful women, yet none of them can penetrate his cold, unfeeling heart? The public eats that sort of thing up."

A muscle in his jaw ticked. Cold. Unfeeling. That's how she saw him? Not driven, or successful, or willing to do anything to secure his family's name? In that way, he and Merina weren't so different.

"I was surprised to learn you had such an aversion to the media since you've played into their hands so nicely," she continued.

"Just because this city is fascinated with the details of my dates doesn't mean I have to pander." His voice came out a grumble, every part of him wanting to argue. It was his habit to keep the walls up, so he'd keep them raised.

"They'll also be fascinated with our lives." A sharp glint lit her eyes. "We're going to be husband and wife. There are things we should talk about. How we met. First date. First time we..."

She let the pause linger in the air and he felt the tension once again settling between them—the good kind.

"...learned each other's middle names," she finished on a soft exhalation. The coy expression dashed from her face when he responded curtly.

"Merina, this is our first date. The rest of it we won't have talked about because the public will assume all we've been doing is fucking."

Her head jerked on her neck and she looked around to see if anyone was listening. As they had the most private table in the room, he wasn't worried. No one was within earshot.

"I've been in the spotlight enough to know that the media assumes I'm sleeping with the women they photograph me with. They're right half the time."

"Only half?" Merina asked drily.

"Seventy percent of the time," he amended with a wry smile. She returned it with one of her own. They ran hot and cold with each other, but no matter the temperature between them, the attraction endured.

Fascinating.

It'd been a while since he'd felt anything. Going through the motions wasn't a polite way to describe what he'd been doing with the women in his past, but accurate.

"The fewer things we have to make up the better," he said. "How did we meet? You stormed into my office to demand I keep the Van Heusen as-is. Then you gave me a doorknob."

Another laugh. She gestured with her glass. "Which I need back, by the way." She lowered her voice. "Won't the public suspect something when I end up with the hotel in my name?"

"By then it won't matter." He shrugged. "The divorce will garner some attention, but will be buried the next day beneath celebrity hoopla."

"Or the next woman you take to an opera." Her words lingered. He let them. He hadn't thought about what he'd do after Merina, but it made sense that after this hiccup, he'd continue dating much the same as he did before.

"Attention for the Van Heusen isn't a bad thing," he said instead of addressing her suggestion. "An article will win you some much needed publicity for the hotel. Mention how charming or quaint or rustic it is. Whatever turns you on about the place."

"You really do hate it, don't you?" Her face twisted into something resembling hurt. He didn't like seeing her hurt. Enraged was one thing; her passion and fight was exhilarating. But this tender look made him uncomfortable. He didn't want to hurt her feelings.

"I don't hate it," he said, telling her the truth. "But why choose a homey hotel over a sleek one?"

"Seriously? Who wouldn't want a relaxing, warm, family atmosphere?"

"Anyone who is trying to work or get laid," he answered frankly.

"I'm not running a brothel, Crane."

Ah, they were back to "Crane."

"Well, I'm not running an orphanage, Merina." Their gazes locked. He broke the connection by blinking. "But there are people who see the world the way you do. When you talk to the media, keep your focus on your passion for the hotel. You'll draw in those bleeding hearts."

Her mouth flinched, taking his comment for what it was—a teasing jab.

Their waiter delivered two small cups of watermelon soup with mint leaves and a crumbling of feta on top.

Merina scowled. "This looks disgusting."

"It tastes worse than it looks," he said, lifting his spoon.

"You don't like it?" She was still making a face as she dragged her spoon through the chilled soup.

"I do not like it," he said.

"Sam I Am?" She looked up, spoon full. "Would you eat it in a box?"

Reese blinked. Of all the references. "Dr. Seuss fan?"

"*Green Eggs and Ham* is the best children's book ever written." She pulled her shoulders as if to challenge him. But he wouldn't argue.

"On this we agree," he said, a note of surprise in his tone.

"I still have my copy from when I was little." She dipped her spoon and lifted it again, still unsure about taking that first bite.

"Me too. My mom used to read it to me before bed. I can't look at that tattered spine without remembering her." The moment it was out of his mouth, he wanted to retract his words. Never, ever was he sentimental on a date. Stick to business, family only as it had to do with business, likes and dislikes in the most general sense.

Rules Merina had obliterated without trying.

"Your mom has passed?" Sincerity leached into her expression.

"A long time ago. Anyway." He scooped up a bite of the chilled soup. Yep. As awful as he remembered.

"There's a gap in our how-we-met story," she said, letting the topic pass. "What will we say happened between the moment I stormed into your office and, say, right now?"

"The truth. I showed up at the Van Heusen in the middle of the night."

"Because . . . ?" she prompted.

"I couldn't stop thinking about you." Apparently champagne made him a drippy sentimentalist. "Your passion," he corrected quickly. "We'll say I was smitten."

"Smitten," she repeated.

"Completely." He held her eyes and she held his, and there, with the worst soup ever concocted in front of them, Reese felt a hit low in his gut. A hit of attraction like nothing he'd ever felt before. No, that wasn't true. He'd felt something like this before. With Gwyneth. He resented the similarity the moment his mind connected those dots.

He needed to get back on point. Like in a meeting when everyone gets off track and needed to be dragged back.

"There are a few details we should discuss tonight," he continued after another putrid bite. "We need to coordinate our schedules. Do you have an assistant?"

"Are you joking?" She took a bite, her eyes scrunched in morbid expectation. Then they opened and the expression on her face faded into *not bad*.

"Am I joking about what? And how could you possibly like that?"

"Are you joking about me having an assistant," she said, then gestured to the soup with her spoon. "What's not to like? It's watermelon. It's refreshing."

"You shouldn't have to drink watermelon. Why don't you have an assistant?"

"Because I like to do everything myself."

He sighed. Hands-on. Bad business, big heart. That should be a saying.

"Very well, I'll send *you* my schedule." He pulled out his phone.

"Now?"

"Why not?" They were a power couple. Any onlookers would think they did this kind of thing as foreplay.

"Okay." She reached into her clutch and came out with her iPhone.

He tapped his e-mail icon and glanced over at her, catching her watching him. "It's Harrington, by the way. My middle name."

Her lips tipped. "Nicole."

"Okay, Merina Nicole Van Heusen. Shall we?"

"Let's."

* * *

Seared scallops with cayenne and a dollop of crème fraîche and caviar followed the watermelon soup. Dessert was chocolate mousse topped with roasted figs served·in an almond tart. She and Reese polished off the champagne, ordered coffee, and camped at the restaurant table until they closed at eleven.

What started out as a nerve-wracking evening with her worrying over what to wear and how she'd handle aphrodisiacs with a man she barely tolerated had ended with Merina feeling better about everything. She and Reese may not be friendly with one another, but in business, they glided. Once their iPhones came out, they'd excitedly shared meeting details and talked shop. They had a lot in common even though her hotel was radically different from his. Although, the head-butting continued when he'd started telling her what to do.

"You'll need to cancel drinks with Lorelei on Tuesday," he'd said after dessert.

"Forget it. I haven't gone out with her in ages."

"New fiancé," he argued, pointing at himself. "Whirlwind romance. Wedding in two weeks."

Okay. That was fair. The discussion had prompted her to point out how he needed to cancel dinner with a woman named Claudia at an upcoming art show.

"Forgot about her," he'd commented, then tapped a quick note into his phone.

"Let me guess? Are you having Bobbie send her flowers?"

"No. No date, no flowers. I sent Bobbie a note to cancel and not reschedule."

Oddly enough, she'd felt a blip of admiration for the

way Reese handled dating. Not the way he tore through women like they were disposable, but how he had the confidence to do whatever he wanted regardless of what people said about him.

After Corbin, part of the reason Merina hadn't dated was because she was beyond embarrassed she'd allowed something so humiliating to happen to her.

The next day at noon on the dot, she strode into Reese's office for their appointment, one with a public relations person who was hired specifically to help this engagement and marriage go off without a hitch. In Merina's opinion, the woman was barely needed. Merina and Reese were professionals who were damn good at their jobs. After the combined first date/business get-together last night, there was only the matter of the prenup, the wedding, and then riding things out until the divorce.

Reese was just pocketing his cell phone when she walked in, with an appointment, thank you very much. Bobbie still hadn't looked happy about letting her through. The doors shut behind her and Merina told him, "Bobbie really hates me."

"No, she doesn't." He strode out from behind the desk, today in a deep gray suit, red tie. "She's too busy to be cordial."

"Like you?" She smiled sweetly.

"Very funny." He made an *after you* gesture and they walked out of his office via a side door, down a hallway and into a conference room. There, a platinum-blond woman sat, wearing a white pantsuit and a scowl. She was young and very pretty and she looked pissed, which meant only one thing.

"Looks like she didn't appreciate your flowers," Merina said as Reese's hand closed over the doorknob.

He frowned, looked through the window at the peeved blonde, and then said, "No. This is our advisor."

Wow. Their advisor was beautiful.

He pulled the door open and announced, "Penelope Brand, I'd like you to meet Merina Van Heusen, my—"

"What were you thinking?" Penelope bolted out of her seat. Taking in her posture, Merina considered that Reese was lying. Because this woman was not happy. Then Penelope turned her scowl on Merina. "You went on your first date in public and not only did you not kiss each other good night, you barely touched each other!"

Reese sighed and Merina blinked over at him, shocked he wasn't having the blonde escorted out by her golden tan.

"I'm sure we can work this out," he said with exaggerated patience. "Merina, have a seat." He nodded at a chair and Merina took the back of it.

"That's what I'm talking about," Penelope exploded. "You just directed your fiancée into her seat with a chin nod." She shook her head, looking disappointed and exasperated. "We can't announce the engagement on the heels of this disaster. I'm going to have to put some spin on your impromptu outing last night to fix this."

Reese and Merina sat.

Penelope, not through yet, lifted her cell phone and read aloud, " '*Reese Crane hit the town with his mystery date, but what started hot quickly moved to tepid as the two stared at their phones over sexy entrées.*' " She paused to send them each a scolding glare, then continued. " '*He and the woman in the red dress shared feisty looks and tantalizing smiles before the evening took on a different tone: one of business as they pecked at their iThings. The scene was set with champagne and caviar, but the aphrodisiacs at Chicago's famed Armande restaurant had no effect on these two office drones. Is Crane's tame date made to distract from the sizable issue of his hashtag? Or is this the one woman in existence who didn't fall at King Crane's feet?'"*

Merina's jaw dropped.

"What paper is that?" Reese asked in a tone that suggested he'd file a lawsuit against them just for fun.

"It's the Chicago Insider—a blog. And it's already been shared across social media about two hundred times." Penelope frowned and her forehead didn't so much as pucker. Her skin was porcelain-smooth, her white suit pristine, and her jewelry winking gold. "The point is, they already smell a rat, and people are paying attention. You two are going to have to up your game."

"We coordinated our calendars. We're on the same page," Merina said, refusing to take the younger woman's abuse silently. "A few more dates and I'm sure the public will see us as a couple. This is just new. They're speculating."

Penelope's fierce expression softened. She came to sit next to Merina, facing her, her smile in place and blue eyes bright. "Merina. You're a vibrant, beautiful woman. You're in love with a gorgeous, hunky billionaire. You were at a restaurant that served everything but sex on those plates. The reporter who happened to be there expected to see Reese and a mystery woman all but fornicate on top of the table."

Merina flinched.

"You two walked in sort of cozy according to this reporter"—Penelope gestured to her phone and then dropped it onto the table—"but you left single file. Reese, you didn't so much as palm her lower back."

"He did so," Merina snapped. "On the way to our table, he placed his palm on my back." She remembered because she'd been aware of that imprint the entire dinner. She cast a glance at Reese, who raised an eyebrow in interest.

"Regardless. Whatever you did wasn't enough to leave an impression on Rose Wells of the Chicago Insider. You two have to do better. The only opinion that matters is the public one."

"So we pander," Reese said through his teeth. Merina was in agreement with him for once. It was ridiculous.

"You hired me to help you convince the world your cold heart has been thawed by a smoking hot romance."

Even though Merina had accused him of something similar last night—being cold and unfeeling—she found herself rising to his defense. There'd been a definite moment of warmth when he talked about his mom. And when he'd confessed his middle name was Harrington. Later she'd even dug out of him that Harrington was a family name. A great-uncle on his mother's side.

"Last night showed how unprepared you two are." Penelope leaned back in her chair and folded her arms. "Kiss her."

"What?" His was a voice of alarm and Merina echoed the sentimentality.

"I want to see if you can pull it off." Penelope shrugged.

"I'm not a performing monkey, Pen."

"We can pull it off," Merina chimed in. Reese looked moderately relieved that he wasn't alone in this battle. First kisses—even ones for show—were not to be trotted out in a boardroom for an audience of one. Merina didn't want a grade, for Pete's sake.

Penelope sat straight. "Good. In that case, let's review

your revised schedule of events, because you two are going to need to sell it. And after the next date, if this happens again"—she waggled her phone—"we will have to reconvene and you will be practicing your PDA for me. Because right now it's PDB."

She stood and pulled a computer from her bag. Merina and Reese exchanged glances.

"PDB?" Merina asked.

Penelope tapped a few keys into her keyboard and didn't look up. "Public displays of boredom."

* * *

"She's intense," Merina said once Penelope swept out of the boardroom, her heels clicked out of the corridor as Reese watched at the window.

"She's the best. And she's trustworthy. She isn't going to run to the papers and sell this story for the highest price." A hint of a smile tickled his mouth. "She hates reporters."

Sounded like a story. It also sounded like relief. Pen was on their side, and apparently they did need someone to help them navigate the choppy waters of the media.

"She's also right," Merina said.

"Yeah," Reese agreed.

"Maybe we *should* practice." She fiddled with her phone, unable to look at him. "So that we're comfortable around each other." Penelope had insisted more than once that they needed to touch and touch often. Hold hands. Stare longingly into each other's eyes. Her words echoed in Merina's head now. *You two should look like you can't stand that you're not alone. Like you could tear each other's clothes off at any moment.*

There was simply no way to do that as long as Reese felt like a stranger.

"I don't have as much experience wooing strangers as you do." She winced at her admission. "I don't mean to say I don't know what I'm doing."

"It's okay, Merina, I know what you mean." He didn't look worried. Then again, did he ever? His face was stone, his hands in his pockets. "What do you suggest?"

His voice came out like a seductive murmur and she could have sworn his eyes dashed to her lips. But she couldn't kiss him here, in his white-and-chrome-and-glass boardroom. On his turf. She needed a few drinks first.

"How about another date tonight?"

"Fine. I'll call Tableau and—"

"No. Not another fancy dinner." Somewhere she was comfortable. "Posh."

"The martini bar?"

"Yeah. We can have drinks and practice there." Off his home turf, and nowhere near hers.

"Seven."

"Seven. And, Reese?" she said as she stood and gathered her purse and phone. "If you pick me up yourself, that may be better."

He dipped his head in a nod and she walked past him. Before she exited the room, she was surprised to feel his hand on her upper arm. His warm palm slid down, cupping her elbow, grasping her fingers, and then lifting her hand. He pressed a soft kiss there, full-lipped and firm, then held her eyes as the air between them sizzled.

Merina's heart did a flip, her stomach joining in.

"Just practicing," he rumbled.

CHAPTER 6

Merina was as nervous getting ready for a date as if she were a teenager. Really, it made no sense. She and Reese were adults, and they both knew what was at stake. There was no reason to fret over the length of her little black dress or worry over the pedicure she'd given herself first thing this morning.

But she did.

She bit her lip. Then she heard the door pop open and the exasperated sounds of her parents arguing about something as they jostled in grocery bags.

Her parents were home?

Merina jogged down the stairs, eyes wide. "What are you two doing here?"

"Like I said, if we would have gone to Fields, we could have saved twenty minutes getting back," her mother told her father as they unloaded the bags on the counter.

"And like *I* said, if we would have gone to the Olive

Garden, we wouldn't be arguing about this at all." He shook a head of lettuce as he spoke.

"We're cooking because we both want to be healthy," her mother said, pulling out fresh tomatoes. "And there's no 'the' in Olive Garden."

"Your mother wants to be healthy. I want to eat at a restaurant." Mark grumbled to Merina while unpacking canned goods from a paper bag.

"I mean what are you doing home? I thought you were working." Reese was due here any minute. Her original plan was to tell her parents she was out with him...after she returned home. Evidently this entire scenario had made her morph into a teenager.

"We're fully staffed if that's what you're asking." Her mother shut the fridge. "You look beautiful."

"Thanks."

And there went the doorbell. Right on time. Reese wasn't so much as thirty seconds late. Merina could have used those thirty seconds to ease her parents into the idea that she was dating the future CEO of the company who'd purchased their hotel and threatened to fire them all.

"Be nice," she said, her eyes trained on her father.

"I'm an angel." He did look harmless with a bunch of bananas in one hand and an avocado in the other.

Merina's parents weren't old-fashioned, and they weren't reserved. But they'd sniff out a wolf in sheep's clothing right away, and Reese was definitely that.

She opened the door to find him dressed in a dark jacket and gray tie, his scruff light but definitely visible, navy eyes matching his designer jeans. Had she ever seen Reese in jeans before? He wore them as well as a suit, and whatever pair he'd chosen had preserved his air of wealth.

Though, she was beginning to wonder if that air was simply *him*.

"Hi." She tracked up from his shiny brown shoes, to a leather belt, to those impossibly long lashes. Then he did something that made her stomach flutter. He grinned.

"Hey, gorgeous." He leaned in, accosting her with a hint of spice from his cologne, and kissed her cheek. On the inside, her nerves rattled, warmth oozing down her spine. On the outside, she was aware of her parents looking on in interest.

She gave Reese a wide-eyed *here we go* look, then turned to her parents. "Mom, Dad, you know Reese Crane."

Her father's mouth compressed. Her mother folded her arms, a worry line bisecting her brow.

"Mr. Crane," she said. "What a surprise."

"We'll be back," Merina said, not stepping into the kitchen. The sooner they left the better.

"Maybe," Reese lashed a possessive arm around her waist. She was pressed flush with a wall of muscle. "Drinks may turn into dinner," he said, his voice low. "And dessert."

Merina swallowed thickly. What was he doing?

"He's kidding," she blurted.

He released her, came deeper into the house until he arrived at the counter. Extending a hand to Merina's father, he said, "Mr. and Mrs. Van Heusen, good to see you. I assume Merina told you the remodel and staffing plans have been put on indefinite hold."

"Hold?" her father asked, taking Reese's hand in a cordial but quick shake. "She didn't tell us."

"Right now we're focused on another building."

"Indefinite?" Jolie parroted. "That's ... interesting news."

"Wonderful," Merina corrected. "It's wonderful news."

"Merina came to my office and made a compelling argument about the Van Heusen." He shot a gaze over his shoulder at her and even though her parents couldn't see his expression, it was a smoldering one. Then he turned back to them. "I stood very corrected. She's a force to be reckoned with."

"That she is." Her father puffed with pride even though he still looked wary of Reese's intentions. Which meant she had some work to do, because her parents had to believe this was real. She hadn't done much to convince them and she wasn't sure the show Reese had put on had convinced anyone.

* * *

"I didn't know Posh took reservations."

"For the upper deck," Reese answered. What did Merina expect, to show up at Posh and smash in with the crowd?

He took his eyes from the road to check on his date. Merina's shoulders were draped in a sheer black wrap over a sleek, short black dress. Her long legs bare and smooth and capped in high heels. He was a leg man and regretted not hiring a driver so he could stare longer. Merina's legs were fantastic.

"Nice effort with the parents. Who knew you could be so smooth?"

"Us sewer rats are able to call up sophistication when we need to." He turned at a light and edged down the street in heavy traffic.

"And that bit about dinner and dessert. Risky." She shifted and he took advantage of a red light to admire the way she recrossed her legs. Her dress inched higher on her thighs.

"Padding the announcement for you," he said. "When you tell them about our engagement, they'll have to believe we were swept up."

She hummed. He had no idea what that meant. He'd bet she had noises for everything. When she was being thoughtful or when she was annoyed. When she was turned on. It'd been a while since he bothered to notice such subtleties with the women he was with. Brief as he was with them, there hadn't been a need.

You've been missing out.

The thought sent the subtlest pang of regret through him. After he'd read Gwyneth wrong—after she'd sold him out for another man—he'd vowed to keep things surface for his heart's and his pride's sake. The idea that he'd robbed himself of experiences in the process didn't settle well.

Not at all.

"I meant it was risky because you implied I might not make it home."

"Well it could be a long evening."

She batted made-up eyes at him and her red lips flinched into a reluctant smile. A surge of attraction shocked his veins. There was something about Merina beyond her physical features that made his libido sit up and beg.

Typically with his past dates, the surge of attraction came later, after he had her clothes off. With Merina, the anticipation of having her clothes off fueled his want.

Keeping things surface was easier in the long run—less messy. So why, in Merina's case, was he looking forward to getting dirty?

"What are you smiling about?"

"Nothing." He whipped his red Ferrari into the valet station. Flashy and just what they needed to snag the attention of the paparazzi. The media thought they could run his and Merina's romance into the dirt, but Reese had a secret weapon. He could ooze charm when necessary. He'd bet Merina could call up her own battery of flirting if needed. More than charming her, though, he found himself looking forward to surprising her.

She sat, hands in her lap, while he came around to her side of the car. Penelope had hammered dents into his ego when she berated him for not touching Merina in the right way. He knew how to treat a woman. It was just that usually the woman on his arm was all over him. Merina wasn't that way. But tonight they were playing things for the cameras. As proven when she didn't shove her way from the car without waiting for him.

Reese opened her door and offered a hand. Merina took it, sliding her softer palm against his, and awareness flooded his veins. Her willingly coming to him was another plus to the evening.

"Darling," he said, laying it on thick.

Her tongue darted out to wet her lips, making the red glisten. She climbed from the car and looped her arm with his. Together they walked in, their eyes peeled for anyone who pointed a cell phone in their direction.

* * *

Reese walked in like he owned the place. The thought alarmed her. What if he *did* own the place? Totally possible.

He swept her through the neon lights and fog to a

semiprivate upper deck. From here, they could see and be seen, which was ideal. Penelope had made it clear they'd better shake off their business-only reputation, and fast. Merina had come ready to play hardball.

She'd asked him here because she felt at home at Posh. The music wasn't so loud that they couldn't talk but loud enough that they wouldn't be overheard.

A cushy couch overlooking the swarm below perched at the edge of a shelflike overhang, surrounded by a glass wall. Up here, with a personal waiter and view of the DJ who was suspended over the center of the bar, she got a glimpse of what it was like to be Reese Crane.

Living the good life high above his minions, his every whim being catered to. She tried to curl her lip at the treatment but couldn't. Being on his arm had its perks. She was going to enjoy them.

"Downstairs, getting to the bartender is a test of endurance and Midwest manners," Merina told him as she watched men attempt to draw the bartenders' attention while women in low-cut tops were served first. "You could learn a thing or two from the people down there."

"That's why I have you." His voice held no challenge, just commanding presence and smooth delivery. Like he meant it. Maybe he did. She was beginning to think she could learn a thing or two from him as well.

Their waiter, flamboyantly dressed in short shorts, a cropped hot pink top, and slatted sunglasses, returned with their drink order. He passed down her cosmopolitan and Reese's scotch. "Anything else, beautiful people?"

"No, thanks, Kevin." Merina winked and he shot his finger like a gun.

"You bet, Mer."

He swayed away and Reese sipped his drink while she waited for his judgment. None came.

"How's your stereotypically feminine cocktail?"

Ah, there it was.

"Fruity. How's your exhaustingly cliché manly drink?"

He took a long draw from the glass, the whiskey rolling over his tongue, his throat bobbing in the most irritatingly tantalizing way as he swallowed.

"It's always what I expect," he said over the music. He dipped his chin at her cocktail. "Yours is to the discretion and capabilities of the bartender. Mine never wavers."

"Do you enjoy getting what you expect, Crane?" She cocked her head. "The expected can be boring."

His features darkened, and in those shadows she saw a man who'd experienced the unexpected once upon a time, and it bit him in the ass. Then the shadows receded and that cocksure, bored mask she'd grown used to slid into place.

What are you hiding, Reese Crane?

"Reliability isn't boring," he stated.

Was it a business failure he'd been turning over in his head, or one of the personal variety?

"Structured childhood?" she guessed.

He shrugged one of his big shoulders. "Yes and no. Dad is ex-military, so he has a side of him that is structured. Mom was more of a free spirit."

Was. He'd mentioned his mother at dinner too. Merina wondered how long ago he'd lost her. How much her loss affected her sons and her husband. She imagined the pain of losing someone that beloved would linger a lifetime.

"You?" He sipped his drink. She wished she could crack open his head and see what he was thinking. His controlled facial expressions hid his thoughts.

"My parents are traditional. They believe in working hard, but they also know money is a tool to provide comfort, not the end-all be-all of existence."

"Do you think my family worships at the altar of the almighty dollar?"

"Not…on purpose," she said with a smile. The challenging glint in his eye told her he knew she was teasing him.

Between them, heat flared. It was the same spark she'd felt each time she was around him. Given her spiking pulse and heated neck, she'd assumed it was rage. Now she was questioning whether the attraction was real. Sure, she was being purposefully receptive to him, but there was something else going on.

Who knew the first time she felt that long-gone spark it would be with a man she shouldn't even *like*? He was impossible not to admire…which was upsetting.

Palpable heat snapped the air between them as he leaned closer.

"Parents are out of the way," Reese said. "What do you want to share next? Schooling? Favorite color? Hobbies?"

"That's pretty dry." She took a drink of her cosmo and savored the sweet, tart flavor before swallowing. The soft green, blue, and pink lighting pulsed with the beat of the song the DJ, hovering from the ceiling, was currently spinning.

They sat in silence while she thought. Dating wasn't something she did often. She was too busy. Busy at the hotel, busy helping her parents, busy being busy with nothing at all. If she stopped for a single second, worry crept in. Worry that she was wasting her life working like a hamster in a wheel, which was why she often didn't stop long enough to think about it.

Dangerous, those thoughts.

There was a very big discussion she and Reese needed to have. And what better place to have it than here, buried under a heavy bass beat?

"What about the emotional hurtles we have to leap?" she asked. "You're a good two feet away from me."

"Maybe I'm shy," he said after gauging the distance on the couch between them. "Or maybe"—he moved closer, lifting his body and bringing it within a foot of hers—"I'm worried I'll frighten you away."

His dark blue eyes sparkled in the club's lighting. She felt something when he scooted closer, but frightened wasn't her dominant emotion.

Intrigued. Interested. Fascinated. There were some words.

"I don't spook easily." Her voice dipped.

"No?" He came closer, so close his jeans brushed her bare knee. He abandoned his drink on the low table in front of him and then did the same with hers, freeing the hand she now didn't know what to do with.

Sifting her hair through his fingers, he leaned closer, firm, but full lips parting as her heart thundered against her breast. Her face went hot. Her throat constricted. This close, he was as powerful as a transformer, causing a buzz she felt in every last one of her neglected erogenous zones.

An inch from her mouth, Reese bit out, "We've been made."

Not . . . what she expected. She blinked, surprised.

"Reporter," he said.

She started to ask where, but a flash among many flashes came from the direction of the crowd below. Then

Reese did something that made her heart lift. He grinned. A natural, easy, toothy grin, paired with a flick of his eyes like he was checking her out.

With his hand, he cupped her nape. Just a light brush before he leaned close and whispered in her ear, "Showtime."

A shiver raced down her spine at the feel of his warm breath against her skin.

"First kiss. Don't screw it up." He pressed his lips to her jaw and for a scant moment she forgot about the reporter snapping away down there. She was too overtaken by the rough scrape of his facial hair on her softer skin, the smell of him enveloping her.

She shut her eyes. This time the flashes of light came from behind her eyelids when his mouth closed over hers. It wasn't hard to lean into him. Her hand grabbed hold of his suit jacket before she realized. And when he slanted his mouth and just the tip of his tongue touched to her bottom lip, she whimpered.

He pulled back too soon. His eyes were heated, his hand moving from her neck and brushing her bared shoulder.

Okay. Kissing Reese Crane was *not* going to be a hardship.

"Not bad," he said, his easygoing smile likely for the paparazzi below.

A pang of disappointment tingled in her breastbone. She shouldn't care that he was acting. This wasn't real. She didn't *want* it to be real.

His fingers continued playing in her hair. He was still close. "We'll discuss timing on the engagement announcement at dinner tonight."

"Dinner?" She blinked.

"And dessert."

"Dessert?" She'd turned into a parrot, squawking his every utterance back at him.

"Though I'm tempted to have my dessert now." He leaned in and pressed his mouth to hers for a quick kiss. Stubble abraded her chin. She reached up and stroked his face, unsure now if the flashing was the club lighting or if this moment would also show up on the Internet tomorrow morning.

"Okay," she whispered, then ran a fingernail down his jawline. "Dinner and dessert."

* * *

Reese felt as if he was vibrating when she scraped his jaw, then his lower lip with her finger. Every inch of him—including the several aching ones in his pants—wanted to take her by the back of the head and kiss her until they were both panting. The need was so visceral, so...*animal*, he sat back some. The idea behind the kiss was to give the reporter some fodder. Penelope may have asked they do a little PDA, not maul Merina in full view of downtown Chicago.

He pulled her hair back into place, all those silken, honey-colored strands falling softly against her shoulders. Everything about her was soft and warm and inviting, except for when she spoke. Then she was barbed and feisty. Both sides did it for him, and he couldn't for the life of him figure out why. Though, this relationship came with a safety net. They could fight all they wanted, and she couldn't go anywhere until the deed was done.

So to speak.

He wasn't sure how they'd survive a six-month marriage

without further exploring the heat that had flared between them. As first kisses went, that one was the most memorable. Hell, he couldn't recall a single kiss in the past that made him as interested in more. With Merina, "more" wasn't guaranteed. Even though a wedding was.

He turned his head to see if the reporter was gone. She wasn't, but she was no longer aiming her camera at them. She was scrolling through her phone, a smile on her face. He went out with her once, years and years ago. Couldn't remember her name now, but she didn't appear the least bit heartbroken. She looked like she was mentally counting the extra zeroes in her paycheck after she sold those photos.

"Oh God," Merina uttered.

"What?" He was on alert, scoping out the club for more reporters or photographers.

"You dated her too."

"What?" Was she psychic or had his thoughts shown so clearly on his face? Either possibility presented problems. He worked hard to keep his feelings buried. It helped with the media and business to be poker-faced. Only his father and brothers knew him well enough to call bullshit. "Why would you say that?"

She shook her head and didn't reward him with an answer.

"How am I going to keep up with your long, long, *long* list of ladies?" She pressed her fingertips between her breasts and his eyes dipped to her cleavage. "If I were the one sleeping with half the men in the city, I would be painted as the slutty girl and they'd say you were slumming."

"Merina." He shook his head. There was a double standard, but he had to call her on that untruth. "No one in their right mind would ever accuse you of being slutty." She was too bright, too poised. Nothing like the one-night-only women he'd been seeing since Gwyneth had incinerated what they had together.

"Wanna bet?" She snagged his tie and tugged, not hard, just enough to see if he'd come the rest of the way. He did, too intrigued not to.

"Sure. I have a few bucks."

"I can't shake your hand because we'd look too businessy, so I had to improvise and go with a tie-tug."

"Good thinking."

She grinned in response before her eyes slipped to his mouth. All he could think of was taking her lips captive again.

"Five dollars says I'm painted as one of your ninnies by night's end," she said.

"You're on."

"You're going down, Crane," and then she answered his fantasy by crushing her lips against his and smothering the life out of his brain.

* * *

REESE CRANE, TAMED?

Merina had never been so glad to lose five dollars. The headline on the blog Monday morning didn't paint her as a hussy, but instead painted Reese as losing a manly peg or two to the siren who wooed him away from all other women. Two dates had been enough for the media to jump to conclusions.

Reese had sent her the headline this morning in a text message reading, *Pay up.*

She wondered how he liked being called "tame" and guessed he didn't, which put a bigger smile on her face.

"Well, you're smiley today," her mother announced as she entered the kitchen via the curved staircase. "And up early."

Merina closed her laptop, not caring to share with her mother how much publicity her "dates" with Reese Crane were garnering.

"I noticed you were home early from your date last Friday." Jolie poured herself a cup of coffee. "Warmer?"

"I'm good." She sipped her half-full cup and debated what to tell her mom about the date, but she didn't have long to think it through when Jolie sat down across from her with her own mug.

After they left Posh, she and Reese went to dinner at a restaurant Merina couldn't remember the name of. Some fancy place with soft lighting and artful blocks of wood acting as tables. Dinner was incredible, and the conversation flowed rather than being forced. It seemed their first for-public kiss had set them both at ease. The evening ended by ten, and he walked her to her door, dropping a kiss on her lips that made her want more.

She wasn't sure what to do with that, so she decided to count it in the plus column for their ruse. It was unlikely but possible there was a paparazzo in the bushes. Better safe than sorry.

She hadn't seen him since and was now mentally readying herself for seeing him tonight. She hoped the meeting-like atmosphere would help quell some of her nerves.

Penelope had requested getting together at Reese's house. At the idea of seeing Reese's private lair, Merina felt fifty shades of nervous. Who knew what lurked behind his gargantuan mostly-unused Lake Shore Drive home? When she received the address via e-mail from Bobbie, Merina Googled it. The aerial view alone was drool-worthy. There was a pool out back. Fountains out front. Three manicured acres surrounded the building. The fifteen-thousand-square-foot house was sold to Reese nine years ago. She'd tried digging up a few pictures of the interior but only found one of the foyer and double staircase sweeping up each side and a small half bath in who knew what part of the house.

"Your father told me not to ask at the risk of being nosy, but... I have to," Jolie said.

Slowly, Merina lowered her mug.

"Why in heaven's name are you dating the man who only a few days ago you called a 'corporate tyrant'? I mean, don't get me wrong, I have eyes and I can see he's terribly attractive." Her mother's lips pursed. "The whole family is. Those three boys got the best of their mother and Big Crane."

She wasn't wrong. Merina had met Tag once before. He was the youngest brother and despite not having an affinity for long hair, she'd been completely taken by his charm and easy smile. Fun-loving Tag was more her style, but she'd received a proposal from the brother who was dark and closed off and irritating.

Until Reese was kissing her. Then he was none of those things. He was delicious and warm and tasted like spice cake. Or maybe that was the scotch.

"We just... hit it off," Merina said, lifting her mug so she wouldn't have to say more.

"Are you seeing more of him?" Her mother's eyebrows crawled up her forehead.

At the mention of "more," she again imagined loosening his tie. Why she was so focused on that one article of clothing, she had no idea. Maybe because she'd never seen him without one.

Merina cleared her throat. "I'm seeing him tonight, actually."

"Tonight." Her mother sighed. "Mer, you do know what you're doing, don't you?"

"Of course." She was marrying a billionaire to gain possession of her family's hotel.

"I worry, sweetheart." Her mother's brow creased further. "Since Corbin—"

"Mom." Merina shook her head. She didn't want to talk about Corbin. Like, ever. It was an embarrassing smudge on an otherwise perfect record. A time when she was blinded by love, or what she thought was love, when the writing was so clearly written on the wall even a blind man could have spotted it.

"Are you and Dad going into the office late?" Merina stood and rinsed her mug in the sink.

"Probably this afternoon. Your father isn't feeling well."

Merina's heart hit the floor. She grasped the counter and waited for bad news. Since his heart attack, she worried he might have another. He didn't eat as healthy as he should and wore stress like a second skin.

"Just a sore throat. Not his heart. He's fine, Mer." Her mother waved a hand but Merina found herself unsure if she could trust her mother's word.

Lately, they had both been doing a lot of lying to each other.

* * *

By seven o'clock, Reese was shaking the hands of a few board members after an impromptu meeting. Their focus now? The restaurants and bars in Crane Hotels nationwide. The bar profits were on a downward turn. In their words, they smelled smoke but didn't see fire. They weren't alarmed yet.

Yet being the operative word. This was Tag's area of expertise and he'd want to get an early stranglehold on it, a tactic Reese was in full support of. Once these vultures left the room, he'd tell his brother just that.

Bob Barber shook his hand next, a smile on his aging face. "Sometimes these things shake out and there's nothing to worry about."

"Sure," Reese said, but Bob's words were meaningless. The forty-minute meeting where they discussed numbers was what mattered. After they closed their leather binders and started talking about drinks downtown, whatever they said was null and void. He refused to feel good about it, but at the same time, this was not his problem.

At least they hadn't brought up his new relationship. He supposed a few more appearances in their vicinity would make them notice.

"Shit," Tag said from behind him after the last board member was out the door.

Reese turned to his brother. Tag scrubbed a hand over his beard. He was frowning. Tag rarely frowned.

"According to them, you have time."

"I don't want to wait until things go tits up." Tag folded his arms over his chest. Stubborn pride ran in the Crane genes.

"We're in agreement."

"I'd like it if they go back to ignoring me."

"Welcome to the club." Reese clapped his younger brother on the back. "Don't worry. Once they hear about the engagement, you'll fade into the background."

"Let's hope." Tag stood. "Come out with me. Been a while since we threw back a few beers."

"Like eight years," Reese said, his tone droll.

Tag chuckled. "Around that."

In truth, he'd love nothing more than to kick back with Tag for a while. He and his brother had a shorthand that didn't require a lot of unnecessary chatter.

"Can't," Reese answered. "I'm seeing Merina tonight, so my drinks will be had with her. And Penelope Brand."

"The cute blonde."

"*No.*"

"Not interested." His brother held out both hands like he was surrendering. "She's a brand of crazy I don't dig." He swept his legal pad off the boardroom table and walked toward the door. "Tell Merina I said hi."

"Will do. And, Tag?"

His brother poked his head back into the room.

"Rain check on the drinks."

"I'll hold you to it, brother." Tag's lips lifted into a smile. Then he was gone.

The drive to his house wasn't far, but Reese felt every mile like it was being branded into his skin. The one thing he hadn't anticipated when Penelope suggested the three of them meet at his Lake Shore Drive home was that his memories of it would rear up and try and take him out.

He'd returned to the house on occasion. It wasn't like he had a phobia, but the structure wasn't what he'd call inviting. The room he and Gwyneth shared, the memories they made were etched into the walls. He wasn't going to cower—but he couldn't say he was pleased about the idea of moving in there with Merina.

His throat went tight at the thought of sharing the space with a woman a second time.

He pulled his shoulders as he drove, mentally compartmentalizing the years he'd spent with Gwyneth. No matter what awaited him behind the front door, he wasn't going to allow himself to be hurt all over again. Especially by old business. He was no longer the hopeful twenty-five-year-old who would get raked in by a purposeful pout. He was a grown man, his legacy within reach. The discomfort he felt at being here was nothing more than an inconvenience.

He pulled up to the gate and pressed his finger to the security touchpad. The iron bars swung outward, opening to the lush garden he hoped survived the cool spring. He'd hired landscapers to plant colorful flowers and clean the fountains and pool, and perform whatever other maintenance was required to get the house wedding-ready. Plenty more flowers were being trucked in for the big day that was in actuality a small affair, but his wedding planner was exuberant and he'd let her talk him into indulging.

"It's your first marriage," she'd told him, hearts mingling with dollar signs in her eyes. He'd thought of Merina and how this was her first marriage, too. Just because he wanted to get this over with was no reason to rob her of doing things right. More flowers were the least he could do.

He parked his car—a Porsche for driving around town—in the garage and walked a path to the front door, his stomach heavy.

The paved walkway to the door was one Gwyneth hated and had complained about often. She'd wanted white stone instead of gray. At the front door, he recalled the Christmas wreath she'd ordered that was so massive, it hid the door-knob.

The doorknob he grabbed now. His palm was damp. His heartbeat erratic.

It's a house.

A gargantuan monstrosity he could barely find his way around in. A piece of real estate he'd purchased because he'd made a lot of money quickly and needed to move out of his father's house. When Gwyneth left and Reese relocated to his suite in Crane Hotel, he still didn't get rid of it.

One of his heroes was Howard Hughes, but it didn't mean Reese had to follow him into lunacy. Papers wrote stories and were always looking for an angle. Sleeping in his suite looked as if he worked a lot of overtime, but living there without an actual home? He didn't need reports that he'd lost his marbles or that he was weak.

He was not weak. This house was a symbol of his success, and it made good business sense to keep it. It also happened to be a place where he'd never really belonged.

He turned the knob just as it began to rain.

* * *

Rain pelted the windows of the formal dining room. Merina sat next to Reese, feeling tension radiate from him. He wore his usual dark suit and neutral expression, but his lips were slightly pursed and the skin around his eyes looked tight. She'd noticed it when he set foot in the foyer where she and Penelope stood chatting. At first she'd thought he must be upset about work, but when Penelope asked for a tour, he'd denied her with a curt "later," then led them into the dining room.

Suspicious.

Then again, he didn't live here. Was it that surprising he didn't like his own house?

So many unanswered questions. All of which she stowed when Penelope announced, "Okay," after tapping her phone in silence for a few minutes.

They'd started the meeting with glasses of wine, Reese's half drunk, Pen's untouched, Merina's gone. Reese had requested the housekeeper, Magda, give them privacy, which was a shame. Merina could use a refill.

She'd expected his mansion to reflect Crane Hotels: white and black and glass. For the most part, she wasn't wrong. Though instead of white, the interior consisted mostly of shining cream-colored floors and thick gold drapes, black furniture and modern-styled lighting. The dining room was considerably warmer with low-hanging shaded lights overhead and a centerpiece with live plants running the length of the black granite table.

Merina hadn't hidden her surprise at the sheer size and beauty of Reese's mansion. She'd lingered out front earlier, admiring her soon-to-be home. She couldn't believe she was actually going to get to *live* here.

"I think we're all set." Penelope rubbed her hands together, a bright smile on her face. The excited gleam in her eyes was even more worrisome than when she'd railed on them back at Reese's office the other day. "You two are on the accelerated plan, which I admit was an aggressive suggestion," she said. "But in just a few dates you've pulled it off. I think after last week's display at Posh, you're going to have a lot of media interest in your wedding on Saturday."

"That came really fast," Merina murmured.

"Whirlwind romance, remember?" Reese said. He was awfully calm. Or something. Normally, he was buttoned up, but today his shoulders were practically under his ears. Whatever issues he'd walked in with hadn't gone anywhere.

"It's fast enough that tongues will be wagging, which is what you want. This needs to be big, a sensation on the gossip outlets. The more attention you get, the more speculation you'll have, so be sure you're always 'on,' no matter what."

"Like our own reality television show," Merina said.

"Exactly." Pen looked pleased. Reese looked...weird. "We are not doing an announcement of engagement," Pen continued, "but, Merina, you should begin wearing your engagement ring as soon as Reese presents it." She looked to Reese. "Where are we with that?"

"Tomorrow." He lifted his glass of white wine and took a hearty drink. It was possible he was as stressed as she was, and who could blame him? Suddenly everything felt really big.

Marriage.

Yikes.

"Perfect," Pen said. "Merina, you'll need to begin moving your things soon. After the wedding, there'll be no more going home for any reason. Happily married couples spend all their time together. You two are infatuated. Remember that." She pointed at Merina with the end of her pen.

"I'll have Bobbie send movers to collect Merina's things." Reese's nostrils flared and his eyes went past the dining room to the foyer, then around, before finally landing on her. "Just let her know what day."

He radiated stress. It was palpable. Twice, her eyes had

gone to his fist on the table, curled into a tight ball. She was tempted to put her hand over his. If they were by themselves, she may have, but in front of Penelope, she felt odd about the display. Odd about the entire thing.

"Merina needs to see the house. Is it later yet? I'd still love a tour," Pen said.

"I'll arrange it." Reese stood abruptly and left the room, back rigid, phone to his ear. He mumbled a few things into it as he wandered into the foyer.

Before Merina could comment on his behavior—and how strange it was for the man of the house not to show his fiancée around—he poked his head back into the dining room.

"I have to get back to the office, but Tilly will show you the house." He pulled back but leaned in again. "She's the house manager. Penelope, good to see you. Merina." With a dip of his chin, he left.

What? He was just...going?

"Don't worry," Penelope said. "I've been coordinating with the wedding planner. You have a fitting appointment for your dress tomorrow afternoon, and I'll forward the other details via e-mail." Penelope pushed a gold embossed business card Merina's her direction announcing that Sash & Satin was expecting her at three o'clock. "Everything is being taken care of. All you have to do is show up."

"I...have to work," Merina said numbly. Reese was behaving more disconnected than before and she was expected to plan everything with Penelope and Bobbie. And what was she going to tell her parents? Suddenly everything was so real. *Too real.*

"Well, honey, this is your big day, so you're going to have to allow time to be a bride."

Those words still echoed in Merina's mind when she went to Sash & Satin the next afternoon. In the dressing room, she slipped into the wedding gown, a backless satin sheath with lace overlays. The straps were made up of fabric flowers skimming over her shoulders. She pulled her hair back, holding it at the nape of her neck and watched a shock of blond fall over one eye.

Then she lost strength in her legs and plunked into the puffy pink chair provided for brides-to-be as devastation washed over her like a rogue wave. Her first wedding. Her first wedding dress. But no one was here, not Lorelei, not her mother. Pen had made the instructions clear last night: until Reese gave Merina a ring (he promised it'd be today), Merina was under a gag order. Even with Lorelei, who Merina had to reveal knew the truth.

"We have to be careful," Pen had warned when she and Merina strolled through the corridors and giant rooms of Reese's house yesterday.

Merina's eyes burned. She had the strong urge to sit in her wedding dress in this boutique and bawl her eyes out. Which was exactly why she gritted her teeth, stood, and smoothed her beautiful wedding gown with both hands. She tucked her hair behind her ears and swallowed the lump of emotion trying to take her down.

She had to remember why she was doing this. Because the hotel meant everything to her and her parents. This was a business arrangement. One she made because the Van Heusen was a landmark and deserved to be treated with respect.

A tap on the door came and a soft feminine voice called, "Ms. Van Heusen, how is it fitting?"

"Almost perfect." Other than a small hem on the straps

and at the skirt, the dress fit, hugging her curves, like it was made for her. "Maybe just a few alter—"

Her words halted as she opened the fitting room door and revealed Reese standing behind the petite woman who worked at the store. He was in a dark suit, but she didn't have a chance to catalog what color tie he was wearing. She was too taken by his face.

He looked as sexy as he ever did, but it wasn't his good looks that floored her. It was his expression.

Reese Crane was stunned.

CHAPTER 7

It made sense in his head. Sash & Satin was on his way back from a meeting downtown. He figured why not? Now that he was looking at Merina, who was poured into a white dress—the same white dress she would be wearing as she walked down the aisle toward him—he felt woozy.

"You're here." Merina sounded as surprised as he felt. Not that he was surprised to be there, but he was surprised by his reaction to her. He knew he would marry this woman come Saturday, and he'd expected her to be in white. But now that he stood there with the wedding band in his pocket, in this room, he was having a hard time remembering that this was an on-paper agreement. He was going to be Merina's husband.

He'd be responsible for her.

The way his father had been responsible for his mother.

The way he'd worked to provide for her. The way he'd kissed her good-bye before going to work and pulled her into his lap on the couch whenever they watched television as a family.

Suddenly Reese was having a difficult time separating what his parents had from what he and Merina would have. The walls felt as if they were closing in.

No.

This wasn't the beginning of a family. Of a life built together. He may share nuptials and a house with Merina, but theirs was a finite arrangement with a very specific end goal: getting him to CEO.

There. Thinking of what was to come outlined with bullet points took his blood pressure down some. Finally, he was able to peel his tongue from the roof of his mouth to speak.

"That's a beautiful dress."

"Mr. Crane." A petite brunette entered the oversized dressing area and delivered a glass of sparkling water. "If you need to sit, there's a bench right behind you. Many of our future grooms experience exactly what you are experiencing right now."

"Excuse me?" He accepted the glass.

She pulled in a deep breath and pressed both palms to her chest. "To see your bride for the first time in the dress you'll be marrying her in is quite something." Then she swept away.

He looked at Merina, one eyebrow raised. Her expression echoed his: perplexed.

"I'll just give you two a minute," the attendant who had been helping Merina said. She left and closed the door behind her.

Predictably, the air in the room thickened the instant they were alone.

"I didn't expect you to be here." Merina knotted her hands together, looking nervous.

"Me neither. I was going to call you tonight, but I was close by. Pen told me about your appointment." He glanced around the enormous room, at the various seats and racks of dresses and wraps, veils, and tiaras. A small side table stood by a chair and he put the glass of water down without taking a drink. "I'm surprised you're here alone." He'd figured Merina would be surrounded by an army of girl-friends, or at the very least her mother.

"Penelope Brand's orders." At that, he spotted some-thing in Merina's eyes he didn't like one bit. Sadness. Again he thought about what his wedding planner said about this being a first wedding. Was Merina's wedding day one she had dreamed of? Had he backed her into a cor-ner and now she couldn't escape?

Without thinking, he stepped closer to her. She lifted her face to his and the sadness deepened into hurt. He felt it like a punch to the kidney.

He was a fucking idiot. She was a strong woman but she was also a vulnerable woman. For years, his responsibility to the women he was with never extended past one night. He was out of practice for anything deeper.

What he wanted to ask her was if she was having sec-ond thoughts. But even if she was, he knew he wouldn't give her an out. Crane Hotels was his legacy. He needed Merina.

So instead, he said, "The only thing you're missing is the ring."

He pulled the felt box from his pocket, the moment

weirdly intimate and definitely backward, considering she was already in the dress. "I wasn't sure what you liked..."

He swallowed past a lump in his throat and cracked the lid on the white gold ring with a princess-cut two-carat diamond.

Merina gasped, touching her chest with one hand, her mouth dropping open. "It's...oh my God, Reese. It's beautiful."

Pride flooded his chest along with that same tight, hot feeling about being responsible for Merina through this ordeal.

"Glad you approve," he said. "Matching wedding band will be at the ceremony."

There was an awkward moment when she reached for the diamond ring at the same time he reached for her hand. "Oh, did you want to...?"

"Let me."

"Okay." She let out what sounded like a cautious laugh.

"This makes it official." Reese plucked the ring from the satin, took her left hand, and slid the band home. "You were right," he said. "Perfect size six."

He released her hand and she smiled down at the ring. Her honey-blond hair was tucked behind her ears, her shapely figure accentuated by the dress, arms bare.

"Wow." She turned toward the mirror to look at the dress again giving him a view of her smooth back. The line of her spine shadowed gently into the low cut of the dress where it then flared out, cupping her ass in a ridiculously sexy way.

He'd lost the strength in his knees once in his life—the moment he'd learned his mother died—but now that familiar weakness returned, threatening to drop him.

He locked his knees and remained steady. It was this room. It was sweltering.

It's not the room.

She turned and his eyes dipped to the subtle *V* in the front, but it wasn't enough to reveal the tattoo he'd gotten a tease of the day she came into his office. He had to know what it was. Either Merina would wear a top revealing the secret ink, or he'd get her out of her shirt and feed his curiosity.

At the idea, his dick throbbed.

Whoa, boy.

"You're sure it's not too much?" she asked, studying the ring he'd had rush-made for her hand.

"Billionaire," he answered.

The joke hit its mark. She laughed and the sadness bled out of her expression. Another wave of pride crowded out the nervousness sharing his chest.

"Okay." She lifted her shoulders and dropped them in adorable acceptance. "Fair enough."

* * *

"That was it," Merina told Lorelei, whose jaw was sitting on the bar. When she called her to tell her she was in possession of a two-carat engagement ring she'd been presented while wearing her wedding gown, Lorelei demanded they meet at O'Leary's, an upscale pub where a girl could get a fancy drink and *not* be accosted by men. It was a good second choice when they weren't in a Posh mood. "Nothing fancy. He just pulled out the velvet box and put it on."

Lorelei was beaming. "What did he saaaaay?"

Merina had to laugh. Lore had been dragging details from her since she got here. It wasn't that she didn't want to tell her, more it felt awkward being excited. While the engagement was real, the sentiment behind it was fake. "You know this is all for pretend, right?" She dropped a consoling hand on Lore's arm.

"If you do not tell me how he proposed"—she stopped to drain her martini, then plucked a blue-cheese-stuffed olive from the glass and pointed at Merina with it—"I will never forgive you."

"He said, 'This makes it official.'"

"Oh." Lorelei chewed thoughtfully.

What Merina didn't tell her was when Reese said it, he'd been smiling one of his wry smiles, the gleam in his navy eyes suggesting he liked that they had a shared secret. And what she further didn't tell Lorelei was that Merina liked having a shared secret too.

"Well. Six months ain't all that long." Lorelei polished off her olives and ordered another round—a pink drink for Merina and a martini for herself.

"The wedding is Saturday and you are officially coming. You and my parents. Bring a date."

"Saturday?" Lorelei shook her head. "Oh, girl. I have to meet with a client..." She shook her head and then smiled. "You know what? She's canceled on me twice already. I'll be there."

"Good. I'd love to see Malcolm again." Merina grinned. She'd been teasing Lore by bringing up her ex-husband, but the moment she did, Lorelei gaped at her like a fish, then pressed her full lips together. "I knew it." Merina wrapped her hand around her refilled drink. "I knew you two weren't over each other."

"It's nothing! Just...exes with benefits. We're not getting into anything like you are." Lorelei waved a dismissive hand.

"Yeah, we'll see."

"Oh? And you know you won't fall into bed with Reese Crane?"

Merina shushed her friend. Reporters could be anywhere. She doubted it, but one could never be too careful.

"Of course I will," she said, batting her eyes in a way that let Lorelei know there was no alluding to the real truth of the situation while they were in public. "He's my almost-husband."

Lorelei caught on and took a careful glance around before winking.

"How do you know we haven't already?" Merina asked, lifting her glass.

"Aw, hell no." Lorelei propped both elbows on the bar and under her breath said, "We're going to need a signal or something so I know when you're being honest with me. I can't take this did-you-or-didn't-you stuff."

Drink in hand, Merina looked over her shoulder and spotted a woman who was trying to pretend she wasn't looking in their direction. Reporter or yet another of Reese's past dates? Maybe both? Enjoying herself, Merina rested her chin in her left hand, angling the hunk of diamond so it sparkled in the overhead lights.

She wanted to see the woman's reaction but didn't want to be obvious. So instead, she just smiled and enjoyed the One Ring of Power sitting not-so-discreetly on her third finger.

* * *

"Tee many martoonis." Merina giggled as she climbed out of the car a few hours later. Lorelei had picked Merina up, but after three and a half hours imbibing drinks at O'Leary's, there was no way Lore trusted herself to drive. So, Uber it was.

"You? Me, girl. I'm a mess. Good night, future Mrs. Reese Crane!" Lorelei shouted from the backseat, then she pulled the door shut. Merina waved and stagger-stumbled up the five steps to her front door.

Soon to be her parents' front door. Because she was moving to Lake Shore into a house big enough to hold her and her family and a few friends, and the entire cast of *Glee*.

She giggled at her own joke and popped open the door, only to be greeted by her dad.

Though "greeted" was the wrong term. Accosted might be a better one.

"Mer," he said, his voice stony. His eyes went to her hand and he sucked in a breath and let it out. He sounded like a hibernating grizzly when he did that. The sound meant trouble and always sent a shiver down her spine.

She hiccupped. Right on cue.

"I need some water," she said, her words running together.

"I'll get it." This the weary voice of her mother, who, like her dad, was in a pair of sweatpants and a T-shirt but also a hoodie.

"You didn't have to wait up," Merina said, and her enunciation hadn't improved.

Her mother handed her a glass of tap water and Merina chugged.

"We received a call from cousin Patty," Jolie said. "She

directed me to a website where your love life has been openly broadcasted."

Great. Her mother's first cousin was a gossip hound. She lived in Missouri and one would swear she was part of the FBI for all the details she excavated about each of her relatives.

"You and Reese were spotted at a bridal shop, and I told her there was no way..." Her mother's words faded out.

Merina blinked, realizing she'd lifted her left hand—with a rock the size of the kitchen table on it—to smooth her hair.

This wasn't the way she wanted her parents to find out.

Jolie moved from behind the counter and took Merina's hand. A gasp sounded in her throat. Behind her, her father let out a sigh that sounded more like a grizzly bear that'd been punched in the nose.

"I wanted to tell you, but everything happened so fast." Which was not exactly a lie. Things were moving at lightning speed.

"I don't like it," he said.

"Well, it's not up to you." Merina spun on him and his face mottled red. She thought of his heart and softened her tone. "I'm sorry. I'm"—she waved her hand as she tried to come up with an excuse for her behavior but couldn't come up with anything but the truth—"drunk."

"Were you drunk when you said yes?" her father asked.

"Dad!"

"Sweetheart, why wouldn't you tell us how serious things were between the two of you?" Jolie asked.

"I couldn't!" That was the truth, anyway. "I was worried you wouldn't approve. Not that I need your approval, because we're getting married on Saturday whether you approve or not." Merina grasped the edge of the counter as the room swayed. She chugged down the rest of her water in greedy gulps before surrendering the glass to the sink.

"Saturday?" Her mother looked aghast.

"Yes. A private affair at his mansion. I only want you and Dad and Lorelei there."

Jolie raced over and grasped Merina's face. "I'd ask if you were pregnant, but surely you wouldn't drink this much if you were."

Merina put a palm over one of her mother's hands. "I'm not pregnant. I"—she swallowed and told another lie, hoping to God she'd remember how to tell the truth once she was through with this charade. "We fell in love."

The phrase came out as if said while her mouth was full of peanut butter, lilting at the end so it sounded more like a question.

"We didn't expect it. I wasn't trying to keep it from you."

"But your dress..." Jolie didn't continue but she didn't have to. Her mother had wanted to be there when Merina tried on her wedding gown, of course she had.

"You were busy at work," Merina mumbled, knowing it was a lame excuse. Then she said, "You'll see it Saturday," which was even lamer.

Jolie moved her hands out from under Merina's, covered her own face, and burst into tears.

Sobriety never came so fast.

Her father curled an arm around her mom, shushing her, and sent Merina a glare. "This is the wrong time to do this. Better head to bed." His glare had definitely not softened.

Merina nodded and let her parents go up ahead of her. She lingered by the sink, refilling the glass and popping two Advil in the hopes she'd stave off the headache that would no doubt hit her tomorrow morning.

She adjusted the ring on her finger, admiring its beauty and hating what it stood for at the same time. A sham of a marriage that was already hurting the ones she loved. *You're doing this for them*, she reminded herself. Then she climbed the steps and fell into bed.

CHAPTER 8

Ideal wedding weather" was how Penelope Brand had described the day when she texted her congratulations on Saturday morning. Merina could state with conviction that the weather was *not* her main concern.

Her goal was simple: Remain in the here and now, standing in front of God and her parents, her best friend, and the man to whom she'd soon be lawfully wed, without passing out or bursting into tears.

And she didn't mean tears of joy.

For most of the ceremony, she'd kept her focus on Reese's bow tie. His tux was stunning black, his dark blue eyes welcoming, his hair perfect. Her dress had been altered, the lace fitted snugly, the back low but not too low. Her ring was now paired with the matching wedding band and the weight of it on her hand was almost overwhelming.

She was in the process of being *married*. Unbelievable.

On her "husband's" side of the room were Reese's father, Alex, his brother Tag, and a man named Bob, who Reese had referred to as a member of the board. Merina didn't like Bob. It was partly his fault she was in this mess.

The officiant's voice was a distant murmur saying words she'd heard before at friends' and family members' weddings, only now those recited promises were coming from her lips. Things like "to have and to hold" and "from this day forward" and "until death do us part."

Part of her screamed from the inside that she was essentially lying and the lying part of her argued that for now, at least, she meant it. This marriage would die when Reese became CEO of Crane Hotels.

So that sort of counted.

The officiant said, "You may kiss your bride," and Merina thought she was ready for Reese's mouth on hers again. She was wrong. His kiss was as heady as it had been before and even in the midst of uncertainty she found herself leaning in. She didn't have to fake her physical attraction to him. Not even a little.

The marriage may be for show, but her reaction to him was very real. How could he taste this good, feel this good if this was supposed to be pretend? He deepened the kiss and she stood on her toes to get closer, aware of Tag cutting in with a sharp whistle and a shout of, "Hell, yeah!"

She lowered to her heels as applause engulfed them. Reese kept his gaze locked to hers, and she wondered if his smile was as genuine as his kiss.

* * *

The reception was a tidy affair, by Reese's choice. He may have let his wedding planner go overboard with the flowers out front, but inside was a neat buffet-style table. Well, mostly neat. She'd littered the table with candles.

Reese plated up a selection of meats and cheeses aside Merina as their guests lined up behind them to do the same. He'd tried to read her during the ceremony as much as he'd tried to manage his facial expressions. He wasn't nervous, but the "till death" part made him twitchy. He didn't take promises or commitments lightly. But then he reminded himself that was why he was marrying Merina in the first place.

Her parents were in attendance, as well as her best friend-slash-lawyer, Lorelei Monson. He'd learned shortly after issuing the prenup that Ms. Monson was in the know about what was really going on between him and Merina, but given her best friend and client had something to gain and plenty to lose, Reese trusted the other woman to keep the knowledge to herself.

She seemed to be on board with the whole thing, save for a few sharp, assessing looks she'd shot him during the ceremony—and oh, look, there was one now. He'd survived steelier scowls than hers.

In the board member department, Bob and a particularly unsavory character, Ronald Dice, stood behind Reese, but Dice had largely ignored them while he plated his food.

"Thank you," Merina said as he handed her a set of silverware wrapped in a cloth napkin.

"Champagne or wine?" he asked. He could use a scotch.

"Oh, um, champagne. We are celebrating." Her smile was faint and her voice heavy.

Reese leaned close and under the guise of placing a kiss at her temple, he said, "This is a party, and, yes, we are celebrating." He heard the sharp intake of breath, watched her breasts lift with the inhale. They may be partying, marrying, for show, but their reaction to each other was so grounded it practically vibrated the floor.

When he'd put his lips to hers during the ceremony, she'd softened, her rigid shoulders lowering, her body loosening. Then she came closer and held on to him. Attraction was not something they'd have to fake—good news, considering they'd need to convince the media as well as the board—but the implications of being truly attracted to the woman he lived with could prove dangerous. *And fun.*

If he allowed himself to have a little.

Correction: If *Merina* allowed him to have a little.

He drew back, pleased to see an answering heat in the depths of her eyes. "Sit." He nodded to their table and handed off their plates to a waiter. "I'll be over with your drink."

"Thank you, Reese." Her voice was soft, her demeanor relaxed.

Before she got away, though, Dice stopped her with a compliment...dressed up as an excuse to bust Reese's balls.

"You make a beautiful bride, Mrs. Crane," Dice said, his beady eyes sharp and shrewd. Of the board members, he'd be the hardest to convince, and exactly why Alex had suggested they invite him. "Quite the speedy nuptials. Making me wonder if you two kids have gotten yourselves into a pickle." He winked and laughed heartily, his gaze going to Merina's belly—flat and streamlined in her gown.

Merina's bare shoulders stiffened and Reese didn't hesitate to wrap an arm around her.

"Ronald Dice. Goes by Dice," Reese said of their unwanted company. "He's been with the board for over twelve years. His wife, Monica, wasn't able to make it. I hear she's on another trip to Cancun?" Reese moved his hand along Merina's bare back. She shuddered beneath his touch.

Dice stiffened, his pompous smile erasing. It was a company rumor that Monica went to Cancun to sleep with other men. Judging by Dice's curled lip, Reese guessed it was true.

"Too bad she couldn't make it," Merina said, her smooth delivery not giving up her nerves. God. This woman. Cool and smooth, yet warm and lush. He allowed his fingertips to tickle her spine, enjoying the way she shifted at the touch.

"Yes. Well." Dice cleared his throat. "Again, congrats." He stepped out of line and scuttled to a table to ruin someone else's day. Reese watched as he made the poor decision to sit next to Lorelei. *Perfect*. She wouldn't let Dice push her around.

One glass of scotch turned into two, and Merina downed two glasses of champagne and finished her plate of food. Next to him, she propped her elbow on the table, chin in her hand, and watched the room.

"Not a bad first wedding," she said after checking to be sure no one was listening. He did the same before responding.

"No one would know it was your first. You handled it like a pro."

She sent him a wry look. "Me? Sure you've never done this before, Crane?"

"Positive." He leaned close and she didn't move an inch. Her eyes flicked to his lips and their guests immediately lifted their forks and rang the silverware against their crystal glasses.

"We have to kiss," she breathed, her face flushing the most attractive shade of pink.

"Shame," he murmured, then leaned the rest of the way to place a soft kiss on her mouth. They lingered and the ringing sound faded into another wolf whistle from Tag and a few female giggles.

Reese pulled his face away to admire his gorgeous bride in white, lit by candlelight.

Kissing for the public was a task he'd expected, but feeling it, responding to it wasn't. He shifted in his seat, attraction lingering between them.

"Cake!" Tag shouted.

The perfect segue. Reese wondered if his brother saw something in the kiss that made him think Reese might need a reprieve.

The formality was quick, Reese slicing the cake, Merina feeding him a bite, and him returning the favor. Whether it was the champagne making her ballsy, or she was trying to kill him, he couldn't be sure, but when he gave her the bite of cake, her lips closed over his finger and sucked. A muscle in his jaw twitched, but his bride didn't let up, pulling his finger from her mouth so slowly, he thought he might die.

Vixen.

Guests came to retrieve slices of cake and congratulate the happy couple if they hadn't already. Merina's father, Mark, offered a hand and said congratulations, along with Jolie, who did the same. Reese accepted their handshakes, but they still didn't look convinced.

"Where is the honeymoon?" Jolie asked, cake plate in hand.

"It's a surprise," Reese answered.

"Will you be home to get your things?" Jolie asked Merina, sadness stealing into her expression.

"Reese is sending movers tomorrow," Merina answered, her tone soothing.

These two were close. Keeping such a big secret from her mother had been a lot to ask.

"Well. I wish you two the best. And do come visit, sweetheart," Jolie said.

"Mom. It's not like I'll never see you again." Merina sighed when they walked away. "I need more champagne."

"Do you?" Reese lashed an arm around her waist and noticed Dice looking at them as if questioning his earlier suspicions. He and Merina had just about convinced the jackhole. Nice. He lowered his mouth to her ear. "We're being watched."

"We should give the people what they want," she replied.

Reese kissed her ear, then her neck, pleased when she tipped her head to give him room. She might not know the effects her bared skin and tempting perfume had on him, but she certainly knew what she was doing when she backed her ass into his crotch and wiggled.

"Merina." He grasped her waist, his voice a low growl.

"Trying to make it believable," she whispered, half turning to give him a saucy wink.

"I can't go to the bar now," he said. "Part of me needs a shield."

"The rocket part?" she asked, pleased with herself.

"Vixen." This time he said it out loud.

* * *

She could blame the champagne for her behavior, but she could also blame the fact that she was now married and could do whatever she wanted to him. Reese had all but forced her hand in marriage, so he deserved every bit of discomfort.

Only now, his discomfort was matched by hers. The warmth in her belly trickled lower and Merina was overly warm in places off-limits to Reese Crane. He could kiss her. He could suggestively touch her. But the contract didn't include sex.

Sex.

Just thinking the word made her chest pulse with longing. Bumping against Reese's erection and hearing his commanding, teasing growl of the word *vixen*, her lips pulled into a smile. Who would have thought she'd wield so much power over the man who ruled them all?

"Is that my pet name?" Smile affixed to her face, she wiggled her hips again and was rewarded with a low, agonized grunt.

Reese's hands tightened on her waist, halting her movements. He lowered his lips and pressed a kiss to her shoulder, then bit her. Just a light scrape of his teeth, but it made Merina's pulse dance and sent her smile on vacation.

Into her ear he muttered, "You'll pay for that."

She heard the humor in his tone and decided whatever the cost, the wiggle was worth it.

"Champagne." Reese loosened his hold. "I'll be back. If pictures of me end up hashtagged by morning, I'm telling everyone it's your fault."

She swallowed a laugh and watched him go, admiring his very fine backside in his tuxedo pants.

"Girrrrl." Lorelei, glass of white wine in hand, approached in a gorgeous plum-colored dress, showing off her legs and large breasts. "He looks good in black." Her hair was pinned back, much like Merina's, in a low twist at her nape. But Lorelei's jewelry was the show-stealer, huge rhinestone earrings and a bracelet for each arm.

"He looks good in everything," Merina mumbled. And probably out of it too.

"Good, yes, but you're beautiful."

Merina leaned forward to accept the kiss on the cheek her friend doled out. "Thank you."

"I'm jealous." Lore looked around the dining room. The doors were opened to the foyer where the ceremony had taken place. Candles were lit, white roses were strung, and every inch of the mansion open to guests was gleaming and warm and romantic. "I can't believe you get to live here."

Her best friend bemoaned her six-hundred-square-foot apartment for the thousandth time, and Merina had to smile. Lore had picked the place, justifying that with her heavy workload she'd be at the office most of the time. But ever since she'd made partner she'd complained about wanting a house.

"Where's Malcolm?" Honestly, Merina was surprised her friend came stag.

Lorelei gave a shrug that said she didn't care, but it was a purposeful deflection. Lore cared too much about Malcolm. And Malcolm not enough about her.

"I'll kill him if he's with another woman," Merina said, meaning it.

"Pfft. Come on." Lorelei made a shooing motion with her hand. "You know that man loves himself too much to make himself look bad. I think he's unsure about us. I can't blame him. I'm unsure."

"Well, Tag's single. Want me to introduce you?"

"No." Lorelei gave her a slow eye blink. "What would I do with him?"

Tag moved in the background, hair down and huge arms straining the confines of his dress shirt.

"Whatever you did would probably be fun," Merina admitted. Tag practically had "for a good time call" stenciled across his broad back.

Reese returned with the champagne right then and Merina accepted the glass. Her brand-new husband radiated control. Confidence. Stubbornness. Each of those qualities more attractive given they were wrapped in such a glorious package.

"I'm going to get myself a refill." Lorelei cordially excused herself. "Reese, you don't take care of my girl, I'll have your balls."

"Exactly what I'd expect you to say, Ms. Monson," Reese replied easily. After she'd gone, he turned to Merina. "She's warming up to me. Any chance your parents will do the same?"

"Ha." Merina sipped her champagne. "My dad isn't convinced. And my mom is not happy."

Mark and Jolie may have experienced their own whirlwind love story, but theirs was rooted in everlasting love. The engagement started on State Street in Chicago around Christmas. Near the ice rink, snow falling, Jolie's tears of joy freezing to her face as Mark knelt before her, ring offered and snow seeping into his dress pants. Merina's mother liked to tell the tale of how she and Mark checked into a high-end hotel in a crappy compact car and handed their duffel bags over to the valet. They didn't belong in this world then, but they'd carved out room for themselves. Her parents saw Chicago as a place they made their own.

"Neither is Bob," Reese said of the friendlier board member Merina was introduced to earlier. "My father will smooth that over." He said this with his voice dropped and his face close to her ear. Goose bumps sprang to life on her arms and legs in response.

Nearly everything about him caused an answering physical reaction.

Tag approached with an easygoing swagger, golden hair rolling over the shoulders of his royal blue button-down almost to the middle of his arms.

"You remember my brother, Tarzan," Reese said.

Tag chuckled good-naturedly, much in the way he approached life. "Congratulations. Though, my brother is an idiot, so I suppose I should be offering condolences." He winked. "Maybe I'll offer those in a few months."

Six months to be exact.

But she didn't say that. Instead she said, "When do I get to meet the elusive Eli Crane?"

"Eli is serving overseas for another few years," Reese said. "He's not one to come home often."

"Eli is in the army?" Her voice sounded hollow. Reese hadn't mentioned his brother was in another country. Shouldn't that have been on his short list of things to tell her? Thank goodness she didn't mention that to the media.

"Marines," Tag corrected. "It's who he is." He looked around the room as if assessing. "He doesn't have a lot of tolerance for this world."

"You mean tolerance for Chicago?" Merina asked.

"Tolerance for the hotel business." One of Tag's eyebrows hitched, then dropped. "Eli's sense of duty overwhelms everything else."

"He's the best of all of us," Reese said, and she could tell he meant it. "He gets that streak of dedication from our father."

"Have Big Crane show you his tats sometime," Tag told her, then clapped Reese on the back. "Brother. I'm off. I have a date."

"Should've brought her." Reese's tone was teasing. Tag smiled in challenge.

"Never. Don't want to give 'em the wrong idea." Tag nodded at Merina. "Sis. See you around."

Sis. Merina blinked as Tag turned, tall and broad and, yes, like Tarzan but with a much better vocabulary.

"He doesn't linger with his dates either, I take it," she said to Reese.

He didn't answer, which was an answer in itself.

"Everyone," Reese announced.

He hadn't lifted his voice much, but the crowd stopped and turned to him the moment he spoke. Reese had a commanding nature. He was someone who drew attention. His palm covered her lower back and warmth transferred from his hand to her skin.

"I'll leave you the run of the house," he told their guests. "Tilly and Magda will get you anything you need. Now, if you'll excuse us, my wife and I have a moonlight cruise to take in."

Low murmurs came from the crowd.

"A cruise?" she asked.

"On my yacht. Your bags are already packed and on

board," Reese said. "Told you the honeymoon was a surprise. You may want to change out of your gown first. I'm losing the tux."

They headed out of the room, Reese accepting handshakes and Merina narrowly avoiding a cheek kiss from Dice. Then they walked upstairs hand-in-hand, winding around hallways until Reese came to a stop in front of a door. Her basic necessities had been moved in yesterday, and unloaded into his room. *Their shared room.*

The door they stood outside of now.

He opened the door, revealing the room she'd seen yesterday when she was putting her clothes and her shoes in one of the closets. Hers was the gargantuan one on the right side of the room, Reese's on the left. She'd fit her dresser, a mirror, and an entire wall of shoes in there. It was almost too much. But then, wasn't this all?

"The honeymoon is on your yacht." She'd walked in ahead of him and turned to find him undoing his cuff links.

"I figured a night away from the house would give us some much needed privacy."

"Privacy to make it look like . . ." Her cheeks grew warm.

He dipped his chin. "Then we'll return to work and life goes back to normal."

Normal. After spending a few days on a cramped boat with the man who made her entire body react like she'd been submerged into a vat of effervescence? She doubted she'd be able to find normal with a map.

"The bonus is on the boat—it'll just be us." He tugged at his bow tie and she froze, anxious to finally see the man out of his tie. "So you won't have to do anything for show."

"No crew?" She had to clear her throat to get the question out when he untied the length of black silk.

"Captain, first mate, and deckhand at your service." Reese left the bow tie dangling and lost the jacket, tossing it haphazardly onto the massive bed. Four fat posts and piles of gold and black bedding stood at the end of the room. Would they share that bed? She assumed they'd have to. The house staff would be suspicious if they didn't.

He crooked a finger for her to come to him.

"What?" It took everything in her not to take a step backward.

"What, what? Come here so I can unzip you."

Oh. Okay, she was being ridiculous. Crane wasn't trying to seduce her. Not even in this luxurious den of sin. That's how she saw it, with its dark wood flooring and rich cedar closets. A bed they could do cartwheels on, Reese's obvious kissing abilities... Yeah, it hadn't taken long for her mind to cannonball into the gutter.

She sashayed—because there was no other way to walk in her floor-length lace-and-satin gown—and turned, having no need to hold her hair up since it was pinned at her nape. Warm fingers brushed there now as he undid the delicate pearl button at the top, then ran his fingers down her bare back before sliding the zipper down. He took his time, pausing at each inch. Her heart thudded as Reese sucked in a deep breath.

"You're truly exquisite, Merina." His low, gravel-laden voice matched her lust-filled thoughts. Being kissed by him was distracting to the nth degree, but being undressed by him? Unparalleled.

"Thank you," she managed.

With the flat of one hand, he touched her shoulder, leaning so close, she could feel the brush of his shirt and the heat radiating off his body. "May I?"

"Crane..."

"The word you're looking for is *yes*." Those words were murmured against the shell of her ear before he closed his lips over the edge of her lobe.

He was a drug. Her eyes fell closed as she gave herself over to the sensation of Reese's broad palms sliding over the bared skin of her back. His fingers tucked beneath the thin flower-laced straps of the dress, then molded her shoulders, pulling those straps down.

"You're so soft." His voice was filled with wonder. He placed another kiss to her neck.

She didn't know what to do with her hands. They were currently pressed to the front of her gown when what she wanted to do was strip herself bare and turn to accept Reese's mouth on every part of her. But she couldn't do that. Selling part of her soul for the Van Heusen didn't include her body.

Snapping out of her trance, she turned abruptly and found Reese's eyes full of lust and his pants tenting impressively.

She wanted to tell him this wasn't part of the deal. That she wasn't going to consummate their fake marriage, but her mouth was dry and her mind busy imagining what his bare chest looked and tasted like, so no words came out. She simply stood, holding her dress to her breasts, where his eyes currently rested.

"No matter what happens, Merina, make me a promise." He looked scary serious, which she didn't like.

"No promises."

The corner of his mouth lifted. "Just one."

As much as she wanted to turn and run to her closet, she didn't.

"Someday," he said, lifting a finger and drawing it over the swell of her right breast, "promise you'll show me that tattoo. It's been driving me crazy since you stormed into my office soaked to the bone and I saw a hint of color through your shirt."

"My...tattoo?" Last thing she expected him to say. It infused this interaction between them with even more tension.

He reached for his top button. "When you're ready."

Before she could satisfy her own curiosity about whether he had chest hair or not, he turned his back and strode into his closet on the opposite side of the room.

She huffed, left with no other choice but to finish the job he'd started and shimmy out of her clothes to change for their yacht honeymoon.

CHAPTER 9

With one last wave to friends and family, amidst polite clapping, and thankfully for her hair absolutely no
rice throwing, she and Reese made their way to the dock
at the back of his house. A boat that looked more like a
mansion floated regally in the moonlight, a fancy cursive
name on the side.

"Luna," she read. "Like *moon*?" Her hand was hooked
on Reese's arm, and she had no trouble navigating now that
she wore a comfortable white summer dress. He'd changed
into trousers and an oxford button-down. He'd left the top
two buttons undone, giving her a peek of his chest hair.
That had fried her brain for a few precious seconds.

"Named after my mother."

"Oh." His raw openness took her by surprise. "It's a
pretty name."

Reese was quiet save for their footfalls on the wooden
dock. He helped her board *Luna* and she couldn't help

thinking she'd left one mansion and climbed onto another. Pristine white and black and gold—Reese's dominant color scheme she was seeing—on the outside and more of the same inside. She entered a lush living room that gave way to an expansive kitchen. A corridor to the left featured more rooms.

"Master and attached bath at the back," he said as he closed the door behind them. "The other has a desk and computer and a smaller bed."

Wow. The massive space had shrunk by half with his heat blanketing her back.

"I don't mind the smaller bed," she said.

"You're in the master," he stated, edging by her for the kitchen. He opened a cabinet and came out with a bottle of liquor. "No one can see in these windows." He gestured around the room at the tinted glass. "There are room-darkening blinds in the bedrooms to keep the sun out if you want to sleep in. No matter what we do, we have complete privacy when we're on the water."

No matter what they did. Didn't that just introduce multiple inappropriate thoughts?

"Your things are already in the master suite," he said, pouring a few inches of the liquor into a glass. "Scotch?"

"Seriously, I can take the smaller room."

He drank, pressing his lips together as he swallowed. Her gaze lingered at the strong column of his neck for a few beats. He looked like he belonged in this opulence, even in his casually unbuttoned shirt, sleeves pushed over his elbows.

"I don't sleep much," he said.

"Something we have in common." The second it was out of her mouth, she realized insomnia wasn't the only thing they had in common. *Green Eggs and Ham* was another. And scotch. "I prefer Glenlivet," she said, tipping her head to the bottle of Macallan scotch on the counter.

His eyebrows rose in blatant surprise. Yes, it seemed they had more in common than just the physical. A factor that threw both of them for a bit of a loop.

"Mind if I use the bathroom first? My mascara is starting to feel like flypaper."

"Help yourself. I'll steer us out and anchor, then I have some work to do."

She nodded and turned to the corridor.

"Merina?"

She looked back at the delicious man in the kitchen and wondered why she hadn't yet crossed the living room to taste the scotch on his lips.

"Penelope suggested we take in the sunrise on the deck. For potential photographers."

"Oh. Yes, good idea." Sunrise with Reese Crane on his yacht. Was she dreaming?

"I'll wake you."

His warm promise followed her all the way into her bedroom.

* * *

Morning came, and for all the sleep she'd gotten, she may as well have stayed awake the entire night. She'd watched out the bedroom window at the waves left in the wake of *Luna*, while thinking through the day. She was married. Reese Crane's wife. Her diamond ring had glittered in the moonlight that made its way through the windows, making her consider what the future would be like. What life would look like when she divorced and went back home to live with her parents.

Wait, no.

She didn't have to move back in with them. She could move out into that apartment like she wanted. She'd make a clean, guilt-free break, and she'd have plenty of money saved, given she wasn't paying rent any longer.

She'd finally fallen asleep for a few hours and woke to a light tap on her door.

"Merina, five minutes. Did you get the text?"

"I'll be right out," she told Reese. Her raspy morning voice wasn't anywhere near as sexy as his. She reread the text in her phone and sighed. Penelope had sent instructions in the middle of the night. *Minimal makeup, respectable but sexy pajamas, coffee optional but would add a nice touch.*

Romantic, Merina thought with a sarcastic chuff.

Penelope hoped a reporter with a long lens would snap a picture and put it online, or heck, maybe even sell it to the *Trib,* preferably with a complimentary headline. Merina had no idea if John Q. Public had bought hers and Reese's relationship, but even if they didn't buy it *today,* they would eventually. She wasn't going anywhere until the board put him in charge and she saw the Van Heusen in her name.

"Really going to have to rough it until then," she said with a laugh. She pushed herself out of bed, which required some doing since it was roughly the size of a small country. She was trying not to think beyond the next few days lest she become completely overwhelmed.

On a typical Sunday morning she would grab a latte from Starbucks and head over to the VH to oversee brunch and catch up on what she didn't get finished from the past week.

This morning was that morning's polar opposite.

She pulled on a pair of comfy cotton pants. She'd slept in her panties and a silky cami she'd found in her luggage—an entire new wardrobe she hadn't chosen, yet fit her style so precisely, it gave her pause. Penelope's doing? The wedding planner's? Or had it been Reese himself? The idea of him choosing her comfortable yet sensual wardrobe was enticing...

Shoving aside the distracting thought, she pulled a long-sleeved shirt perfect for the chilly morning over her cami and finger-combed her hair. Obeying Penelope's orders about makeup, she splashed water on her face and dusted on a little powder. Just as she did, another light rap came at the door.

Reese was on the other side in sweatpants and a sweat-shirt—both gray—his hair slightly rumpled, his face in need of a trim, and looking more devastating than she thought possible. "Ready?"

"Um..." Words. She couldn't call up enough to string into a sentence, so she went with a slightly coherent reply. "Yeah. Yes."

With a nod, he reached past her and snagged the fluffy comforter from the bed, rolling it into a big ball. Then he took her hand—cold—in his—insanely warm—and said, "Let's go see that sunrise."

Emerging from the softly lit cabin of the boat to the dark, frigid wind on the deck made her suck air through her teeth. She considered dashing back to bed—after she snatched that heavenly blanket from Reese's arms—but seeing as this was their first appearance as a married couple, fleeing his presence the morning after wouldn't be well received. Still, she couldn't help voicing a complaint.

"Oh my God! It's freezing out here," she said, her teeth chattering.

"Worth it, I promise." Wind kicked his hair. He looked almost rugged with the overgrown stubble and those casual clothes. Like him, but a homier him. She'd never really thought of Reese Crane as "homey."

"When was the last time you took in a sunrise on a yacht?" he asked, shaking out the blanket.

"Never. You?"

"The morning after I proposed to you." His mouth quirked and she had no idea if he was joking or not.

"Really?"

"Really. Took the boat out and sat on the water until morning." He spread the blanket over a bench facing the water and sat.

"Were you having second thoughts?" She'd had about a million.

"Come get warm," he said instead of answering her. He held the blanket out like a cape and obeying his request, she sat next to him. He rerouted her, lifting her onto his lap, then closed the blanket over her. She snuggled into his heat, moving until she was comfortable.

He grunted when she bumped his—*ahem*—man part a little too aggressively.

"Sorry." This time, her wiggle was met with his palms closing over her waist. He turned her to the side where her hip met several inches of steel.

"Hold still," he said, his voice just as hard. "Before you kill me."

She bit back a smile. Not because him being turned on

was funny, but because she couldn't remember the last time she'd had that effect on a man.

"Laugh it up," he encouraged, one hand moving up her leg.

"It's not you. I just...this is...weird."

"It's a human reaction," he said simply.

She gazed at him and wrapped her arms around his neck. Was this how he categorized the one-night-only dates he was so well known for? As "human reactions"? She almost asked but he interrupted her thoughts.

"We're supposed to look in love," he said drily. "Consider this my effort to help that along."

She let herself giggle, startled at how easy it was to sit on Reese Crane's lap and laugh. It was as if she'd fallen into an episode of the *Twilight Zone*.

"That's better," he said, his hand coming to rest on her thigh.

She'd brushed her teeth before she came out and was pleased to pick up the hint of mint on his breath as well. They were being so careful. So very careful. And now they were being tasked with indulging. Something Reese was skilled at, but she hadn't given in to much in her life.

So, go for it.

"Thick hair." She pushed her fingers through the strands the way she'd wanted to since he'd appeared outside her bedroom door. Wavy, dark brown, but in the coming daylight, she could see the flecks of gold. "No gray yet," she observed. "Surprising since your father has a head full."

Unwavering navy eyes stayed on her. So this was what it was like to have his full attention. Since he hadn't stopped her, she gave in to another whim and ran her fingers down his jaw and over scruff that was soft to the touch. Against her breast, she felt his heart pound.

She dipped her fingers into the collar of his sweatshirt, holding his gaze. His nostrils flared and his jaw tightened. The steel beneath the blanket bobbed against her hip.

"Chest hair," she whispered, exploring carefully. "I like that."

"Do you." He tightened his arms around her.

It wasn't a question, but she nodded anyway. The sun peeked over the water, casting golden light over his face, but neither of them looked away from each other to take in the morning making its grand entrance. Reese's hand came out from under the blanket and cupped her neck, pulling her mouth close to his.

"So fucking soft," he whispered against his lips. "I've never felt skin so smooth."

"Not ever?" Her tongue darted out to lick her lips. They were so close she could almost taste him.

"Never."

She gave in, erasing the scant space between them, telling herself kissing him was for the benefit of the camera. On contact, Reese crushed her against him, and that's when she knew.

They weren't pretending. This kiss was *real*.

Merina speared one hand up through the back of his hair, her arms still linked around his neck. She needed him as close as possible. His tongue delved into her mouth and she accepted, kissing him as passionately. They made out for long minutes, so long that by the time they separated, she was out of breath. Sunlight had washed over the deck, heating the boat, though they'd done a pretty decent job of heating it themselves.

His Adam's apple bobbed as he swallowed, his eyes hooded and his lips pursed.

"Honey." She stroked his face. "You look...flushed."

He didn't smile at her teasing. In fact, his face went harder than the insistent erection pulsing against her backside.

"That should do it," he growled.

"Do what?"

"Give the photographers what they need." He moved her hand from his face and kissed her palm, but it was a flat kiss, his expression equally so. He shifted out from under her and stood.

She didn't like this "business as usual" guy. She liked rumpled, sexy, kissing guy. She liked couldn't-control-himself guy.

"I'm going to grab a quick shower." A twitch of his lips didn't give way to a real smile before he vanished belowdecks.

Picturing him in the shower without anything on sent a flood of warmth to her belly. Reese had lost control with her and he didn't like it. She pressed her fingertips to her lips to smother a smile.

She liked it.

Too much.

* * *

Reese rested his fingertips on the blotter of his desk, nostrils flared, his mind a tangle of silken skin and sex and hot kisses that stole the breath from his very lungs.

Only two of which he'd sampled this past weekend.

He'd spent a total of two days aboard *Luna*, but after the

sunrise that accompanied his dick-rise, he'd spent a lot of time avoiding his wife. He'd returned to the deck with coffee for each of them, his body under its best behavior.

He couldn't afford to let go of his control. There was too much at stake. Crane Hotels. CEO. His legacy. The position he was born and bred and groomed to take. He wouldn't lose it over an attraction of convenience.

She's more than convenient and you know it.

Merina was a long game: lasting months, not one night. The attraction between them was as volatile and unstoppable as a brush fire in California's dry season. *Dangerous*.

He frowned.

As of this morning, he could take solace in the fact that their ruse did its job. A gossip column in the local paper had offered up photos of spring in Chicago. A section called "Love Is in the Air" featuring budding trees and flowers and a photo of Reese and Merina's sunrise kiss.

The shot was from too far back to see much more than their faces pressed together aboard *Luna*. But the headline was key and what had Penelope phoning him first thing this morning to punch the air in triumph.

REESE'S ROCKET UNDER NEW MANAGEMENT!

To be fair, he may have felt less homicidal today if his "rocket" had been well tended to.

"No to dinner with the city council," he answered Bobbie, who was standing in front of his desk jotting things onto a pad of paper. "I'm not in the business of being a social puppet."

"Yes, sir." She finished writing, overlooking his bad mood. But he knew she could tell. *He* could tell. The idea had been to go right back to work after the wedding and carry on as usual, but ever since he'd unzipped his bride's dress in their shared bedroom, he hadn't stopped wondering what it'd be like to get her out of her clothes and into his arms. Even when he wasn't thinking about it, he thought about it. Which was inconvenient. Ill-advised.

Unexpected.

That last description irked him the most. He thought he'd known what to expect from Merina when he'd offered this arrangement. Now life was throwing him a curve ball and he did not like it. Not even a little. Worse, he'd be going "home" tonight, which meant his current method of dealing—avoidance—was about to come to an abrupt end. Workdays didn't last all day. Not anymore.

Given the mansion's sheer size, he should have enough breathing space to ignore the potent attraction and get his brain back in the game. But there was no way around sharing a bedroom. The house staff may not be there at night, but come morning, they'd see the sheets disturbed in two separate bedrooms and suspicions would be raised. For the most part, he trusted his staff, but when it came to getting fifteen minutes of fame, he only trusted Magda implicitly. He had one shot at making the public believe in him and Merina. They'd have to keep their guard up in front of everyone.

Bobbie left, but the doors didn't swing shut before Tag strolled in.

"Would it kill you to wear a fucking suit?" Reese barked.

Tag waited for the doors to shut completely behind him, then crossed his arms over his chest and raised one eyebrow. "Bro. You have got to find a way to work off this sexual energy or everyone is going to know the truth in a day or two."

Reese let out a breath that was loud enough to rattle the windows behind him. "Is it that obvious?"

"Yes."

Dammit.

"You are crouched like Wolverine ready to pounce."

Reese took in his posture, hunching over his desk, fingernails white from the amount of pressure he was applying. He was strung tight. He stood, rolled his shoulders, and cracked his neck.

"Guess you should've taken a mistress alongside your bride," Tag observed, coming to the guest chair and plunking into it. A half-smile suggested he was kidding, but Reese didn't find it funny. The only woman he could picture beneath him, legs spread, back arched, face flushed as he drove into her, the air filled with her moans of pleasure, was Merina. What horrible irony that he'd married the one woman he couldn't fuck.

"I know why you're stressed," Tag pointed out, because he was being oh-so-helpful today.

"It's work."

"No, it's not."

Reese didn't sit; he was too wired. He affected a bored expression. "Fine. What is it? Enlighten me."

"You have to go back to the house and live there," his brother answered matter-of-factly.

"And?" But Reese knew where this was going.

"And your suite here at the hotel will be neglected for the first time in years. You're returning to the scene of the crime, man, and don't think that's not going to affect you. Having Gwyneth take off was one thing, but having her take off with Hayes was the fuck-you to end all fuck-yous."

Hayes. The second-to-last person Reese wanted to think about was his ex-best friend. The first being Gwyneth.

"Ancient history," Reese said. The mention of their names sent a wave of regret through him, but most of that sting was because he'd been taken advantage of—had *allowed* himself to be taken advantage of—and hadn't stopped it. "Right now my focus is on surviving the next six months." Or less. Maybe the board could be wooed before then and they could divorce before his dick shriveled and dropped off. He repressed a shudder.

"Is she not cooperating?"

If by "not cooperating" Tag meant she was "not having sex with him," he was spot-on. Like Reese, Tag dated often, only when Tag dumped his date it wasn't with a curt conversation and delivered flowers. Tag did it with a wink, a smile, and a playful bump on the jaw, and the line that worked best for him: *Let's save ourselves the trouble.* The blow-off matched his easygoing attitude, so girls most often left with a matching smile.

"Meaning?" Reese asked.

"Meaning is she bitching at you all the time? You two have this volatile energy." He wiggled his fingers in front of him. "Combustible. If you're not screwing it away, you have to be arguing." He shook his head curtly. "Not good for the public."

Hmm. Great point.

"We'll manage."

"I didn't come in here to razz you, believe it or not," Tag said. "I wanted to suggest you come with me to play racquetball. Burn off some of your rage before you climb this building and start swiping at low-flying planes."

"Racquetball." The idea of pounding a little blue ball

into the wall sounded like a great way to forget about his own pair. At least for a few hours. "You're on."

"Was that a *yes*?" Tag put a hand over his heart and pretended to have a heart attack.

"Don't make me change my mind," Reese said, instantly feeling his mood lift.

It'd been a while since Reese had walked away from his desk on a weeknight.

He was overdue.

* * *

By eleven o'clock, Merina was uncharacteristically beat. Typically, she'd just now be getting going. A day running the Van Heusen pulled her attention in nineteen thousand different directions, so it was during the late hours she was able to catch up.

Car window rolled down, she opened the gate via fingerprint, a detail set up this morning before she'd left for work, and parked in the massive garage next to Reese's fleet of billionaire-mobiles. She sneered. Those cars were like the women he used to date. Ridiculous, silly excuses for attention, only to be discarded or replaced the moment he tired of them.

Wow. Along with being beat, she was grouchy too. Purse on her shoulder, she stepped from her non-flashy sedan and moved to the side entrance to the mansion, which she was pretty sure opened to a cloakroom... or the kitchen? She couldn't remember. She'd had a hurried run-through of a tour twice now and determined that the house was a maze.

Before she could open the door, it popped open before

her, revealing a portly, smiling woman wearing a black uniform, a white shirt, and a tired smile.

"Magda," Merina greeted, fingers mentally crossed that she'd gotten the woman's name right.

"Mrs. Crane." Magda's accent was pure Chicago. "Late night for you. Were you able to work the gate and the garage door okay?"

"Yes, thank you. Everything hums like a well-oiled machine around here."

"Thank you for saying so." She pointed over her shoulder to the kitchen. "Your dinner is in the oven. Tamales, or if you don't care for those, a small tray of spinach lasagna."

Yum.

"I'll probably have both," Merina said. She could get used to coming home to dinner. Typically, she ate room service in her office, and as good as the food was at the Van Heusen, there was only so much spring-mix salad and seared ahi a girl could eat.

"Good night, Mrs. Crane."

"Good night."

Magda left via the open garage door and Merina punched the button to close it. She ended up opening the wrong garage doors *twice* before figuring out what buttons to push to close them again.

"Pull it together, *Mrs. Crane*," she chided herself as she walked inside. She set the alarm code on the door and strolled through the kitchen, the smells as tantalizing as promised. And, as she'd promised Magda, she sat down to a healthy portion of both lasagna and tamales before rinsing her dish and fork and depositing them into the empty dishwasher.

"For my next trick, I'll find my room." She'd been trying to be funny, but it wasn't so funny when she got turned around in the staircase that led from the kitchen to the opposite side of the house, and then in attempting to reroute to the other hallway, ended up in an upstairs office instead.

Tall, rich mahogany shelves lined the walls, books clogging them. An arched window faced the lake, taking up half the wall. A desk dominated the space, and the man facing the window dominated the desk. She couldn't see Reese's face, just the back of his head, chair turned, hand propping up his head. She had no idea if he'd heard her approach until he spoke.

"Evening."

"I'm lost. I was on my way to the bedroom and made a wrong turn in Albuquerque."

"How do you think I ended up in here?" He turned, dropping his elbow and facing her. He was in his signature dark suit, this one with a subtle pinstripe design visible thanks to the moonlight, and his tie knot had been loosened, his top button opened. His scruff was short, his hair perfectly styled, and that crooked tie was about the sexiest thing she'd ever seen him wear. It bespoke of his loss of control, and she was quickly learning "uncontrolled" was the way she preferred him.

"So you gave up?" She walked to the desk and Reese's eyes dropped to her feet before skimming up her pencil skirt and lingering at her silk shirt. That's when she remembered his comment about her tattoo. Was that why his eyes so often strayed to her chest?

"I thought if I sat awhile, it'd come to me." She liked his dry sense of humor, but beneath it was another emotion. One she couldn't place. He wrenched his eyes to hers when she came closer.

"You really want to see it, don't you?" she asked, her voice husky.

He rested his palms on his suit pants, fingers splayed, chin up as he kept his gaze fused with hers. He did. She could feel that need vibrating from him.

"You might be disappointed." She fingered a delicate button on her shirt and watched his fingertips dig into his legs. "It's not much."

"I'll be the judge of that." Purposefully, slowly, he leaned back in his leather chair and watched as she undid first one button, then the second. One more open button over the center of her bra gave her enough clearance to show him.

"You're going to kind of get flashed," she said, the quiet ticking of the clock and Reese's face in shadow making her heart hammer. She pulled the shirt open, moonbeams highlighting the bit of ink she'd added to her body five years ago.

Reese reached up, fingers brushing from the tip of the arrow, down the shaft, and over the flames that made up the fletching. He moved quickly, standing and lashing an arm low around her waist and pulling her against him.

She braced herself on the desk with one hand, her other flattening against his chest. They lingered there and listened as the clock in the room ticked three times. She swiped her fingertip along his neck, the touch of her bare skin to his setting him off.

Like a rocket.

He kissed her. A punishing and exciting kiss, a kiss she'd wanted more of since they locked lips on the deck of the *Luna*. But this time, there was no one watching.

* * *

Merina's shirt was open, her mouth on his, and Reese forgot about the speech he'd been intending to give her the moment she set foot in his house. He'd been in this room mulling it over for a very long time. He'd decided on a clear set of rules for their marriage. Rules involving him and her and separations so that they wouldn't muddy the waters with sex. It made sense until she'd come in here, smooth skin cool in the moonlight, amber eyes shining. Then she'd unbuttoned her shirt, and his speech was buried under the only two words he'd thought before he sprang out of his chair.

"Fuck it," he said against her mouth after a devouring kiss.

"Fuck what?" she breathed.

"Fuck *you*. Preferably on this desk. Preferably two minutes ago." He felt the curve of her smile all the way down to his rigid cock.

She panted as he moved his mouth to her jaw, then to the side of her neck. He pushed her hair aside to give himself room as she squirmed beneath his insistence. He enjoyed the dance. She couldn't help herself when it came to him and he couldn't do anything about wanting her whenever she was near.

"Futile," he said, tugging at her shirt to bare one shoulder.

"What is?" Her voice was a wisp in the dark room, a breathy siren's call steering him right into the rocks.

"Resistance." He worked the buttons on her shirt, pulled it from her arms, then tossed it aside. He pressed his lips to her tattoo. A flaming arrow he wanted to know the meaning behind, but now was not the time. Any questions he had could be asked later. Now they were lost under the pounding of blood passing by his eardrums. He had to have her. No more delays.

"I can't wait to take this off," she said, pulling on the knot of his tie. He raised his head and saw the heat in her eyes mirroring his and couldn't help smiling.

"The tie?"

"I like you in it, but I like you out of it more." She slipped the silk knot loose. "And the shirt." She flattened her hands on his chest and pushed. He sat obediently, which was new. If she were any other woman, he'd have had her completely nude and spread across his desk before his tie was off. He preferred control. With Merina, he'd become insatiably curious. He was willing to give in to her for the moment, if only to satisfy his lingering curiosity.

She reached behind her to unhook her black lace bra, pushing her breasts out. He admired the swells, the mystery tattoo. Delicate but aggressive, the flames licking across her chest. Then she unzipped her slim skirt and shimmied out of it—taking her time until the material fell to her feet. She left her tall black heels on, which saved him stopping her from taking them off. She was just how he wanted her.

"Ready?" He reached for her hips and her eyes widened, her chest lifting with each hectic breath.

"For?"

His answer was to spin her to face the desk, place her hands on the surface, and stroke one palm down her spine. Then he bent and took a gentle bite of one ass cheek.

"Oh!" She whipped her hair and glared over her shoulder at him.

Behind her, he ground his erection into a pair of matching black lace panties he considered tearing off with his teeth.

"Oh." Her glare faded into a heavy-lidded gaze.

"Do you like this, Merina?" She did. He could see it. "What's your pleasure?" Her bent over the desk, balanced on her elbows was definitely his pleasure, but he wanted their first time to be what she wanted as well.

"What do you think?" She backed her lush ass into his crotch and moved in an erotic sway.

The attraction between them was like flames spreading to the carpet and climbing the walls. He didn't delay another second. He released her hips to remove his belt, a quick slide of leather through buckle. Halfway to his goal of freeing himself from his pants, he had an incredibly important, if not unfortunate thought. He swore, the word an incoherent growl.

"Condom?" Merina's voice was filled with hope. But Reese couldn't give her the answer they both wanted.

"Not until we find the bedroom." He stepped away from her, propping his hands on his hips and regarding the ceiling. One deep breath turned into two as Merina stood and tugged on her clothes. She offered his shirt.

He snatched it, lowered his head, and kissed her, tasting her mouth and wishing they'd started this in a room where prophylactics were in reach.

When she opened her eyes, she was looking smug, if not a little proud at causing his massive lack of control.

"Vixen." He smoothed his hand over her skirt, then gave her a slap on the ass. For a second they stood in a clinch smiling at each other like idiots. "Follow me."

Several wrong turns later, Merina giggled from beside him. He stopped in a corridor and pressed her flat to the wall with his body. Much as he wanted to kiss her, he hovered inches from her tempting lips.

"Something funny?" he asked.

Her high heels dangled from her fingers. She reached up and pushed her hair from her face with her free hand.

"You mean besides you getting lost in your own house?" She grinned.

"Your mouth."

Lips pursed, she purred, "What about my mouth?"

He leaned closer, closer until the only thing separating them was a breath. "I can think of better ways to put it to use."

Her sharp exhale tickled his lower lip, but he forced himself to back away. "We're close. Trust me." He took her hand.

"You need a bloodhound," she offered. The smart-ass.

"Merina." His blood had gone from boiling to simmering, but his cock hadn't received the memo. If she didn't stop teasing him, he'd throw her down right here in the . . . Where the hell were they, anyway?

"You have two kitchens?"

"Apparently." He blinked around at the smaller kitchen area, which, of course, he knew he had. Then he tightened his hold on Merina's hand and dragged her with him, picking up the pace as her laughter echoed through another open, empty room.

The moment they passed a downstairs bedroom, the one overlooking the pool, he had his bearings. But those bearings had come with a memory of the last time he'd set foot in that room.

Five years ago . . .

"I'm not sleeping in the same house as you. You can

fucking keep it!" Reese shouted as Gwyneth tossed her clothes from the closet to the bed. She was sobbing and part of him wanted to go to her. He refused. He was the one whose world had been torn to shreds. He was the one who had been betrayed. It was Gwyneth who chose to take their four years together and throw them into the incinerator.

"You're being unfair!" She pointed at him with a dress on a hanger.

"Me?" He stepped back into their shared bedroom, the one overlooking the pool because she liked to swim in the morning. "Hayes, Gwyneth?" His voice rose, but pain had eked into his tone. "You could have chosen anyone to fuck me over for, and you chose goddamn Hayes Lerner?"

Her lip trembled but he didn't let himself care what she was feeling. He couldn't. If he gave her an opening, she'd talk her way back into his life and he couldn't afford to be this wrong. Not ever again. Whatever she was going through paled in comparison to the earthquake now splitting his entire being in two.

"Anyone!" His voice cracked and he forced down a lump of misery. He would not let her see him wounded. He would come back from this. When he did, she and Hayes could fuck in public for all he cared. The problem was that right now, he did care.

Later that night, when he escaped to Crane Hotel and the uppermost suite on the same floor as his office, he realized the mistake that had been made was his.

He'd watched his father after his mother died. Watched him wall up and move forward. Alex's mind was on his business, his sights honed in on profits, numbers, and facts. Things that could be measured and quantified. Things that could be counted and delegated. Alex marched onward for a decade after losing Lunette, and in the process Reese had learned an invaluable lesson.

Women were not for keeps.

His mother's death had left all her boys unprepared. Scrambling. When fifteen-year-old Reese would have collapsed under the weight of grief, when Eli, just a year younger, would have beat the shit out of every kid in school for fun, and when Tag, at the tender age of eleven would have hidden from the world instead of cashing in on his big personality, Alex had stepped up and done what his family needed.

He'd soldiered on. They didn't call the man Big Crane for nothing. Yes, he was in charge, but it also took a big man to move past what would have put a lesser man in the grave alongside his wife.

Reese knew that lesson but temporarily forgot it over what amounted to a pair of great tits and a swish of strawberry hair. Gwyneth had made him forget his purpose. Forget his priorities. Heartbreak was his payment, and he'd earned every shattered piece. With it came the reinforcement of that long-ago learned lesson. Women weren't for keeps. Women didn't stay.

That night, he made a decision. Focus on building his future on something tangible, something that wouldn't go anywhere. Crane Hotels. Alex would retire in the next five or ten years and the board would be looking to appoint one of his sons the new CEO. Big shoes to fill, but Reese had big feet. He was going to be the one, and he wouldn't let a woman stand in his way.

Not ever again.

Merina's aerated laughter cut into his thoughts the moment Reese opened a door and ushered them into the foyer.

"Thank God," Merina said, dropping his hand. "I thought we'd end up in the garage next."

He turned and found her smiling, her shirt buttoned wrong, the edge of her tattoo peeking out. She was tempting and made him want to bury his bad memories in every inch of her smooth skin. To forget what had happened long ago and take the reprieve.

But his body had grown cold at the memory that had assaulted him, and he wouldn't be put in a position of explaining it to Merina.

Whiskey could be his bedmate tonight. It worked almost as well as sex to help him forget the past.

"You can find your way from here, I assume," he muttered, taking a step away from her.

"I can." She cocked her head inquisitively, sensing the change in him.

"Then do it." Moonbeams sliced across the foyer, and he backed from the light into the shadow of the kitchen.

CHAPTER 10

Reese never came to their shared bedroom last night, so when Merina woke in the morning, it was to a strange room in a strange bed by herself. Which was pretty much par for the course since her marriage. But last night was especially odd.

She'd gone from stripping for him, to accepting his kisses, to nearly having sex on a desk, to...nothing. She'd peeled back another layer of her husband in that moonlit office. Heat had sizzled between them as per their usual, but this time he'd been almost...dare she say it? *Fun.*

By the time he'd turned on her in the foyer, shooting her with a cold glare and snarling lip, she was completely confused. And the last thing she'd been willing to do was chase after him when he stomped into the kitchen. She'd instead watched his retreating figure wondering what had set him off.

Getting lost in the house had them laughing and

bantering—it was more funny than frustrating, so she didn't think that was what turned him. After that near-kiss in the corridor, she'd expected him to haul her upstairs over his shoulder and have his wicked way with her. Instead, he'd clicked like a switch. All over her one minute and disinterested the next.

No, not disinterested. There had been something else freezing the air between them. Something he hadn't been willing to talk about. Something that had sent him running from her instead of to her.

She tried to tell herself she didn't care as she dressed for work. Tried to convince herself that whatever had happened between them, it was for the best that they hadn't acted on their desires. But the moment her heels clicked from the foyer to the kitchen, she'd gone from contemplative to enraged.

She spotted him the moment she entered the kitchen. Pressed suit, facial hair trimmed, tie in place. His profile was to her as he filled his mug with coffee.

"Well. Look who's up," she said coolly.

He turned and her heart dipped just a little. There was so much fatigue in his eyes, she almost felt bad for him. Had he slept at all? Then she remembered the shit he'd pulled last night and allowed her anger to take the driver's seat. No matter what they should or shouldn't be doing, his rejection and the way he'd shut her out stung.

"Good morning," he replied, frowning.

What.

Ever.

"My bed was lonely. Care to share where you spent last night? Here at the table? On your yacht? Or did you..." She trailed off when he tipped his head subtly to the side.

She heard the crinkle of a plastic bag and slowly turned to find Magda on the other side of the room, fresh trash bag in hand, cabinet door open. Merina hadn't seen her there. And now someone else knew Reese hadn't slept in the same bed as his wife last night.

"I'm sorry, darling," he replied, coming to her. "I ended up working until almost four in the morning and slept in the office." He pressed a kiss to her forehead and tipped her chin. "You were so exhausted last night, I didn't want to wake you."

Her anger morphed into disappointment, which was less sharp but cut deeper. She'd washed in here on a wave of anger, ready to hash things out. Share what was really bothering her. He owed her his honesty behind closed doors. If she was expected to live here with him and pretend to be his blushing bride, the least he could do is treat her with respect.

He offered his coffee mug. "Cream?"

Apparently, her husband was content to carry on business as usual.

"Not today," she answered, covering for the fact that Reese didn't know how she took her coffee.

"Keeping me on my toes, I see," he said, his voice annoyingly light.

How long had he stayed awake turning over whatever upset him? Or had he compartmentalized it completely and not think about it at all?

"Can I drop you at work?" he asked.

You can drop dead, she thought, then bit her sharp tongue.

"I'd prefer to drive," she said, not bothering to pretend for Magda's sake.

"All right, then. See you tonight." With a nod, he walked out to the garage, perfectly unaffected as he told her to "have a nice day."

Mug in hand, Merina watched a sporty silver car she'd never seen speed out of the drive and out the open gate. Then she exchanged a glance with Magda and without bothering to speak to the older woman, turned on her heel and left the kitchen.

* * *

The next couple of weeks reminded Merina of the way she and Reese were when they'd first met. Cool and disconnected. The biggest difference was that now she shared a house with him. And a bedroom. Reese and Merina agreed that sleeping in the same room was paramount so as not to have a repeat of that morning in the kitchen and make Magda more suspicious. "I trust her," he'd said, "but I do want to give her the benefit of plausible deniability."

Reese ordered a couch for the bedroom to be delivered that very day, and since then had spent his nights on it getting the few hours he did sleep after he came in from the office.

Merina took the bed, though she didn't sleep much more than he did now that she'd set up a work-from-home office in the room across from their bedroom. She still went to the Van Heusen to care for the day-to-day, but after hours were no longer spent in the bar with a cup of tea. Now she was expected to be here, where anyone who cared to wonder what she and Reese were up to would assume they were up to their eyes in each other.

Which couldn't be further from the truth.

Rather than keep late hours in his office at the hotel, Reese worked from home at night so as not to raise suspicions with the board. The press hadn't written anything new about their marriage, but Reese expected that to change after Alex Crane's upcoming retirement party.

Over dinner Magda prepared—lemon risotto, salmon scaloppini with truffles, and a crisp white wine—he sat at the head of the table, Merina at his left elbow. Magda had already gone home, leaving them to their meal.

"Dad's party will require a bit of acting," he murmured, picking at his rice.

"On your part, you mean?" It was him who'd walked away from her and hadn't pursued or so much as kissed her on the mouth since that night in the moonlight. The night she'd allowed him to strip her almost bare and bend her over the desk. Part of her felt embarrassed and angry that she'd let him that close, but another more dominant part still pulsed with rejection that he hadn't sent her a sideways glance since.

"Both our parts," he corrected. "Lately we've been distant. Understandable, seeing as how busy we've been."

"Busy?" She let out a sharp laugh. "You tore me out of my clothes and left me by the stairs." She pressed her lips together before she said too much. The last thing she needed was for him to know how she felt. In the race for control, she needed to hold on to as much as possible. Reese was a predator, and she refused to be the wounded, weaker prey.

"We agreed getting physical would be confusing," he said, seeing right through her.

"Who agreed?" she asked, dropping her fork.

Reese sent her a blank look that pissed her right off. How

inconvenient he had to live with a woman who demanded they have "real" feelings and "real" conversations. How silly of her, expecting to be treated like a human being.

"It's not ideal, I admit," he said while she silently fumed. "I can have the house staff reduce their hours so they're here when we're not. That way, we can— Where are you going?" he asked when she pushed away from the table.

"I'm tired," she clipped, feeling a swell of emotion hit her like an anvil. She had to get out of here before he saw her cry. She darted from the dining room and ran up the stairs, trying to quell the tears that burned the backs of her eyes.

She was so damn lonely she couldn't stand it. No more morning coffees with her mother, no more late-night chats when she returned home and found her father waiting by the television. She even missed talking to Arnold at the desk when she worked late at the Van Heusen. When she was at work, she was busy, and when she was out to dinner with Reese, she couldn't completely be herself, and when she was here in the house, she was alone. Even with him in the same room, she felt utterly alone.

In the bedroom's en suite, she stripped out of her work clothes and stepped into a hot shower, allowing the tears to come as she softly sobbed under the water. When she'd met Corbin, he was attentive and fun and always smiling. He was complimentary and, yes, completely and utterly imma-ture. But he'd filled an emotional need she'd been trying to ignore since he split with everything she had in her bank account.

Since then, she'd stayed busy, occasionally dating and being she-woman, able to handle her job, work overtime, and date the occasional underwhelming prospect. But to-day, just weeks into her marriage, Merina was exception-ally fragile. She couldn't be she-woman today. She just wanted to be a woman. She wanted to be vulnerable and open and emotional and unreasonable.

She wanted someone to hold her while she was all of those things.

But there was no one.

* * *

He gave Merina a few minutes before following in the di-rection she'd disappeared. When he reached their bedroom and heard the shower on, he started to retreat. Until he picked out another sound beneath the pounding water.

Crying.

Soft, tender sobs he could tell she was trying to hide. Trying to *stop*. And they absolutely froze him in his tracks.

He hadn't taken her emotions into consideration since the night he ran from his past demons. He'd walled up, closed in, focused on work, and figured she was doing the same.

But Merina wasn't like him. That was her most beauti-ful attribute. She was led by her heart, not her sense of duty and business. He'd held the Van Heusen over her head, but it was ultimately her caring nature that had made her say "I do." He'd taken that good faith, and the real connection they'd forged, then frozen it solid.

Part of which pissed him off—he wasn't good for her, good for anyone, and she should avoid getting involved with him any more than necessary. He'd lost control in that darkened office when he kissed her, but vowed not to go there again. He respected her enough to leave her alone. His chest crumpled as another soft sob came from the other room. Not the staged cries of his ex, who would have turned on the waterworks to gain sympathy or her way, but real, soul-rending sadness Merina was desperately trying to hide.

Maybe she didn't want to be alone.

He hovered in the middle of the room, unsure what to do next. Indecision in general made him uncomfortable. Rarely did he not know the next step. Silently, he turned over his options. Leave her to herself or wait for her to come out. The latter would risk her lashing out, but he wasn't that big of a dick that he didn't realize this was his fault, at least in part.

The man in him who was used to delegating the messy emotions of his past relationships wanted the latter. He was embarrassingly bad at these sorts of things, and it showed. But the husband in him knew he'd hurt her and wanted her to be okay. That, he wouldn't run away from.

Even though he had no idea what the fuck he'd say when she same out, he took off his suit jacket, rested it over the arm of the couch, sat, and waited. He didn't have to wait long.

Within a few minutes, the water shut off, and a few minutes after that, Merina exited the bathroom, a white towel wrapped around her body. His eyes went to the tattoo peeking out over one covered breast, the arrow whose meaning he didn't know. Her shoulders were beaded with water droplets from her damp hair, the golden hue darker because it was wet.

Her red-rimmed eyes went wide, surprised to see him, no doubt.

He felt a physical pain he didn't know what to do with in the vicinity of his heart. In the minutes he sat here, he hadn't thought of how to start the conversation. Turned out there was no need, because she spoke first.

"What are you doing up here?" Her anger snapped into place. He knew the diversion well, since he often used anger to mask his true feelings. She wanted him to believe that's all this was, her being upset because he was an ass. His instincts told him this was deeper than that. More complicated than that.

Exactly what he'd been running from for two weeks— technically for five years. But Merina wasn't Gwyneth, and if he thought for a second he could handle Merina the same way, he was a bigger idiot than she thought he was.

He didn't answer, knowing his words wouldn't be heard, so instead he followed her to her closet.

"Do you mind?" She spun on him, anger flashing in her eyes.

"We need to resolve this," he started, but the words felt wrong. A second later he learned they were.

"Oh, did you come up here to renegotiate?" She opened a drawer and rifled through the pile of lace and silk panties. One hand holding the towel over her breasts, she shook black lace at him. "So we can impress your stupid board tomorrow?" Her cheeks reddened. "What if I don't feel like playing dancing monkey to your organ? What if I decide to be my real, true self instead of the plastic me you insist on?"

"Are you forgetting the purpose of this marriage, Merina?" Also the wrong thing to say, but she'd lit his temper the second she'd issued the threat. Real or not, he didn't care for her dangling her loyalty over his head. That crumpling feeling in his chest turned into a cave-in, the walls falling down around him.

"You endure me until I'm named CEO and receive the Van Heusen in return. Is it so hard?" He couldn't lose CEO, not now that he'd come this far.

"It's occurring to me I didn't negotiate enough into my end of the deal, Crane. Enduring you is more difficult than I anticipated."

The moment she spoke, her mouth froze open. He could see the hint of apology in the way she averted her gaze, but a second later, she pressed her lips together and elevated her chin. Committed to her path.

"Don't worry about my feelings, Merina. I have none." Again, her eyes slipped to the side. She was unaccustomed to being nasty. "Tell me again how hard your life is." He lifted his arms to gesture around the massive master bedroom. "Your meals are made. You can sleep in any one of ten bedrooms. Your food is prepared by someone else, your messes cleaned for you. You have access to a *yacht* and a spending account to do with as you please."

"Is this a guilt trip?" she snapped. He didn't acknowledge her interruption. He'd worked hard for what he had—what he was practically handing her—and refused to let her off the hook so easily.

"At the end of your time served," he bit out, "you will have the hotel I purchased at market value free and clear. What more could you have possibly asked for?" He hadn't pegged her for a gold digger but damn. What fucking else?

She wrestled on her panties, her movements jerky, the towel slipping slightly and giving him a view of one luscious thigh.

"What else, indeed?" she grumbled, her voice wavering

the slightest bit. "That's all there is to life, isn't there?" She speared him with those red eyes again.

"That about covers it," he answered.

"What about family?" Her eyebrows lifted and dropped. She took a step closer to him. "Emotional connection?"

Cold sweat prickled along his shirt collar.

"Sex. Closeness. A night spent in someone's arms instead of being alone." With each example, she came closer. Until she was standing in front of him, chin elevated, holding his eyes unwavering.

Closeness.

If there was one thing he was not capable of giving, it was friendship. He'd buy her the moon. He'd fuck her silly. But that kind of closeness wasn't up for grabs. Not even in exchange for the coveted CEO of Crane Hotels. Not for anything.

"I'm just tired." She retreated and wrestled into a T-shirt without flashing him, then dropped the towel, exposing her legs briefly before she jammed them into a pair of long, stretchy pants. "Never mind."

"Never mind," he repeated as she bumped past him. "Is that like *fine*?" Because as he'd learned, *fine* was bad. *Never mind* didn't sound much better.

She shot him a confused look before climbing into bed and snatching a book off the nightstand. "I'll probably read a little, then call Lorelei. I need someone to talk to." She looked up after opening the book in the middle. "Apparently that's not in my *contract*. Do I need to go elsewhere or will you be leaving this room soon?"

Oh, hell no.

He stalked to the bed, took the book from her hand, and tossed it onto the couch that had been his bed for the last few weeks, but of course she'd ignored that sacrifice on his part.

"Hey!" she protested.

He bent over her, hands fisted on the bed at either side of her gorgeous, hidden body. "Who do you think you're talking to, *Mrs. Crane*?"

Her eyes flared, but not from anger and not from fear. From lust so thick he could taste it on his tongue.

"Will sex fix it?" he asked.

She looked infuriated, then slightly chagrined.

"Will it?" he demanded.

"Of course not," she murmured, unable to look anywhere but at his mouth.

He leaned closer, then a little closer, until his lips pressed hers. He slanted his mouth, but gently, giving her every opportunity to shove him away. To tell him no.

She did neither.

Instead, she reached for the back of his neck and tugged him close, until he was forced to shift his weight or lose his balance.

Hand under her ass, he moved her to the center of the bed, pressing every hardening inch of his body against every giving inch of hers.

"I made you cry," he said when he pulled away. Her fingers threaded into the back of his hair.

"Yes," she whispered.

"I don't like that I made you cry."

"So don't do it again." She laid the softest kiss on his mouth. "Sex might not fix it, but it's worth a shot."

The hold on his libido slipped.

"God, I want you." He tightened his grip on her ass.

"Then take me." She fisted his shirt and dragged him

closer. Seconds later, his tie was tossed aside, the buttons undone one by one.

He continued moving his tongue against hers, tasting the salt from her tears and the heady, spicy flavor of her mouth. She smelled of shampoo and soap and all he wanted to do was bury his nose between her thighs and absolutely devour her. He didn't know how to fix her hurts deep down, but he knew how to make her forget them for now. And so far, she was willing to concede that point.

He'd take it.

But this wasn't just for her. No, there was a selfish part of him that needed her to cover his deep hurts as well. Forget what led them to this point, what would be waiting for him when it was over. His need for her was unlike any he'd felt before.

He was a starving man, and she was his feast.

* * *

This is crazy.

This is crazy.

But the words were drowned by the pulsating demands of her body. Reese was turning her inside out. She needed what he was offering. She needed to be taken, kissed hard, held down, fucked until she was begging for it.

Her emotions couldn't be trusted in his care, this she knew, but her body . . . her body was a different story. Reese Crane was an expert—knew exactly what a woman wanted, what a woman needed. She happened to be a wanting, needing woman.

He lifted her shirt over her head, his talented mouth closing over her nipple. Her hands dug into his hair, anchoring herself to him. Where before she was filled with despair and loneliness, now she was filled with longing and anticipation.

So much better.

He reached between her legs and cupped her sex and let her nipple go with a subtle *pop*. "Hot."

"Wet," she returned on a breath. Being hidden away with him here, having a shared secret...she liked it way more than she should. It was indulgent in the best possible way.

His lips met hers again, the rough scrape of his jaw welcome. She parted her legs where he was still touching her while she explored the planes of his muscled, bare chest. His golden skin, an army of abdominal muscles, and the scant trail of hair arrowing straight for the part of him she wanted to see most of all.

She cupped the erection straining his suit pants and he grunted, increasing the friction of his hand between her legs. She squirmed, all but coming on the spot—with her top off and her pants on.

"Not yet, you don't." The playful side of him intrigued her and only made her want him more. "Wait for me."

She wanted to wait. She wanted him inside her before she allowed her control to ebb, her body to uncoil. Given the buzz in her limbs, her orgasm would be all-consuming and she wanted to consume him with it.

She was tired of doing things alone.

Quickly, she unthreaded his belt, and when she reached for his zipper, he grunted a warning. "Careful."

She went slowly, unzipping as she slipped her other hand into his pants to protect his bare skin from the angry metal teeth. He was hard and heavy against her palm.

"Reese's rocket," she said against his mouth. His eyes closed, robbing her of the pleasure simmering there. "In the flesh."

His eyes opened. "What am I going to do with you, Merina?"

"I think you know."

Proving he did, his mouth dropped to hers briefly, then he was up, peeling off his clothes and yanking open the nightstand drawer on the opposite side of the bed. Merina kicked out of her yoga pants, eyes on the gold foil packet between Reese's teeth.

The promise of what was to come rattled her nerves and set her aflame. Maybe she was wrong earlier. Sex with him might fix everything after all.

Panties off, she tossed them to the floor. Reese rolled the condom on, stroking himself once more, twice more. She bit down on her bottom lip, her eyes on those coveted inches wrapped in his strong fist. He depressed the bed with a knee and came to her.

"Say yes, Merina." Her name rolled off his tongue, his deep timbre seducing her ears. He parted her legs with one knee and settled between her thighs.

At the same time the word *yes* hissed from between her teeth, he buried himself to the hilt. Every. Last. Inch.

She crossed her ankles at his back, holding him close. With powerful thrusts he plunged into her again and again. This need had been vibrating between them for the last few weeks—hell, maybe the last month. The attraction between them had always an inferno they'd tried futilely to keep from lighting.

Pity. Because this was damn good.

One hand at her lower back, he canted her hips and

pushed into her again. Her eyelids slid shut as a moan of encouragement eked from her throat.

"Finally," he said through labored breaths. Then he smiled, inordinately pleased with himself. "Found it."

"We'll see," she lied. Because he had. Each sharp thrust pinged an innermost part of her, snapping another thread on her control.

"Give it to me, Merina," he demanded, still working, still thrusting.

"Not until…" Droves of tingles ran a race from her toes to her face. "…you."

"Ladies first. I insist." He drew out slowly before driving into her, and a sharp cry of pleasure came from her parted lips.

They had sex the same way they fought, fighting to maintain control as long as possible. But just as the thought came that she wouldn't let him win this battle, she surrendered. Another thrust and her back arched, an orgasm rocking her. He followed, surrendering with her, his groans of pleasure loud in her ears.

Lights exploded behind her eyes and part of her registered that she was being *loud*. Which Reese probably ate up with a spoon. *Egomaniac*. Even that snide thought couldn't erase the buoyancy that overtook her chest, the pleasant blankness that covered her mind, the feeling of being a part of someone else—the closeness she'd mentioned earlier.

Seconds, minutes—hell, who knew how long—passed before she opened her eyes, feeling as if she'd surfaced from a drugged haze. Reese was propped on his elbows over her, eyes hooded, breathing heavy. From inside her, his cock pulsed. She gave him a squeeze.

It drew a smile to his brilliantly handsome face. "You know a few tricks."

She smiled back at him, unable to keep from it.

"That"—he kissed the tip of her nose—"was a good idea."

Merina hummed. It really was. The feeling of lost and lonely had been replaced with light and happy. She couldn't remember the last time she'd felt this way and could stand to feel it much more often. Reese Crane, as she'd assumed, was dynamite in the sack.

Not that she'd tell him that. Though he looked like he might already know.

"No bragging." She pressed a finger to his lips. He nipped her fingertip.

"No need." He drew out of her, taking her sated groan with him, and he chuckled. "Your body tells me everything I need to know."

There was a thought. Her body was giving away her secrets without her having to say them. Which made sex a bad idea. She rolled to face him as he slipped out of bed.

"Don't worry." He winked. "I won't tell."

She picked up a pillow and tossed it at his naked ass, burying her smile in her elbow, because watching his backside clench and release as he paced to the bathroom was a sight she'd not soon forget.

CHAPTER 11

The board members ambled from the conference room table, and as per their usual, Alex, Reese, and Tag stayed behind. Alex filled his coffee mug to the brim then lifted and dropped the newspaper onto the table. "Subtle."

"I thought it was nice." Tag shrugged one massive shoulder. The "nice" headline he was referring to was in a Chicago socialite magazine. Not exactly the *Trib* but anyone who cared about gossip paid attention to *Elegant Elite*. They were the ones who started photographing Reese with his dates at every charity and dinner function, and they'd mentioned *#ReesesRocket* on their Twitter feed several times last week. The headline HONEYMOON'S ON! was definitely a step up.

"It's flashy," Alex told Reese.

"Penelope assures me turning the media will convince the board."

Alex grunted.

"Tomorrow night's the retirement party," Reese said. "They'll see then." Reese didn't think anyone would suspect he and Merina were anything but in love after they'd blown each other's minds in bed last night. This morning had been as peaceful as monks. Shared orgasms had put some slack into the tension between them. Getting along behind the scenes was bound to make it easier to parade around in public.

Always productive after sex, he'd typically excuse himself to his office, but when he'd come out of the bathroom, his wife had beat him to it. Merina was up, dressed in her stretchy pants and T-shirt again, and pulling on a pair of sneakers.

"Thanks for the recharge, Crane." She'd grinned. "I have monthly reports to review."

Then she was off, wiggling her round, delicious ass away from him and into the office down the hall. He retreated to his own office but concentration wasn't as smooth as usual. Typically sex freed his brain and he could work, but last night, his mind kept returning to the wonder that was Merina's face during sex. The neat little pleat between her golden brown eyebrows. The parting of her pink mouth when she blew out a ragged breath of enjoyment. Her normally smooth, tamed hair a wild mess over the pillow, a few strands thrown over half her face while she writhed.

Incredible.

Fingers snapped in front of Reese's face and he blinked to see Tag's surly expression and their father standing to leave.

"Anyway, I'm off," Alex declared. Only after he'd gone did Tag speak.

"You fucking did it. You had sex with Merina."

"She's my wife." Reese pushed his chair away from the conference room table unable to hide a very wide, very proud grin. He buttoned his jacket and Tag stood with him.

"Proud of you, Clip." Tag nodded his approval, using an old nickname.

Clip was short for *paperclip*, and Tag had started in on Reese the day he put on his first suit. Being teasingly labeled as the pencil pusher back in his twenties had irked Reese, and Tag had been happy to needle him. Now the title held no venom.

"Careful," Tag continued. "Girls get attached. They want more."

"Thank you, Tag. I'm sure as a man who has perfected the hookup and breakup, you have loads of advice." Reese lifted an eyebrow.

"Hey, I'm just looking out for you. There is a reason Dad is still single."

"Because he's focused on work," Reese said.

"And there's a reason you've had Bobbie send flowers and a note of cease and desist to every date you've had since Gwyneth..." Tag trailed off. "Sorry."

"Relax." He put a palm on his brother's shoulder. Mom had been a worrier. Tag came by it honestly. "This marriage has an expiration date. When it's over, so is the sex. Merina understands that."

Not only had they sweated out their problems in bed, but she'd also hopped up and went right to work afterward. She hadn't been clingy or emotional, and was no longer crying in the shower, so he was glad about that. She more than understood what was between them, and Reese was happy to let her use him physically.

"There are always strings," Tag said, genuine worry fusing his features into a mask. "Once you're crowned CEO, she might not appreciate you blowing her off."

"She's making out like a bandit, Tag." Reese pulled the office door open. "Her hotel will be in her name, free and clear. She couldn't care less about my position at Crane save for the fact it's getting her what she wants."

The second it was out of his mouth, a niggle of doubt reared in the back of his head. Was that true? Merina wasn't cold or calculating, and she'd put her personal reputation on the line to help him reach his goal. Marrying him was a great sacrifice on her part.

Despite his doubts, Reese said, "I'm sure of it."

"You deserve to be CEO." Tag stepped out of the office door, his voice just above a whisper. "Just . . . make sure you don't get too attached to your 'wife.'"

"I know what I'm doing." Reese stared Tag in the eye until his brother ran a hand through his long hair and sighed his exasperation.

"I know you do." Tag nodded and started down the hall, Reese behind him. Before they crossed the threshold into the foyer, he turned to give one last harbinger of what was to come. "And, Clip?"

Reese stopped.

"You can fuck her. But don't fuck her over. She's not one of your one-nighters."

On that, they agreed. Merina was something else entirely.

* * *

Merina stopped advancing across the hotel lobby when she heard her name. She turned to find Arnold's kind, smiling face.

"Your cards came." He lifted one from the business card holder on the front desk.

She plucked the card from his fingers. There, beneath the Van Heusen's regal gold Phoenix logo, was her name. Her *new* name.

Merina Crane, Manager

Seeing her new last name in black and white made her palms sweat. Somehow that business card made things more official than her marriage certificate.

Because you had sex with him.

Yeah, well, she refused to feel guilty about that. Already, three people pointed out how nice she looked today, one of them her bar manager who'd commented, "Marriage looks good on you, Merina."

If they were in this together, they may as well enjoy themselves.

"Thank you, Arnold. I didn't even think to change the cards." Especially since she'd change them back in a few months.

"You have your mother to thank." After a long pause, she returned the card but before she could leave, he spoke again. "I always wondered how different marriage was for women than men." His smile turned wistful. "My wife had to leave her family and move to my house. Change her name to my last name. And let me tell you, she was not excited about becoming a Woodcock." A deep, warm chuckle reverberated from his chest.

She laughed with him and faced the desk. He rarely spoke of his wife. If he had a story to tell about her, Merina wanted to hear it.

"Adeline was a strong woman, but she was old-fashioned. She said that things were supposed to be like that according to God. A woman submitting to her husband. Did you know that verse doesn't mean what people think it means?"

Merina rested her elbows on the high counter, taking advantage of the quiet lobby to listen to another of Arnold's life lessons.

"People think it means to come under someone's control, but that's not the translation. If a wife submits to a husband, she's giving him a gift. She's giving him the opportunity to be a man. Without that lesson, he won't be strong. Instead, he will be weak and in response, she will feel as if she has to protect herself. That's not the way it's supposed to be." He shook his graying head. "Just because you women can protect yourselves and be your own warriors doesn't mean you should. Men need a chance to do that too. To protect and love you makes us better."

"I...never thought of it that way," she admitted. But then again, had she ever dated a man who wasn't perfectly willing to let her handle the hard things? To let her handle *everything*? Corbin came to mind. He was definitely not the chivalrous type. He had no problem watching her work hard and taking her money.

Reese on the other hand...

Her face heated as she remembered him saying *Ladies first* in bed last night.

"Love suits you, Mrs. Crane." Arnold smiled and handed her the business card she'd just put back. "Hang on to that."

"Adeline was a lucky lady," she said with a sad smile.

Would she find a pure love like Adeline and Arnold had shared?

"I was lucky," he said. "I wasn't this man before I knew her."

That conversation had been a nice reprieve in what turned out to be a hell of a day. Particularly her new bartender, Heather, who'd developed a fascination with a recently hired single bellman who was a consummate flirt. Several times, Merina was forced to split up their conversations and redirect them back to work.

Arnold had joked about it being "spring" and everyone being "frisky," which made Merina smile. That theory went belly-up when her chef walked out midshift. Leonard wasn't frisky or in love. He was pissed at his staff and the world and about a recent notice he'd received to vacate his apartment. He'd stomped out, threw his chef's coat in the lobby, and left a string of profanities lingering in the air.

Containing that sort of shitstorm was well outside of her capabilities. Everyone loved a good story, and that drama would make for tongue-wagging fodder for weeks, maybe months to come.

By the time Reese arrived at the Van Heusen at seven, Merina was frazzled, crazed, and a bit surprised to find his presence brought comfort. She'd forgotten he'd driven her to work this morning.

"I texted you," he said, cutting through the lobby with a long-legged gait, his eyes on her unerringly. A shiver made its way up her spine, then down. That look. That approach. It reminded her of being taken last night, the way she'd enjoyed every single second of it. She'd needed to cash in her sexual frustration and Reese had been the perfect outlet.

Sure, that's all it was...

"Things have been nuts." She reached for her phone and saw three texts from him. *Ready?* Followed by: *Be there in 20.* And the final: *Here. Coming in.*

"Let me take you to dinner." He came close and she tipped her head to take in his height. She couldn't remember the last time she ate—she seemed to remember a packet of instant oatmeal sometime late morning—and had pretty much been running on coffee. Now her brain was having trouble processing, her soaring stress level not having yet begun its descent.

"Hello, Reese." Merina's mother strode toward them, no doubt to intervene.

"Mrs. Van Heusen." He dipped his chin in greeting but his eyes tracked right back to Merina. "I was going to say drinks first, but you look as if you need to eat."

"You can call me Jolie, Reese. Or Mom, I guess. Since you're technically our son now."

Oh my God.

"Mom." She tried to communicate with a glare that Jolie was overstepping her bounds.

"Did you see your new business cards?" Jolie asked Merina.

"I did. Thank you."

"Did Reese?"

Merina snatched one up and delivered it to Reese, who took it, read it, and said absolutely nothing. "He has now. I'll just grab my things," Merina told him, and then cupped her mother's elbow and led her to the office.

"What are you doing?" Jolie asked.

She released her mother and grabbed her purse and packed a few files she'd need to work on at home. "I'm not sure what you're up to, but please try and behave yourself."

"You married him." Jolie shrugged. "Do you not want me to be friendly?"

"Friendly, yes, but fake, no." At that pronouncement, a ping echoed in her chest. Fake was exactly what this was. At least, on the outside. God. What a mess.

"Just because I'm not sure why you married him so quickly doesn't mean I won't welcome him like I would any son-in-law. We'll be spending cookouts and holidays together for years to come." Jolie's smile warmed her entire face. "And maybe celebrating with grandbabies in the future."

"Mom!" Merina nearly choked. "I just got married! We're still finding our way around."

"I bet you are." Her mother elbowed her.

If only she could tell her the truth. That the only reason she'd agreed was to secure her family's future—the Van Heusen's future.

"I can't do this right now. I love you. I'm going to dinner with Reese."

"Have fun, sweetie. Love you too."

Years to come. Grandbabies.

Oy.

* * *

The check took its sweet time coming to the table, then the valet spent precious minutes locating the car, and *then* when Reese arrived at the mansion, Magda took more of his time relaying household details he really didn't want to hear right now.

Reason being, during dinner, Merina had leaned close and whispered, "How about a repeat of last night?"

Forgetting his steak dinner, he threw his napkin on the table and signaled the waiter for the check.

"I meant after dinner," she'd quietly reprimanded.

Merina had eaten some of the shrimp appetizer, a salad, and a dinner roll, so he knew she wasn't starving. Tonight, he could subsist on her alone. So his reply was a curt but heartfelt, "Fuck dinner."

Watching her bite her lip sent fire pouring through his veins. He hadn't had enough of her and tonight was testing his patience. As evidenced when Magda said good night. The moment she was out the door, Reese cupped the back of Merina's head and backed her through the foyer to the staircase, his mouth on hers. He took the banister with his other hand and walked her up the stairs, refusing to unseal his mouth from hers until they were close to the bedroom.

They didn't make it.

He pressed her against the wall, his self-control dwindling, his erection pulsing. Fingers fumbling, he managed to open two delicate buttons of her shirt before she reached up and finished the job for him, dropping it to the ground and greedily seeking his kisses.

He liked her greedy. He liked her half naked.

Burying his fingers into her hair, he reached around and flicked her bra open with the other. Then he freed her breasts, lowering his lips to taste first one nipple, then the next. The sensitive bud tightened on his tongue. He continued laving her, loving the way she writhed and the way her breath caught as he suckled her.

"Reese, God," she moaned, her hand in his hair, and arched her back. "I've wanted you all day."

"Same." He unzipped her skirt and shoved it down her legs.

He'd never spent an entire day wanting to see someone. Flashes of her naked, the sound of her tender moans in his ear, had assaulted him during meetings, while on the phone, and while drafting e-mails.

There was a corner of his mind that she occupied, and with her back into his arms tonight, he could build on what he'd learned—give her more of what she'd enjoyed the most.

And try a few new things.

He dropped to his knees and stripped her panties next, holding his breath for the sight that was about to be his. Soft folds, completely bare save for a neatly trimmed patch of hair hiding those luscious lips between her thighs. He put his face there now and slicked his tongue inside. She fisted his hair and tugged, eliciting a sharp shout of satisfaction.

"No, not out here," she said.

Yes, here. His hallway. His house. His wife.

He didn't argue, but delivered blow after blow. Lick after lick. And when he found her clit, he sucked, to see what her reaction would be. She arched her back and pulled his hair, and he decided he'd make her come, right here against the wall.

He explored her with a finger, then two, stroking in time as he savored her with his tongue. She tasted heavenly— the kind of taste you sample and never, ever forget.

"Please, oh please," she panted now, begging for release. Thrusting against his face, with one hand on the wall for leverage and the other on the back of his head as she guided him.

Greedy. Demanding.

He couldn't get enough.

Slipping his fingers into her warm wetness again, he stroked her clit slowly.

"Come, beautiful," he instructed. He sped up his strokes, repeating the smooth, slick motion until he watched her eyes pinch closed. Then he lowered his mouth to her again and on contact, her thighs locked.

Her shouts of ecstasy would have brought the entire house staff running had they been on the clock. Those shouts turned to whimpers as her tightened thigh muscles grew useless. She collapsed against the wall and began to slide.

Reese didn't let her fall.

He stood, scooped her into his arms, and smiled down at the woman now holding on to his neck. Hooded eyes brimmed with satisfaction. Her smile was foxy and slightly embarrassed.

"I suppose you're proud of yourself," she grumbled as he carried her to the bedroom.

"Damn straight," he said, then deposited her on the bed. Naked, sated. Goddamn beautiful. And for tonight. His. All his.

* * *

"No wonder the girls want you to call them back," Merina said half to herself as she lay on the bed. Realizing Reese heard her, and that her comment was as nakedly honest as she was, she attempted to cover by adding, "Dinner was nice. What I ate of it, anyway."

"Hmm." He sent a gaze down her body and up. Chills rose on her skin in response. "I don't know about dinner but dessert was five-star."

When he reached for his tie, her breath snagged. His

hand halted over the knot. "What is with you and getting me out of this tie?"

Merina pushed to her knees and tugged the length of striped silk, bringing his face to hers. "I like when you come undone, Crane."

"Control freak." His warm breath tickled her lips and she smothered his words with her mouth. He cupped her breasts, not the least bit shy about touching her. She made quick work of his tie, untucked his shirt, and shoved his hands away in the race to undo his belt.

"Turnabout is fair play," she breathed, her hands shakily unzipping his pants. When she'd leaned over the table at dinner to whisper into his ear, she'd had one thing in mind.

Tasting him.

"I didn't expect..." Whatever he'd been about to say was lost in a long, deep sigh when Merina closed her mouth over his bare cock. He was hard and getting harder under her attention, and he tasted heady and spicy.

One warm palm tracked down her back while she worked, stroking a sensual line over her spine, closing over her bottom and then up again. His movements slowed hers, taking her from racing to savoring, and rather than be in a hurry, she enjoyed every second.

When the fingers of his other hand speared her hair, it wasn't to hold her mouth in place, but to gently touch the underside of her jaw, massage her scalp, and issue words of praise that tangled around her heart.

"Merina." His voice broke on her name.

When he was close, he spoke her name again, gently pulling from her mouth. She allowed him to slip away, sitting up on her knees and cupping his backside—almost as steely as his front side.

And because she hadn't had enough of feeling how hard he was everywhere, she let go of his ass and trailed her hands beneath the shirt hanging loosely from his shoulders. Rocky abs and concrete chest and rounded, thick shoulders. She pushed his shirt off his arms, running her hands over his warm muscles.

"I like you like this," she told him. "Take your pants off." She sat back on her heels and watched as he stomped out of his pants and discarded his shoes and socks.

He lowered over her and she pushed on his chest, forcing him to his back. "Oh no you don't."

"You want control tonight, Merina?" He cupped her hips in his large hands, making her want to take back those words, but then she remembered that most of her fantasies had included her on top, so the answer was yes.

She wanted control tonight.

Sliding one leg over his, she pushed her breasts out as she straddled him. When he raised his hand to touch her, it was to draw a line over her tattoo. His eyes locked on hers, filled to the brim with heat, and he lifted his head slightly off the pillow. She kissed him, a soft sigh tickling her throat as his hands moved to her breasts.

Reese took control from her, sliding his tongue along hers and slowing the pace. He turned her inside out with each thick, delicious, drugging kiss, and she found her hold loosening. Her body softening. Her mind melting.

Before she knew what happened, the world was rotating and she was on her back again. When she opened her eyes, Reese was rolling on a condom. Before she could complain that this was *not* his show to run, he was between her thighs and sliding home in one strong stroke.

Slow.

Then out again even slower.

"Yes." Holding on to him, Merina uttered the name she'd avoided using as much as possible. "Reese."

* * *

Reese returned from disposing of the condom and collapsed facedown next to Merina, who was lying on her back, arm over her eyes. She hummed and he heard the smile there. Then he lifted his head and saw it too. Propped on his arms, he leaned over and kissed the corner of that smile.

"You want to compliment me," he pointed out, "but it goes against your code of ethics. Am I right?"

She lifted her arm and peeked out at him, a smudge of mascara under her eyes. He reached over with his thumb and swiped it away. It took a few gentle tugs, but eventually she was perfect again instead of raccoon-eyed. Although, raccoon-eyed, she was pretty damn perfect too.

"You need a compliment, Crane? Who knew you were so needy?"

"Back to Crane?" She'd called him by his name a moment ago, and not just once. He liked hearing his first name roll off her lips, especially since she snapped at him by using his last name so often. "I don't need a compliment," he said honestly. "I know how good I am in bed."

"Whatever." She snorted.

"Your mouth lies but your body doesn't, Merina."

Something fragile flickered in her eyes. Not hurt or anger, but vulnerability. It caused an answering thud in his chest and a simultaneous wave of panic.

When they'd agreed to marry for show, he didn't expect to have sex with her, and he'd bet his fortune she wasn't planning on having sex with him. That mystery unearthed, they were now stuck in the light with each other.

"You like sex," he said. He was learning about her, having slept with her more than once. The prospect of sleeping with her again made him want to know more. What made her tick? What did she like done to her? What did she like to do?

"Who doesn't?" She rolled to face him, goose bumps puckering her arms. He maneuvered off the comforter and tossed it over her. He stroked her blanket-covered arm, warming her from the room's chilly air.

"Plenty of women think they like sex," he answered, "but they're timid about asking for what they want. Hell, you don't even ask. You take it."

"You're referring to the blow job, I presume." Her cheekbones dashed with color. Not used to talking dirty, he'd bet. Another intriguing fact about her he catalogued for later. "I'm sure you've had plenty of those."

Belatedly, he realized his "plenty of women" comment had alluded to the women he'd slept with. Not the best topic to bring up in bed. "I won't talk about the women I've been with in the past."

"Like I'm jealous of those ridiculous women?"

"Ridiculous?" He felt his eyebrows lift.

"Silly. Vapid. Take your pick of adjectives."

"Some of the women I dated have been decent," he said in his own defense. "Kind, intelligent, and not at all interested in what I could give them."

"I guess I sort of fit into that category now..." She winced.

"That's different. We had a business agreement for the hotel, for CEO. This..." He again ran a hand over her arm. "This wasn't part of the deal."

"No." Her eyes found his. "I guess not."

"I'm not going to use it against you. You know that, don't you?" He'd asked because he wasn't sure she'd ever been able to give of herself freely without someone taking advantage.

His thought paired with a stab of regret. He'd done exactly that.

"I know." Her voice was tiny, and she wouldn't look at him. She wasn't sure, but he was. She could trust him not to hold this over her head when things ended.

I'll miss it, though, came the wayward thought. A thought he shooed away with a subject change.

"Let's talk about this, then." He pulled the blanket away and kissed the arrow inked over her breast. "I should know what this means."

"Oh, should you?" Feisty. Just the way he liked her.

"Given the amount of times I plan on kissing it and admiring it while we're together, I should know what it means. Then I can concentrate on your pleasure rather than spending precious brain cells guessing."

"You're good." Her laugh washed over him, making him smile.

"Thank you."

"It's...nothing. Something I wanted when I was younger."

"What are you hiding?" He'd been trying to tease another laugh from her but the question made her guard go up.

"I think we should talk less." She lifted the blanket and

wrapped her hand around his cock, stroking him from base to tip.

His arm lashed around her, moving her closer. She stroked again, this time running her thumb over the head, which felt so much like her tongue, his body bucked.

"Why, yes," she purred. "I believe part of you is ready." With a wicked smile, she threw the blanket off and went down on him without an ounce of warning.

Unable to resist, his hips thrust forward. She cupped his balls and held his length, popping him out of her mouth and licking. Then she lifted her eyes to meet his briefly before taking him into her mouth again. Reese grasped the sheets, tearing them from the corners and knocking pillows to the ground. Every nerve ending in his body shot off like fireworks.

There was too much pleasure to contain. Merina's mouth was hot and wet, and she knew exactly how much pressure to put on his balls. She knew how hard to suck him, gently jerking him off at the end while her tongue swirled the tip.

He lost his ability to hold on to control, bucking off the bed. She tore his orgasm from him. His hand fisted in her hair, he pumped into her mouth. She swallowed every drop, licking him from base to tip when he collapsed to his back.

His muscles gradually loosened, his world a series of hazy sensations. Blackness covered him, or maybe that was the blanket. A featherlight kiss landed on his lips.

"Your tattoo," he mouthed, unsure where the unhinged thought had come from. At the end of the most amazing sex of his life, he realized he'd been manipulated. She hadn't wanted to answer him and distracted him in the most effective way possible.

Clever girl.

The only answer that came was a *click* as the light shut off. For the first time in years, he slipped into a slumber that wasn't alcohol- or exhaustion-induced.

CHAPTER 12

Shit." Reese yanked the knot out of the bow tie and started over.

"You're on edge tonight." Merina appeared behind him in the doorway of his closet, balancing on one foot to pull on her other silver high heel. Her gown was blue and sparkly and short enough to display succulent thighs that made his mouth water.

"You're in danger of being stripped bare." Bow tie forgotten, he went to her, scooping her close and kissing her. A line had been crossed. One where he grabbed her up without hesitation, and one where she came to him, no questions asked.

"How the hell do you tie one of these things?" Her hands went to the tie and she frowned, perplexed.

"Very carefully." He let go and resumed his battle with the strip of silk while Merina went to the mirror to straighten her skirt. Of all things, he thought back to Tag's words of warning. Because life with Merina was suddenly very cozy. Once they divorced, he'd miss not only the sex, but the relaxing moments that followed. He didn't anticipate this type of casual banter once he resumed his casual dating status.

At that thought, he nearly recoiled. Casual dating had never sounded so...off-putting. He wouldn't do it right away, of course. He'd have to have a cooling period. And figure out a way to settle for less, considering sex had never been this good before Merina.

Whoa.

Probably that was his cock talking. It bobbed in the direction of the woman unknowingly torturing him in a very short dress.

"Easy, fella," he murmured, succeeding at the knot and straightening the bow tie at his throat. "We can't let her lead us around like that."

"Hmm?" Merina said. "Did you say something?"

He left the closet, snagging his jacket on the way out. "Yeah. I said, beware the board. They have sharp, pointy teeth." He made the two-fingered gesture and Merina rolled her eyes.

"Monty Python? Really?" She lifted a silver clutch off the bed and swayed out of the room. Like a puppy, Reese followed, mentally high-fiving himself because she knew Monty Python.

* * *

Okay, this was beyond nerve-wracking. Merina had been confident about the retirement dinner and her ability to look as if she belonged on Reese's arm. Then she arrived and nearly every pair of eyes in the room zoomed in on them. She hadn't anticipated this much attention. Not at a private function.

Now, she worried the entire room could see the sexual satisfaction painted on both their faces. As great as last night was, how were they not supposed to wake up and partake this morning? She'd stepped out of the shower, only to find Reese stalk in naked and ready. He'd pushed her back in, pressed her against the shower wall, and entered her again and again.

And when he'd kissed her while he was getting ready tonight, she could have easily gone for one more round. Hair and makeup be damned. If they weren't already cutting it close, she may have taken him then and there.

The rigid businessman she'd seen before she moved in with him—the same man everyone else saw—wasn't nearly so rigid or unyielding when they were alone together. It made her want to spend more time with him—both in bed and out.

Reese's warm palm splayed over her dress and she was glad the dress had a back. She'd been charged with acting like she was madly in love with him, and she'd rather not everyone see the very real goose bumps he brought to the surface of her skin. Or the way her eyes fluttered closed when he kissed her neck. Sex had muddied what they had together, which she'd have to sort out when it came time to end things. For now, she'd use it to her advantage.

"Merina, I'd like you meet a few members of the board. I don't believe you've had the honor yet," Reese said in front of a group of men, one eyebrow raised, communicating, *Don't you love how full of shit I am?*

She offered a bland smile to say, *Impressive how full of it you are yet still smell like heaven.*

She shook hands with one of the older men, feeling on display for his approval when he swept assessing eyes over her dress, then to Reese. She didn't want to sell it too hard, so she wasn't plastered to her husband, yet she didn't want to merely drape her hand over his forearm because that seemed too formal.

While they watched with hawklike eyes, she turned and lifted her fingers to Reese's hair and stroked a lock of it away from his forehead. He looked down at her, a flicker of awareness in his dark blue eyes.

"There. Now you're perfect." The air between them snapped, a palpable charge. Her smile shaky, she stood on her toes and kissed his cheek, her voice going to a low murmur to say, "I only like you rumpled in one place, Crane."

Reese didn't let her sink to her heels immediately, cupping her waist and lowering his head to steal another kiss. "Thanks, baby," he muttered against her parted lips.

He released her and Merina's heart pattered. Endearments weren't Reese's style. As she recalled, he'd never once called her "sweetheart" or "honey" or "baby."

She liked it way more than she should.

Like, *a lot*.

"Better leave these two alone." One of the board members shoved his glass of scotch against another man's arm. "Come, Barnes, a refill is in order."

"And they're off," she said when the men shuffled away.

"How are you holding up? Only three or four more hours to go," Reese said. "Champagne?"

"White wine is safer. Makes me less giggly."

"You? Giggly? That I've got to see." He pressed a kiss to her forehead, and Merina leaned into him. A moment later, his hand stiffened against her back. In fact, all of him went rigid. Arms, legs, head, neck. Merina searched the room, her eyes landing on a petite woman with strawberry-blond hair. Freckles dotted her tanned skin, and lips that looked as if they'd had some cosmetic plumping smiled as she sauntered in their direction. Merina heard a word come from Reese's mouth she was pretty sure was profanity but couldn't quite make it out.

"Reese," the woman said, her plastic smile glued on. Her eyes—green—flicked to Merina before fixing on him again. "It's been ages."

"What are you doing here?" Reese asked, doing a terrible job of being courteous.

"Hayes is here too. You know we wouldn't miss the chance to wish Alex well on his big day." The animosity hung thick in the air. This redhead knew exactly what she was doing.

In Reese's defense, Merina's back went up.

"Merina Crane." Rather than offer a hand, she held her clutch in both hands. "And you are?"

"Gwyneth. Sutton. Well, formerly Sutton, now Lerner."

Gwyneth Sutton Lerner rang zero bells. Clearly this woman and Reese had a history. And she refused to let Gwyneth think that Merina was in the dark.

"My apologies for not recognizing you." Merina slid a gaze down the woman's lithe figure and back up to see Gwyneth's mouth slide into a sneer. "Excuse us, we were just visiting the bar."

Merina steered toward a wine cart, Reese's arm under her hand as rigid as rebar.

"Care to share?" she asked as they strolled. Well, she strolled; Reese marched since he was too tense to stroll.

"No," he answered.

"Well, if I'm going to help you out here, you need to give me something."

"I said no, Merina."

The air between them had gone from sizzling to frigid—like someone had opened the door on an industrial-sized freezer. Merina doubted the freak ice storm had been caused by a one-night stand gone wrong. No, this Gwyneth woman had been *more*. A thought that didn't sit well with Merina at all.

Reese shifted away from her and ordered a glass of wine, delivering it instantly. "I'm going to grab a scotch." He dipped his head at the other bar across the room where spirits were lined. Before she could protest, Reese walked away.

In full view of the board, what else could she do but sip and smile and pretend her husband wasn't hiding something from her? And that was what bothered her the most. She'd never seen Reese hurt. Given his reaction—closing down when hurt crept in was his defense mechanism.

Across the room, Gwyneth locked arms with a bulky blond guy, his hair sharply cut, his facial features severe. He wasn't unattractive, but his choice of arm candy made Merina dislike him instantly. Yes, there was a story there, and she intended to find out what it was. But for the moment, she was forced to mingle.

Reese hadn't given her much choice.

* * *

Pull it together, Crane.

Reese, fists balled at his sides, stalked across the Crane Hotel ballroom. Not so much for whiskey but to escape his ex-girlfriend, who had ambushed his father's retirement party. It'd been years since he'd seen her, since he'd punched Hayes in the face and demanded that Alex fire him.

It was the act of a desperate man. A younger man. A less in-control man. But Reese didn't care how unfair it'd been to take Hayes's job away from him. Reese's former best friend took his girlfriend, so it seemed only fair. After years of not seeing either one of them, finding himself faced with one was enough. Hearing that the other one was around the corner was too much.

This was the problem with the unexpected. Reese *thought* he knew what to expect tonight. He knew his efforts and energy would be focused on Merina and the board and making sure his marriage appeared legit. Now he needed to regroup. It was obvious Merina knew something was up, but he wasn't anywhere near ready to give her the short version.

"Scotch neat," he ordered. "Actually, make it a double."

The woman behind the bar poured what could be considered a triple. Reese jammed cash into the tip jar—could've been a five or a fifty, he had no idea—then lifted the scotch to his lips.

Before he took a drink, Tag appeared in front of him, grabbed the glass, and set it on the bar. "Hi."

"Do you want to die?" Reese asked under his breath. The bartender cleared her throat and gave them some privacy. One of the benefits to being a Crane was that the staff tended to respect them.

"Do this." An easy grin appeared on Tag's face. "You want to look as if you don't want to kill me since people are looking."

"I don't give a shit who's looking."

"I can see that." Tag deposited the glass behind the bar and pointed across the room. "Over there is better. For a lot of reasons."

He turned to walk away and Reese followed. Tag kept up conversation, talking about absolutely nothing as they cut through the crowd, pausing to say hello to a few people Reese hadn't greeted yet. Once they were at a bar lined with taps, Tag ordered a few beers. From this part of the room, they could see the crowd, and no one was close enough to overhear.

"Let's talk about why you abandoned your gorgeous new wife after she met your despicable ex-girlfriend." Tag took a drink of his beer, filling his cheeks with the brew before he swallowed.

"Merina has questions I can't answer right now." Questions like who was Gwyneth to him, how long did they date, and what about her presence turned Reese into an overly starched shirt?

"And you think walking away is going keep her from asking? If anything, you're making it worse. Merina knows Gwyneth has something on you, or was something to you. She's going to want answers." Tag lost his easy grin.

"You forget I have things under control."

"You forget I know a hell of a lot more about women than you do. Your wife is by herself after you introduced her to your ex-girlfriend." Tag spoke purposefully, making sure Reese heard every syllable. "I'm not the only one noticing, Reese."

He glanced around the room. Merina was alone, drinking her wine and trying to look casual. Board members were dotted throughout the party, the one female board member standing in a huddle of other women whispering. Was she talking about Merina?

"I suggest you sweep Merina in your arms and start dancing. Better yet, take her into one of the side rooms and have sex with her up against a wall."

Reese's eyes snapped back to his brother.

"Thought that'd grab your attention." Tag gave him a brief smile. "Anything is better than everyone witnessing you nursing your wounds after Gwyneth dive-bombed you."

"Can't we tell her to leave?" Reese growled.

"No, you cannot." This came from their father. The man of the hour was wearing an all-black tuxedo, tuxedo shirt, and bow tie. The stark contrast against his white beard and white hair made him look that much more regal. "I saw her, son. And Hayes. They are not here to cause trouble."

"Bullshit," Reese said, turning to face his old man. He wouldn't censor himself when it came to Hayes and Gwyneth. His father may have seen it as post–high school drama, but Reese knew better. It was the only time he'd ever been in love, had ever seen his future hovering ahead of him. The only time he saw potential for a family of his own. Marriage. A home. And then all of it was gone. In the blink of an eye.

Just like Mom.

"All due respect," Reese told his father, "you don't know what you're talking about when it comes to them and you never did."

Alex's cheeks mottled in anger.

"Reese." Tag's voice was a gentle reprimand. "Dad."

Alex's attention snapped from Reese to Tag.

"Eyes all around," Tag muttered.

"I'm sick of the show," Reese said. He'd prefer to drown his fury in scotch and crack the empty bottle over Hayes's head. The asshole.

"You need to say hello to him, Reese. Tag is right. People are watching," Alex said. He didn't smile, but his face relaxed as if he was having a cordial conversation with his sons and nothing more. "Grow up."

Reese ground his molars together.

"Watch him." Alex told Tag, then strolled into the party, arms up to receive more congratulations.

"Breathe, Reese."

"Fuck off, Tag." Reese turned on his heel and went to the other bar, where the female bartender was about to empty his abandoned scotch down the drain. He snatched the glass from her and drank it down in three burning swallows. "Refill that, will you?"

At the same time, a cool hand slid over his tuxedo jacket. He turned his head to find a freckled hand resting on his forearm, a very big diamond ring on her finger.

He lifted his chin and met Gwyneth's green eyes.

"Hey, sailor." Her lips bowed into a smile. "Buy me a drink?"

* * *

Oh. My. God.

Watching Reese medicate himself with scotch was one thing, but standing idly by while Gwyneth kamikazed him was another.

Merina wasn't going to allow the skinny redhead to hit on her husband. She finished her wine and relinquished the glass, but before she took two steps toward Reese, Tag stepped in front of her.

"May I have this dance?" A smile lifted his trimmed beard.

"No. I have a redhead's ass to kick." She smiled sweetly.

"Ah. Yes, that would be good for the media." He offered his hand. She regarded it suspiciously.

"Are you going to give me more answers than he did?"

"I doubt it." He took her hand and she sent a look across the room at Gwyneth and Reese, wanting nothing more than to bust through the crowd like ten-pins before that woman could sink her teeth in him.

Again.

Funny how defensive Merina was and she didn't know what had gone down between them. But something. Her intuition was spot-on even on her worst day.

She allowed Tag to lead her to the center of the ballroom amidst a few couples dancing and chatting. He expertly turned her so her back was to Reese.

"Just remember to smile."

She forced a grin and spoke between her teeth. "How's that?"

His mouth pulled into a grimace.

When she went to move away from him, he laughed and towed her back in. "I kid, I kid. Come on, Sis, relax. I promise it's not as big of a deal as you're making it."

"Really?"

"Probably."

Tag's eyes were lighter blue than Reese's, his hair sun-kissed and golden, the waves hanging over a white button-down shirt that had to have been custom-tailored to cover the expanse of his shoulders.

She'd met Tag once before at a conference. Towering over everyone, dressed in a tight T-shirt hugging his rounded muscles and sporting a bearded smile that was oh-so-genuine, he wasn't an easy person to overlook. He carried the Crane air of confidence and moved like he was in charge. And he was not bad on the eyes. She'd noticed that as well, though her danger-o-meter went off the moment he came near. This guy was a player.

He towered over Merina, even taller than Reese by a few inches, so she had to tilt her head a little more than usual to talk to him.

"Who is she?" she asked.

"Who?" Tag's eyes flicked to the side, then back. He grinned. How full of shit was he? Merina rolled her eyes to let him know she wasn't buying it. "Oh, her."

"Yeah, *her*."

"That's Reese's story to tell, Sis." True, but she didn't feel like being fair. She wanted to know the truth and Reese wasn't talking.

"Obviously they dated and she's horrible."

Tag laughed and squeezed her hand in his. Merina stole a casual look over her shoulder, making out Reese's arm and Gwyneth's dress before Tag moved her again and blocked her view with his huge body.

Merina pegged him with a glare. "Is she a socialite?"

"You could say that. She cares a great deal about money," Tag said.

"Were his flowers not well received?" she fished.

"No can do on the intel." Tag shook his head. "I have a suggestion, though. When he comes back over here, seduce him. Make him a little hot under the collar in front of everyone and then take him home and"—he winked—"you know."

"Kiss my ass, Tag!" She kept her voice down, but she didn't hide her anger. "You don't have any right to tell me what to do and what not to when it comes to Reese."

"Did I hear my name?" Reese appeared between them. His voice was low and soothing, his eyes tight at the corners. He'd escaped the clutches of Gwyneth Sutton Lerner, apparently. He offered a palm to Merina. "May I?"

"Please." She pulled away from Tag, who released her waist and gave his brother a look of concern.

"Sure you're okay?" Tag asked.

"I'm good. Thank you." Reese gave his brother a nod and Tag nodded back. In the midst of that subtle exchange, she guessed these two would do anything for each other.

"I don't need Tag to run interference," she told Reese as she narrowed her eyes at Tag's retreating figure. Several women's heads turned and several of them were with dates or husbands. She clucked her tongue.

"Go easy on him." Reese tucked her against his body, and she instantly subdued, settling against him like she fit there. Tag was attractive, yes, but nothing was as electric as being held by Reese. All of her tingled. *Sizzled.*

"He's looking out for me."

"I saw her talking to you." She moved one hand into the back of his hair, staking her claim to anyone watching.

Reese studied her for the count of three before saying, "She told me where she and Hayes were sitting so I could say hello."

His words were carefully measured, almost robotic.

"It looked more intimate than that," Merina mumbled to his bow tie.

"After this song, I'll introduce you. You shouldn't have been in the position to introduce yourself and I apologize for that."

His avoidance was bothering her. "Reese."

"Merina." He pulled her close, splaying his hand across her back.

Lost in his eyes for a few staggering seconds, she almost forgot what she was going to say. Then she remembered.

"Do you want to talk about it?" *Whatever put that truck-load of hurt in your eyes?*

"Not here," he said after a few beats. She'd take it. That was better than the staunch "no" she'd received earlier. "I won't give you a reason to worry again, Merina."

But he wasn't doing her any favors by shielding her. She didn't want Reese hiding his anguish from her. She'd rather him lay it on her lap so she could help him with it.

A tiny voice of warning rose up and refused to be ignored. Hadn't she tried to "help" Corbin by letting him move in with her? The last thing she needed to know was Reese's messy history with any of the women he'd had in his life or his bed.

Especially since Merina would be leaving both sooner rather than later.

* * *

The music slowed and Reese released Merina, most of him not wanting to. Holding her comforted him and allowed him to put off playing nice with the last two people on earth he wanted to be cordial with. Unfortunately, his father and brother were right. Reese couldn't avoid them. Or he *shouldn't*, anyway.

What would the CEO of Crane Hotels do?

He sighed and Merina took his hand, offering her steady brand of comfort. It was a novelty to have a woman at his side for anything other than business or pleasure. This was neither. She offered her friendship and support and nothing about her was faking it. She was here for him.

He kept hold of her hand, and as they crossed the room, he told her the truncated truth. "Gwyneth and I used to be together. We ended things amicably. Hayes was an employee of Crane Hotels—manager of quality control for a while—until my father let him go."

She was quiet as they drew closer to the couple that had irrevocably changed Reese's life.

"Sounds like there's more to that story," Merina said, not fully accepting his offered half measure. But then, he hadn't expected her to. She was smart and sharp and unafraid to speak her mind. Three things Gwyneth never was. The redhead who used to share Reese's bed had nothing on the suave blonde at his side today.

He pulled Merina closer, resting her hand at the crook of his arm and glancing down into amber eyes. "There is, but now's not the time."

"Fair enough." They shared a polite smile, but hers had a hint of heat behind it. Camaraderie. Silly as it sounded, her walking with him gave him strength.

Hayes looked up from his food and swiped his mouth with a cloth napkin.

Surprised, you bastard? Hayes had known Reese would be here, but he was probably surprised to see Reese venturing over to say hello.

Hayes sipped from a glass filled with clear liquid with a lime floating in it. Club soda or vodka tonic? He'd celebrated his one-year sobriety the day before he was fired for being a douche. Hard saying if he'd stayed on the wagon since then. So much had changed.

"I guess congratulations are in order," Hayes said, speaking first. "On your marriage and I assume you're taking over for your dad."

"One of those for sure, the other is to be determined," Reese replied, his tone smooth.

Hayes's eyebrows jumped in consideration. He still had a small white scar on his lip from where Reese had clocked him. He'd landed a hit on his nose, too, but the bump on the bridge had predated Reese's fury. Probably some other boyfriend he'd pissed off in the past.

"Hayes Lerner." He offered a hand to Merina, but she wrapped both hands around Reese's biceps and smiled instead of touching him.

Reese admired the hell out of her for it.

"Mr. Lerner." She didn't make an excuse for not shaking his hand, and there was nothing rude in her words or expression. Hayes, realizing she wasn't going to be cordial, awkwardly pulled his hand away.

Reese wanted to kiss her. Later, he'd show his appreciation.

"Your lovely wife and I met earlier," Merina told Hayes.

From the chair beside her husband, Gwyneth looked down her nose. Merina unwaveringly held her gaze.

"It was kind of you to come out and wish Alex well," Merina said. "I'm sure it wasn't easy for either of you to show your faces here."

Reese smothered a smile, practically hearing the mic drop.

"I have no problem being here," Gwyneth hissed. But she was way out of her league. Her freckled cheeks went ruddy, betraying her anger. She'd never been good at hiding her temper. She and Reese had gone round and round over the stupidest shit when they'd dated. And then they'd gone round and round over Hayes, which turned out was even stupider.

"Alex taught me a lot," Hayes interjected, putting his hand over his wife's to calm her. "Gwynnie reminded me that I was the bigger man by showing up here. Which is why we came. We'd never miss Alex's retirement. No matter how you feel about us being here."

Pompous prick. That was the exact reason Reese bounced his fist off Hayes's face all those years ago. He flexed his hand with the temptation to do it now too.

Smarmy dickweed.

"Alex is a good man." Merina stroked Reese's arm, bringing his temper down a notch. "I'm sure he can see exactly what you are trying to accomplish by being here. If you'll excuse us." In a stage whisper, she added, "I'm going to sneak out of here for a moment with Reese. You remember how hard it was to keep your hands off him, I'm sure."

Merina gave Gwyneth a saucy wink and snatched a cube of cheese off Gwyneth's plate and ate it. She sucked on the tip of her thumb in what had to be the sexiest move Reese had ever seen. "Mmm. Thank you. I know that wasn't mine, but I saw it and just had to have it. You know what that's like. Try the crab bites. To die for."

Her arm wrapped around his, Merina turned. He walked with her, a smile tickling the edge of his mouth and a twitch coming from the recesses of his tuxedo pants. Bawdy and refined. That was his Merina.

His.

At least for now.

"Now find us a closet so I can kiss you," she said as they left the ballroom.

Right fucking now.

"No closet." He flattened her back to the wall outside the door. Her eyes flared, her mouth curving into a pleased smile. He leaned close and brushed her nose with his. "Let 'em watch."

Then he tipped her jaw and covered her lips with his and kissed her for all he was worth.

CHAPTER 13

Monday morning, Reese surfaced from sleep when a soft sigh paired with tugging the covers from his shoulder reminded him that he had company.

He usually slept on the couch next to the bed, save for the time after Merina had gone down on him and left him prostrate and dead to the world. Even then he hadn't woken up next to her. She'd risen before him and he'd found her downstairs sipping coffee out of his favorite mug.

Well, that and Saturday night after the retirement party. He'd gone from kissing her in that hallway (and getting busted by Bob) to going back in for the party until they could make their escape. After, they'd gone straight to bed, but then, too, Merina had been up and reading the *Wall Street Journal* when his eyes opened.

This morning she hadn't scampered out of bed, for reasons he guessed he was responsible for, and that made him proud. He felt her finger touch his lips and opened his eyes.

"Cocky bastard," she grumbled. Merina was rumpled and sleepy, her eyes barely open, her hair in complete disarray. And so gorgeous with the sun filtering in behind her, he had to blink to make sure she was real. "Do you always wake up smiling?"

He pulled her close, because in his huge bed, she was too far away. Then he rolled, threw a leg over her body, wrapped an arm tightly at her back, and kissed her neck.

"I wake smiling," he said, kissing her ear next, "whenever the woman I go to bed with has six screaming orgasms."

"Six!" she protested, pushing against his bare chest with both hands.

"Was it seven? I lost count." He loosened his hold on her and pulled back to find her rolling her eyes.

"Hardly." She wiggled away from him, then climbed out of bed. She was wearing almost nothing: a barely-there pair of panties and a silky tank top. When she was on her feet, she grabbed a pillow and tossed it over his face.

"I'm still smiling," he said, his voice muffled.

She grumbled something else and he moved the pillow in time to watch her fantastic ass wiggle into the bathroom. Then he rolled over, and despite the shining sun, closed his eyes and went back to sleep.

* * *

An hour later, Reese emerged wearing a suit and tie, looking bright-eyed and bushy-tailed and ready to take over hotel chains and turn them into dust. Merina was dressed in her usual uniform of pencil-skirt-and-blouse but doubted she looked either bright or bushy. Unless you counted her hair, which she'd wrestled with for nearly twenty minutes before giving up and pinning it back in a low ponytail.

"I was going to run this morning, but you wiped me out last night." he said in greeting, moving to the coffeepot. His gaze strayed to the mug in her hands.

"What?"

"I have a cabinet full of mugs and that's the one you choose."

"I like it." She cradled her coffee protectively.

"Of course you do."

"It's comforting."

"Of course it is."

The black mug with gold writing on it was the last thing she'd ever expected to find in Reese's sterile, clean environment. It added a touch of whimsy, which was shocking.

"You mean this is... *yours*?" She turned the mug and read the message aloud. "'Sometimes all you need is a billion dollars.'"

Reese grinned and Merina almost had to reach behind her to grab the chair for support. He was ridiculously gorgeous, and remembering the sight of him between her thighs last night wringing orgasms from her made her want to grab his tie and lead him upstairs now too. And, yeah, her orgasms had numbered around seven, but she wasn't ready to admit he could separate her body from her brain so thoroughly.

"Tag bought it," Reese said. "He thinks he's funny."

At the mention of her brother-in-law, she hummed.

Reese came to her, his own mug white and plain and boring. For the first time, she thought how that didn't fit him. Which made her frown. She didn't like that he kept surprising her.

"What did he say at the party that pissed you off so much?"

"It wasn't what he said. It was...I don't know."

But she did know. She didn't want to admit it, but she knew. It was the way Tag instructed her to seduce Reese. The suggestion that what she and Reese had was for show...which it was. But she didn't like to talk about him or what they had in such obvious, sterile terms. Tag had made their marriage sound cold, but with her, Reese wasn't cold. That night, last night, and hell, even this morning, there was considerable warmth between them.

"I was just pissed about Gwyneth," she fibbed.

"Ah." Satisfied with that answer, he nodded. "You handled her and Hayes beautifully, which was why you received so many presents last night." He stole a kiss. "Like I said, I was going to go for a run today, but you let me sleep in."

"You needed it. We had a stressful weekend." Though yesterday had been an almost lazy Sunday by comparison. Reese took calls, and she did some work on her laptop, but mostly, they sat in the sunroom and watched it rain. Magda delivered lunch to the room and had left a casserole in the oven for dinner. Merina and Reese ate at the counter rather than at the table and ended up going up to bed sooner than either of them expected for the sex he'd previously been bragging about.

"Are you sure you don't want to tell me more about your sordid past?" She fluttered her lashes. She didn't know the story behind Gwyneth and Hayes, only the bleached, censored version Reese had mumbled at the party. But as the woman who had thwarted Dumb and Dumber at the party, she was due an explanation.

Reese disagreed.

"Nice try." He finished his coffee and put the mug in the sink. "I can drop you at work, but I have to go to a dinner meeting at eight, so you'll have to find your own way home."

"No, that's okay. I have to run a few errands while I'm at work. I'll take my car." Including an overdue therapeutic lunch date with Lorelei.

"Okay. By the way, you should try that sometime."

She narrowed her eyes in confusion. He pointed to the mug.

"Having a billion dollars. It's handy." He kissed her again, lingering long enough that she had to pull air through her nose. "See you tonight."

He left and Merina shook her head, worried that her current set of problems couldn't be solved by a billion dollars. Arguably, her problems were *caused* by a billion dollars. Which was the reason for her meeting with Lorelei. Things with Reese were getting complicated where her emotions were concerned. And since she knew her best friend was re-seeing her ex-husband (though Lore had yet to officially admit it), she could help Merina compartmentalize when it came to Reese.

Merina needed to keep her heart separate from the sex. Because the sex was great and she refused to give up the best perk to this arrangement.

* * *

"I'm in love with him."

Her fork halfway to her mouth, Merina lowered it back into her salad bowl and gaped at her best friend. "Malcolm?"

"I know!" Lorelei hadn't touched her salad, but she had downed a glass of Riesling in record time, and she never drank alcohol before five. She dropped her face into her hands. "I didn't mean to."

"This is awful," Merina muttered, abandoning the salad in favor of her own glass of wine.

Lorelei peeked from her hands, an expression of devastation decorating her flawless brown skin. "It is, isn't it?"

"I meant for me. You were supposed to be the voice of reason. I came here to talk to you about keeping my heart out of the equation with Reese since we've..." She looked around at the restaurant and leaned in to say quietly, "Crossed a few boundaries."

Lorelei stopped looking devastated and started looking interested. "Boundaries?"

Merina nodded.

"Did he earn his hashtag?"

"Lore! Seriously?" She lowered her voice when a pair of well-dressed women shot twin evil looks at her. "That's what you want to know? Out of everything I said, *that's* what you're most interested in."

Lorelei folded her arms on the table and shrugged one shoulder unapologetically.

"Yes, okay? *Yes*, he earned it and honestly, it's terribly uninventive and a lame descriptor for what he's capable of."

"Well, maybe you are the only one who knows what he's capable of since he's kept you in his bed for more than one night."

There was a thought. Merina bit her lip. Of everything they'd done together, she hadn't stopped once to consider she was blazing some sort of trail. Reese was now a one-woman man after being a one-woman-for-a-night man. That was scary. She wasn't ready to start a real one-on-one relationship. Not with the man she'd temporarily married.

"Listen, you're going to be fine." Lorelei, bless her gorgeous lying face. She had snapped into lawyer mode, saying exactly what Merina needed to hear, and Merina was not going to argue.

"Hit me."

"First off." Lorelei held up a finger. "Malcolm and I were married." Her smile fell. "Of course, so are you and Reese. Maybe that's a bad place to start. You know what I mean. We were *really* married. Like, for real."

"I'm with you." Merina waved a hand. She didn't feel better yet, but she had faith her friend would arrive at a point.

"Malcolm and I have a relationship that is volatile," Lore continued. "You know, the kind where everyone has a quip for everything. Bickering became like foreplay with us."

Merina sighed. Yeah. Not helping her feel better at all.

"Plus he had a rep before he met me of being quite the ladies' man. Once he met me, he quit those bitches cold and I was the only one he had eyes for. He went from player to a good husband and the only reason we split was because I was too stubborn to—" Lorelei cut off her own speech, seeing the same thing Merina saw: that Lorelei's and Malcolm's story was eerily similar to Merina's and Reese's.

And Lorelei had fallen back in love with Malcolm.

"Sorry, honey." Lore offered her condolences with a hand over Merina's on the table. Then she waved over the waitress and ordered two double chocolate mousses and espressos. "It's not for sure yet," Lorelei said when Merina's shoulders slumped. "Maybe he'll turn back into a dick. Like...Cinderella at the stroke of midnight. Give him time and he'll give you a reason to hate him."

"Okay," Merina said, but that didn't make her feel any better. Because maybe...just maybe, she was enjoying herself too much. Enjoying Reese too much to be willing to hate him.

If she ever had.

* * *

"With the exit of Alex, we'll be deciding who to appoint within the next month," Bob said at the board meeting.

Reese fisted the pen in his hand, willing himself not to throw it like a dart and hit one of them with it. Any of them. He wasn't picky.

"You know my preference, gentlemen," Alex said, leaning back in his chair. How did he do that? Always look so damned calm? "Reese is my number one. He's been groomed for this role since he was a young man. He's good at his job. He works hard."

"We're aware," Frank, the blowhard, said.

Reese looked to his left, but Tag's chair was empty. Usually his younger brother's careless expression was calming. Tag was visiting the Crane Hotel resort in Hawaii to assess the bar situation the board had bellyached about. Nitpicking bastards.

"I will say," Bob interjected, casting a smile of encouragement at Reese, "that the few stockholders I've spoken to have been impressed with his recent turnaround."

"Yes, and the few I've talked to," Frank said, "are suspicious of this sudden marriage and abrupt change in Mr. Crane's behavior."

"The state of my personal life has nothing to do with my business ethics," Reese growled, unable to play nice any longer. At his right, his father sighed in resignation. "Leave my wife out of this."

"And yet, you've been sure to include her at the most opportune time," Lilith said. "Don't get me wrong, Reese, I'm all for a reformed man, but who's to say this isn't a ruse to earn favor and land the CEO?"

It was on the tip of Reese's tongue to ask if that would be so bad, but he was relieved of that urge by Bob's interjection. "Come on, Lilith. You saw them at the retirement party."

"Could be an act," she said.

Reese's nostrils flared.

"Well you can't expect them to consummate on the boardroom table for you to see how serious they are," Frank, who hated Lilith, replied, oddly on Reese's side.

"Over the line." Reese stood and pressed his palms into the table. "If you think I'd pander to you or the stockholders, you're out of your mind."

He may have married Merina for favor, but that had since changed. No longer was it a show. The hugs and kisses—the sex—everything between them had shifted from pretend to real.

"My father is right. I've been groomed for CEO my entire life. Lilith, as someone who used to be friends with my mother, I'd think you'd have more respect for my choice of woman to settle down with. She would approve."

"She would," Lilith said gently.

Alex put his elbow on the table and stroked his hand

over his mustache, probably to keep himself from interrupting.

"And, Frank, unless you'd like the entire room to imagine what you'd look like having sex with that twenty-eight-
year-old wannabe actress you're dating, I'd thank you to
never paint a visual like you just did about Merina. As for
the rest of you serpents, if you could call on whatever professionalism still clinging to your recently shed skin, you
might consider my talents, my motivation, and my work
record rather than who I take to bed every night."

Reese straightened, buttoned his jacket, and scooped his
phone off the table. "If you'll excuse me, I have to prepare
for a *real* meeting this evening."

No one added anything, not even his father. Reese all
but strutted from that room, mentally picturing his own mic
drop.

Merina would have been proud.

* * *

"What a bunch of cockroaches," Merina commented after
Reese told her how far south the meeting had slipped. She
opened a drawer, then another, then one after that. "Where
is a knife in this kitchen?"

He shrugged. "How would I know?"

She gave him a bland look.

"Does not require a knife." He lifted his glass of scotch.
"Anyway, Magda does all the cooking around here, don't
you, Magda?"

"Top left, next to the refrigerator," his housekeeper answered as began filling the dishwasher. The woman was
crazy efficient.

"What are you doing, anyway?" he asked as Merina carved into an avocado.

"I'm making guacamole."

"Why?"

"Why am I making guacamole?" She quit carving and gave him a confused, possibly miffed look. She was too damned attractive.

"I don't want to know why you're making guacamole. I want to know why you don't have *Magda* make guacamole? She likes to make things. That's why she works here. Right, Magda?"

Magda, who'd known him nearly his entire life, smiled one of her supremely tolerant smiles. "I do indeed, Mr. Crane. It's nice to cook for someone again, seeing as how you've been away from the mansion for so long."

He tilted his head and arched an eyebrow, hoping she read his silent communication to curb that discussion. Not that there was a need. Magda wasn't one to gossip.

"Sometimes it's fun to do things for yourself," Merina said, halving the fruit…or was avocado a vegetable? Something to ask Siri later.

"But most of the time it's nice to have things done to you," Reese said. "I mean, for you."

Merina shot him a glare, catching his intentional reference to the things he'd like done to him. Things she did with her mouth and hands, involving her wearing a hell of lot less clothing than she was now.

"You weren't born with a silver spoon in your mouth, Crane." She pointed at him with the tip of the knife. "You were born with an entire cutlery drawer in there."

Magda chuckled and Merina smiled in triumph. He abandoned his scotch and stalked to his wife, lashing an arm around her middle and pressing her against the counter from behind.

"What was that?" he rumbled into her ear. She smelled good today. She smelled good every day, but today there was something light and intoxicating about the fragrance on her neck. "New perfume?"

"Yes, you bought it."

"You're welcome."

"No, *you're* welcome," she breathed.

"Magda, I'm going to need a moment with my wife." He lowered his lips to Merina's neck and she dropped the knife with a clatter, her hands gripping the edge of the counter. He closed his hands over her hips and squeezed.

Merina rubbed her ass against his crotch.

"Second thought, take the evening off," he told Magda, not wanting to expose his housekeeper to more.

"Just like your parents." Magda tsked and pressed a button to start the dishwasher. "Good night."

That comment was one he chose to ignore.

Once Magda was out of sight, Merina turned to face him and this time rubbed her front against his front. He wound his fingers around her ponytail and dragged the elastic from the strands, freeing her hair, enjoying the soft feel of every part of her and the easy attention she gave him.

"Why is it"—he lowered his lips to hers—"that when you sass me, all I want to do is fuck you?"

Her hands rose and spread over his chest, sending an answering heat flooding his veins. Because Merina liked sex, because she'd initiated it, and because she'd made it a point to show her enjoyment, he didn't have to mince his words. He could tell her what he wanted, and she would respond.

She brushed her lips against his, but instead of kissing him, whispered, "What did Magda mean we're like your parents?" Then she grinned, knowing his balls were aching. She lifted herself to sit on the counter. "Tell me. I want to know."

He let out a sigh, but she grabbed his tie and pulled him to stand between her legs. Once he was there, he wasn't inclined to leave.

"Mom and Dad were a nightmare," he said, teasing. "They were insanely in love, but in a house full of boys, the gross-out factor was high. "All over each other. Kissing in the kitchen, making out in the pool. Once I walked in on them on the couch in the living room and they said they were cuddling. After I aged up a few years, I knew exactly what they were doing."

"So Magda means we're demonstrative." She loosened the knot of his tie, which had never in his life been sexy until Merina started doing it. "Hmm."

Hmm. That sounded as dangerous as "fine" and "never mind."

"She's known you a long time, then?"

"Since I was ten. She was part-time then, raising her own kids."

"I didn't know she has children," Merina said, eyes brightening.

"I didn't know you cared," he said as Merina finished undoing his tie. "She has three." Merina unbuttoned his top button and then one more and stroked her fingers down his throat.

"My parents kiss each other on the cheek and on the forehead," she said, continuing to drive him wild. "They lovingly bicker. But I can't say I've ever seen them pas-

THE BILLIONAIRE BACHELOR   233

sionate with each other." She screwed her face into a cute look of disgust. "Eww."

"You aren't missing out." His hands moved down her back and over her bra. With the flick of a thumb, he unclasped it.

"You're good at that." She pursed her lips. "I guess you've had a lot of practice."

"A trap I refuse to walk into."

"Smart man." Holding both sides of his tie, she tugged him closer, but still didn't kiss him. "Tell me about your mom."

"Merina." He backed away but she had a grip on his tie and he didn't get far.

"Other than the fact you named your boat after her."

"It's a yacht." He pulled a hand through his hair, feeling uncomfortable. None of them talked about Mom. Not because of a written code, they just... didn't.

"How did she die? I don't need gory details, just the facts."

"You mean you don't know?"

"How would I know?" she asked.

He was stalling and she wasn't letting it go, or letting him out of it. And really, what was the harm in discussing Lunette Crane? But the urge to hide, to keep the details of his personal life private, was strong.

Habits. Years and years of habits. Merina's fingers stroked over his skin again. He met her eyes and told her the truth.

"She was driving to work one day and was involved in a three-car pileup involving two semis."

Merina winced, and before he could stop himself, he told her the gory details anyway.

"Hers was the compact car in the middle."

"Reese..." She shook her head, pain searing her pretty face.

"One day she was sending us out the door to school, and that night she wasn't home. A few days later I was saying good-bye to a wooden box." He didn't know if the position of his mouth was a sad smile or a grimace. "She was a beautiful woman, but there wasn't enough left of her to reconstruct for the funeral."

One of Merina's hands left his tie to cover her mouth. Something about her reaction—her shock, the pain in her eyes, the tenderness she showed him when she gently rested a palm on his chest—drew him in instead of pushing him away. The last five years had been about enjoying a woman's company for the short-term, and conversations rarely if ever veered into "how did your mom die" territory.

Keeping Merina at arm's length was something he'd thought he could do, but that idea was becoming less and less desirable. The more she was around, the more he realized he liked talking to her. He moved her hair over one shoulder and stroked a finger over super-soft skin and along the collar of her shirt. Once there, he undid one of the delicate pearl buttons.

"I shouldn't have asked." Her eyes were glassy, her mind no doubt locked on the horrors he'd described.

"You deserve to know. It's something a wife should know about her husband." He wanted to distract her. To erase her pain. Especially since it was for him. Seeing it sliced into him. *Deep.* He undid another button and parted her shirt. "Your turn."

"My turn?" Distraught, her mouth sagged.

So he did what came naturally, lowered his lips to the edge of her tattoo and pressed a kiss against the ink.

She caught his head and breathed a heated sigh into his ear.

"You have a story, Merina." He took the kiss she wouldn't give him earlier. When she tried to deepen it, he denied her, robbing her of his mouth. "Tell me. I've earned it."

* * *

Reese swept broad fingers over her tattoo. The point at one end down to the bright flames streaking from the end.

"What's it mean?" he asked, his voice low. He ran the tip of his finger back over her body art.

"You wouldn't appreciate it." Her voice came out husky, his touch turning her on. Truthfully, he'd been turning her on since he mentioned wanting to "fuck her." A phrase she was sure she didn't like before she'd met Reese Crane. What was it about this man that flipped her world upside down?

"Try me." Navy eyes snapped to hers. His fingers dipped between her breasts and then over one of her nipples.

She sucked in a breath, locking her high-heeled shoes behind his knees. She supposed she owed him a personal story. Being physical with him was easy, sharing...not so much. They'd come this far. He hadn't pulled punches when he told her of his mother, a story that absolutely broke her heart.

"I grew up in the Van Heusen hotel," she told him. "Part-time. The VH was my home in a lot of ways. I played in the hallways, helped the housekeepers with laundry. Sat with Arnold for hours while he worked the desk."

"The older man. I've seen him."

"He's been there for years. The flames"—she undid another button and slipped the shirt off her shoulder, revealing the arrow in full—"are a theme."

His eyes held hers for an impressive few seconds before recognition sparked, then he moved to her tattoo and his lips curved into a small smile.

"The Phoenix." He opened another button on her shirt. "That building rose from the ashes."

"Yes."

"Did you rise from the ashes, too, Merina?" The last button open, he removed the shirt from her arms, his gaze finding hers unerringly.

"In a way." Cool air hit her bare breasts when he took her bra off. Her heart hammered, half afraid he would ask her about her past, half relieved when he didn't.

"Why an arrow?" Both hands covering her breasts, he lowered his head and forged a trail of kisses down her neck.

Her eyes on the ceiling, she had to remind her tongue how to form words as he dragged his tantalizing mouth to her collarbone.

"It's a popular symbol," she breathed, goose bumps dotting her skin. A small squeak left her lips when he lightly licked one nipple. He tweaked them with his fingers, kissing her and swallowing her sounds of satisfaction.

"I want to know what it means to *you*, Merina." Oh, the way he said her name. Low and tender and filled with authority. He tugged her nipples, sending a flood of heat to the apex of her thighs. "Tell me, or I'll stop."

His tug turned into a tweak.

"Okay." Merina tightened her legs around his. She didn't want him to stop. Which he must've figured out, because next, he grinned. One of those Reese Crane grins that weakened her knees and made her want to punch him in the throat.

"An arrow...can only move forward...by being pulled back," she answered in between breaths and the pulls of his distracting, kneading fingers. "It's stronger for it."

"You're driven." Mouth covering the pulse at her neck, he sucked her skin for a mind-melting second before speaking against her damp flesh. "A quality I admire."

Head lifted, he zoomed in on her again, and she squirmed. Not only from his sexual attention but also the way he seemed to see her in that moment. Like he was *really* seeing her. It made her feel more naked than when she was actually naked.

"Not surprising." She jerked her eyes to another spot in the room. "You're equally driven."

"The Van Heusen is more than a building to you." Fingers on her jaw, he guided her face back to his.

"Yes. Isn't the Crane more to you?"

His eyes went to the side in thought, giving her a brief reprieve from his intense focus. "Not really."

"You mean if someone wanted to redesign your building, you would let them?" She found that hard to believe.

"No one would redesign my building without my permission."

"Because you'd never bankrupt yourself and have to sell it to the local vultures who—" A gasp swallowed the rest of her words. Reese had dipped his attention to her breasts again. She was beginning to think they were the most sensitive to his kisses.

A few mind-numbing ministrations later, and she'd forgotten what they were talking about.

"Stop teasing me." Clutching the back of his hair, she kissed him hard, driving her tongue into his mouth. She tore at his shirt, rewarded by the sound of two buttons plinking off the edge of the stainless steel sink.

He responded by kissing her just as hard, his hands moving her skirt up and finding her panties before tearing them down her legs. She worked his belt open but didn't get further before he stepped back. He took care of freeing himself, his erection pointing out and up in all its powerful glory.

Her mouth watered. His physicality paired with his formidability her own personal catnip.

Hands on her hips, he tugged her ass to the edge of the counter. She rested a hand on his cheek and his expression softened.

"You okay?" His voice was low with concern, his brows closing in slightly. She wasn't okay. She was in a fantastically compromising position with Reese and she didn't mean because she was perched on the counter. It was the last several minutes that had her chest pinging in warning. They'd discussed private things—not business, but how they felt. Intimacy on a new level, and now they were going to seal it with sex.

Danger, danger, her mind chanted.

She ignored it. She could handle the split between being physical and emotional. She could. She *would.*

"Condom."

He blinked twice as if snapping out of a trance.

"Wallet." He dug out the foil packet, a few hundred-dollar bills fluttering free of the money clip and sailing to the floor. He ignored them. She laughed. That was so . . . him.

"I need to get back on the pill," she said to cover for her amusement.

"No shit," he said, the condom packet clamped between his teeth.

He was disgustingly handsome. They smiled at each other, then Reese tore open the packet and put on the protection neither of them wanted to use.

She opened her legs wider and welcomed her against his body. When he needed more space to maneuver, he swept the cutting board, knife, and avocado into the sink and pulled her down on his hardness.

Yes.

Eyes closed, she clung to his neck and shoulders and enjoyed the feel of his big hands on her bare ass. She lost one of her shoes as she attempted to grip him tighter, and Reese had a near miss with the cabinet handle just over her shoulder. He cupped her head between thrusts to protect her from a similar fate.

"Dangerous," she breathed, but the word had double meaning. It wasn't as dangerous to have sex with Reese amidst knives and cabinets as it was to do it after talking about his intimate family history and her private tattoo not even her parents knew about. It was dangerous to discuss birth control and having sex with nothing between them.

Except a contract.

Yeah, except for that.

"Merina." He hoisted her in his arms and drove deep, teeth bared and eyes heated. There was another emotion mingling there she couldn't place. Heat, yes, passion, you bet, but almost . . . solace.

Like she was his refuge.

"I'm here." She ran her fingertip over his lips.

His intense gaze suggested he'd noticed her mind wandered. She wondered if he'd figured out in which direction...or if his had wandered down the same path.

Dangerous.

* * *

Back flat on the kitchen floor, Reese threw an arm over his face and caught his breath. His shirt was still on, his pants around his knees, and the floor was freezing his backside. Marble wasn't known for its warmth, but the rest of him was buzzing and humming enough to heat every inch of him.

Merina.

Sex with her might be the death of him. Or at least the man he'd become post-Gwyneth.

Merina's subtle touch rippled over his abdomen. His muscles clenched as he tried to channel whatever strength he could to keep from reacting. If she found out he was ticklish, he was screwed. Her fingers stilled.

"Oh, come on," she said, her voice husky. *Sexy*. She placed a kiss on his belly button and his muscles tightened again.

"What are you doing?" He tried to sound and look pissed when he moved his arm and grimaced at her, but his composure was shaky. And she knew it.

"You are!" She grinned wide. "Oh my God!" She raked her fingers lightly over his stomach and he let out a half-grunt. He snatched her wrists and called up every ounce of control he possessed.

"Merina, stop it."

But she didn't stop it. Apparently his "mad" tone needed work.

She threw her naked body over his partially clothed one and wrestled one of her hands free. He swiped the air in an attempt to grab her, but not before she dug her fingers into his ribs. Unable to keep from it, he let out a howl of a laugh. She didn't let up and soon he was laughing so hard, he feared he might break something. Especially after a potentially bone-breaking orgasm that had left him devoid of enough strength to resist.

"Please," he wheezed, reaching for her tickling hand again and missing it.

"He begs," Merina said between elated giggles.

"For the love of Christ!" That came out in a shaky whisper. He'd finally lost his damn voice from laughter. That was a first. *Finally*, he got a vise grip on her other hand. Rolling her onto her back, he trapped her beneath him. He watched as her eyes smiled along with her mouth.

When he managed a full breath, he grumbled, "You're impossible."

"And *you're* ticklish." So damn proud of herself. He liked that look. Too much. Enough to want to see her proud of her accomplishments again. Would she feel that way when he handed over the Van Heusen? Would she be proud she'd earned it back at the cost of marrying him for a few soul-stealing months?

The thought made him frown.

"I'm not ticklish," he argued. "That was a rare postcoital reaction."

"Did you just use the word *postcoital*?" She laughed the word and something in the center of his chest unfurled.

He felt light and happy and...weird. Weird because

feeling both light and happy wasn't what he was accustomed to.

"You'd think after the counter, the kitchen chair"—her eyes rolled up and to the left, where Reese had taken her on his lap a few minutes ago—"then sliding me halfway across this ice-cold floor, you'd have a dirtier word for it."

"You'd like that, wouldn't you?" he sneered, but secretly he admired her teasing tone as much as he'd admired her puckering nipples.

"I would like to warm up," she said.

"Fair enough." He kept hold of her wrists and pulled her up so that she was sitting. "That, I can fix." When he knew he could scramble away safely, he let her go. Then he stood and tore off the remainder of his suit. Once he was bare-assed naked and Merina had climbed to her feet, he lifted her into his arms. He carried her out of the kitchen, around to the back of the house, and into the enclosed pool room.

"Hot tub," she breathed. He put her down and opened the door to the enclosure.

"Second best way to warm up." The first being sex.

"I forgot we had a hot tub."

We.

Here came the feeling of "weird" all over again.

"You're genius." She lifted to her toes, sliding her body along the length of his, to put a soft kiss on his mouth. For a change he wasn't thinking of his dick or the fact that he'd be between her legs soon. He was thinking of how he'd pleased her. How she'd referred to what they had together. The *we* could have been a slip of the tongue, and yeah, it was just a hot tub, but that implied co-ownership was something he hadn't experienced in…a while.

Then she was off, strolling around the edge of the pool to the hot tub and stepping down into the square of hot water. He watched her curvy, naked body sink lower and lower.

"Coming?" she called, not bothering to hide her breasts beneath the bubbles.

God. This woman.

"Hell yes," he answered, trying to sound like his old cocky self and not like the unhinged sap he was turning into. He sank into the water. She glided over, breasts slicking over his chest, her leg rubbing his thigh. His dormant cock sprang to life.

There. Good old-fashioned lust. That, he knew what to do with.

"Your stamina..." She didn't finish her sentence, but she looked impressed with her mouth forming a little "O."

"Still can't pay me a compliment?" He almost said "After all we've been through" but bit his tongue in time.

"You don't need one," she said flatly. Since it was smart to feed that assumption, he did.

"You're right. I have my own hashtag."

She laughed, a sensual chuckle, and moved to sit next to him. He leaned back, his arm resting behind her head. She hummed a low, pleased sound and he closed his eyes, enjoying holding her.

"There's a bedroom over here," she pointed out, a fact he didn't need or want to be reminded of. He hadn't thought of his and Gwyneth's former bedroom since the night he and Merina were lost in the bowels of this house. "Why didn't you choose this as the master suite? It's huge and opens to the pool."

His eyes opened and his chest expanded as he took a

steamy breath. So many reasons. "I used to sleep in there," he answered, his tone final.

She stayed quiet, which was suspiciously out of character. He turned his head. She watched him with amber eyes that held no judgment but a lot of questions. Questions he didn't want to answer. Wasn't ready to answer.

She curled into him, hands on his shoulders, and kissed him. He kissed her back and waited for her to ask, but she didn't. Not even when she pulled away and rested her damp cheek on his shoulder. They sat quietly, her half on his lap, the water lapping around them, warm and silky.

It came naturally to wrap her up in his arms, so he did. Just held her, and closed his eyes, and enjoyed not talking.

CHAPTER 14

I don't know why he's doing this. We never go to his house," Reese grumbled, hands tightly wrapped around the steering wheel. He mumbled under his breath that he'd rather stay home.

When she'd met Reese for the first time, Merina would've concluded that this was him being a spoiled baby who didn't want to drive outside the city to his father's house and deal with a cookout on a random June weekend. But knowing the man she shared a home with now, she didn't think it was so simple.

Like the night in the hot tub when she'd pointed out the bedroom on the other side of the glass. He'd walled up and fallen silent. She used to believe he was a one-ply, super absorbed a-hole. Now she saw he was more complicated, had more depth. Even a sense of humor, and dare she think it? *Feelings.*

Feelings she suspected were unresolved and maybe un-excavated in some circumstances.

It's not your job to fix him.

It wasn't. And it would do her good to remember that.

She had practically felt him retreating from what would likely be a painful discussion.

He'd never expounded on the "I used to sleep there," but it wasn't hard to guess that he probably slept in that room with someone he'd rather not talk about. Maybe several *someones*. Didn't that thought make Merina's stomach twist.

She'd called and talked to Lorelei about it, too afraid to text her in case the conversation was pinched and printed at the *Spread*, the latest gossip blog to pick up every bit of non-news about the new Cranes. Lore listened between bites of a rushed lunch before her next meeting. The conclusion they'd arrived at was to "let it go" much in the same vein of that overplayed song from *Frozen*, and so that's what Merina had done.

Whatever lay behind his reasons for leaving the largest room with the best view in the house unoccupied were his and his alone. She'd had to remind herself that more often than she liked.

Today, though...today was a different beast, but possibly the same species. Pain waited for Reese at the end of this trip. It tightened his eyes and pulled at his firm mouth. He hadn't prepared for today emotionally, and had attempted to avoid it by going to work today even though he should have taken the day off.

Men.

"Great," he added at the end of his grumbling tirade as he parked at the end of a long driveway. Rows and rows of expensive, shiny cars—several of them convertibles—lined the massive parking area to the left of a large, three-story house. "I see Frank's car. Maybe he brought his girlfriend. You'd like her. She's your age."

Well, this promised to be fun.

Merina would have grabbed his tie to get his attention, but he wasn't wearing one. Reese was dressed in a casual collared shirt and khakis, and with the exception of hair to his elbows, closely resembled his brother Tag. In lieu of the aforementioned tie, she put her hand to his face and ran her fingers down the barely-there scruff that lined his sharp jaw.

He held his frown, his eyes scrunched in frustration.

She leaned closer and his expression softened, those scrunched eyes opening enough to dip and take inventory of her ample cleavage. She had gone with a summery turquoise dress that wrapped in the middle, low-cut enough to give the girls a day in the sun.

"Your tattoo." He stroked the skin above her breast.

Okay, so the cleavage wasn't front and center. He continued to surprise her.

"Shit." She fussed with the material. That was the problem with this dress. "Maybe if I tighten my belt I can hide it."

"Let them see it." Reese captured her hands. "Let everyone see it. It's you." His eyes were warm until his gaze snapped to the house and another flash of pain darted across his features. So quickly, if she hadn't been this close to him, she may have missed it. "Let's get this over with."

He came around to her side of the Lamborghini, a car she'd admit was damn sexy and aside of Reese's sour mood, pretty damn fun to ride in. She accepted his hand and watched as he took in her tat again.

"Who knew you had a thing for bad girls," she joked, draping her hand over his arm so she didn't wobble up the cobblestone.

"There's a first time for everything." She wasn't a bad girl per se, but knowing she'd taken Reese to his knees—both during a blow job and while tickling him—made her pull her shoulders back with pride.

After Corbin, she'd stopped thinking of herself as confident—as a catch. But a man as powerful as Reese Crane succumbing to her specific brand of femininity was proof she still had it.

They walked up the drive and cut across a flower and rock garden, over the lush lawn, and along a path leading to the front door. They passed cute round bushes and red feathery ones. Pink and purple and yellow flowers lined the dark mulch interspersed with spiky green-leaved plants.

Where Reese's mansion was decadent and regal, Alex Crane's house was homey, despite being gargantuan. The siding was a rust-cinnamon color, the windows and roof slate gray. She spotted three balconies—two on the top floor leading out from opposite rooms and one on the middle floor. Downstairs was reserved for a massive patio, the outdoor furniture as clean as if it'd been bought today. Hell, maybe it had.

"This is beautiful," she said. "And a pool house?"

"Heated."

"Like yours."

"Like father like son. I guess I got used to it and wanted one of my own."

She chewed on that thought. "So, you grew up here?"

"Yep." He reached for the door. "Only house I ever lived in until I bought the estate."

Interesting. Was it memories of his mother that made him dread coming here today?

He swung open the door and they were greeted by an attractive red-haired woman wearing a white shirt and black vest and skirt.

"Welcome to Big Crane's home. May I take your handbag and lock it in the private coatroom?" she asked Merina.

"Oh...sure." Wow. Formal.

"I'm Reese," he said. "You must be new."

The woman did look a dash chagrined before her professionalism snapped back into place. "Mr. Crane's oldest son. You must be Merina Crane."

Merina smiled. "I am."

"I was hired for the event. My apologies for not recognizing you, Mr. Crane." She handed Merina's purse off to an attendant. "Right this way. I'll show you to the backyard."

"I can find it, thanks." Reese took Merina's hand. "He goes through house staff like underwear."

Merina sent the redhead an apologetic smile and shuffled alongside her husband out to the yard.

* * *

This house had been his home since Reese Harrington Crane had returned from the hospital swaddled in yellow because his parents didn't find out if he was a boy or a girl until he popped out. His room had been on the third floor, the windows replaced by balconies and sliding doors only after Eli had stopped sleepwalking. Now Alex lived here, though his assistant and house staff occupied the house most of the time as well.

A third of the square footage as Reese's home, it was still huge but his father had never downsized after Lunette had died. If it were Reese who'd lost his wife in a car accident, he couldn't have moved fast enough. Hell, when Gwyneth cheated on him, he hadn't been able to set foot into the mansion without remembering her sorting mail in the foyer, or drinking tea in the kitchen. Or opening his eyes in the morning and watching out the window as she dove into the deep end of the pool.

Similarly, his father's house was haunted by as many painful memories. Reese remembered his mother in the kitchen, rushing back and forth to throw lunches together for the three of them. They could afford to eat the private school lunches, seeing as money had never been a problem, but she'd insisted on packing homemade sandwiches on bread that Magda had baked from scratch.

Outside, the covered back patio sprawled the length of the house, providing welcome shade from the hot sun. As if Alex had phoned up God himself and requested good weather, above were blue skies and only the occasional puffy cloud.

"This is a beautiful house," Merina commented, her hand squeezing his.

"It was." He lifted her hand and brushed his lips along her knuckles, pleased when she sent him a smile that calmed some of the torrential feelings inside him.

When his mother was alive, life was as close to perfect as the family of five could've come. After she'd passed, the kitchen held memories of frozen casseroles and lasagna that neighbors and friends brought for them to eat. The pool house the room where Reese would sit for hours, feet in the water wondering if he fell in and drowned if it would relieve the pain his mother's death left behind.

It was emo-teenage kid stuff he thought he'd outgrown. Being back here or encountering his and Gwyneth's former bedroom hadn't made him want to drown himself, but a familiar, black cloud hung ominously above his head.

A few years after his mother died, Reese started shadowing his father at work. It took a week for him to decide that his college major would be whatever gave him the proper education he needed to take over Crane Hotels someday.

His legacy.

The woman next to him was a crucial spoke in the wheel of his journey. Thanks to her, he was on his way to a future that burned so brightly, it shut out the hurt. Merina also shut out the hurt, because that black cloud didn't hold the weight it had before she was here.

He didn't have the time or desire to take a long vision of that thought.

Hand in hand with Merina, he walked through the grass to where his father stood, dressed in white pants and a navy shirt, his white hair lifting in the breeze.

"Reese. There he is." Alex was standing with Frank and Bob, and a quick glance around the party determined there were a handful of other board members in attendance.

"Gang's all here," Reese muttered. Merina moved her hand to his elbow, possibly warning him to behave himself.

An hour into mingling, she'd made the rounds with him to greet guests and friends of the family. They parted with a kiss he'd assumed was for the crowd, yet when her hands lingered on his neck, and his eyes sank closed, the kiss felt like it was only for them.

That'd been happening often, and in this setting, surrounded by gawking onlookers, he itched with the urge to leave. Partly because he'd rather be alone with Merina, and partly because being here reminded him of the deal he'd made with her in the first place.

They'd moved beyond a deal and a marriage for show. They had slipped from the precarious ledge of staged kisses and convenient sex. Their relationship was more than signatures on a contract.

He hadn't meant for it to happen, but now that it had, he had no idea what to do about it.

His father approached, carrying two bottles of beer. He offered one to Reese, who stood next to a small algae-filled pond.

"Frog," Alex said as the tiny green thing leapt into the water with a *bloop*. "Can't pour the algae killer in there or else the frog will die."

"Isn't that natural selection?" Reese asked drily, accepting the brew and tipping the bottle back for a long, wet sip. He'd laid off the alcohol while wandering around the party, and now it tasted damn good going down.

Alex chuckled. "So. Enjoying yourself?"

Beer bottle to his lips, Reese grunted.

"Penelope thought a cookout would be the nudge you need." Alex lowered his voice, his eyes moving around the yard. "One more casual affair for the board to see you with your wife."

"You're talking to my advisor?"

"She's on the Crane payroll."

"She's on *my* payroll."

"I'm not retired yet." Alex broke into a grin. "Eager to see me in checkered golf pants?"

"You never did know how to relax." Reese nodded at his father's hearty build and flat stomach. "Time to let yourself go. Get paunchy."

"Shit." Alex laughed the word.

His old man deserved the break. After raising three boys alone—who'd grown into three hard-working, dedicated men—Alex deserved to kick back and not be responsible for anyone but himself.

"I have to stay fit for the ladies." Alex pulled a hand over his chest, his mustache stretching as he smiled.

Reese nearly spit out his beer. "You? Date?"

"Never know. I'm hot for a senior."

"And apparently senile."

His dad flipped him off and Reese laughed, which helped him relax. Alex had always, always been on Reese's side. Even when he became surly or short-tempered at work, there was nothing he wouldn't do for his boys.

"I owe you," Reese said, looking down at the grass.

"For?"

He met his father's blue eyes. Dark blue like his own. "For always making sure I knew that Crane Hotels was my destiny."

Alex blinked in surprise, or maybe he was moved.

"You didn't let me hand you anything, son. You demanded an interview."

That was true. "I didn't want to be handed anything."

"So proud of that. You wanted to prove you deserved your position at Crane Hotels, and soon enough you will be the head the company." Alex put a hand on Reese's shoulder and Reese felt the horrifying burn of tears at the back of his eyes. "Where you belong."

"Who are all these people, anyway?" Reese asked,

changing the subject before this bizarre display of tenderness revoked his man card. He recognized half of the guests, but the other half were either people he'd never met or had met in passing and forgotten.

"Filler," Alex answered. "So the board doesn't think this is a setup."

"Penelope's idea?" Reese guessed.

"She's sharp. Single?"

"Don't even think about it."

Alex chuckled, then his eyes went past Reese. "Ah, and here are the rest of them."

Merina's parents walked onto the patio. Merina, who was carrying a glass of white wine and standing next to Lilith, cast him a wide-eyed look from across the yard.

The desperate gaze told him she needed him to stand with her when they said hello. To feel needed, to be needed by her was as welcome as her needing him in every other way.

"Better greet your outlaws," Alex joked, lifting a glass. "If you only win two people over today, it should be them." His raised eyebrow told him Alex didn't believe that the Van Heusens were convinced.

But the real problem was that Reese wasn't convinced he was faking any longer.

* * *

Things had been strained between her and her parents since the wedding. Mom had tried to accept Reese without judgment and her father rarely brought it up. She hadn't prepared for seeing them today, but Merina was determined to make the best of it. After a few months of scrutiny during a marriage "for show," the strain was wearing on her in a way she was afraid had begun to show.

Thankfully, Reese was gliding her way, staggeringly powerful even dressed down for a faux casual cookout. As she'd learned since she set foot in the yard this afternoon, this get-together was anything but casual. Big Crane entertained his guests, his eyes lingering whenever they landed on Reese and Merina. He was watching the board and watching them in equal measure.

"You didn't tell me," she said as Reese looped an arm around her waist and turned with her to face her incoming parents.

"I didn't know," he replied. "Penelope."

In other words, this *shebang* was courtesy of their own personal public relations department. At least she had Reese. That thought struck her a little dumb. She'd come to rely on his presence. Lean on it, even.

Before those warning bells could trigger an alarm, Jolie and Mark sent a few uncomfortable glances across the lawn. They were nervous in the obscenely wealthy crowd, and now Merina was one of the flock. She'd fulfilled the whole "leave and cleave" order with a billionaire husband and her parents came an inch away from filing for bankruptcy.

Merina's heart ached for them. She wanted to assure them that they would be working at the Van Heusen as they liked. That they wouldn't have to change a single thing. Soon, she would.

"Well, this is quite the party," Jolie said as she approached. She was dressed in a floral dress, cut to flatter her plump-around-the-middle figure. Mark wore khakis and a golf shirt, trying but not quite hitting the fashionable mark.

"Hi, dear." Mark nodded at Reese next. "Reese."

Reese greeted them by name and pulled Merina flush to his hard, warm body. She rested her hand on his stomach, not realizing she'd done it until her father's eyes dropped to her hand, then raked up her dress and locked on her tattoo. His mouth frowned.

Right. The tattoo. Today was fun.

"I didn't know you were coming," Merina said. "I would have thought you'd have mentioned it at work on Friday."

"Well we were only invited this morning," Jolie said.

"I insisted we attend. I have something to talk to Reese about," Mark stated.

"About what?" It had better not involve Reese's intentions or she'd die.

"Don't worry," Mark said with one of his calming *Dad* smiles. "It's business not pleasure. Unless there are cigars?"

"There are cigars," Reese confirmed, his tone much more friendly than on the drive over here. "I prefer business with my pleasure."

His comment paired with the subtle slide of his fingers along her side. Merina felt her cheeks go up in flames, her mind retreating back to the many pleasurable encounters they'd had, all thanks to the business of this marriage.

"I'm sure you and your mom would like to eat while we talk," Reese said, his voice a seductive murmur. He pressed a kiss to her waiting lips, and then whispered into her ear, "If I don't come back in an hour, run."

She swallowed a smile and saw he was wearing one when he backed away. Several layers of gloom had lifted from him, and she'd like to think she had something to do with his improved mood.

"We'll be fine," Merina said for all of their sakes.

"Jolie, I highly recommend the artichoke dip," Reese said, then turned to Mark and gestured for him to follow.

Merina watched her husband walk away in that strong, long-legged swagger she'd grown accustomed to before facing her mother. "What was that about?"

"You know your father. He needs to be involved." Jolie's expression was calm and accepting. "Let's let the boys take care of that and you can show me to that dip."

More secrets. Merina put her arm in her mother's and led her to the chilled buffet bar on the patio, wishing she could tell her mother the truth about her and Reese. Though she wasn't sure what the truth was anymore. She'd married him for ownership of the VH, but now she was enjoying the perks that came with their marriage.

The biggest of which was Reese himself and who she was when she was with him.

Later, Mark and Reese emerged with smiles and scotches in hand, and Jolie and Merina mingled with the various women present who either worked for Crane or were friends of the family.

After her parents left, Tag arrived late, which was not surprising in the least. He nodded at Merina but beelined for his brother, and he and Reese hung at the bar on the patio. One by one, women turned their heads to take in so much sexy testosterone in a small space.

Lights on strings and soft music playing through speakers had drawn the dwindling crowd to the patio. The board members had gone, and the remaining few consisted of Alex's family, his assistant, and another older couple. Tag and Reese were chatting so Merina made a trip to the bathroom, catching sight of a cozy side room on her way back.

Curious, she veered into there instead of going outside right away.

Too bright to be a den, the room featured a pair of French doors leading out to a flower garden with a bench in the center. The blooms were fresh, as if they were purchased recently, but for all Merina knew, Alex had a full-time gardener tending to every inch of this place.

The house was spotless. There wasn't a twinkle of dust sitting on the shelves or the desk. She went to those shelves now, loaded mostly with picture frames, though a few books—fiction like Clancy and Patterson—stood off to the side. A box of cigars sat next to a small urn that read XAVIER CRANE, FATHER, SOLDIER.

By the age of the photo, Merina guessed he was Alex's father, Reese's grandfather.

She perused the pictures in the frames next. Various photos of the three boys fishing, or dressed for Halloween, or sitting at a picnic table eating slices of watermelon in the backyard. They were young, Reese probably only twelve or so. The only recent photos were one of Reese's corporate grimace, the same picture on the Crane Hotels website, and Tag's, though he was smiling. Eli's most recent photo was a military one. Him in front of a flag, clean-shaven, hair cropped beneath his hat. His mouth wasn't smiling and there was a hardness about him. She wondered when he'd be on leave. If she'd ever meet him.

She abandoned the frames for the back doors, admiring the lush flowers and greenery. Night was falling, the sun dipping low and giving everything a grainy quality.

"Are you driving home?" came a deep voice from behind her.

Guiltily, Merina turned. Alex—hands in his pockets, reminding her of the way Reese stood most of the time—lingered in the doorway.

"Sorry?"

"Tag and Reese." He made a drinking motion with his hand. "Sauced, the both of them."

"That's...unexpected." She couldn't say she'd ever seen Reese "sauced."

"Unless you're driving, you should bunk here."

"Oh, um...okay."

"Good. I'd like that." Alex offered a genuine smile. Not a single part of him looked as if he was upset she'd been snooping, but she had the urge to explain.

"I'm...uh...I saw photos and wanted to see the boys when they were boys."

"Ah. There are some good ones in here." Alex ambled into the room. "Arguably, Tag never grew up," he joked, elbowing her arm gently. "But, yeah, that's them when they were younger. That one is my favorite." He nodded at the picture of the three of them shirtless and eating watermelon. Reese's eyes were thick with lashes like now, but Tag was notably skinny and had certainly outgrown that trait. Eli sat off to the side, slice of watermelon in one hand, petting a cat with the other.

"The yard hasn't changed much, but they have," she commented, unsure what to say. Alex filled the silence with the last topic on earth she thought he'd breach.

"Luna's death hit Reese the hardest." His voice took on a soft quality, pain outlining every word. Pictures of Alex's late wife were notably missing from this room.

"Which of your sons looks the most like her?" she asked.

Alex left her side and pulled open a desk drawer. He approached with a gilded silver frame, an 8 x 10 of a woman behind the glass.

"This was a few years before she died," he said quietly.

"She's beautiful." Merina traced the slope of the woman's nose and over her blue eyes. "Reese."

Alex put one blunt finger over her forehead and drew the line down her long, fair hair. "Tag."

She laughed softly.

"Eli has her sensitivity."

"A sensitive marine?"

"We exist," Alex said, returning it to its drawer. He came back to stand beside her again. "Reese doesn't like being here."

"I noticed."

"Maybe because he's the oldest and knew her longer, or maybe because I handled things better with Tag and Eli. Either way, he prefers not to visit."

"But he does because he loves you," Merina said.

"He's a good boy." Alex's dark blue eyes trained on hers. "Remember that when everything's through. Will you?"

"I will."

He nodded, ending that topic. "I'll make a phone call to Magda to let her know you're staying. Have her drop a change of clothes for each of you."

Wow. Handy being rich. Alex must have recognized her surprise because he offered an explanation.

"Magda knows him. Loves him. She looks out for him." Alex put his hands in his pockets. "When Reese bought his house, I sent her there to work for him. And let me tell you"—he shook his head in earnest—"I did not want to give up those tamales."

"Oh, I had those. I don't blame you." They shared a smile and she realized this was the first lengthy conversation she'd had with Alex. From afar he'd seemed both serious and cunning, but it turned out he had a lot of warmth. Like the way Reese's charm had been buried beneath his surly exterior. How much more could she unearth in her time with him?

"He needed Magda more than I did," Alex said. His love for his sons was genuine. Strong. He was a man who'd do anything for them. She wondered if his idea to retire had anything to do with ushering Reese in sooner than later.

"Since you're staying, more wine?" Alex asked, heading for the door.

"Always more wine," she said, following.

"You fit in here, you know that?" Alex offering an arm and together they rejoined the party.

CHAPTER 15

The hearty, rich sound of male laughter made Merina smile. Reese and Tag had moved from the bar to a pair of chairs next to a stone fireplace. Scotch glasses in hand, they sat and talked about stories from when they were kids.

It was a rare occasion to see Reese so open and warm...like when she learned he was ticklish. His laughter ebbed and the smile lines stayed on his face briefly before fading. Her heart wrenched. She'd liked seeing him with his guard down.

"Chardonnay," a soft voice announced next to her.

Merina accepted the glass from a cute waitress. She wore a tiny black dress and strappy heels, her black hair pulled into a ponytail. She'd been here since dinner, clearing dishes and doling out drinks. How did someone land a cushy gig like this, anyway? Her job was to hang out on a billionaire's porch and serve drinks to the five people left: Tag, Reese, Alex, and Rhona. Merina had talked to Rhona briefly. She was Alex's personal assistant, around his age, and almost exclusively spoke to Alex. And the lovelorn look in her eyes when she did it suggested Rhona had been looking at Alex like that a long, *long* time. Alex, on the other hand, didn't appear to have a clue his PA had the hots for him.

Men. Seriously.

Clueless.

"Excuse me." The waitress came closer to the barstool where Merina sat. "I know this is really inappropriate"— she looked around the porch before continuing—"but is there any way you could introduce me to the guy with the long hair?"

"You want to meet Tag?" Merina's eyebrows went up in surprise. The other woman had to be at least twenty-one to serve the drinks, so at least they were in the safe zone there.

"I could lose my job, but..." She bit her lip and gazed over at Tag, hearts blooming in her eyes. "God, he'd be worth it, I bet."

Tag was laughing, Adam's apple bobbing. His casual button-up shirt was open one more button than necessary, revealing the top of his golden chest. His hair was down and ran over his shoulders, his beard proving he had no problem growing body hair.

"He is very attractive," Merina said as the waitress, still staring, gave a mute nod.

But when Merina's eyes tracked to Reese, leaning back, feet crossed at the ankles and his hand gripping the arm of the deck chair, her mouth watered and heart stuttered. If that was anywhere near the way this sweet college-aged girl saw Tag, then she was right. Hell yeah, he'd be worth it. How long would she have the dumb job anyway?

"I'm Merina," she introduced.

"Taylor." Her dark eyes swept over to Tag and she sighed with longing.

Adorable.

"You've never worked for the Cranes before, I take it?"

"Oh, yeah. But..." She wrenched her eyes off Tag but it took some effort. "I've never talked to him."

Maybe it was the wine, or maybe Merina felt bold since Alex had told her she fit in here, but she decided to make this girl's Cinderella dreams come true.

"Lucky for you, I know him well." Merina stood and looped her hand around Taylor's arm. "Ready?"

Taylor blushed, her smile dazzling. "Ready."

* * *

"You baited him," Reese said, feeling loose after way too much to drink. It was nice relaxing with his brother and dad. In this house of all places. And Merina had let him do it. Not once did she ask to go home, or excuse herself to bed early. At the end of the night when Tag vanished with one of the waitresses, she came to sit with Reese by the fire. He'd sat, his fingers woven with hers as Alex told a war story he'd heard a dozen times. Merina was rapt, orange firelight bouncing off her gorgeous face, her hand lazily resting in his.

He'd felt more at home with her next to him, a thought he'd blamed on the booze. It'd better be the booze or he was in big fucking trouble.

"I didn't bait him," Merina said. "I made an introduction. Taylor wanted to know what kind of shampoo he used." She grinned at her own joke and took the cosmetic bag Magda had dropped off earlier into the bathroom.

"Baited." But his firm tone didn't scare her. Not that he ever scared her, but she *really* didn't react now.

He'd been certain when this day started that it'd end with him in a much more sour mood, but so far, he didn't feel anything but glad to be here.

"Did she put my mouthwash in there?" He peeked over her shoulder as she dug through the bag.

"Yes, Your Highness." She offered a travel-sized bottle over her shoulder. He took it and went to the second sink, and side by side, he and his wife participated in a nighttime ritual they'd never done together. They brushed their teeth. At one point, Merina looked over, her mouth foaming like Cujo, and smiled.

He smiled back, curious at his own reaction, because moments like these didn't make him sentimental. Especially after he'd been forced to strut around like a damned prize poodle for the attending members of the board.

"That was brief," Merina commented after she rinsed her mouth and pulled her hair down. Honeyed strands fell like silk, wavy from the day's humidity.

"What was brief?" He toweled off his mouth.

"Your light mood." She still wore her dress but had undone the belt at her waist and a matching turquoise bra peeked from behind the material.

He absolutely wasn't going to broach this topic. Not while his veins were flooded with scotch. God knew what he'd wind up admitting.

He stepped forward and swept open her dress, resting his hands on her waist. Being with Merina physically was easy. He could give her what she needed physically. Emotionally, not so much.

"Softest fucking skin I've ever felt." Yep, still a little

drunk. He wasn't slurring but the words came slowly and weren't easy to enunciate.

"Ever?" she breathed.

He kissed her collarbone, ran his tongue over her tattoo. She was fishing, but he decided to answer her anyway.

"Ever." He closed his lips over her hectic pulse.

"What'd you and Dad talk about?"

He stopped his exploration to shake his head. "We're not talking about family while I'm seducing you."

"I'm not having sex with you here." Her eyes widened in alarm. "This is your childhood bedroom."

"Actually, this one was Eli's, so no worries."

"That's worse!" She gave his arm a playful slap. "I haven't met him yet."

Reese's shoulders stiffened. Would Merina ever meet him? Unlikely. Eli wasn't due back soon. He e-mailed and called every few months, but by the time he came home, Merina would be out of Reese's life. Permanently, he imagined. He didn't see how they'd remain friends. A sudden surge of melancholy made him frown.

"I don't want to talk about my brother." He smoothed his hands over her shoulders and pushed the dress off her body. Lace panties matched her bra. He plucked one of the little black bows decorating them. "I don't want to talk at all."

"I can't ask about my parents—"

"Nope." He kissed her neck.

"—or your family?" Her fingers in his hair sent a surge of warmth through his limbs. This was working. Under the attention of his fingers and his mouth she caved every time. She trusted him enough to let down her guard, which made him uncharacteristically humble.

"Correct." He placed an openmouthed kiss on the top side of one breast.

"Share a shower?" she gasped, gripping his hair.

"Always." He tugged the cup of her bra down and pulled her nipple into his mouth, the word echoing in his head. With Merina, "always" only meant "until," and he didn't want to think about how soon the end would come.

* * *

Merina toweled off, Reese next to her doing the same. They shared an almost shy smile, which was insane considering what had happened under the spray. He'd stripped them both naked, then hustled her into the smallish stand-up shower in the corner of the room. After doing a thorough job of soaping and rinsing her into a heated frenzy, he'd shut off the water.

"We can't do this," she said, but she barely meant it.

"Oh, we're doing this." He was damned attractive with his damp hair sticking up from running a towel haphazardly over the strands. His chest was bare and glistening with droplets of water. Between a pair of strong thighs, his cock hung heavily, tempting her in a million different ways.

Sex with Reese was so many things. Fun. Fantastic. Mind-erasing. But the idea of being in bed with him while his family was in the house—his brother, his father . . .

Merina was supposed to be pretending to be wifely, not actually *doing* the wifely things with him. Or sordid, wicked things with him.

"You're doing that on purpose," he growled, and she realized her eyes were glued to his impressive manhood and that it'd grown even more impressive now that her teeth were resting on her bottom lip.

"I'm not." She tracked her eyes up his body and met his navy gaze.

He took a step closer, steam rolling around them, and speared his fingers into her wet hair. "Are too." He kissed her gently, pushing his tongue past her lips to tangle with hers. He backed them from the bathroom to the bedroom, the moonlight arcing across the floor lighting their way.

His moves were familiar. He had a pattern of seduction and she played into it like a well-rehearsed dance. And right now he was doing one of her favorite things: raking his whiskered chin over her sensitive skin as he left a trail of damp kisses on her neck.

"Have fun trying to keep quiet," he mumbled against her mouth. He tasted of scotch and spice and she could swear she was getting drunk off his tongue.

He dropped her to the bed and laid over her, pressing his erection into her thigh.

"Who says I'll try and keep it down?" She cupped one of his rock-hard ass cheeks.

"Your Midwest manners, remember?" He dragged his tongue over one breast and Merina's back arched. When he sucked her nipple into his mouth, heat weaved down her spine. Taking his time, he dragged his tongue to her other breast. "You'll have to go downstairs and face them in the morning."

He continued torturing her, suckling her deeply as warmth flooded between her legs. She hissed, pushing him away when she couldn't stand another second.

"Really quiet sex," she conceded.

"The quiet part is up to you," he said, lifting an eyebrow. Eyes on her, he moved from her breasts to her ribs, down to— Oh no...

"No, no." She clasped his head when he ran his tongue over her belly button.

"Yes." He nipped and licked where her thigh met her... Oh, God. He was going to kill her.

"Reese, please," she pled. "I... you're right. I don't want to embarrass myself."

An evil glint in his eyes, he lifted and dropped one eyebrow before slicking her center with his tongue.

Her pushing hands turned into kneading, threading his soft hair between her fingers. She steered his mouth where she wanted as he laved her again and again. He continued sending ripples of delight through her until she clutched and came on a quiet whimper.

He climbed her body, placing kisses here and there until he was lying on the pillow next to her. Content, she rolled over and rested her chin on his chest.

"Nice work. I don't think you woke anyone up," he said with a lazy, pleased smile.

She smiled back at him, the light from the moon slanting across his bare chest.

"Well, I don't think Tag's sleeping, so maybe he and that waitress are the ones waking Dad tonight."

"Ugh. I can't think about it."

He laughed, bouncing her where she rested.

It wasn't right to take advantage of Reese in his slightly boozed state...But she was a woman and as a woman knew the best way to extract information from a man was at a time exactly like this one.

She ran a finger through the scant hair on his chest,

making circles and watching his eyes drift closed. *Oh, no, you don't.*

"So what did you and Dad decide, again?" Merina opted to ask the question as a leading one, hoping Reese might think she knew more than she did.

"That's between us men," he said, his eyes still closed.

"Reese!"

"I made him promise not to tell your mother or you and then we drank scotch."

She huffed.

"Why do you care what we talked about?" He opened one eye. "Afraid he asked me about you?"

"Did he?" There was a mortifying thought. She didn't think her father would ask Reese to divorce her to give her a chance at finding a husband who loved her, but what if he had? What if Mark saw right through them?

How can he? Even you can't see where the fake stops and the real begins.

"We talked about business. None of which is yours." He touched the tip of her nose with his finger.

"Do you think the board will make you CEO?" she asked, wondering if they'd done a good job at convincing them.

"Worried you'll lose the Van Heusen?" It was a fair question since that's what she stood to gain.

"You deserve CEO."

"I'll get it." He twirled a piece of her hair around his finger. "Don't worry."

"One more question." Because he hadn't answered any of them to her satisfaction yet.

He blinked his eyes slowly, clearly tired. "The interrogation continues."

She took a breath and asked the question she'd wondered about since the night of the retirement party. It came out as a demand. "Tell me about you and Gwyneth."

His fingers stilled in her hair.

"I assumed she was more than a one-night thing when she cornered you. And you dislike Hayes. I'm guessing because he dated her after you did?"

"I'm not talking about this, Merina." Reese didn't sound angry so much as serious, but she wasn't going to let him off the hook.

"You force me to draw my own conclusions."

His eyes sank shut but it looked like a tactical move to her.

Okay. She could rise to a challenge. "After a torrid threesome, you became insanely jealous because Hayes was much better at—"

Reese's hand covered her mouth. His expression wasn't furious or amused. Hurt sliced into his eyes and contorted his handsome features. She mumbled his name against his palm and with a sigh, he took his hand from her mouth.

"It's not nearly that adventurous." He grew quiet for so many seconds, she'd begun counting them in her head. When she got to thirty-one, he drew in a breath to speak.

* * *

He couldn't cower forever. He knew that. What had happened with Gwyneth happened and his wife wanted to know. Half of him wondered if it'd be therapeutic to tell her, the other half warning him not to traipse down Emotional Lane and crack his chest open so she could investigate the scars in there.

"It's old news," he said. Hell, it was ancient news. "But if you really want to know..."

"I do." She shifted on his chest, pillowy breasts on his ribs, her comforting weight against his bare skin. What was it about her that made him able to tell her things he swore never to talk about?

He could do this. He just had to stick to the facts, spit it out, and then it'd be done.

"Gwyneth and I dated when I was younger. She was after money, and not a little amount—she wanted the lifestyle." All true. The socialite in her wanted to maintain her status, increase her position in the years to come. Her mother had taught her well. In Reese she'd seen opportunity and nothing more. He just hadn't been privy to her plan until she fucked his best friend.

Loving someone who didn't love him had hurt like a bitch. He'd attempted to ignore it, to anesthetize the pain by pretending it wasn't there. But the numbness always wore off.

"The short of it," he said with forced boredom, "was that Gwyneth was shallow and I was too young to know what to do with my money. I gave her whatever she wanted."

Money. Jewelry. His heart.

"She took advantage of you." Merina's fingers moved soothingly over his skin, grounding him.

"I'm the man, honey. She didn't take advantage of me. Suckered me maybe."

She let him have the deflection.

"Did you date long?" she asked.

Four years was a long time. Age twenty-four to twenty-eight for him, and while they weren't formative years, they were the years he'd started to discover who he was, who he would become.

But that fell under the category of sharing far too much, so he shrugged and said, "Not really."

"A month? A year?" she pushed.

"A handful of months," he muttered. *Or fifty of them.* Admitting the truth was embarrassing. He had been blissfully blind to Gwyneth's intentions. Believing she loved him for him, not for what he could give her. To this day it made him feel foolish. And foolish men did not run successful companies.

He looked to the window rather than at her when he fudged the truth. "I learned a lesson I needed to learn, and she moved on to greener pastures. Hayes was an up-and-comer, or was until he was fired from Crane Hotels."

"Scandal," Merina whispered, trying to lighten the mood.

"Not quite." That was a flat-out lie. He'd felt scandalized. Used. Pissed. Hurt. All at once and in overwhelming equal measures. He moved Merina's hair from her forehead, admiring her beauty and the honesty brimming in her eyes. Since she'd met him, she'd been lying to everyone she cared about—and to people she didn't. It didn't escape him that he'd given her little to no choice in the matter.

It bothered him now more than before.

"Is she the reason you dated all of Chicago one night at a time?" Merina blinked sweetly, teasing him, which he appreciated. She didn't want to see him hurting. Good thing she couldn't read his mind because a large part of him was hurting for her; for what he'd done to her.

He wanted Merina to believe that Gwyneth had stung his ego, not demolished his ability to commit to someone.

And really, he couldn't give Gwyneth that much credit. He'd made a series of choices after she left—purposeful decisions with an end goal in mind. Plus, if anyone had kept him from settling down, he could lay that blame at his mother's feet. Her death had practically inoculated him.

Whatever he had with Merina, he was grateful the end date was on the horizon. The hurt he'd feel letting her go as planned would be easier than learning she'd left him or never loved him or died.

That thought didn't do much to settle him. No relief came from imagining himself in bed alone, no Merina draped over his body.

"It's easier to trust a woman for a night," Reese answered belatedly. He brushed her cheek with the back of his knuckle. She was achingly beautiful, her eyes warm in the moonlight. "Most I could lose was the contents of my wallet. But my 401(k) remains intact."

She hummed. "Who says I won't drain your accounts, Crane? Maybe I'm money and power hungry."

He laughed, and some of that coveted relief came. "You're in love with a hotel. You inked the theme for the building onto your breast. You worry about your father's health. You're concerned about the college girl who more than happily went to bed with my brother tonight. I doubt, even though you 'don't like me,'" he added, air quoting the words she'd said to him when he proposed, "that you'd tempt karma by doing something as lowly as robbing me."

The corner of her mouth curved and he touched her smile with the tip of his finger.

"You're a good person, Merina." In the silence of the room, he counted her heartbeats.

"You're a better person than you give yourself credit for,

Reese," she said, her honesty flooring him. "And I like you more than I used to."

He liked her more than was healthy. He liked her in his bed. He liked her swathed over his chest. He liked her in the wrapped dress and especially out of it. He liked her way more than he'd anticipated.

Essentially, that was the problem, wasn't it?

He'd vowed to never take a woman to bed more than once after Gwyneth destroyed everything between them. He'd talked himself into the idea that Merina was just a long one-night stand. But he'd shared things with her he'd never shared with one-night stands.

They were in his childhood home, for God's sake.

"Hey." She put her finger on his chin to turn his face to hers. When their eyes locked, he had a premonition. It had claws. Fangs. It was one word with seven letters.

FOREVER.

Forever was a myth. *Always* wasn't real. His future was CEO and eighty-hour weeks and living on the same floor of his office at Crane Hotel. What he had with Merina was...

Ah, fuck. He couldn't categorize it and he wasn't sure if it was because he didn't want to or because he already knew and didn't want to admit it.

"I do like you," she murmured, interrupting his hectic thoughts. "A lot."

His heart rapped a hectic beat. Try as he might to ignore it, he couldn't escape the idea that in the last ten seconds things between them had changed irrevocably.

He liked her a lot too. A whole damn lot.

She shifted from his chest to her pillow, and side by side, they looked up at the ceiling.

"Good night, Crane."

"Good night, Merina."

They didn't speak after that, but neither of them slept, either.

* * *

Waking in a bed that wasn't hers, and without Reese next to her, Merina lay on her back for a few minutes and thought through last night.

But instead of enjoying fantastic memories of the shower, followed by more fantastic memories of them in bed, she found herself replaying the tape of her awkward admission.

I like you. A lot.

Because they were in high school.

She wasn't in love with him, but if she were being honest with herself, it wouldn't take more than a nudge to get her there.

What started out as a business agreement had morphed into sex as a perk but had since—dare she say it—*grown*. Reese had become more than a one-dimensional character.

He was a dedicated son, a loving brother. He was funny and had moments of kindness. She'd been too blind to see it—too angry to see it.

Reese worked hard and was even harder on himself. There was a boy inside the man who missed his mother, and seeing his sadness had flayed her. Together, they'd built a marriage on a bargain, but the life they'd built around it was starting to look very real.

Was starting to *feel* very real.

After years of living at home—and a brief stint with Corbin in that same house—Merina had never lived on her own. And Reese, a workaholic who lived at his hotel, had never bothered to make a home. But since Merina moved into the mansion, they had turned it into a home. Together.

And last night, in Alex Crane's home where he'd raised his three boys through their tumultuous teenage years without his wife, Merina saw that this family was more than the headlines gave them credit for. They were, at least for a little while, her family too.

The board was being picky about who would acquire the role of CEO. They were holding it over Reese's head, which was abhorrent, but on the bright side, their indecision gave her time. Time to show her husband that not all women were like Gwyneth. Merina was after his heart, not what he could give her.

If he gave them a chance, a real one, maybe they'd have a shot at something more. But she was getting ahead of herself. They had a few more months to figure things out. She threw the covers off and climbed out of bed, the thought comforting.

Twenty minutes later, she'd put on the jeans and shirt Magda had packed her, slipped her feet into her tennis shoes, and did a quickie makeup-and-hair session. Because she was reasonably sure no one heard her moans from last night, except for Reese who had earned them, Merina walked downstairs with her head held high. The long staircase led to a living room that opened to the kitchen... where she saw two people.

Tag and Taylor.

Awkward, party of three.

The second to last step she took was to back away, but Taylor already spotted her. So did Tag. Their smiles didn't waver. Especially Taylor's, which slipped only briefly to mouth the words "thank you" to Merina.

Tag meandered to the door with his hand on Taylor's back, his voice low and rumbly and sounding as if he was breaking unpleasant news to her in the gentlest way possible.

Merina hoped she hadn't caused the girl any kind of undue heartache. The front door shut and before she could decide whether or not to scamper upstairs and avoid a conversation with Tag, Reese came in from outside, an empty coffee mug in his hand.

"Not even going to feed her breakfast?" he asked his brother. Then his eyes landed on her and heated to a distracting degree. "Morning."

"She's all right," Tag answered. He slid a knowing glance first at Reese, then back to her. "Merina, you're looking...refreshed."

He grinned and her cheeks grew hot.

Reese didn't hide his own smile as he crossed the room, rounded the counter, and refilled his mug. He placed the coffee in front of her and she stepped forward to grasp the handle.

"And sharing a mug? You two are adorable," Tag said, getting himself a glass of water.

"How do you know she's all right?" Merina asked, desperate for a subject change. She hoped Tag hadn't overheard her and Reese last night. Then again, how could he have overheard anything but what he and Taylor had been doing? "What if she's feeling used?"

"Trust me, Sis." Tag leaned his elbows on the counter in front of her. "She's going back to Berkeley in a few weeks. She doesn't want anything more than I gave her."

"Which was what, an STD?" Merina asked with a sweet smile.

Reese choked on a laugh.

"Hey, I am squeaky clean." Tag straightened. "Which I assume you would assume given the way you practically threw Taylor into my arms last night." A hoisted golden-brown eyebrow suggested Tag knew how things had gone down. Which meant Taylor probably, *definitely* did not feel used. "But enough about me. You two seem to be taking your roles as husband and wife seriously."

"Don't." Reese's single-word command was paired with a murderous glare. One Merina supported. Mainly because what Tag had said was dangerously close to the truth. The "roles" of husband and wife weren't like roles. They were better at being a couple than she could have imagined.

The front door squeaked and the three of them looked over, the room sinking into silence. Despite her deciding Taylor was a-okay, Merina half expected the younger woman to make a tearful entrance. Instead, it was Alex, in navy shorts and a tight gray T-shirt, huffing and puffing like he'd run a mile. Or ten.

Big Crane was in amazing shape. Merina thought about adding "for an older guy," but he was in amazing shape for *any* guy. Rounded shoulders that reminded her of Reese's and thick, muscular thighs that echoed Tag's build. Her eyes perused the tattoos on the side of his arm, a black pictorial faded because of his tan and likely the age of the ink. Woven in the pattern, she made out the words *semper fi.*

He left the door open and Rhona, his PA, stepped in behind him, dressed in pink pants and a matching pink hoodie. Her blond hair had a natural gray streak running from the front of her ponytail to the back. The look suited her.

"I'm going to grab a shower," she told Alex, touching his shoulder before slipping her hand away. "Morning, everyone," she said with a smile before taking the stairs.

Had no one noticed that Alex's PA had a thing for her employer? Reese and Tag were fascinated with the contents of the refrigerator, paying their father no mind. Alex paced into the room and pulled the earbuds from his ears. He disconnected them from his phone, tapping the screen as his breathing regulated.

Tag offered a green smoothie in a plastic bottle, and Alex accepted, cracking the lid and taking several deep swallows.

"Good run?" Reese asked his father, defecting from his plan to drink something other than coffee and grabbing a fresh mug.

"Yeah. Rhona pushes me."

That wasn't all Rhona wanted to do with him.

"I have news," Alex said, setting his smoothie on the counter.

Her mind caught up in the love story she was currently writing in her head, Merina waited for him to announce that he and Rhona were running off to the Bahamas to tie the knot.

"Bob called me while I was jogging and told me the board is not interested in any new candidates for CEO."

The room went silent. Reese, in sweats and a T-shirt, leaned one hand against the counter, the other white-knuckling his coffee mug.

"Congratulations, son. They're naming you next week."

Next week.

"Well done. To both of you," Alex added, dipping his chin in Merina's direction and pairing it with a wink.

She blinked as she tried to sort the feelings rushing through her. Dread paired with a visual of sand running through an hourglass. She'd thought she and Reese had time, but now that he was being named CEO, did that mean things between them were...over?

"Nice fucking work." Tag broke the silence first, clapping his brother hard on the back.

Reese didn't say anything for a few seconds, eyes staring unseeing at the floor in front of him. Then he smiled. Genuine and unfettered, joy burst from him and encompassed the room.

Merina wanted to wrap her arms around him and share in the moment, but she didn't quite fit in the huddle of Crane men. This was their celebration.

In a fatherly show of affection, Alex cupped Reese's face and bumped his forehead with his own. Tag's laughter followed. Reese absolutely beamed.

Before Merina started feeling shut out completely, Reese shot that beaming smile over to her and held her eyes for a very long time.

She returned it, feeling included and, despite the feeling of running out of time, proud.

CHAPTER 16

CRANE HOTELS NAMES REESE CRANE CEO.

The headline in the *Tribune* wasn't as splashy as what the gossip rags had been writing about him, but that large black print may well have been a golden road leading straight to heaven.

The board had taken nearly as long to announce as it took them to reach the damn decision. It'd been two weeks since his father told him the news and the article appeared in the paper just today.

He'd been desperate when he'd concocted the idea of marrying Merina. Fully prepared to prove to the board he could settle down and be viewed as responsible enough to run the company he'd already been running at his father's side for years. Six months, and he knew he could convince them.

But it didn't take that long.

Because he and Merina delivered Oscar-worthy performances? Or because of something much scarier: They were no longer performing.

The article was full of encouraging phrases like *Alex Crane's eldest son was born for this* and *Naysayers will now be forced to take a backseat and watch*, and Reese's personal favorite, *a unanimous decision by the board of directors*. Still, the win felt bittersweet. Even paired with an ass-kissing quote by Frank and Lilith praising Reese's hard work, which he couldn't have imagined her saying unless she had a loaded gun to her head.

The bittersweet part was that he'd arrived at CEO sooner than expected, and it was the right thing to do to sign over the hotel to Merina and quietly divorce. The board may have taken their sweet time announcing who was CEO, and Reese knew why. They didn't want a ripple of doubt on the surface of their decision. They were a careful and proud bunch, representing stockholders who were twitchy. A divorce, especially a quiet one, would not throw them into a search for Reese's replacement. Hell, at this point, Reese doubted anything short of a scandal involving him and a few farm animals would threaten his position.

But he didn't want a divorce. Not yet. He preferred to stick to the original plan—the six-month plan. His being appointed to CEO was accelerated, yes, but no reason to cut things short prematurely with Merina.

Because you aren't ready to let her go.

He frowned down at the article that should have him popping champagne.

He didn't like the feeling uncertain. Merina staying had never been permanent—not for her, not for him. He had everything he wanted...everything he needed.

His phone pinged, reminding him of a lunch with the president of Strategies, who wanted to upgrade every keycard entry in every Crane Hotel across the country. It was Reese's first big decision as head of this company, and despite the potentially bland content—keycards didn't exactly turn him on—he was jazzed.

This was it.

Everything he'd wanted for nearly a decade, here for the execution. He turned his focus to his upcoming meeting and mentally curbed thoughts of Merina and his marriage. This was his destiny. His legacy.

He was going to nail it.

* * *

"Mr. Crane, Mrs. Crane is here," came Bobbie's voice over the intercom.

Reese blinked up from the e-mail he was typing to check the time at the top of the screen. It was eight? At night? The day had flown and for much of it, he'd been in the zone. Busy, handling his current position as well as delegating work since they hadn't yet found anyone to take over his former position as COO.

"You don't have to announce she's here, Bobbie. Just let her in." Good Lord. That woman was a robot.

"Yes, sir."

A few seconds later, Merina swept in looking fresh and beautiful in a deep purple dress and tall, tall shoes. Since he hadn't dropped her at work this morning, he hadn't seen what she was wearing. So infatuated with the cut of the dress and curve of her hips, he noticed belatedly, that she was carrying a very large frame.

"To what do I owe this honor?" He stood and came out from behind his desk.

"For your trophy room." She flipped the frame around. It was the newspaper article. He grinned like an idiot.

"I don't have a trophy room." He accepted the frame, his eyes perusing the article there. The article he'd unabashedly read five times and stopped short of highlighting his favorite parts.

"Start one," she said.

He put the frame on his desk and swept Merina into his arms. She slipped her hands around his neck and tilted her head, her blond hair sweeping off her face.

"We did it," she said, her voice tender.

We. He and Merina had been a team, still were a team. This was what had been missing since he spotted the article this morning. He'd yet to share it with Merina.

Now he felt...whole.

"Yeah, we did." He kissed her. Hard yet soft, loving the way she clung to him and pressed her body against his. Loving that she'd come down here, hefting a frame in those high-heeled shoes of hers, to deliver his gift. She didn't have it sent. She hadn't waited until he arrived home. She brought it up here with her own two hands.

Hands now resting on the back of his neck while he tasted her mouth. With a deep intake of breath, he slanted his head the other way and accepted her tongue, sliding his palms from her back to her front where he cupped a breast, then shaped her ribs and hips with his hands.

She hummed in the back of her throat and only then did he pull away to look her in the eyes.

"I guess you like it?" she asked. Her lips were slightly pink from sparring with his five o'clock shadow.

"You're very hands-on."

She slid those hands to his chest. "Which you have enjoyed many times."

Not what he meant, but he let her have the innuendo. What he'd implied was that she cared. About her hotel. About her parents. About people in general. About his accomplishments. She cared...about *him*. He cupped her hands in one of his and trapped them against his heart.

He cared about her, too, but there wasn't a safe place to lay those words. Nowhere to store them considering he and Merina were nearly at the finish line.

"Don't go mushy on me, Crane." Her smile shook at the edges, possibly concerned he might say some of the words she'd seen reflected in his eyes.

There was a safe space for them, and it started and ended with sex. He'd stick to the program, as requested. For both their sakes.

"Not capable of mush," he said, then further demonstrated by bending at the knees and sliding one hand beneath her skirt. "Tell me, Merina. Have you ever harbored a fantasy about having sex with the CEO of Crane Hotels in his office?"

She rolled her eyes but her face colored. If she hadn't thought of it before, she was definitely thinking about it now. Better than her trying to guess what he'd been thinking—which was that regardless of a contract or a wedding band, he liked the idea of sharing things with her. Drinks, dinners, and sex were givens, but smiles and jokes and conversation had been added to the mix.

He liked them all. He molded his hands along her bare thigh and over the silky material of her panties. "Are they purple?" he asked with a groan.

She had a proclivity to match her underwear to her outfit.

"They are." Her fingernails raked through his hair, and much as he hated to do it, he moved away from her to punch a button on his phone. "Bobbie, go home."

"Yes, sir," came her reply.

"I assumed we'd celebrate more formally, but this works too." Merina's eyebrows rose in challenge when he returned to her.

"We should do what we do best, don't you think?"

"I do." She reached behind her back and he listened to the *snick-snick* of the zipper as she slowly drew it down her back. He watched hungrily as the front of her dress loosened at her breasts. Seconds later, she was pulling it from her shoulders and dropping it to the floor. His eyes were glued to the purple bra shoving her breasts together, perfectly contrasting the bright orange and yellow flames licking the end of her arrow tattoo.

"Tell me," she said, her voice a seductive purr. "Are *you* the one with the fantasy of having sex as CEO of Crane Hotels?" She took a bold step toward him.

"Definitely." He caught her hips.

"I won't ask if you've ever had sex in this office because I don't want to know. I could still be your first as the man in charge, which counts for something."

"It's a first on both counts." He could tell by her relaxed expression she liked being his first. "You're a lot of firsts for me, Merina." He unclasped her bra. "My first hostile takeover." Her eyelids narrowed, so he added, "My first wife." He dragged the bra off her arms, sliding his fingertips along her skin and watching as her nipples pebbled in the cool air. "My first—"

She caught his mouth to stop his words and he was glad, because he wasn't sure what would have followed those words. Soon there was pulling and tugging, unbuttoning and unzipping. He closed his lips over her breast as she stroked him into a fevered frenzy.

Whatever happened between them, he'd forever have this memory. Pain shot through his heart. He didn't like thinking of her as a memory. She was his for now, and that's where he'd stay.

If they were creating a memory, he'd create one she wouldn't soon forget. He spun her so she faced the windows. Mirrored, no one was seeing in, but she never brought it up. Either she trusted him or simply didn't care if anyone looked. Both of those worked for him.

"Beautiful," he murmured against her ear, watching as he cupped her breasts in the reflection. She arched seductively. "And mine."

Her eyes opened and clashed with his. Night had fallen and dots of light from neighboring office windows created a faux sea of stars. They stood at his desk, bared completely.

He put a kiss on her shoulder, then bent to retrieve a condom from his wallet.

"Hurry," came her plea.

"Moving as fast as I can, honey." He felt her pain. He wasn't drawing out the anticipation of any longer. They needed this—needed to celebrate how far they'd come.

Hell. He needed her, period.

She bent, hands on top of his desk, ass in the air. He reached for her hips, the tip of his cock stroking her slick folds. She was wet and ready.

He traced the delicate line of her back with his fingertips. Her hair fell over smooth shoulders when she lifted her chin. He memorized her like this—eyes closed, elbows on the desk, breasts full. She opened her eyes and her smoky, fuzzy twin had matching lust in her eyes.

Tilting his hips, he entered her and a sharp shout of "yes" left her lips.

"Tell me what you need." He gripped her tightly, unwilling to let her give him more before taking what she came for.

"This," she said. He slid into her again. "You."

He repeated the movement, hands wrapped around her hips as he drove her back against his thighs again.

"You," she gasped.

She needed *him*. Those words wound around and tickled a part of him he was desperately trying to ignore. The part of him that knew he wasn't what Merina should need.

She grasped his hand when he slowed down, and issued another command.

"Harder, Reese." Her reflection smiled. "I need you to give it to me harder."

That, he could oblige. Holding her, he pounded them both into oblivion, his mind buried under the sensation of her tight warmth and the sweet sounds of her release. She was shouting now, his name, the word *yes* and *oh God* and a *please* thrown in for good measure. If he could have gotten his tongue to work, he'd have shouted with her.

Merina knocked a stapler and the contents of his inbox to the floor, throwing her head to the side in a gorgeous display of ecstasy. One that accompanied her inner muscles spasming. Reese was caught, trapped there within her. As she took her orgasm, she drew his from him.

He came hard, so hard he had to bend over her to rest

a hand on the desk, the other cupping her ass as he finished with a few final pumps. Chin on her back, he lightly scraped her flesh with his teeth.

She sighed, contented.

For several minutes the only sound in the room was hectic breathing. Until Merina cut in with that droll, joking tone of hers. "Remind me to bring you gifts more often."

He drew out of her, slowly, and discarded the condom in the wastebasket under his desk. That ought to be fun for the cleaning staff. Merina began collecting her clothes from the floor.

"Going somewhere?" He took the panties and bra from her hands and threw them on his desk.

"I was going to get dressed so we could go home."

"Soon." He lifted her into his arms, his own words curling around his heart like smoke. Just as delicate. Just as impermanent.

He carried her to the leather couch on the opposite side of the room and pulled her onto his lap.

"What's this?" She sat prettily across his legs, her arms looped around his neck.

He stroked the shape of her tattoo and watched goose bumps light her skin. So sensitive. So soft. So strong. Because it took a powerful person to be this soft yet assert herself as Merina had. And she was coming home with *him*.

A man who hadn't gone home in years.

He held her breast, stroking her nipple lightly with one thumb. When she shuddered, he kissed her. Softly, slowly, silently thanking her for bringing him to this point. Then he said it aloud.

"Thank you."

A bemused expression, then, "You're thanking me for sex?"

"No, smart-ass," he said, and that earned him the cocksure tilt of her mouth. "I'm being sincere. For a change." Her smile turned to a cute laugh. He gave her a brief kiss. "Thank you for doing this . . . whole thing."

"Oh." Her fingers twined in his hair.

"I held the VH over your head because I needed this," he admitted. "I needed you . . ." His throat grew tight when those words came out, and he had to swallow and force the rest. "I needed you, Merina. I've wanted CEO for as long as I can remember. Crane Hotels is in my blood. This company is my lifeline, my legacy. If Crane Hotels had gone to someone else . . ." He shook his head. "It's my worst nightmare."

His admission had left him feeling bare, ironic considering he was wearing zero articles of clothing. Merina gave his words room to linger, not speaking for a few moments.

"I used to see Crane Hotels as big and impersonal. Cold without personality. Like you."

"Ouch." He winced.

"I was wrong about you. About this hotel." Her lips pursed in humility as she glanced around the room. "You love this place the way I love the Van Heusen. It shows in the way you traded your life to live here. To oversee every part. To put yourself on the line and do whatever it took for CEO." She stroked his hair again. "You weren't going to let it go without a fight."

Just like she'd done for her hotel. Another thing they had in common.

She palmed his cheek. "And you're welcome."

He accepted another kiss and sank down onto the couch, comfortable with her on top of him.

"Was it all it was cracked up to be?" he asked as her hands wandered over his chest and down his torso.

"Sex with the CEO?" She palmed his erection and his mouth fell open. "Better than I imagined."

Like everything with her. Merina was better than *he'd* ever imagined. Better at handling his ex. Better at taking things in stride. Better at knowing what he needed— knowing when to forgive him.

Soon, her kisses turned hungry and his hands wandered to the space between her legs. Minutes after that, she was under him and he driving into her once again.

Her eyes on his, he lost himself in their amber depths, thanking her with more than just his words. With nothing to prove and nothing between them but a thin layer of latex, Reese took his time. Her orgasm came in gentle waves, her eyebrows pinching over her nose and her swollen mouth open and saying his name.

"Oh God, Reese. Yes." Eyes on his. "Yes, Reese. *Yes.*"

Because he liked hearing that, and seeing her come apart beneath him, he held on until he was fairly certain he'd given her two—maybe three—more, before letting himself go. When he let go, he pressed his mouth over hers and drank her in, even as he lost himself in her body, his mind a tapestry of pleasure.

* * *

Merina was chewing on the side of her finger, eyes on her computer, mind turning over the image on the screen. What she'd meant to do was peek at the article, close the website, then shrug it off as no big deal. For she was a strong, independent woman who was very much in charge of her faculties.

Instead, she was staring at an image of Reese that was seven or eight years old and feeling a sharp pain in the center of her chest. Like now, in the photo he was devastatingly attractive. He was bare-chested, possibly naked, and lying on a pile of stark white bedding. His grin was infectious and achingly happy, his eyes bright in the sunlight streaming in from behind him. Seeing it—knowing where it came from—was just plain heartbreaking.

Penelope Brand had texted her this morning and let her know "so that you're prepared" that Gwyneth Sutton Lerner had hopped onto Twitter the night before and posted the photo with Reese's infamous hashtag (thankfully, that particular part of his anatomy was not featured), as well as one of her own choosing: *#Loveofmylife*.

By lunch, the tweet had been deleted, and Penelope had guessed that Gwyneth was drunk when she posted it, or at the very least pissed off at Hayes for whatever reason and seeking revenge. But nothing on the Internet ever truly went away, even after the delete button was pushed.

It made Merina think back to Alex's retirement party when Gwyneth had scuttled over to Reese and Merina had wanted nothing more than to go pry them apart.

The *Spread* had snagged a snapshot of the tweet and splashed it onto their column. Penelope's phone call had also included some additional unpleasant news: the television show *Inside Edition* had called for an official comment, which Penelope had denied them. Which meant she expected the photo, paired with a *whooshing* sound effect, to be featured alongside Gwyneth's tweets tonight.

Understanding that this was yet another of Reese's conquests who had a thorn in her side—one who'd lobotomized her brain since tweeting an old intimate photo was the height of stupidity—Merina fully expected to continue with her day like nothing happened.

That was twenty minutes ago.

Initially, she did scoff and close the window, but working was impossible when she kept seeing that photo on the screen of her distracted mind. So she found it and opened it again in her phone. Then she opened it on her computer screen so she could see it bigger.

The part carving out a tiny piece of her soul was the expression on Reese's face. So light, happy, *carefree*. A good five minutes into staring at the smile lines bracketing his mouth—the mouth she'd kissed repeatedly—she finally put her finger on what was bothering her.

Reese had let someone into his heart, and that person had been Gwyneth. The woman he'd played off like she was no big deal, when clearly, the look on his face in this picture had BIG DEAL written all over it.

When she'd asked if Gwyneth had been the one responsible for him sleeping with all of Chicago, she'd been joking. Now she couldn't bring herself to laugh. The look on his face—that was a man in love. Which meant Gwyneth had meant something to him and had left him heartbroken.

At his parents' house, at his office when she'd taken him the framed article, Merina had thought she'd seen him open up. There had been a few moments of stark connection, where she could swear she'd seen in his eyes how much she'd come to mean to him.

Things had been so, so good. Reese coming home from

work, practically skipping because of his newfound position. Merina couldn't be anything less than happy for him, because she thought she'd understood. She thought she'd finally uncovered the man who had hidden from her—peeled back one of his final layers.

Gwyneth's photo of Reese proved Merina hadn't scratched the surface. Because she was obsessed, she went to the *Spread*'s blog (after swearing for months she wouldn't read that garbage) and read every word of what they reported. Including something that made her feel even worse about the current state of affairs.

As far as the Spread *can tell, this picture of Reese (sans rocket, boo-hoo!) was taken when he was at the ripe and sexy age of twenty-four. We had to dig through the archives, but our sleuths here uncovered a few early photos of this couple. It seems their four-year affair ended suddenly (even scandalously!) since Gwyneth was photographed with Hayes shortly after her and Reese's appearance at an art show in downtown Chicago. We reached out to Gwyneth Sutton Lerner as well as Reese Crane for comment but haven't heard back yet. We'll let you know as soon as we do!*

Four years.

Four.

Years.

It was the only thing Merina could focus on. She'd asked Reese how long he and Gwyneth had dated and he'd brushed it off with an evasive "a handful of months." It wasn't that she was upset he'd lied to her. It was *why* he'd lied to her.

Why hadn't he told her the truth? Why did he lie, play Gwyneth down? Was he trying to protect Merina from the truth...or worse? Trying to hide how much he still loved Gwyneth Sutton Lerner...

Her heart hit her throat and she swallowed around it, choking back the urge to burst into tears.

After all Merina and Reese been through together, he hadn't trusted her with the truth. After she'd put herself— her heart—on the line, he'd lied to her.

This had happened once before—with Corbin. Lorelei had insisted that Reese was not Corbin. In many cases, he wasn't. But that chickenshit move to dodge instead of manning up and telling her the truth had proven one thing.

Reese had kept his distance, while she'd been trying to erase it.

* * *

Today wasn't going smoothly. Pure adrenaline paired with excitement over his new position last week led to an overwhelming need to put his fist through a wall this week. Work was busy, which he enjoyed, but the level of stupidity he was currently wrangling bordered on criminal.

After handling a board of directors meeting without his father or Tag, Reese realized his biggest challenge with them would be keeping from hurling one of them down the elevator shaft. Which wasn't a good idea, though it would make him feel better.

Bobbie had called in sick, probably for the first time since she'd started working for him, so he'd left the phone messages unchecked. He wasn't retrieving them and sure as shit didn't have time to deal with a temp.

Penelope Brand had texted, then called, then texted again to say "check your e-mail"; all of this he'd registered while sitting across from Ingrid Belter. Ingrid was a powerful woman who held the keys to the city of Austin, where he was currently working with her to open two new hotels. And he wouldn't undermine her or their meeting to answer Penelope. Pen worked for him, not the other way around, and did a damn good job of panicking often and early.

Once Ingrid was on a plane back to Texas, Reese finished up what he could for the day, ignoring the belligerent red light blinking on Bobbie's desk. Even if he did know how to tap into voice mail, he was far too spent to go through dozens or hundreds—who knew how many of them Bobbie handled that he never saw?—of messages.

He climbed onto the elevator and by the time he hit the lobby, his phone gave an insistent ring. Penelope. *Again.* He should have remembered what curiosity did to the proverbial cat before he hit the ANSWER button.

"What?" he barked.

"I'm guessing you didn't check your e-mail or my text messages," Penelope said.

"Pen—"

"There's no time. Are you near a television? Your segment is up next."

"My—"

"*Inside Edition*," she said, then rattled off the channel.

"Mike," Reese said to the man at the front desk. He instructed him to pull up the channel on the lobby television. There was a small alcove of chairs in a corner by the TV, and Reese took one. He was still on the phone with Penelope, who was blathering about how she'd tried to reach him sooner to warn him.

Warn him about—?

A second later, his mind went blank.

Reese felt his shoulders go rigid as he saw a picture of himself—naked in Gwyneth's apartment bedroom—shortly after they'd started dating. He was bright-eyed and fresh-faced and may as well have had the word SUCKER written across his forehead.

"Young and in love Reese Crane, photographed by then girlfriend, Gwyneth Sutton Lerner, has recently taken over Crane Hotels," the news anchor said. She went on to question the timing of a tweeted (now deleted) photograph, guessing it was a desperate attempt by Gwyneth to win him back now that he'd landed the coveted position.

"Hard telling how the news has hit Reese's current wife, Merina, seen here leaving a coffee shop wearing an over-size pair of sunglasses…"

A photograph taken a few weeks ago, Reese remembered, and one they'd chuckled about one morning over the coffee in their own kitchen.

"Gwyneth did remove the photo from Twitter sometime this morning, but since then has tweeted the following message: 'I regret nothing, including the four years I spent with Reese Crane. #ReesesRocket, #Loveofmylife.'"

The reporter wrapped up by showing the photo of him for the *fourth* fucking time and mentioning there was no word of what Gwyneth's husband, Hayes Lerner, thought of his wife's revelation to the public at large.

Reese, numb, had forgotten the phone was to his ear until Penelope spoke.

"Not as bad as I thought," she said.

"Is that a joke?" he asked, voice flat. "I'm naked on national television."

"This is a small matter of spin. We'll say your desperate ex-girlfriend is having marital problems. I already briefed

Merina, so she's prepared for a possible run-in with the press. If you happen to run into a reporter, just remember to..." Penelope continued with her instructions.

Reese, in rigid monosyllabic replies, agreed to do as she suggested: smile and shrug it off.

Smile.

Yeah, right. Gwyneth's betrayal was thick and bitter, and the timing was abysmal.

He pressed END on the call, noticing Mike still standing behind him awkwardly, remote in hand. "Mr. Crane, did you want me to—"

"Turn it off," he said, managing to add, "Thanks."

Stiffly, he made his way to his car, mind on what he'd be dealing with tonight and the days to come, and not the least bit happy about it. By the time he pulled his Porsche into the garage and went inside, he was thirsty for scotch and more scotch.

CHAPTER 17

Not knowing what else to do, Merina had come home from the Van Heusen, laced up her athletic shoes, and gone for a jog. She'd wanted to pound something, may as well be the ground.

Fifteen minutes later, she gave up trying to run off her disappointment—both in herself and for trusting Reese, the dirty liar.

She'd slowed to a walk, holding her aching side while watching her shoes cut through the plush grass when she heard his voice.

"You look like you need a break." Reese was dressed in his suit from work, tie knotted at his neck. The article of clothing she couldn't wait to take off him had become the one she wanted to strangle him with.

"I'm more of a stationary bike kind of girl." She blew out a breath and walked to the cooler outside, getting herself a bottle of water. "At the gym at the Van Heusen."

"So why are you running?"

The back patio faced the lawn surrounded by trees, and she took a seat on a cushy chair beneath the awning, tugging her sagging ponytail free. He sat next to her.

"I thought it would calm me down," she answered truthfully. One of them may as well be honest. "Seeing that picture of you..." In the end, she couldn't lay herself open. She let her voice trail off.

Her eyes had adjusted to the dark, though there was enough ambient light—some from the gardens surrounding the house, most from the interior of the mansion—so that it wasn't pitch black.

Reese remained quiet. Evidently, he wasn't going to broach the subject if she didn't. Merina wasn't feeling as magnanimous.

"It was serious between you two," she said. "You and Gwyneth."

He stared into the distance for a minute before leaning his elbows on his knees.

"Four years," she said when he said nothing.

"Is there something you'd like to say, Merina?" It was a question he didn't want answered. She could tell by every tense line on his face. "I don't have the patience to let you poke me with a stick until I respond the way you'd like."

Okay. Fair enough.

"You were in love with her."

If she thought he looked angry before, it was nothing compared to how he looked now. It made her heart sink to her stomach. If ever there was a time she didn't want to be right, it was now and about Gwyneth. Merina had believed he'd confided in her the night at his father's house when she'd asked about his past, but he'd been hiding from her the whole time.

"Why did you let me believe she was just a girl you dated for a *handful of months*?" She was angry now, the questions coming at a rapid-fire pace. "Did she live here with you? Is that why you never came back to the mansion? Did she sleep with you in the bedroom you refuse to talk about?" She pointed to the room where sliding patio doors overlooked the pool.

"I see that you're under the assumption we're talking about this." Reese stood from the chair, scraping the legs on the concrete as he did. She didn't like when the cold crept in, when his shutters slammed down. When he refused to deal with messy feelings, namely hers.

"Why won't you tell me the truth? What is it you're so desperate to hide?" She stood also, fists curling at her sides. She'd kept her cool in an effort to do as Penelope had suggested since this was supposed to be "rolling off her back." Well, fuck that. *Gwyneth* wasn't rolling off her back.

"I'm not hiding anything from you. I just don't want to talk about it." His tone was so controlled. Did he *not* regret lying to her?

"Why don't you trust me? I'm sleeping with you for God's sake…" Then she laughed, a humorless sound, and added, "Not that sex means anything to you."

His expression went from angry to borderline hurt.

"Silly me to have thought things changed since the night at your father's. Since the night in your office. Since—"

"I'm broken, Merina! Okay? Is that what you want to hear?" Reese was shouting but the hurt still brimmed in his dark blue eyes.

It took her a moment to digest those words. The truest words he'd ever said.

"Yes. I do want to hear it. I want to know."

"You want to know," he repeated with a grunt. "There is a reason I had to draw up a contract to force someone to marry me for show. I'm not equipped to do it for real."

She blinked, half stunned he admitted as much and half disappointed he couldn't see how wrong he was. Couldn't he see what they had was so much more than a "contract"?

"That's not true—" she started.

"It's true," he clipped. "After Gwyneth, I vowed never to stay at this house. She made me look like a grade A jackass. Humiliated me in front of my father, my coworkers, and anyone who suspected she'd dropped me for Hayes. It's not an easy thing to recover from."

"Reese—"

"Have you forgotten the purpose of that ring being on your hand?" He stalked over to her and captured her wrist. Her blood iced at his frigid tone.

"The deal: My being appointed to CEO in exchange for not tearing your family's hotel to the studs. It never included more."

But they'd been more, at least to her they had.

"Do you know what I told your father at the cookout?"

She didn't. Reese never told her. She didn't like the idea of him telling her now when he was this upset.

I'm broken.

She didn't want him to be broken.

You can't fix him. That sensible voice in her head kept her quiet. She wouldn't take on Reese as a project.

"I told Mark I was giving you control of the Van Heusen as a surprise," he said. "That's what he asked me at the cookout. If I was planning on continuing the remodel, or if I'd give you control of the hotel."

"That took some nerve," she mumbled, not liking that her father hadn't come to her.

"The papers are ready," Reese said. "It's a done deal once you sign."

"I thought…the Van Heusen was part of the divorce settlement…"

"Surprise."

But this wasn't a playful, celebratory surprise. This was him shoving her away.

"Hey." She tugged his tie, looking up at his face. Her Reese was under that rigid exterior. *Somewhere.* "Talk to me."

"There's nothing else to say."

"There is." She hadn't told him about Corbin, and in a way that made her as guilty as Reese. She'd been holding back, protecting herself. "I had an ex-boyfriend who… well, he lived with me in my parents' house."

Reese's mouth compressed, looking unhappy. About her living with a guy before him or because she was continuing this discussion, it was hard to say.

"I told myself I loved him, and I guess in a way I did. He took advantage of me. He used me. Emptied my bank account and left with my money."

Eyes downcast, he took her hand. "I can replace the cash."

"You could." This was his way of empathizing, but couldn't he see he was more to her than a means to an end? "I don't care about the cash. I did, but I don't now. He made off with my pride, and that's hard to find once you've lost it. I understand what Gwyneth put you through." She gave his hand a squeeze. "I've been there."

"Why do people do that?" His cheeks tightened, lip curling in disgust. He dropped her hand. "Pretend they understand what you're going through. Like when someone dies."

Like his mother? Her heart crushed.

"You don't know what it was like, Merina. You aren't a man who strived to be great and had a setback that could cost him his destiny."

"Excuse me?" She almost laughed. "You *took* my destiny!"

"I bought it. And now you have it back. You're whole."

And he was an idiot.

"You know why no one 'understands' you, Crane? Because you don't bother sharing. If you opened your mouth to do something other than get me off, we might have the occasional conversation and understand each other!" She was shouting now, fists at her sides. "Your pain doesn't outweigh mine because you can't talk about it."

"Fine. You want to talk? You want to devolve what we have into messy relationship territory? I'll talk." Reese said, his voice raised again. "I was in love with her, okay? I found out she was fucking my best friend, and for the second time in my life, my thoughts bordered on suicidal. The only time I ever felt that way was when my mother died. I thought I'd outgrown it, yet here I was in a big house I owned, the weight of a future company on my shoulders. In an instant"—he leaned in, his fingers pressed together to make his point—"I was fifteen again. Unsure. Scared. *Desperate*."

Merina's stomach flipped. She closed her eyes for a moment, trying to block out the pain in his words.

"I vowed never to set foot in this house again. Every

room reminded me of Gwyneth. I made plans to build a life with her and she..." A muscle in his jaw flickered and Merina's heart sank. He'd planned a life with Gwyneth. Here. In this house. "I was willing to risk my future, the company I am now running, to pander to love."

Merina had fallen in love with him. Completely, no take-backs. What a shitty time to have that revelation.

It hurt to hear he loved Gwyneth, but it hurt more to hear him slot love into the category of "inconvenient." Reese equated love with being weak. Who needed love now that he had his precious company?

"That future existed only in my imagination," Reese continued, his voice eerily calm.

"What about your new future? You have a chance at something here... *We* have a chance to build on what we've started."

"No, Merina." Those two words were so final. "Seeing my photo splashed on television was more than inconvenient and embarrassing. It was a reminder of a very important decision I made. The reason I dated random women and broke it off after one date for the last five years was because I never want to feel like that again. That's why our arrangement is and always was going to be temporary."

It was a low blow. One she felt in her heart. Because she was the moron who went ahead and fell for him while they were under "contract."

"Women are temporary. Gwyneth was temporary. Those one-night stands? Each one as forgettable as the last." He took a step away from her as if illustrating his point.

"Reese—"

"And so are we."

Her face went cold. A part of her saw what he was doing and hated him for it. But a larger part loved him and hated to see how much he was hurting. That part of her spoke next.

"Goddammit, Reese, don't do this." She wanted to touch him and if she thought he'd allow it, she would have. As close as she thought they had become, she now saw she didn't know his heart at all. "You can't tell me out of all the times we slept together, you never once wondered if we might work out. You can't tell me you never thought 'what if?' You can't...because I was there, Reese. I was..."

She had to stop talking when a lump seized her throat. And that lump came because her husband's face hadn't changed. His brows didn't bow in sympathy and he didn't come a single step closer to her. His navy eyes were dark and emotionless.

Which meant she was wrong.

He'd never considered them working out. He'd never asked "what if?" She loved him and yet he couldn't see them as more than an arrangement.

She was another in a long line. Soon to be forgotten.

"I'm getting a shower." His face was studiously flat. "I'll sleep in the guest bedroom so you don't have to worry about me bothering you."

He went inside and she watched him go. Everything had escalated so quickly. Or maybe it hadn't. Maybe this had been building since the night she laid eyes on Gwyneth at Alex's retirement party. That should have been her clue that Reese couldn't handle a relationship. She'd patted herself on the back for handling his ex like a pro, and *he* hadn't handled it at all.

Every part of her wanted to run after him now and finish

this fight, but instead she rooted her feet to the ground and let him go.

She'd risked too much tonight. If he didn't know how she felt after that tirade, then he was a bigger idiot than she was. He may be protecting himself, but she needed to protect herself as well.

She'd been taken advantage of once before and as a result had become stronger. She could deal with this. Even though her stupid heart had the worst taste in men, she would survive this. She'd come out stronger.

Eventually.

* * *

Nothing was working.

Reese dropped his pen and leaned back in his chair, face to his hands. The massive headache behind his eyes had cropped up before lunch, and nothing he'd done to stave it off had helped. Not the ten minutes he laid down on his couch and tried to rest his eyes, not the painkillers he swallowed, and not trying to ignore it by getting back to work.

In the week that had passed since the fight with Merina, work hadn't been the same. The exhilaration of CEO he'd felt initially had dulled. Now he just felt busy.

He pulled a hand down his face. God. He felt like shit for the things he'd said to her. The way he'd walked away. She stood there on his back patio her vulnerability on display when she asked him to give "them" a shot. Them as in him and Merina. The "we" he'd recognized when she'd dropped off the frame wasn't in his imagination.

But it wasn't the right thing to do. In a rare moment of

word vomit, he'd told her the truth. He was broken. Merina should be with someone who suited her, and while they were compatible as hell in bed, out of it . . . they weren't.

She was passion and vibrance and truth, and he was fear and cages and avoidance. At least when it came to relationships. She needed someone to bloom with—to thrive.

He wasn't that guy.

He'd slept in the guest bedroom every night since the argument and while he didn't care what the house staff thought about having to make up two different beds in the morning, he *did* care that Merina hadn't chased him down. A big part of him expected her to demand he talk about things. When she didn't, he figured she'd given up, thereby giving him what he asked for. Saving herself and leaving him to himself.

Only today, right now, that wasn't what he fucking wanted. She gave him space and he, for a change, wanted none. The night they'd argued, the next night, and every night after, Merina's bedroom door remained closed. She remained behind it.

This morning, outside her bedroom door he hesitated, hand poised to knock, but in the end walked away. The things he'd told her weren't nice, but they were true. If they were always meant to be temporary, he may as well let her begin disconnecting now. He'd told her so much truth, he was sick from it. He and Merina had grown closer than he'd anticipated. If he let himself think for a second "what if" . . . well. He wouldn't go there with her.

He couldn't.

He blew out a breath now, his head still aching. No woman made him feel the way Merina Van Heusen did.

Merina Crane, his mind corrected.

Right. His wife.

The outside world wasn't privy to their marital squabble, however. No, for the world they'd become actors. Merina played the part and so did he. It was the way he'd imagined things would be the day she'd signed the premarital agreement, but after all they'd been through, the distance felt wrong.

The day after the argument, Penelope had called an emergency meeting at Crane Hotel. Merina showed up, looking fresh and beautiful, and Reese sat there with a mouthful of apologies he'd had to swallow down. For the sake of business. For the sake of the future.

Pen made it clear them being seen together was paramount. *"You can't let Gwyneth get any more mileage out of this. Keep doing what you're doing. Go places together. Let people see you kissing, holding hands, smiling."*

Merina accepted the challenge gracefully. Head up, with a curt nod, her viciously dominant spirit in charge. She'd done a convincing job pretending to like him, which he assumed she didn't. How could she after what he'd said to her?

He made it a point to drop her off and pick her up at work, placing a kiss on her lips for the waiting paparazzi. The *Spread* was milking Gwyneth's tweet. Pen had sent him a text with a link to an article featuring him and Merina at dinner yesterday. In the photo, Merina was leaning on the table, breasts on display, tattoo bare, smiling at him.

He'd sat with his arm around her as she told him about her day and toyed with the knot of his tie. Her act was so genuine, he thought he was off the hook. He'd taken her hand, hell-bent on dragging her to the single bathroom to devour her, but then she'd mumbled under her breath, "Reporter at the bar."

That's when he'd realized it was all for show. The woman who had warmly touched him and showed off the tattoo she'd previously hidden was simply enduring him until they could call it quits.

It was frustrating and irritating...and exactly what she needed to do.

He was all for pretending when he was part of the game, but the game had changed. She'd closed off the part of her he'd grown used to. Not just the sex part. The genuine Merina part. Now he was left with...he didn't know. Some cardboard version of her.

The wife he'd spent the last week with was not the same woman who, drenched, had carried a doorknob into his office and called him a suited sewer rat. He smiled at the memory, but then his smile faded as pain lanced his chest. He missed her.

And had no idea how to fix it.

After their explosive argument, he assumed Merina felt something for him that was strictly unadvised. He'd thought for a terrifying minute that she'd fallen for him... or was about to. Fear hit him like a safe dropped from the top of a building. Being responsible for her heart...he couldn't. He'd fail. Miserably and completely. Even thinking of her vulnerability in his hands now made his chest constrict.

But things hadn't worked out that way after all. Merina soldiered on, respecting his boundaries. He would have thought he'd be thrilled when she stopped hassling him about his "feelings."

In general, he didn't like to share. He didn't want to talk

about things. He was better living in the present. Step 1, Step 2, Step 3...and on and on until the goal was reached. Along the way, Merina pulled information out of him. No. He'd offered. He'd wanted her to know about him. She was in his life, in his house...

In my heart.

She had a way of making him less mechanical and more open. Which was one of the reasons he asked her to do this with him in the first place. She was great with the press, with people in general. If anyone would believe the cold heart of the playboy had been won, Merina could convince them.

So either he was a great actor, or she was really convincing, or...

Or nothing.

He sure as fuck wasn't going there.

There was a light tap at the door, followed by Bobbie's voice. "Mr. Crane."

His skull pulsed and he closed his eyes against in pain. He'd asked his assistant not to use the intercom given that his brains kept trying to bust out of his cranium.

She poked her head through a crack in the door. "Did you need a change of clothing for tonight? You're due at the Van Heusen in an hour, and I wasn't sure if you're planning on going home first."

An hour? This day had vanished. He looked over the papers spread on his desk and the many pink notes from Bobbie with phone calls he'd yet to return.

"Uh, no. I'm...I'll clean up here and head straight over."

"Very well, sir." Bobbie nodded, then pulled the door shut.

Dread covered him like a heavy blanket.

Merina's parents were celebrating their anniversary at the Van Heusen hotel.

"You have to be there," Penelope had told him when he mentioned he was going to skip it. He'd thought it best to let Merina go alone and tell everyone he was at a work meeting. Faking for the press was one thing, but her family...

He wasn't that good of an actor.

When he'd argued with Penelope, she'd again insisted he go. "You're her husband. This is her parents' anniversary. It's a no-miss, Reese."

She was right, of course. He was tired of the women in his life being right.

Reese shut down his computer, the pressure behind his eyes making his teeth ache. In an hour he'd be standing in the Van Heusen's ballroom with Merina's parents. Two people who were in love and had been for years.

Reese hadn't told Merina the whole truth of what he and Mark had shared at that cookout. Yes, Mark had asked about the hotel and Reese's plans, saying, "Merina loves it so very much," but he'd also asked Reese not to hurt her.

"I'm not sure what's going on with the two of you," Mark had said, "but you should know my daughter has a tenderness about her that has been taken advantage of before. Don't hurt her, Reese."

Reese wasn't planning on hurting her, but he could see the potential there. Hurting her was staying with her. Letting her believe in him, expecting him to change and be the man she needed. His telling her she was temporary was to honor her father's request.

So tonight. He'd do this for her. He'd endure a family

gathering, one guaranteed to remind him of his own fractured family—of his mother's loss—and he'd make sure Mark and Jolie saw that no matter what, Merina's wholeness was his priority.

But as his heart pounded fast behind his ribs, he feared giving her what she needed would cost him what he needed.

Her.

CHAPTER 18

CITY lights moved outside the tinted windows on the quiet ride back from her parents' anniversary party. The air in the backseat of the town car was thick and restrictive. The interior as dark as the deep furrow in Reese's brow.

Merina was exhausted from an evening spent putting on a show for her parents' guests. Forced to look happy and in love—only one of which was true. Who knew she could be miserable and in love? That was a first.

Her parents danced, toasted, and regaled the crowd with a retelling of their engagement. State Street, the ice skating rink, her father on bended knee in freshly fallen snow. It was a story she'd heard a hundred times and one that always made her heart full. Tonight, it made her chest feel like it was filled with cement, the weight of it sagging her shoulders. Could have been Reese's reaction. She'd watched him while her parents spoke. The way his lips were rigid when he forced a smile. The way he white-knuckled his scotch glass. How stiffly he'd held her when he danced with her out of obligation.

"All in all not a bad night," she lied, picking a speck of lint from her skirt. Someone had to break the suffocating silence.

Reese emitted a noncommittal grunt.

This week had been chipping away at her soul. Not because she'd had to pretend to want to touch him, talk to him, and spend time with him for the press's sake. The hideous truth was that she *wanted* to touch him, talk to him, and spend time with him. Even after he'd made it clear that he didn't want her.

Resisting him had been harder than she'd imagined. That same ache of loneliness when she'd first moved in with him attacked again. Only now she was lonely *for* him.

Sleeping in separate bedrooms was one of the hardest adjustments of her life. She'd grown used to that closeness, his warmth and hardness at her back. She'd come to miss him teasing her about using his coffee mug in the morning. Now he was gone by the time she got up.

Reese put his hand to his head and massaged his temple. It wasn't the first time he'd done it tonight.

"Still not feeling well?" she asked. The more she tried not to care, the more she was reminded she did.

"It's the same headache I've had for days." He adjusted his tie—purple and paired with a dark gray suit and pale gray shirt. His face was trimmed close, his hair in its usual state of perfection. He smelled good, looked great, and knowing she wasn't free to touch him in private made her heart squeeze painfully.

No doubt her parents' invitation at the end of the

evening hadn't helped his aching head. Hell, Merina felt a migraine of her own brewing the moment her father opened his mouth.

"Merina is a very important part of our love story," Mark said. *"And you, Reese, are now an important part of hers."*

Oh God. Oh no. Her father was a sap, and he was about to make a huge mistake.

"Dad."

But he kept talking. Kept digging.

"This year, we want to include you two in our tradition."

She didn't dare look up at Reese, who stood stock-still and stone silent next to her.

Jolie leaned over and kissed Merina's cheek. "Wait until you've been together twenty-five years and have a daughter of your own to embarrass."

They'd invited Reese and Merina to the ice rink on State Street in December. It was her parent's annual tradition, though now they sipped hot cocoa instead of lacing up their skates.

She and Reese had endured the invitation as graciously as two people who knew they would be divorced by then could. Shortly after, they made their escape from the Van Heusen ballroom where a town car, complete with driver, waited.

Now they rode in the backseat, ensconced in silence. Someone needed to address what had happened tonight. May as well be her.

"They genuinely like you, you know." Not what she'd meant to say, but it was true. He should know that her parents weren't putting on a show. "We had a rough start but you won them over."

Reese shifted in his seat, mouth a grim line as he stared straight ahead.

"Can you at least talk to me?" she whispered.

He faced her, handsome and hard, and she couldn't bear it any longer. She'd cracked through this façade once before. She could do it again.

"Reese. Let's—"

"We're here," Reese said as the car pulled into the driveway of their Lake Shore Drive mansion.

So they were. She looked out the window at the home she'd soon be leaving.

"Driver," Reese said. "I'll need to go straight to the Crane Hotel."

"Very well, sir," the man said, eyes dashing to the rearview mirror.

"Reese—" But once again he cut her off.

"Darling, I'll be late," he said, his voice as flat as his expression. As empty as his heart.

There was no getting him back. The only thing she could do now was move on.

"Take your time," she snapped, then pushed her way out of the town car and went inside. Alone.

* * *

Merina hadn't been able to sleep that night, which was nothing new. What was new was the combination of being angry and worried about Reese—because he wasn't "late" as he'd said he'd be.

He never came home.

If they were in a real marriage, he'd owe her an explanation. At the very least a phone call from atop the Crane

Hotel where her husband had gone to brood. She refused to chase him.

Or so she thought.

By Monday morning she found herself outside of the Crane, thinking about how this morning was vastly different from the ones before it. Before Reese Crane filled her thoughts. Before she loved him. The sight of his big, stupid hotel looming overhead made her want to grab a handful of rocks and vandalize it. Shatter all that perfect, pretty glass.

Perfection was a lie.

Inside the pristine shining interior of the Crane, she bypassed the lobby and punched the elevator button. She rode to the top floor, arms folded, eyes staring unseeing as the doors opened and closed again, letting various guests on and off.

Finally she arrived at the top floor. Bobbie was at her desk, guarding the double doors of Crane's office as usual.

"Is he in there?" Merina asked as she walked out of the elevator.

"He's in his suite, but—"

Merina held up a hand. Part of her flooded with relief that he was here and safe.

Bobbie called after her, offering to phone Reese's room, but Merina refused. He'd ignored her for the entire weekend. She wouldn't be ignored any longer.

Real marriage or not, she deserved to know why he was hiding.

Leaving the office behind, she stepped into a corridor that opened to the only suite on this floor. She'd never been inside but had known it was here. The idea of what he'd spent his nights doing before he and Merina were "together" and who he'd spent them with made her stomach burn.

A pair of double doors with gold handles split the corridor in half. No doubt locked, but maybe she'd get lucky.

The square button on the handle depressed as her thumb brushed it. She jerked away when the door swung inward. Then she froze, her heart thundering and her stomach sinking. A lithe redhead came out, eyes and nose red, tears streaking her makeup.

Gwyneth.

Not a single encouraging thought ran through her mind at the sight of Reese's ex-girlfriend leaving his private suite. Especially when Reese came into focus over Gwyneth's shoulder, wearing nothing but boxers and tugging a T-shirt over his head.

No, no, no.

The look on his face when he saw Merina was placid acceptance. Not shock, not anger. His hands were resting on his hips as if challenging her to walk in and give him hell.

Gwyneth muttered, "Excuse me," but Merina barely registered her slipping out. At the threshold of Reese's room, she stood as he waited inside, their eyes locked in challenge.

Behind him, his bedsheets were tangled. White sheets like in the photograph Gwyneth had shared on Twitter.

Don't go there.

Merina needed to leave. As soon as she was able to tear her eyes off him and turn on her heel, she'd march out of the hotel. Just as soon as her brain made sense of the scene she'd walked into. Right now, nothing was computing.

Before she could, he spoke, his tone even. His words weren't even all that surprising.

"I want a divorce."

Instead of turning, she rushed into the room, unsure what she'd do when she reached him. When her hand came up to slap his face, he caught her wrist.

"You...chickenshit!" Tears flooded her eyes, and then she crumbled. Giving in to the feelings of hope and devastation she'd been trying to pretend hadn't existed for the last week plus.

She tugged her arm but he held fast.

"Merina."

"Fucking idiot!" she managed through a hot stream of tears. He said her name again and she stopped struggling.

"A reporter from the *Spread* somehow gained access to your parents' party. They ran a post with a photo of us standing apart, speculating that we weren't getting along." His hold loosened, but he didn't let her go. "It would be unwise not to use this as momentum. The announcement of a divorce would be a logical next step."

Logical. Why did that word hurt more than the others?

"So this is out of convenience?" Or had he sabotaged what they had, burned it right to the ground? That theme kept making an appearance in her life.

"Ironic how the press ended up being our ally," he said.

He was too calm. Too controlled.

"Gwyneth looked upset." Mimicking his cold tone, Merina shook her arm from his grip. He ran a hand through his hair, perfectly disheveled. There was a time not so long ago she'd made a mess of his hair. Now the only mess was the one he'd made of her.

"She was upset," he said. He snatched a pair of jeans lying across the bed and slid into them. "What are you doing here?" He zipped up, then fastened his belt.

Sabotaging. Most definitely. He wanted her to believe he and Gwyneth had slept together but Merina wasn't that stupid. He was pushing her away. Drawing those steel shutters down tight and cowering behind them.

He was broken, all right. But she wasn't going to let him sit here in pieces while she had to go out into the world stitched together.

"You never came home," she pointed out.

"No." He tucked his hands into his pockets and just... stood there.

"Are you seriously not going to explain this?" She gestured around the room, taking in the state of it for the first time. Messy. Reese wasn't messy. There was a room service tray pushed off to the side, the remains of a steak on a plate. One plate. More evidence he'd spent the evening alone. There were dirty coffee mugs littering his desk and his wrinkled suit was a draped over a chair. "What's going on with you?"

"Don't."

She didn't heed his advice. If he was pushing her, then she would push him back. It was risky, but she'd bet the part he was hiding was the part of him that felt something for her.

Was it possible she could get through one final time? *For good?*

She came close, breasts brushing his T-shirt-covered chest. He seemed to will himself to stand still instead of run the other direction.

"You look like shit," she said, truly seeing him for the first time. He didn't look sexily rumpled from rolling around in bed with his ex. He looked exhausted. Spent. Like he hadn't slept in two nights. His normally perfect scruff bordered on scraggly.

"I'm fine."

"No." She shook her head slowly. "You're not." But she could see, even in his worn-out state, that he'd made a decision and the decision was final. He was backing out of their marriage sooner rather than later. He was done. "You're quitting. Despite what you feel. Despite what you *know*."

"It's better we do this now before your parents make any further holiday plans."

Crack!

He hadn't seen it coming, so when her hand finally connected with a sharp slap to his cheek, he looked stunned, then furious. He lashed both her wrists with his hands and yanked her against his body.

"Leave before I have you thrown out." His lip curled, but the anger in his eyes wasn't all anger. There was something else in there. Heat and loss and *want*.

"I love you, you idiot," she said, tears welling as she saw fear etch into Reese's tired face. Fear so prevalent, she could practically taste it.

"Gwyneth and Hayes are getting a divorce," he said.

Merina blinked once. Then twice. Last thing in the world she expected him to say. "What?"

"She came to see if I'd take her back."

Merina couldn't feel her face. Or her limbs. It was like her soul had snapped free and was floating overhead.

"What did you tell her?" she whispered.

"I said 'fuck you.'"

"Good answer."

Reese hadn't let her go, and his eyes hadn't left hers. She wanted to ask why he was giving up on them. Why he was determined to go through with the divorce. Why he'd ignored her admission and changed the subject. But even as she thought those questions, she could guess his answers.

He'd say his new position as CEO was demanding. That he didn't have time for a relationship. That he'd vowed years ago never to get hurt again. Or maybe he'd go the "contract" route and remind her again that she was temporary.

In other words, he was going to lie.

"Do you want me to go?" She was as afraid of his answer as she was not to ask. If they were ending things, she wasn't going to leave without first showing him what he was losing.

"No." The truth. Finally. "I just want you."

"Then have me."

* * *

Reese rerouted Merina's hands to the back of his neck. She put her fingers in his hair and gazed up at him with so much want and hope that his heart threatened to cave in.

He'd tried. God help him, he'd tried to get her to think something had happened between him and Gwyneth. Selfishly, he wanted Merina to leave angry and make things easier for him to end. But where she was concerned, he was weak. Her invitation that he could have her was far too tempting to pass up.

One last time.

Anticipation made his arms shake as he lowered his mouth to hers. Merina tasted like heaven. He'd been missing her taste for far too long. When he saw her standing at the door of his suite, he couldn't remember ever being devastated and glad to see someone at the same time.

Gwyneth had come to his suite earlier and he had just stumbled from the bathroom after about an hour of sleep last night. At first, he thought he was hallucinating. Then he wondered if *she* was. What she was asking was certifiable. He'd never in a million years take her back. He couldn't believe she'd come here to ask. Even if he hadn't been second place to Hayes all those years ago, it was too much to ask. Gwyneth tearfully shared that Hayes was cheating on her, which served her right. She wanted to know if Reese had seen her tweeted photo, and then she let him know she meant the "love of her life" thing.

"Yes, I did," was his response, followed by that colorful FU he'd told Merina about.

That interaction had left him pissed and Gwyneth in tears. Seeing Merina had hit him like a blast of cool air on overheated skin. He missed her. Two damn days apart had left him lonely and lost.

Hadn't he put her through enough loops on this marital roller coaster? The divorce papers were drawn up. They sat on the desk behind Merina, but now that Merina was in his arms, he wasn't inclined to point them out.

Now that he was kissing her, he couldn't stop. She loved him. Even after he'd lied. And left. After she'd seen Gwyneth leave his suite. Could he do nothing to deter her?

A million excuses tumbled through his head but not a single one left his mouth. There was no way he'd deny them this moment. No way he'd let her leave without taking her in every way possible.

Scent.

Touch.

Smell.

He lifted her shirt over her head. Beneath his T-shirt,

she explored his torso with her hands, showing no signs of hurry. He grabbed his shirt by the neck and pulled it off, adding it to a pile of clothes in the corner. Life had been hell without her. If forty-eight hours had reduced him to a pitiful slob who couldn't say no, what would the next forty-eight hours bring? Or forty-eight *days*?

He wouldn't think about that either. He buried those fears the same way he buried his hands in her hair, slanting his mouth over hers and taking what he needed. But he wouldn't rush. He refused to rush.

Slowly, intentionally, his hands went to work on the clasp of her bra.

Then lower, to the zipper at the side of her skirt.

Panties were peeled down her legs, his lips following as he placed kisses on her thighs, the insides of her knees. High heels were slipped off and kisses delivered to her ankles. To the arch of one foot.

Once Merina was nude, she started on him. Smoothing her hands over his chest, cupping his manhood over his jeans and giving him a gentle squeeze. She went to work on the fly, the zipper, pulled the denim down his legs. When her hand wrapped around his cock, Reese's mind blanked.

No woman could replace her, and he hated that he had to let her go. But he didn't dwell in that unpleasant future.

Not when she kissed him deeply and commanded, "Take these off."

He stripped off his clothes, but when her hands came to his chest to shove him onto the bed, he stopped her. With a shake of his head, he lifted her into his arms and placed her on the blankets gently. So delicately. She never took her eyes off his.

He started at her tattoo, kissing the flames, and then moving his mouth between her breasts. One irresistible kiss to each peach-pink nipple, he ran a hand down her ribs, over her hip, and lifted one leg.

"So perfect," he mumbled against the silken skin of her stomach.

"I want it hard," she said.

"You'll get it slow." He lifted his head to make sure she saw he was serious.

Her head moved back and forth into a slight shake. "Reese."

It was a plea. A plea for him to take her at a feverishly fast pace and give them the release she was begging for. If this was his last time with her, he refused to let her leave without knowing—on some level—what she'd come to mean to him over these last few months.

"You owe me, Crane."

"What happened to 'Reese'?" he grunted when she gripped his erection.

The expression on her face melted into one of sadness. *What did happen to him?* it seemed to ask.

Fuck if he knew.

Rather than answer that unspoken question, he gripped one of her hips and slid in to the hilt. The moment he lost himself in the heat of her, in the sounds she made in his ear, time stopped.

His eyes rolled back, his lids closing.

His mind splintered. His chest cracked open.

There was only her.

Only him.

Only *them*.

"We're not fucking," she said.

"No." He palmed her jaw, making sure she saw him, truly saw him. "I'm making love to my wife."

He parted her legs wider, thrusting once, twice. When he plunged deep again, tears leaked down her cheeks. He raised a thumb to her face and wiped the wetness away.

She licked her lips, and voice thick with emotion, she flayed him with, "I love you, Reese."

He couldn't say it.

He *wouldn't* say it.

His next thrust was one long, wet slide, paired with his lips over his. She kissed him back. Against every last bit of his own advice, and in his private suite at the top of the Crane Hotel, Reese made love to his wife.

The woman he loved.

CHAPTER 19

All set." Lorelei slid the divorce agreement across her desk. "Since you already have the Van Heusen squared away, this is pretty straightforward. There's really nothing else do to but sign it."

There wasn't. Merina had already moved her things out of the mansion. She did so tearfully, not caring that Magda and the come-and-go staff saw her wearing sweats, bawling as she packed up her things.

Almost four weeks ago, in Reese's private suite, he'd made love to her. She let him, unable to stop herself from telling him she loved him.

Twice.

Immediately after, he'd led her into the shower. Silently, they stood in the steam, Reese soaping her body as she shivered, feeling everything too much. He didn't confess that he loved her, which she assumed meant he didn't. He'd done it for her. He'd given her one last hit of

Reese Crane before he asked her to say good-bye to him permanently.

"Take the divorce papers with you when you go," he'd said, scrubbing her back with a washcloth as she stood in the water. "The sooner we wrap up loose ends, the easier the transition will be."

She still didn't know if he meant for her, him, or the press.

She hadn't seen him since.

There was no reason to. She didn't live in the mansion any longer, and there was no reason to go to the hotel. Lore was right. The Van Heusen was squared away, so there wasn't anything left to do but sign on the bottom line.

Lorelei handed her a pen.

"It's been a month, Mer," she said. "Put yourself out of your misery and move on."

According to the *Spread,* Reese had. They posted a photo of him and Penelope having lunch and reported that the blonde had "fallen hard for her sexy employer."

Merina didn't think it was true, but it made her feel a little better to imagine it was. Hating him was easier. After she'd slapped him, she should've turned and walked out.

Then she wouldn't have dangling "I love yous" to contend with.

"Mer."

"I know." Merina tried to smile, but the reflected pain in her best friend's eyes was so prevalent, tears welled in her own. Crying hadn't solved a damn thing, so Merina accepted the pen and scrawled her name next to Reese's.

"He never called or texted. Not even to see if I'd signed yet," Merina said numbly.

"I'm sorry."

"So am I."

Everything they'd had, gone with the stroke of a pen.

"I'll drop these off for you," Lorelei called as Merina left.

Merina didn't respond. She walked out of Lore's office and headed straight back to the Van Heusen.

* * *

The rustling of plastic sounded in the room and Reese cracked his eyes open. Sunlight pierced his retinas, so he slammed them shut again.

"No housekeeping," he grumbled, unsure why the maid was here. He'd instructed her to come by once a week, and he remembered before he broke the seal on a bottle of sixty-year-old scotch last night that he'd hung the DO NOT DISTURB sign.

The numbers on the clock blurred, focused, then blurred again: 11:43. He couldn't remember the last time he's slept past eight. Well, whatever. He was due a sick day, probably had a hundred of them in queue. Hungover counted as sick. And anyway he was in charge.

He turned his face into the pillow, his skull aching like someone had split it with an axe. Today's hangover wasn't something he felt like dealing with. Neither was yesterday's. Or the one he'd had the day before. They'd become his new routine.

He heard more rustling, but rather than deal with it, he pulled another pillow over his head. If she wanted to take the trash out so damn badly, *fine*.

* * *

The next time he opened his eyes, it was to the patter of rain on the windows. The room was dimmer, so that was a plus.

His head still hurt when he opened his eyes, so it would make sense not much time had passed. Through a glass of water—where had that come from?—he made out the wavy numbers on the clock. The first number was a three. In the afternoon, he presumed.

Since his tongue was glued to the roof of his mouth, he pushed up on one elbow and reached for the glass. Two aspirin sat next to the water, Bobbie's doing no doubt. He took them both, drank the water, then closed his eyes again to sleep hopefully another four or five hours. Then he could climb out of bed, order a pizza, and start drinking.

But before he could sink into sleep, the sound of his cell phone pierced the air. A purring ringer he'd turned off three days ago. He reached blindly for the phone and silenced it. Phone calls were the one thing he refused to let interrupt him. If the damn thing started ringing, it would never stop. He didn't feel like dealing with anything.

Not people.

Not work.

None of it.

He hadn't shown up for a single meeting, had delegated most busy work, and Bobbie was handling his e-mails. If the board tried to shit-can him, Reese would deal with it then. Right now only one thing mattered. Getting through the worst heartbreak of his life and coming out the other side.

There had to be another side.

God help him, there had to be.

* * *

The smell of coffee permeated the air, and this time, his eyes sprang open. Okay, coffee was going too far. Even for Bobbie. Evening time was for drinking. With a groan, he pushed up to sitting and scrubbed his face with his hands. He was disoriented and thirsty, but at least his headache was gone.

Eight p.m. He'd made it through another day.

Cell phone in hand, he squinted at the screen, fumbling through the menu to make sure the ringer was off.

"Click the button on the side," a woman's voice cut into the air.

"Thanks." He flipped it with his thumb and the screen showed it was on mute.

Wait. That voice wasn't Bobbie or the maid. He turned his head to find a slim redhead standing at the window, arms crossed over a pale pink suit.

"You missed the board of directors meeting today," Gwyneth said, taking a few steps toward the bed. When she reached his side, she sat on the edge of the mattress. "I told them you had the flu." Her nose wrinkled. "You smell awful. When is the last time you showered?"

"I don't know. What's today?"

She gave him a small smile.

"What are you doing here?" After she'd begged him back post-Twitterpocalypse and he had dropped the F-bomb and made her cry, he'd been certain he'd never see her again.

"Bobbie called me. She couldn't reach Tag or Alex," she said.

"Remind me to fire her." He slipped a second pillow behind his back and shoved a hand through his hair. "I was asking *why* you are here."

"I know what you meant. That love of my life thing?"

she said, referring to the hashtag heard 'round the world. "That was an exaggeration. I was lonely. I was also mad because Hayes slept with his twenty-two-year-old assistant, Candi with an *i*. In retrospect, I should've taken a little time to myself before I sought you out."

"You think?"

"Then I saw Merina," she continued. "Everything I should have felt for you was reflected in her eyes." Her smile faded quickly. "Only my feelings were more about myself." Gwyneth shook her head softly, but not out of animosity, more like she was having a really late epiphany. Her eyes snapped over to him. "She loves you."

"*Loved*. Past tense." He pointed to his desk where an unopened envelope sat. "Divorce papers."

He hadn't opened the envelope yet. Why bother? Bobbie had brought them in three days ago...maybe four days at this point. Merina's lawyer-slash-best-friend had dropped them off. He was glad he didn't have to face Lorelei. She no doubt had an opinion about what he could do to himself using which body part, and he didn't want her to demonstrate.

"You must have really hurt her if she signed them." Gwyneth stood and moved to the kitchenette. She returned with a mug and Reese frowned.

"That had better be scotch." Steam curled from the mug, so probably not.

"You won't sleep tonight anyway. Drink it." Once again, she sat on the edge of the bed.

It smelled good, which was why he accepted the mug and took a sip.

"Still waiting to find out why you're really here," he said. "You aren't the most magnanimous person I know."

A wry smile lifted half her mouth. Gwyneth had been out of his life so long, everything about her felt foreign. Her face, her voice...that she cared enough about him to intervene so he wasn't fired.

"You mean am I here to try and convince you to take me back again?"

"Are you?"

"No." To her credit, she didn't look the least bit upset about the prospect of being turned down.

As miserable and heartbroken as he was, he still wouldn't say yes to Gwyneth. Once a cheater always a cheater. As Hayes had recently proven to her. At that thought, he couldn't help but offer his condolences.

"I'm sorry he hurt you. It sucks to be lied to." He didn't hate her. He didn't like her, but he didn't hate her. He'd take that as progress.

"Thanks." She sent a glance around his hotel room. "You know...I could see that Merina loved you when I saw her at your father's retirement party. What I didn't know until I arrived here to your pigsty was that you loved her back. This isn't like you."

True. He'd handled heartbreak in the past by staying busy. Losing Merina made his heartbreak over Gwyneth look insignificant. He opted not to be petty and point that out. More progress.

"The night I met her, I figured the marriage was a stunt. You needed to clean up your reputation to land CEO and she's such a fantastic businesswoman. The perfect candidate for a wife."

"It was a stunt." No need to hide it now. "Or...it was supposed to be a stunt."

"I should have known. You'd never choose someone

like her without a purpose. Then you fell for her," Gwyneth
added with a pitying shake of her head. "Since we split,
your dates were temporary and easy to blow off. Merina is
neither of those things."

"She was supposed to be *both* of those things," he said,
remembering the moment of genius when he'd hatched his
plan.

"Well." Gwyneth stood. "You're an idiot."

"On that, you and Merina see eye to eye."

"Take a shower." She stood and took his coffee. "I'm
leaving."

"That's it? You came here to dole out your unsolicited
advice and now you're leaving?"

"Make sure you shave. Women don't like too much
scruff." She gestured to his face and he scowled.

"Merina does." He ran his fingers over his bristled jaw,
remembering all the times she'd done the same. She once
commented how she liked the scrape of his chin over the
inside of her thighs. He smiled to himself.

Goddamn. He loved her so much even that smile hurt.

Gwyneth rinsed his mug in the sink as he stood and half
hobbled across the room. She wasn't kidding. He needed a
shower. He paused, hand on the bathroom door. "Hey."

She looked up.

"Hayes is a dick," he said. And because he would be
downing scotch by the mouthful right now if Gwyneth
hadn't barged in, he added, "Thank you."

A small nod. "You're welcome."

He took a fast but thorough shower, emerging into his
suite with a towel around his waist and scrubbing his hair
with another. Gwyneth was gone, his coffee mug upside
down, drying on a dishtowel.

His lips quirked when he saw one of his dress shirts tossed over his desk. A Post-it note stuck to the collar read, *"you faced your past, now go get your future."* He slipped the shirt on, his smile falling the moment he spotted what was on his bed. The divorce papers.

She'd opened the envelope. An envelope containing more than their decree. On top of Merina's signature was a wedding ring.

His wife's ring. *Now your ex-wife.*

Panic seized his chest as reality sank in. *Finally*, and deep enough that his heart cracked right down the middle. He remembered the day he'd given it to her.

The moment he'd seen her wearing the wedding dress in the shop. The instant he slid the soldered bands onto her hand during the ceremony. And when she kissed him, feeling the coolness of the ring on his cheek. The way the diamond glinted at the Van Heusen when she handed him the business card that read *Merina Crane.*

Their shared past flashed in his memory.

The nights in their bedroom. The mornings in the shower. That day in the kitchen. The evening she'd come here and slapped him in the face.

His knees threatened to give, and he grabbed the night-stand to keep from dropping. His hands shook. This wasn't panic. This was devastation.

Similar to when he lost his mom, a veil of dread cloaked him. He remembered when she died, thinking he'd never hug her again. He'd never hear her voice again, and worst of all, he'd never have the chance to tell her he loved her. Not ever again.

With Merina, he was a chance to do all of those things. Hug her. Hear her voice. And no matter what she felt for him now, even if she didn't want to hear it, he'd tell her for the first time that he loved her.

That he'd been lying, to her and to himself, for too long.

Even if she didn't love him any longer, she deserved to know. And he wouldn't let another minute pass without telling her.

He snagged a pair of jeans off the floor as lightning streaked the sky. Rain poured down in sheets and he let out a dry laugh.

Perfect.

CHAPTER 20

Merina didn't wear heartbreak well. She knew because each and every person who'd seen her recently had told her she looked tired or asked if she was getting sick.

The UPS guy, the mailman. The linen delivery guy. Her mother. Her father. Arnold, who usually minded his own business, had taken to checking on her regularly. Heather had brought Merina a cup of hot tea every evening without being asked.

Merina pretty much lived in her office. The more she worked, the easier it would be to forget she was grieving. Right?

Wrong.

Lorelei had dropped off the papers to Reese's secretary three days ago. Merina had told herself she wasn't expecting a response, but she'd waited to hear from him. No way could he allow this to happen.

He'd remained distant and silent. Nothing had changed him. Not the moment she put her heart in his hands, or given him her body one final time. Not putting off signing the divorce papers on a marriage she was far more invested in than she should've been. Not finally signing them.

He was gone.

Merina accepted this horrible fact and felt every painful prick of it like a thousand needles in her skin.

Heather had shut down the bar and Merina's parents had gone home hours ago. In her office, door cracked open, no one to witness her misery, Merina decided to feel her feels. Every last miserable one of them. An audible sob left her lips, the sound so lonely, it beckoned more sadness.

Her last period had been a relief, because the last time she and Reese slept together, neither of them had the presence of mind to use a condom. For a few terrifying days, she was sure she was pregnant. The gods had smiled on her misfortune, deciding it'd be a dick move to add a baby on top of a divorce.

So. That was good, she guessed.

She reached for a tissue and dabbed her cheeks, vowing this the last surge of emotion she'd allow to wreck her. One final torrential downpour of a cry. Which, ironically, was what it was doing outside now. The papers were signed. She'd crossed the finish line. Only a little longer and she'd soon begin to heal.

She hoped.

Merina swiped her fingers under her eyes and decided to go out to the bar for something stronger than the tepid tea on her desk. She'd been drinking too much wine lately, but she'd read an article that "situational alcoholism" was a thing.

Tonight, especially, she'd earned a glass of wine. Hell, a bottle.

Thunder rattled the walls as she slipped by the front desk, relieved to find Arnold waylaid by a late check-in. While his attention was diverted, Merina bolted around the CLOSED sign at the doorway of the bar.

Yes. A bottle of wine would do fine. Maybe she'd go into the banquet room and drink it in there. She grabbed an open bottle, and a wineglass. Tempting to drink it directly from the source, but she did have some sense of decorum.

She took two steps and stopped cold when a man wearing jeans, a T-shirt, and a suit jacket stepped past the CLOSED sign. Water dripped on the carpet with a soft *tap-tap* from his soaking clothes.

Like the first time she'd met him, his posture was straight. In a weird gender flip of that same scenario, his clothes were adhered to his skin. His typically perfect hair was in disarray on his head, water curling the ends and dripping from his forehead down the tip of his nose.

She tried to speak. Failed.

The ladder she had been mentally climbing shook, threatening her path to recovery. She imagined herself sliding down a neighboring chute instead. *No. No chutes. Only ladders.*

Up, up, and a-fucking-way.

"Reese." She squared her shoulders and called up every ounce of strength she possessed, which wasn't a lot. But fake it till you make it, right? "I assume you received the papers. Later than you wanted them, I'm sure." *So* not the issue, but she had to keep the facts in the forefront. "I would have had them to you sooner but I wanted the timing to be right for—"

"Cut the horseshit, Crane," he cut in.

She'd said exactly those words to him once.

He walked to the bar and plunked a doorknob onto the surface. The same one she'd left on his desk the first time she'd met him. She stared at it, mouth dropped open.

"You forgot this," he said.

Her heart lunged for him and she mentally restrained it. She hated him. Or was trying to.

"Celebrating?" He dipped his chin at the bottle of wine in her hand.

She told him the truth. "Coping."

"I went with scotch. A lot of it."

"Another popular choice."

A damn doorknob was not a peace offering. She refused to see it as one.

"What do you want?" She held up a hand. "You know what? I don't want to know. I'm going to allow myself to believe you came here to drop off the Van Heusen's doorknob and be on your way." She made a shooing motion. "Go on. Swim back to your lair."

He didn't leave, though. Only rested his hands on the bar. She backed up and stood behind it, so afraid if he touched her, she'd let him get away with murder.

"Merina."

"You're not the only one who's broken," she said, her voice hard. "You broke me."

His face melted into a mask of hurt. The exact emotion she'd wanted to see the night she stood in his hotel shower. When she got dressed to leave his suite, the divorce papers in hand. Instead, he'd been stoic and cold, while inside she'd been dying. She couldn't afford to hear his excuses and reasoning now. She had to keep climbing out of the pit, not sink back into it.

"If you're here for closure, I'm not interested," she said. "You might feel better after you say whatever it is you came here to say, but I'll only feel worse." She pointed at him with the wineglass, holding it out like a weapon to keep him from coming closer. "Finish your unfinished business on your own. Or in the company of a bottle of scotch. But...I'm not...I can't listen while you explain why you couldn't..."

Her words faltered as Reese closed the gap between them, one slow step at a time. He took the wine bottle and glass from her hand, and placed them on the bar.

"I'm not ready to forgive you," she continued. Desperately. "And...and even if I was, I'm not giving you the satisfaction of—" He placed his palm on her face, brushing her bottom lip with his thumb. "What are you doing?"

He didn't answer her, only stared down at her mouth.

"Reese?"

"You still love me. I wasn't sure until I walked in, but I can see it."

She shook her head. No. *No.* She couldn't accept this. Not after an agonizing month and an even more agonizing last couple of days. She'd made the decision to kill off the part of herself that still loved him...Only it hadn't died. She would find a way to let it go, though. She would. Because Reese didn't fall in love and she couldn't be in love alone.

"I don't," she whispered.

"Yes, you do," he said.

She opened her mouth to argue, but he didn't give her a chance.

"You were right. I am a chickenshit. Too terrified to try, so I thought cutting us short would be less painful. But it's not painful, Merina. It's worse. I haven't felt a goddamn thing in weeks." He rested one hand over her heart. No. Over her tattoo. "Until right now. I feel this."

His voice cracked and she lifted her eyes to his. Dampness from his hand seeped through the material of her shirt.

She shivered, but not because she was cold.

"Do you feel this?" he asked.

She bit down on her cheek to keep from crying, her eyes sliding shut in bald surrender. She felt it. God, how she felt it.

Soft kisses brushed her closed lids, first one, then the other. His warm breath in her ear, he said, "You feel it. I know you do. I feel it."

"You can't..." Finally. Her voice. Thank God. For a moment she thought she'd stand here completely mute and let his words cover her like a warm blanket.

"Can't what? Love you?" He drew back so he could conquer her soul with his navy blues. "Too late. I love you. I've loved you even longer than I dared admit. And you still love me, Merina."

"I don't."

"It's okay." He smiled gently, looking handsome.

"It's not!" she said, tears of anger, of confusion streaming down her cheeks. Because she did love him, dammit. She loved him, but she hated him for doing this. "It's not okay."

Weakly, she shoved his chest with her hands but he only pulled her closer.

"I missed a board meeting today. I missed a lot of meetings. A lot of work."

She frowned.

"Laser focused on my legacy, I would have done anything to attain CEO. Like marry a woman and threaten to gut her hotel because I knew how much it meant to her. But now I have what I want, and without that woman by my side, my legacy means nothing. I was working so hard to fulfill my destiny, I failed to see that you, Merina, are a part of it. Without you, I have nothing. Without you, I am nothing."

She simply stared.

"The day you stormed into my office with that"—he pointed at the doorknob—"you changed me. I was never the same after you. But I'm stubborn, and I'm stupid. I let myself believe letting you go was better for both of us. No matter how much it hurt me, I knew you were better off without me."

She wanted to be.

"But you're not, are you?" He touched her face again. "Did I really break you, Merina? Won't you let me fix it? Fix us?"

"I'm terrified," she admitted, her voice choked with unshed tears. "I'm so scared you'll freak out and leave again. I can't take it. I won't go through this again."

"You won't have to."

"I don't know that." She couldn't trust that he wouldn't shut her out all over again.

He licked his lips, nodding at his shoes. When his shoulders rose and dropped with a deep breath, she could see he understood where she was coming from.

"I need to be rebuilt," he muttered.

"Sorry?"

"Like the Van Heusen." He lowered onto one of the barstools and looked around the room, at the ceiling medallions, the shelves lined with bottles, the antique sconces. He put his fingers on the brass doorknob. "I was gutted before I met you. I was a shell, my foundation shaky. I'm better than the man you met the first time. Because of you, I'm better."

She thought of Arnold's words about his wife. *I wasn't this man before I knew her.*

But that didn't change one indelible fact.

"I can't fix you," she said.

"I don't want you to fix me," Reese said. "I want you to stand beside me. You see beauty in this place, and you made me see it too. You see charm where there are cracks. I'm cracked in a hundred places, but the biggest one happened when I saw your ring on top of those papers."

She told herself not to go to him but found she was drawn in by what he said. This strong, cocky, coldhearted billionaire had been softened by her. He was asking for a chance. The same man who looked at this room with disgust now held nothing but warmth in his eyes.

She reached for him, watching as her palm touched the damp scruff on his face.

"You're a mess," she told him.

"I'm on the mend." His eyes looked as wet as the rest of him when he fisted her silk shirt. His sodden hold was strained, as if he wanted to pull her to him but resisted. He only waited.

"You can rise from the ashes on your own, Reese."

His face fell. He gave her a sad nod and released her shirt. As much as it hurt, she backed away from him, and waved good-bye. This time, for real.

She heard him stand, the shift of material as he walked behind her. When she reached the doorway, he spoke.

"I found home with you."

She turned. He stood, arms at his sides, shoulders slumped. She never thought she'd see Reese Crane look dejected.

"Home was a safe place when my mom was alive. Then she died and I never found it again. Not with dad and my brothers. Family, trust, love, yes. But not home. That place you feel safe naked." He gave her a slight eyebrow lift. "Figuratively."

Her lips flinched the slightest bit.

"The mansion was never more than a place to live. Once I left it behind and moved to the hotel, I forgot about needing a space where I could be me." He dipped his chin and walked closer to her. "Until you."

She didn't retreat. Not this time.

"We built more than a business, Merina. We accomplished more than fooling the world. We made a house into a home. I want that with you. But this time, a safe space for both of us."

"To be naked," she said.

"Preferably."

She smiled, just a small one.

"Come home with me, Merina." He tipped her chin. "For tonight. For good."

He bled sincerity. And her heart couldn't deny that what he'd said was the truth.

They had built a home together.

Her life hadn't made sense for weeks, but instantly, the fog cleared. She could see clearly. She could see him. See *them*. She wrapped her arms around his waist and felt a rush of air leave his lungs in a grateful huff as he folded her against him.

"Come back." he said against her hair, his voice tight. "Come back and I swear I'll spend the rest of my life making this up to you."

She lifted her face and saw the love reflected in his eyes. Beneath the suited sewer rat, there was a man. The man she'd fallen in love with. The man she'd never recover from no matter how long he stayed away.

"Okay."

"Okay?" His smile was cautious. Adorably unsure. He blinked back what looked like tears as her own eyes blurred with them.

He squeezed her close and she could feel how right this was, how right they were together. She knew him. She believed in him.

"Come on, Crane," she said. "Take me home."

EPILOGUE

Rumpled and sexy, Reese's head rested on the pillow, his firm mouth smiling. The Chicago sun was shining, bouncing off the fresh blanket of snow in the backyard. Merina had climbed out of bed and taken the robe off the Van Heusen doorknob now hanging on the wall like a hook. She stood at the sliding doors looking out at the pool and beyond from their first-floor bedroom.

She turned and squared her fingers, framing him.

"What are you doing?" Reese propped his head on his hand.

"Hashtag love of my life," she said.

"Get in here." His smile widened.

She hopped to the bed, sliding into white sheets and into his warm, waiting arms.

"Let's see it," he said.

She lifted her left hand, turning her fingers so he could see the engagement ring he put on her finger last week. On

State Street. When they met her parents there to ice skate and celebrate their very special anniversary.

"I can't wait to marry you." He kissed her knuckles. "Again." He threaded their fingers together, pressing their palms flat and leveling her with a heated, sincere gaze.

She leaned in and kissed his nose.

"Thank you." He kissed her lips.

"For?"

"For making me." He tugged her closer as they lay side by side. "They say behind every good man is a strong woman."

"I think the saying goes 'Behind every good man is a woman rolling her eyes.'"

"Well, I was close."

She held her index finger and thumb an inch apart.

He moved in to kiss her again and she interrupted with, "Oh! I forgot to tell you."

He pulled his chin back to focus on her.

"I decided to have a team of decorators tackle that whitewashed lobby of Crane Hotel."

"You what?"

"Bo-ring," she sang. "When they're done, your glass and stone shrine will be Bohemian and full of personality."

"I don't like personality." His mouth turned down.

Enjoying teasing him, she rolled out of bed. "I should confirm we would like the tapestries after all." She tapped her lips and pretended to think. "And the beaded curtains."

"Merina, you'd better be kidding." He threw the sheets aside and stood.

She backed across the room as she continued. "Do you think the addition of bean bag chairs in the lobby is too much?"

A hint of a smile curved the stubble around his mouth, making her grow warm and her heart leap. He knew she was kidding.

"Only if you promise to have a Tarot reader present on Saturdays. No live chickens, though, it'll freak out the suits." He caught her, fisting the knot in her robe and pulling her close.

"I had you going, admit it." She laughed.

"I'll admit nothing."

"You'll tell me everything, Reese Crane." She wrapped her arms around his neck as he splayed one wide palm over her back.

"Let's try you saying my name again." He put his lips against hers and murmured, "Only this time louder, and with more enthusiasm."

This time her laughter was joined by his. She kissed his smile. Her husband—er, soon-to-be husband—in her home. Their home.

She ran her fingers through his hair but when she met his gaze, she found him looking scarily serious.

"I love you, Merina Van Heusen."

Her chest expanded as she pulled in a breath, that same breath clogging her throat.

"I love you, Reese Crane."

To overhaul the pool bars in Oahu's Crane Hotel, Tag enlists the help of his neighbor-slash-bartender Rachel Foster to help with the design. Several sultry nights later, their relationship deepens, but Rachel knows a player is always a player. Now that she's fallen for the billionaire prince, is she willing to walk away?

Please see the next page
for a preview of

The Billionaire Next Door.

CHAPTER 1

Eyes closed, Rachel Foster drew in a steeling breath, shut out the din of voices at the surrounding tables in the bar, and said these words aloud for the first time ever: "Mom, Dad, I resigned from my position at the design firm after Shaun took credit for my work, moved out of our shared apartment, and took a job as a bartender instead."

She held her breath for a few seconds before opening her eyes. "Should I start with my ex taking credit for my work, then move to the resignation? Or is it best to open with the bartender bit?"

"I think they'll love you no matter what." The fiftysomething-year-old man in front of her, who was playing the role of "Mom and Dad" chuckled and shook his head.

Oliver something. He had kind green eyes, a plain face, and a head full of hair dyed a shade too dark for his age and skin tone. He was a regular at the bar where she worked, enjoying the same exact meal (turkey club, no mayo) each and every weeknight. He always ate, but never drank alcohol, only soda. And he had a big, beautiful Great Dane, a dog she would soon be in charge of while living in his gorgeous apartment. She really needed to learn Oliver's last name.

"You say that because you've never met them," she said, grabbing the soda gun from behind the bar and refilling his Diet Coke.

He brushed his hands on a paper napkin and shook his head. "I'm old enough to be your father."

"Uncle," she corrected, being generous.

"*Older* uncle," he reiterated. "Either way, I have longer perspective than you and I'm advising you to tell your folks what's going on."

"I will." Eventually. Right now, she couldn't call her family in Ohio and drop in their lap that their successful city-dwelling daughter was *not* watching the gold nameplate go up on her office door. Instead, she was stacking dirty dishes in a bus tub and cleaning that sticky, disgusting stuff out of the rubber mat over which she poured libations for eight hours a night, five days a week.

She took Oliver's plate as he reached for his wallet. He extracted a credit card, which he used to pay everything and get miles for his many business trips, and set a gold key next to it.

"Front desk knows to expect you tomorrow," he said, then brought up the Great Dane with whom he shared a life. "Adonis has been asking about you since you stopped by last week."

She pocketed the key with a smile and settled the bill, swiping the card on the machine a few feet down the bar.

"The front desk was incredibly thorough and scares me a little." Last week when she was there, they required two forms of ID, then took a photo of her to put in their database. "I'm surprised they didn't ask for fingerprints." She tore off the receipts and handed them over with a pen. "And Adonis is gorgeous, and only loves me because you gave me liver treats to feed him."

Oliver laughed as he signed the receipt. "His loyalty is easily bought," he said of his dog. "He's a gentle giant."

"That he is." She accepted the pen and the receipt, glancing at the tip line to see that Oliver had once again tipped the amount of his meal, which she used to yell at him for, but now accepted that he wasn't going to listen to her no matter what.

"Thank you for doing this, Rachel," he said. "I didn't expect to be in Japan an entire month."

"You're welcome." She'd confided in Oliver one late night how her roommate situation wasn't working and she needed to find a new place, never imagining he'd offer to solve her problem for her. As it turned out, he was due to go away on business and his house sitter had another job lined up. He asked Rachel if she'd take the gig, saying he couldn't stomach the idea of Adonis in a kennel. Then he told her his address and Rachel nearly drooled all over the bar in front of him.

Crane Tower. *Ooh la la.*

Not only would she get to live in his glorious fifteen-hundred-square-foot apartment, but he was paying her. *Generously.* She could add the money Oliver was paying her to her savings and find her own place. It was either that or move back home, and she wasn't willing to concede that battle yet.

She'd find a better gig than bartending. Something professional and brag-worthy. Not because bragging about her job was important for her, but for her parents. They were ones who were so proud of their daughter the "city girl."

Once Oliver left, her roommate-slash-coworker Breanna sidled up next to her.

"Soooo. How's Daddy Warbucks?" she asked with a grin.

"Bree." Rachel laughed as she washed a beer glass in the double sink. The roommate situation that wasn't working had nothing to do with Bree or her significant other, Dean. Rachel adored Bree, and vice versa. They'd become close in the two months since Rachel moved in with her, and really Rachel thought they'd be roomies much longer than this. So did Bree. But then Bree's boyfriend, Dean, proposed and she said yes and he moved in and well...Rachel was now a third wheel.

She didn't want to be in the way of what her friends had, and she could tell what they had was really special. She could tell because she knew what a relationship looked like when it wasn't right. What Bree and Dean had was right.

"I'm going to miss you." Bree pouted, pushing her full lips out. Her chin-length brown hair was smooth tonight, her eyes sparkling thanks to glittery eye shadow.

"No, you won't. You and Dean will probably run around naked the moment I leave."

She grinned. Rachel was so happy for her friend. They'd bonded almost instantly, which she did with almost no one. Not men, not women. No one. She was an island, and leaving Ohio for Chicago was the scariest thing she'd ever done in her life. But she'd succeeded.

Sort of.

Breaking up with her boyfriend of two years, being homeless, and losing the job for which she attained her degree were minor setbacks.

At least she hoped so.

* * *

"The term 'acceptable losses' isn't bad news, Tag." Reese Crane, CEO of Crane Hotels and Tag Crane's oldest brother, arched an eyebrow.

"It should be," Tag growled. Loss should never be "acceptable."

The board had started talking about wanting to increase profits in the hotel bars last year, but they'd downgraded their assessment since Tag brought up the idea of upgrading the bars nationwide.

Ever the underestimated brother, he shouldn't be surprised at the board's reaction to his move. He'd stepped up with an announcement that he was going to fix the bar issue, and the board had shrugged, stated it was not necessary, and then moved forth with their agenda. By the time they'd adjourned, Tag had nearly snapped his pencil in half.

He dropped the unused No. 2 to push a hand through his hair and then remembered it was pulled back. Long, nearly to his elbows, he preferred wearing it down, but for board meetings he wrangled it into a low-hanging pony-man-bun. He also wedged his wide shoulders into an uncomfortable button-down and wrapped his bulky thighs in trousers.

He felt...wrong. Not himself. When confronted with the news a few months back that the board wasn't happy about the bars, he'd prepared for his job to become a lot harder. He sent his effective but blasé behavior on vacation. Readied himself to step up and make Guest and Restaurant Services shine by taking home the bound report they'd slapped onto the table that day.

As a rule, he liked easy. He thrived on easy. Rules were not his favorite things, unlike Reese, who loved rules. He was a rule *maker*. In fact, Reese had landed his wife—now ex-wife, and soon to be his wife again (long story)—thanks to a carefully drawn-up prenup and a penchant for outlining everything with bullet points.

Tag did his job, was damn good at his job, but didn't like too much structure. The bound report before him, the one he'd received months ago, complete with spreadsheets, numbers, and projected targets, was seriously structured. And seriously pissing him off.

"Why the fuck did they give me this if they weren't going to follow through?" He lifted the report. The cover read "Fiscal Projections for Food & Alcohol". The word *fiscal* was enough to give Tag hives, but he'd pored over those sheets, those numbers, until his eyes bled. He'd come in here ready to throw down, then they just...brushed him off.

"It's your department," Reese said with a shrug. "You know what's best."

"I'm going to make the profits sing. *Acceptable loss* doesn't factor into my plans for Crane Hotels."

Reese's lip curved, an almost proud expression that reminded Tag of their father.

"I'll do things my way," Tag stated. "This"—he held up the report then dropped it into the wastebasket by the door—"is bullshit."

Reese followed him to the door and flipped off the light.

They walked silently through the hall and out into the reception area where Reese's secretary, Bobbie, was typing, her fingers flying over the keyboard.

"Look forward to hearing more." Reese slapped Tag's shoulder, then turned and vanished into his office, where he was most of the time. The Cranes—Reese, Tag, Eli, who was still overseas serving in the Marines, and their father, Alex—were in this battle together. They'd never bail on each other.

Tag preferred his home office, where he could focus on something other than the purring of the receptionist's phone and the pompous chatter of the suits occasionally prowling the floors. When he wasn't there, he was traveling to one of the Crane hotels to oversee a grand opening or cut the ribbon on a new restaurant.

He said good-bye to Bobbie, collecting his coat and scarf from the coatrack next to the elevator, then rode down to the lobby.

The Chicago home base for Crane Hotels was regal. Tall and shining, white and glass. The Crane was their great-grandfather's very first new build, and that made Tag proud. Over the years, Tag had risen in the ranks and learned how to invest. He worked for Crane not because he needed to, but because it was his purpose. Each of his father's sons felt they had a part to play in preserving their family's legacy.

Typically, he'd take a car, but he looked forward to the chill. It was a rare day that the Windy City had no wind, but the cold air was crisp and calm when he strode out onto Superior. He pulled up his collar and plunged his hands into his black coat's pockets and, head down, marched home.

Crane Tower stood exactly three blocks west of the Crane, and was Tag's proudest accomplishment. His brother may have purchased a mansion, but Tag had purchased an entire damn building. He'd done so quietly, buying it from his father so as not to get too much attention for the sale about a year ago. His penthouse was at the top floor, forty-nine, and overlooked a sea of buildings. He liked the vantage point. He loved being on top. Ask any of his past girlfriends. Well, dates. *Girlfriends* was a strong word.

Crane Tower's doorman, a middle-aged guy whose name Tag did not remember, pulled open the door as Tag angled to get inside. The respite from wind was brief, and kicked up now, blowing his hair over his face and temporarily blotting out the vision exiting the luxury apartment building.

She was blond. He swept his hair behind his ear and stopped dead in his tracks. Petite, which put her on his "no" list since he was six-and-a-half feet tall, and wearing high-heeled, knee-high boots that met the edge of a long dark coat, belted at the waist. The wind chose that moment to bless him, parting her coat and revealing her legs, covered in gray leggings, beneath a short, short black skirt. He followed up to where she was closing the coat over her like Marilyn Monroe trying to push down her dress, and then she caught him looking.

And looked back.

Shiny lipstick. Thick, black lashes. A pair of black leather gloves came to her mouth where she pulled her hair away from her lips and Tag felt a definite stir of interest in his pressed-for-work pants.

Then she was gone, hoofing it to a car waiting on the

curb. He watched the maroon sedan pull away from the curb, a woman in the front seat, and blinked as the taillights dwindled in the distance. Then to the doorman, he smiled.

"Mr. Crane," the man greeted.

"Hey...uh. Man. Who was that?"

A brief look of panic colored the doorman's features like Tag might fire him for not knowing. "I don't know, sir. Would you like me to find out?"

"No." Tag looked in the direction of where the car vanished. He liked not knowing. Liked the idea of running into the blonde again by chance.

Maybe in the gym or the lobby. Or the elevator. Yeah, he'd rather stumble across her.

"No, that's okay. Thanks." He nodded to the doorman and strode in, stepping onto the elevator a few minutes later. On the ride up, he realized he was leaning in the corner, smiling like a dope, the bar upgrade issue the furthest thing from his mind.

Fall in Love with Forever Romance

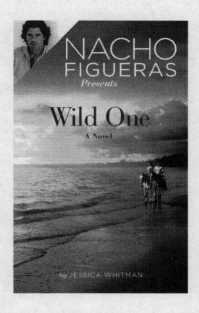

NACHO FIGUERAS PRESENTS: WILD ONE

Ralph Lauren model and world-renowned polo player Ignacio "Nacho" Figueras dives into scandal and seduction in the glamorous, treacherous, jet-setting world of high-stakes polo competition. Sebastian Del Campo is a tabloid regular as polo's biggest bad boy, but with an injury sidelining him, he's forced to figure out what really matters...including how to win the heart of the first woman who's ever truly understood him.

Fall in Love with Forever Romance

"Will get you in the spirit for love all year long."
—Jill Shalvis, *New York Times* bestselling author

Happy Ever After
in
Christmas

GREAT
LOW
PRICE!

Debbie Mason

USA TODAY BESTSELLING AUTHOR

HAPPY EVER AFTER IN CHRISTMAS
By Debbie Mason

USA Today bestselling author Debbie Mason brings us back to Christmas, Colorado, where no one in town suspects that playboy Sawyer Anderson has been yearning to settle down and have a family. But when his best friend finds out the bride Sawyer has in mind is his off-limits baby sister, it might be a hot summer in Christmas in more ways than one...

Fall in Love with Forever Romance

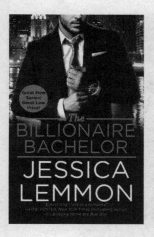

THE BILLIONAIRE BACHELOR
By Jessica Lemmon

Bad boy billionaire Reese Crane needs a wife to convince the board of Crane Hotel that he's settled enough to handle being CEO. And beautiful Merina Van Heusen needs money to save the boutique hotel she runs. But what will they do when love intrudes into their sham marriage? Fans of Jessica Clare and Samantha Young will love this new series from Jessica Lemmon.

A SUMMER TO REMEMBER
By Marilyn Pappano

In the tradition of RaeAnne Thayne and Emily March comes the sixth book in Marilyn Pappano's Tallgrass series. Can Elliot Ross teach the widow Fia Thomas to love again? Or will the secret she's hiding destroy her second chance at forever?

Fall in Love with Forever Romance

FOREVERMORE
By Kristen Callihan

Sin Evernight is one of the most powerful supernatural creatures in heaven and on earth, and when his long-lost friend Layla Starling needs him, he vows to become her protector. Desperate to avoid losing her a second time, Sin will face a test of all his powers to defeat an unstoppable foe—and to win an eternity with the woman he loves. Don't miss the stunning conclusion to *USA Today* bestselling author Kristen Callihan's Darkest London series!